Havana's Secret

Guntis Goncarovs

ISBN: 1475232861
ISBN-13: 978-1475232868

DEDICATION

Havana's Secret is dedicated to the men of the *USS Maine*, ACR-1, who lost their lives in service of our country.

Behind every good book are a number of people who help, cajole, encourage, suggest, and even read and critique drafts after drafts after drafts. Havana's Secret is no exception. So, thank you Joan, Susan, Bekki, Sean, Kristi, Mike, Nina, Brian, Jamie and Tanya for tolerating this curmudgeon. If I forgot anyone else, it was inadvertent.

Prologue
August 1897
Mondragón, Spain

Mondragón offered temperate warmth for late summer in northern Spain, but Michele Angiolillo never cared much for warmth or summer. The factory where he worked in Paris was an inhospitable oven that trapped the sun's heat and wilted him as it did every worker on the floor, regardless of the season. His paltry wages kept him in the factory from sunrise to sunset, leaving him little time for anything but recovery in order to drudge through next day's toil. He didn't have the luxury of time to relax; he had his destiny to fulfill.

Angiolillo was angry — angry enough that even death by garrote which stood as the punishment for his intended actions held him steadfast in his conviction. He wanted revenge for the gruesome nightmare of medieval, inquisitional tortures meted out as retribution for striking in Montjuïch where he witnessed scars from burned flesh on the bodies of jailed survivors. He wanted revenge for their disfigured limbs and missing appendages. Over three hundred comrades were arrested that day.

He disparaged that in this modern day, where factories were crammed with machines, workers like him enjoyed few freedoms from hand chosen despots of the European monarchies. Workers in his homeland were exploited in the same ways as in the other parts of Europe. Had he been English, German, or French and not Italian, worker persecution was the same. Originally he had planned to seek revenge on members of the Spanish Royal family, but a fellow revolutionary — a comrade associated with the Cuban insurgency — suggested a different target. Spain's Prime Minister Cánovas del Castillo, whose bloody hands ravaged Europe, then spanned the Atlantic to create death camps in Cuba, where thousands there suffered and died, would serve a more adequate statement. To assassinate him would avenge the atrocities at Montjuïch, for which he was more likely responsible. His death would reverberate throughout the entire world.

His objective now Cánovas, he still needed to find a way to eliminate him. Resolution arrived serendipitously. When he attended a small worker's rally in Paris, a meeting with a quiet and rather furtive German worker by the name of Ziegler offered the precise information he needed. The thin bearded comrade knew where to find Cánovas, and offered help avoiding police and border guards along their route through the Spanish mountains.

Pompous, Angiolillo thought when he stopped directly in front of Santa Águeda, the posh-looking thermal bath resort outside the mountainous Mondragón. Ziegler disappeared immediately after they arrived after indicating Cánovas would be lounging at the edge of the steaming pool sized bath. For a brief moment, Angiolillo drank ancestral pride for a few moments the way Italians feel when they see high Renaissance architecture. The resort sprawled from the massive main building to smaller, connected chalets. Mist laden clouds drifted at the rooftops as they meandered, depositing dew on every surface. Angiolillo inhaled the mountain air deeply and regained focus on the object of his revenge, reaching underneath his armpit for the well-oiled revolver Ziegler had provided. Straightening his back, he marched in through the foyer to find the great room. Inside were sitting chairs centered on the rippling blue-green water of the steaming thermal bath. As he had been assured, there sat Cánovas, back to him, reading silently. Angiolillo quietly inched closer.

They were alone.

Reaching into his jacket, he silently eased out the fully loaded revolver and stepped closer. No sound rose from the worn soles of his shoes. He drew in and held a breath. Five feet from his target — two arms' lengths — he leveled the barrel directly at the back of Cánovas' head and cocked the action.

Crack! Flame spit from the barrel. Blood spurt from the small hole at the nape of the Minister's neck. A maroon stream spit forward until Cánovas' head slumped forward and pinched it off. Angiolillo stepped closer, close enough to place the barrel of the revolver on the back of Cánovas' head.

"For my brothers at Montjuïch, I repay you," Angiolillo said, then pulled the trigger again.

The Spaniard's head twitched.

Angiolillo fired again for good measure. Cánovas' body crumbled to the floor.

Footfalls echoed from under hurried shoes across the expansive room, then stopped. Angiolillo calmly turned, placed his revolver away under his arm, and started walking out toward the foyer.

"¡*Asesino*!" screamed Señora Cánovas. Angiolillo stopped, filled his chest with the moist air, and turned back toward her. "¡*Asesino*!" she cried out again, waving

3

her bent finger directly at him.

Angiolillo glared at Señora Cánovas, now quivering as she watched the slumped body of her husband inch toward the floor. She covered her face with her hands and began to sob. Showing no regret for his action, Angiolillo bowed politely, and with a firm voice in Spanish said, "*Pardone, Señora.* You were the wife of a monster," then turned back toward the foyer when a trio of police officers rushed into the room. He stopped and stood tall.

"*Canalla.*" Señora Cánovas screamed as she pointed. One police officer rushed toward Angiolillo, who offered no resistance. They poised their guns at the balcony for confederates. Señora Cánovas stumbled toward her husband, and as she melted into him, sobbing hysterically.

"*Quien mas,*" barked the lead officer when he forcefully ripped the revolver from Angiolillo's hand.

"…No one but the souls of the dead at Montjuïch," was all that Angiolillo could utter as the officers dragged him out through the foyer. He looked up and made brief eye contact with a well-dressed man who was standing at the desk, who quickly turned away as Angiolillo was hustled out of the building.

"Wilhelm Ziegler," the man at the desk turned back and said to the shaken concierge. "I would like to send a message home."

Crowned as *Kaiser Wilhelm II*, the former Prince Frederick now enjoyed his position. Early in his reign, he needed to direct his energy to the business of Otto von Bismarck's tenure. The "Iron Chancellor" was an old man now, who plodded through decisions concerning international affairs. Wilhelm demanded quicker, personal control over these matters, and so forced Bismarck to resign. This allowed Wilhelm to replace Bismarck with someone he could ply more easily. He harbored no regrets.

His strong army and navy offered him primacy, affording him ventures to far away conquests, making Germany the envy of his European cousins. His incursions into China and Africa restored the proper respect his stature deserved. Wilhelm inherited a strong network of experienced and cunning operatives, Ziegler being one of his favorite intelligence gatherers. The Kaiser grinned as he read the latest cable from the youthful Ziegler. Cánovas was now gone. An anarchist had resolved a bothersome obstacle. With the strong-willed Prime Minister out of the way, he could now ply Maria Christina, Spain's Queen Regent into a more useful ally, rendering her to become little hindrance to the growth of his influence and power.

The more nagging issue to be resolved, he thought as he stood over and looked down to the world map he used to cover for his massive oak desk, was expansion outside European borders. To maintain his primacy over the seas, he required more useable colonies — ones that could service his naval force adequately. What few colonies he did control had little in the way of resources. Cuba was the gem he needed for his crown. It had been untouchable with Cánovas in power. *Until now*, he mused. Cuba could be his sooner than he planned.

"Frederick!" Wilhelm yelled through his open door. Scuffling shoes brought a scrambling personal correspondent to his expansive office.

"Yes, Your Majesty," the thin, young telegrapher said as he bent at his waist.

"Send a return cable to Ziegler — a simple message. 'Virginia.'"

"Yes, Your Imperial Majesty," the telegrapher snapped his heels and bowed again before heading toward the doorway.

"... In addition, send for Admiral von Tirpitz. I wish to speak to him," Wilhelm demanded brusquely. He unlocked the top left drawer on his desk where he maintained several of his private papers. He extracted the top file and dropped it on top of the map, directly to the east of the Virginia coast.

The title of the file read: "Sea-borne invasion at Norfolk," a report outlining details written by his top naval officers. He grinned — it would be his penultimate conquest — one which no one else would envision. He skimmed through several pages, and then mumbled to no one else in the room, "Tirpitz can add the final touches to this one."

The wet Havana evening had turned into a stifling night, which Domingo Villaverde could not wade. It was already three o'clock. Instead of wasting more time tossing in a damp cot, he got dressed, left his flat, and worked his way through Havana's quiet, wet streets. He slipped into the Governor-General's Palace, walked directly to the telegraph office, and unlocked the door. He knew he did not have to look around first — no one would be awake at this hour. The Spanish government censors always left promptly at nine and never returned until eight the following morning. He closed the door behind him, and habitually locked it before sitting down at the teletype to send a message to Tom Warren, his old friend in Key West.

Villaverde was a small statured, dark skinned Cuban, but his skill as a telegrapher earned him a prime position within Governor-General Weyler's palace staff. The Spaniards were ignorant of the covert reality that he was actively engaged with U.S. Consul-General Fitzhugh Lee, stealing sensitive messages from the Spaniards, which he forwarded to Lee or directly to his old friend in Key West. He wound up the magneto just as the teletype began hammering on its own.

Madrid, he thought. Most of the cables during the past few weeks had been nothing more than routine messages between Prime Minister Cánovas and Governor-General Weyler. This one was not routine, not just that it was being sent during the early morning hours when everyone in Havana would obviously be sleeping, but also that it had come from the Prime Minister's office — and from Práxedas Mateo Sagasta, not Cánovas: '*Cánovas assassinated by anarchist this morning at Mondragón. Sagasta now Minister in charge,*' Villaverde translated.

The teletype fell silent again. This single event could change the complexion in Havana. Even all of Cuba. He knew Sagasta. He was Cánovas' antithesis. Sagasta had pacifist leanings, and because of that, he would be more inclined than Cánovas to negotiate a peaceful settlement to the hell that raged in colonial Cuba; perhaps even some easing of the brutality that haunted Cuba.

What had happened was not sensitive news. What the Spanish would be doing about it was which made this information urgent. Lee and Warren needed to know. He quickly scribbled the information down and stuffed it away in his shirt pocket to deliver first thing in the morning. He then tapped out a less urgent message to his friend in Key West.

Part One
September 1897
Havana, Cuba

Chapter 1

"Reduce speed to one-third," ordered the Captain. His young pilot swung the polished brass engine room telegraph smartly to full span and then pulled it back to one-third. Captain McManus then announced his vessel's intended entry into Havana harbor with two long and very distinct tones from her air horn. The engine room telegraph handle moved as it rang twice, signaling the engine room complied. Gray-black water that sheeted off the cutwater dissipated as the coastal steamer *Olivette* slowed, responding promptly when the inlet valves directing steam to the engines were throttled down.

Captain Cyrus McManus, short, bowlegged, and grayed at his temples, was a former Confederate naval officer in line for a captaincy just as the war drew to a close. Even at his advanced age, he maintained himself in such superb physical condition that no one dared countermand his orders for fear of an old-fashioned butt kicking. He never returned to military service following the war, despite incessant recruiting and the demand for experienced sea captains in the re-constituted U.S. Navy. He chose to ply his trade with the new generation of coal-fired passenger steamers. Working along the Eastern coast, he built a reputation as a master of steam engines. As newer and larger vessels were built, he turned down offers for commands, preferring to stay in charge of the engine room, the heart and soul of the vessels.

The *Olivette* and her two sister ships were the brainchild of an old colleague, shipping magnate Henry B. Plant, who specifically required that the building contractor use McManus as a consultant in construction of the vessels, particularly for the design and production of the engines. When the *Olivette* was completed, McManus willingly served under Captain McKay for ten years, further honing the vessel's power plant. When McKay retired, Plant and the other owners convinced McManus to assume his rightful and long overdue position at the *Olivette*'s helm.

"Ninety to starboard," McManus directed. The *Olivette* made him proud. She may have been ten years old but her engines ran with exacting specifications and still ran as smoothly as they did the first time she spun her iron screw. No other passenger steamer could even compare. She was a stately vessel, three hundred feet from stem to stern, and thirty-five feet at the beam, which gave her passengers a wide promenade deck with a clear and full view of the ocean expanse while en route. Moreover, she was reliable.

"Aye, sir. Ninety to starboard," the helm officer replied briskly. The *Olivette* was a frequent visitor to Havana, a workhorse in Plant's shipping company, robust enough that she seldom missed her three runs per week schedule between Havana, Key West and Port Tampa. The vessel slid directly into the center of the channel. McManus smiled as he sauntered to the pilothouse port side windows and craned his neck to follow the imposing edifice rock on which perched Castle Morro some fifty feet above.

At the top of the massive block wall, he caught a glimpse of a group of Spanish soldiers, their rifles shouldered, lined along the edge of the castle's defensive walls, staring back down at him as he directed his vessel to another on-time, mid-day mooring.

"Get over it," McManus grumbled angrily at the voyeurs. He held them culpable for the personal embarrassment he endured from the *Olivette* Incident, as it was publicly called by the Yellow Press. It was all because a young Cuban woman was taken into custody and searched by a Spanish police matron on his vessel. Led by newspaper mogul Randolph Hearst, the American press exaggerated the incident into three nubile Cuban women strip-searched by a male police officer on his vessel as he stood by unwilling and unable to come to their aid. McManus still smarted over the newspaper story now nearly six months later. He hated being portrayed as a Captain "helpless" against the Spanish authorities.

"Give 'em a show, Chief," he then mumbled over his shoulder to his crew Chief.

"Aye, Cap'n!" Chief O'Connor, a grizzled old Scotsman, winked as he growled. His lumbered walk betrayed arthritic hips.

"And hoist the Gadsden on the jack mast," McManus added.

"Fly 'em! Fly 'em all! Gadsden on the jack!" the chief called as he stepped out the side portal and onto the narrow Captain's walk around the pilothouse to monitor his charges. White clad crewmembers scurried into action, hands flying over ropes and rigging, hoisting the blanched triangular sheets up to their full-open position on the foremast. The sails had no real function anymore. They were mostly for show, since the *Olivette*'s heartbeat came from a triple expansion steam engine.

The Gadsden flag, a rattlesnake on a yellow background, a symbol of the American War of Independence, was shimmied up the jack mast. McManus sneered. "Don't tread on me, you rat bastards," while passing the fortress. He held back shaking his fist. "Maybe the only good thing to come out of the north," he mumbled as the flag snapped to attention at the top of the mast.

McManus turned back into the pilothouse, but as he looked over his papers, realized he still had one more preparation for coming into port. "Chief, where's the damned Purser?" he called out the open window.

"Right behind you sir," Ames, the ship's purser calmly replied, standing just inside the side portal. A wry grin curled his lips.

"Should 'a known..." McManus's comment was as much an apology as any crewmember would get on board his vessel. He handed Ames a thick yellow envelope, then added with a wink, "Find out from our guest if we expect any return mail."

11

"I know there will be sir," Ames replied, taking the envelope.

McManus enjoyed the cloak and dagger-like mission with his old friend, Havana's Consul-General Fitzhugh Lee — right under the noses of the Spanish authorities. The nimble purser disappeared as quickly as he had arrived, double-timing his way down the metal stairway to the dining saloon.

Samuel Carter looked up from his coffee when Ames entered. The purser scanned the room as he approached. *'Unnecessary,'* Carter thought. Most of the passengers were watching the Captain's mooring maneuver from the open area at the bow.

"You will see the Green House tomorrow?" Ames asked, his slight British accent tainting his words as he slipped the envelope to Carter.

Carter nodded yes, understanding the message clearly. Ames twitched the corner of his mouth, then scurried back to the pilothouse as Carter stuffed the envelope into his jacket pocket and continued slurping at his coffee. He would move it to his secret hidden pocket when he was sure no one would notice. He already knew Domingo Villaverde had intercepted some very sensitive cabled messages from Madrid that were too risky to be directly cabled back to Key West. Villaverde must have cabled Tom Warren, his telegrapher counterpart in Key West, that he had a "hot one." Warren relayed the message to Ames, who acted as the go-between, that another secret from Havana required delivery. That was the ruse, and the *Olivette* and her timely schedule became the perfect courier.

Carter watched Castle Morro fade into the distance on the port side while Havana harbor widened. Underneath the bright blue sky, the glassy black water perfectly mirrored a flotilla of vessels of all sizes: fishing boats, orphaned dinghies, cockleshells held at anchor close to shore, peeking out from behind massive iron-hulled ocean and coastal steamers moored at the buoyed deeper water stations. Even larger Spanish warships nested amidst the flotilla with their gray hulls and big guns peering toward the shore as if on guard for unwarranted landward approach.

Alone with just his thoughts, Carter mused about his past six months, most of it spent in Cuba. Originally assigned here as an experienced counterfeiting sleuth for the U.S. Treasury, his charge was to sort through the activities of some less than honest Americans looking to wheedle advantages to further their illicit activities. He never expected to be drawn into espionage under the auspices of Consul-General Fitzhugh Lee. Protocol demanded he report to him while in Cuba. Lee drew him deep into his cobbled web of covert operatives who monitored the insidious Spanish infection now brutally spiraling out of control. Whether his boss in Washington, Treasury Director Hazen, was or was not aware of the redirection was unclear to Carter, he reckoned there must have been at least a tacit acceptance.

A refreshing breeze slipped through the open windows of the saloon and whisked kindly across his skin, already beading up with sweat. He took another drink from his coffee, cooled enough to take by the mouthful, and mused the rules in this new game of espionage. Lee, an ex-Confederate cavalryman was tutoring him in this new venture. The rules were disparate enough from his previous undercover work and felt made up as he went, with one exception — don't get caught. His lessons at the Citadel gave him some insight to the tactics of espionage, but this was new for America and for him.

Carter took another drink as he heard the distinctive *ring-ring* of the ship's engine room telegraph. He felt the rumble of *Olivette*'s engines quell to a pleasant, lulling hum. Another double ring. The engines reversed. No jolt. *Captain McManus and his crew were quite adept at smooth moorings,* Carter thought. Out over the convergence of passengers at the bow, a pack of motorized tugs and ferries headed out to meet them. Steam-powered tugs kissed the *Olivette* port and starboard and together worked the steamer to her mooring while rickety looking ferries hovered nearby.

As the *Olivette* finally stopped and dropped anchor, Carter downed the last bit of his coffee, complete with the bitter grounds, and stood up. He worked his wide-brimmed Panama style hat that shaded his fair skin from the sun on his bristly red hair and hand pressed his suit jacket. As was his habit, he scanned the room. He noticed a rather stout, older man in a seersucker suit helping a well-dressed younger woman up from her chair at a table across the dining salon. Her head turned slightly toward Carter. Her alluring green eyes, framed by her long, auburn hair, appeared to smile at him. Slowly shouldering his old, carpetbag type satchel, Carter smiled back. She turned away with the older man then melded into the pack of American businessmen and visitors queuing for departure.

Carter regrouped his thoughts. There were enough Americans embarking on their own Cuban adventure that he knew his features would not stand out. So long as he maintained a neat outward appearance, Spanish authorities and Cubans loyal to Spain would not suspect him as a spy. Carter realized though, that despite blending in, he still needed to maintain vigilance.

On shore, Carter queued into the line and waited his turn on the dock for routine inspection by the Spanish authorities. He didn't have to worry — he had left his weapon squirreled away at the Consulate before he left for the States. Most of the people in front of him in line were processed efficiently, one officer inspecting papers while the other questioned and cursorily checked bags for contraband, leaving Carter's wait short.

"*Dale tu bolsa a él, ya mí tu cuenta de pasaporte,*" the taller of the two officers barked. Carter complied, relinquishing his bag and papers. The officer inspected the small hard-covered passport, then looked up. "*¿Su nombre es* William Alexander?"

"The Third," Carter replied, one-liner like, presenting three fingers to the officer asking his name.

As long as he added the designation 'III', Carter's stepfather agreed to him using the alias. He tipped up the brim of his hat. The shorter officer looked up as he finished rummaging through Carter's satchel.

"*Nada,*" he mumbled, then dropped the satchel at Carter's feet. He then thrust his arm forward, grabbed the yellowed envelope peeking out from under the American's jacket flap and surrendered it to his superior.

"*¿Lleva algo para declarar*, Señor Alexander?" the officer asked, not trying to speak to him in English. He waved the envelope at Carter, and then opened it. After he scanned them, he slapped them back at Carter without replacing the blank sheets back into the envelope. Carter shook his head and shrugged his shoulders.

"Just wanted some real paper to write home with... didn't think I needed to declare that," he quipped as he picked up the papers and put them away.

"*Vaya*," the officers barked and turned back to the waiting queue. "*Siguiente*," one ordered, pointing to the next person in line.

"*Gracias, señores*," Carter replied, swung his satchel over his shoulder then moved on, distancing himself from the dock area, where many of the Americans stopped to ask passing locals for directions in unrehearsed, grammatically pitiful Spanish. Carter sucked in some of the thickness that was the air this time of year in Cuba. Havana was vibrant, and when not, completely quiet. There were few indications of the desolation, distress, misery and rampant starvation under the Spanish occupation.

He continued on to a café across the main street, the Café Luz. It wasn't his favorite place in Havana. In fact, he probably would not even stop here but for its location — a position that provided full view of the harbor traffic and a focal point where intelligence could be harvested. This rat hole allowed him an unsullied view and protected him from stumbling into the crosshairs of the Spanish junta. The Spanish did appreciate his assigned position as Treasury agent, since it left the local policemen one less issue they would need to deal with. They neither cared for nor tolerated espionage. Criminality was more acceptable than espionage in this milieu.

"*Buenas tardes, señor. ¿Un café?*" a faceless voice asked. Carter turned and saw the familiar wispy physique of Ramón standing behind him, his hands folded fig leaf in front of his yellowed apron. Carter removed his wide brimmed hat, wiped beaded sweat off his brow, and then nodded "*Sí*" in reply.

Ramón disappeared into the sea of table umbrellas. As Carter settled into a white, multi-layered painted wrought iron chair at a small table and gazed out at the *Olivette,* Ramón reappeared. The young Cuban placed a steaming cup of coffee on the table then chinked a water-spotted spoon onto the saucer. Thick, sweet Cuban coffee here was an added attraction. It the most flavorful he had found in Havana, served hot and sweetened with a generous dose of native sugar cane. Even the late summer swelter's stifling humidity, drawn in over the island by a tropical storm departing to the west, could not curb his desire for wanting this coffee hot. The flavor was worth the extra perspiration that bled from his pores as he drank.

"Some bread with your coffee, Señor?" Ramón asked, in English this time. "Perhaps toasted?"

"*No. Gracias*, Ramon." Carter replied as he looked up and considered his waiter more closely. Ramón's left arm was laced with white keloid scars, traces that stood out next to his dark skin, reminders of his incarceration by the Spanish authorities. He was still not sure if Ramón was his given name, but that really did not matter. No one seemed to use given names here anymore. Ramón's imprisonment failed its purpose, as it had with most Cubans since it simply cultivated stronger anti-Spanish sentiment and among most Cubans he knew. As Ramón returned a smile to Carter, his parted lips betrayed a missing front tooth.

Carter took out the yellowed envelope from his jacket and set it on the table so that Ramón would notice. He looked around to be sure no one, especially Spanish authorities watched him, then replaced the blank paper with the authentic messages he had hidden from the inspectors in his trousers. Ramón took the envelope, slipped it into the pocket on his apron then disappeared. Carter waited; sipping at his coffee until Ramón walked by and casually set the envelope back onto the table. Carter retuned the envelope to his jacket pocket, finished his coffee, and left the bistro, continuing on to the Consulate, which was now more or less, his home.

He regarded his life as it was now. He enjoyed the assignment as an intelligence scout for Fitzhugh Lee and understood his upbringing better than most of the Northerners he worked with in Washington, all of who were as thick as thieves. The General seemed more like a father, not just because of their comparative ages, but also that the old man was versed in the details of what he desperately wanted to know — details about the *Hunley*, a secret Confederate submarine. Carter had discovered only a few years back that his real father had served on that infernal machine and was presumed dead following an incident off Charleston. Few people, even his mother and stepfather spoke much about this vessel. Lee explained why the *Hunley* was critical in the bitter fight to extend Charleston's life, revealing facts about which his history professors at the Citadel fell short during their lectures.

Carter turned and headed due west, about a block away from the Consulate. He reached the gate that led into the compound, and approached the rather large building that resembled an antebellum plantation house. After slipping through the gates, he headed up the worn carpet covering squeaky wooden stairs, past the first floor offices of the New York Herald that set up shop for several reporters, and into the Consulate proper.

"Well, I'll be. Welcome back, Mr. Carter. I was hopin' you'd catch the *Olivette*," Consul-General Fitzhugh Lee said as he waved to hurry Carter in. His thick southern drawl and aristocratic paunch betrayed both his Confederate bloodline and fondness for the local cuisine.

"I reckon the storm that blew by did nothing for the weather. Still feels like hell out there," Carter followed Lee and entered the great room of the Consulate, a room replete with plush, aristocratic furniture and gold leafing. Hallways webbed out from the Great Room, which led to what they had converted into offices.

"You ain't lyin', son, but I was thinkin' an Alabama boy like you would feel at home in this soup we got for air down here," Lee chuckled through his words as he melted into his chair, slipped off his unbuckled boots and thumped his stocking feet onto the corner of his Victorian styled desk.

Carter settled into a cushioned chair in front of Lee's desk as he regarded the formulaic former Confederate cavalry commander. Lee could only be carried into battle by draught horse these days, but his demeanor and suit remained meticulous and diplomatic. He fired up the end of a long, Cuban cigar, offering Carter one while blue smoke boiled from his nostrils. The ecstasy of his inhale could be discerned by his wriggling toes.

"I understand the *Seneca* will be arriving in two days," Carter then prompted as he sat back in his chair.

"Excellent. You've done some homework," Lee chirped as he spun an ambrotype across his cluttered desk. Carter immediately recognized the young, sultry eyed beauty in the picture. Evangelina Cisneros, as he recalled, was the daughter of Colonel Cosio y Cisneros, a former insurgency President and revolutionary arrested by the Spanish authorities. His old friend, General Calixto Garcia had spoken of him many times. According to the Hearst papers, Evangelina was skirted away with him to the Isle of Pines, an off shore prison south of Cuba, more as a result of her guileless support of her father than any specific insurgent activity. The American press chronicled a sordid tale of Evangelina's suffering and relentless pandering by her Spanish captors with enough fervor to rattle the McKinley administration into higher-level negotiations to facilitate a release. The negotiations failed.

When Colonel Cisneros took very ill, the Spanish authorities moved him to an on shore medical facility. At that time, Governor-General Weyler ordered father and daughter to be separated, moving Evangelina to a women's prison in Havana where the Governor-General decreed mandatory incarceration for the city's prostitutes; in reality, Weyler cordoned them off for his own sordid benefit and for the delight of his minions. Over a hundred women were jailed, and Carter thought that Evangelina Cisneros shouldn't have been subjected to such detritus.

"So let me understand this whole caper," Carter dropped the ambrotype back on the desk while Lee poured himself three fingers of Scotch into a crystal tumbler.

"Hush, son, and let me finish," Lee interrupted, raising his open palm, cigar wedged between his forefingers like a pointer. "McKinley and his bunch up in Washington haven't gotten off square one on getting her released. The presses in New York have called on him to release her, along with other political prisoners, mind you. My bride has filed a personal plea with Governor-General Weyler. Nothin'. Even Mrs. McKinley, bless her heart as infirm as she is, petitioned Weyler. Still nothin'."

"Why her?" Carter could not hold back his question. "Why *her* in particular?"

"Strike while the iron's hot, son!" Lee slammed his open hand on the desk and vaulted up from his chair. Shoeless, he slid around the room in a rather awkward march. He stopped at a world map on his wall pointed to places as he spoke. "With Cánovas gone and Sagasta is in control over, here; Weyler no longer has the full support from Madrid, here. By the way, I am sure Villaverde's stolen cables confirm that, since this not something the Spaniards would want us to know. McKinley, here, ain't doin' crap to take advantage of Weyler's weakness, here. So if we can embarrass Weyler by sneakin' out the most talked about prisoner in the world, maybe Madrid will finally recall the damned "Butcher" and we can get on with some real negotiations for *Cuba Libre*."

"And why me?"

"I know those damned cowboy reporters are running along with this scheme with or without us, and we can't have that. Especially since I can't trust them to pull it off without stumbling. And those clowns stumbling could expose everything we are doing here."

Carter mulled over the comments for a moment as he fondled his cigar.

"And I know you can get it done right, son," Lee added before sucking deeply on his cigar.

"So I'm going to kidnap this woman and skirt her over to the *Seneca* right under the authorities' noses?" asked Carter.

Lee turned and grinned from ear to ear. "You got it, son." Carter scrunched his lips and continued a fixed stare on Lee.

"You know, son. You look like you could use a drink and some rest. Why don't you slip in there and get in a quick nap before we get this thing rolling?" Lee noted as he pointed to a room Carter had been using.

Sam Carter took his morning walk around the harbor and noticed that the *Seneca* still had not arrived. It would have been a day early today, he thought, but the ship's arrival was clearly the most important piece of this cockamamie plan Lee had coerced him into executing. And if they completed their job before the ship arrived, hiding an escaped prisoner in Havana might just become the more dangerous part of the plan's agenda.

There was little he could do about the *Seneca*, he thought as he stopped in front of the Café Luz for a coffee. He settled into a bent iron chair at a small table and continued his gaze out onto the murky waters of Havana harbor. If there was any solace to the polluted darkness, it was now. Ferries and fishing boats would soon split the surface like plows in a cotton field, spreading wakes meandering toward the shoreline and seawalls, which would then disappear as they kissed the land.

"*Buenos Dias, señor. ¿Un café?*" Carter turned and saw Ramón standing behind him. Mauve colored stains streaked down the Cuban's same yellowed apron made Carter wonder if anyone considered washing them. As Carter removed his wide brimmed hat, he nodded, and Ramón once again disappeared into the sea of table dew-laden dripping umbrellas. Carter's mind wandered aimlessly until he noticed the young lady that had been on the *Olivette* seated at a table across the veranda. She was alone and interestingly dressed in more casual clothes than the fine dresses she wore on the ship. Carter's curiosity was stirred as he watched the young woman scribble notes in a bound brown booklet between sips of coffee.

"Your coffee, señor," Ramon's voice startled Carter. He set the steaming coffee on the table.

"Any news?" Carter asked. Ramón quickly stiffened. His eyes wandered around to be sure no one was within ear shot before leaning over Carter's right shoulder.

"*Casa de Recojidas*. Plans delivered this morning," Ramón whispered as he unfolded Carter's napkin.

"Yes, it will be hot today." Carter avoided a direct reply, speaking with an arrogant flair and much louder than his waiter. He mopped his brow again with a handkerchief.

"And guard schedules."

"Yes, we have been very fortunate no storms have ruined this wonderful weather," Ramón flashed an asymmetrical smile and nodded at Carter. He stuffed his yellowed dishtowel in the loosely tied string holding his apron from falling below his waist, then turned and limped away, back toward the café's kitchen.

Carter got what he needed. He sipped at his coffee and monitored the locals as they meandered through narrow streets. In spite of the oppressive heat, women knew enough to dress modestly so not to incite wandering packs of soldiers. Not even the sensationalized Caribbean machismo compared to what he had heard of their brutal and lustful demands for satiation.

Others, like Ramón, failed to hide the examples of retribution for their dissidence; disfigured limbs, scars from bullets, and burns from torture. Their eyes remained hollow. Their disposition echoed disparagingly hopeless against what appeared to be the invincible and brutal overlord which the Spanish military had become. He reckoned that most of the locals knew not what he knew; that their own patriots, insurgent Generals Calixto Garcia and Máximo Gómez were in fact, making slow but forward progress against the oppressively strangling Spanish rule. Carter would have rather buoyed their hopes with that revelation, but the insurgency needed the element of surprise on their side.

Carter set his cup down and let the coffee cool just a bit more. As he drank in the sights, he noticed that the table where the young lady had been sitting was now vacant. He brooded for a moment, realizing he had lost his chance to approach. It would have been a welcome diversion for his morning. When he dropped his gaze to the ground though, a leaflet lying under the table caught his attention. He picked it up, turned it over and noticed that it was a copy of the *Ensayo Obrera*, a socialist paper. Mulling over the paper as he milked his coffee, he reckoned that in a place as chaotic as Cuba had become, messages like this could fuel anarchy and spread like fire through a dry cane field. That however, was of little concern to him for now, he noted as he checked his pocket-watch.

"Damn," he mumbled as he realized he was running late. He bottomed-up the cup, letting the residual grounds of the coffee slide into his mouth, since they would allow him to continue savoring the taste. Stuffing the leaflet into his jacket pocket, he fished out a few coins, dropped them onto the table, and left the cafe.

"Sam, we've been waiting for you," Consul-General Fitzhugh Lee called as Carter entered the Consulate. He waved Carter to follow him down the easternmost hallway. "We're in the main office." Carter trailed the paunch Consul until they turned into a wide-open conference room where two men stood. They turned and stared at Carter. Instead of shying away from their owl-like glances, Carter approached with a wide smile.

"Sam Carter. Glad to meet you," Carter stated. He recognized Karl Decker from his Nordic features, athletic build, and distinct hairless scar that followed his jaw line, surrounded by week old stubble. Decker obtained that wound when he was trampled while reporting on a violent coalmine strike two years back. Sam assumed Decker would have probably forgotten that it was he that pulled the reporter out of the fray that night. Probably even saved his life.

"Karl Decker." The well-dressed reporter shook Carter's hand vigorously and strongly, as if to emphasize his fitness.

Carter reckoned he was about thirty, a year or two younger than he was. "Reporter, correct?"

"That I am." Decker puffed up, as if trying to intimidate Carter, but it only served as amusement.

"And this is Carlos Carbonell," Lee quickly moved to separate Sam from Decker. Carbonell was distinctly Cuban, with dark eyes much friendlier than Decker's.

"Señor Carter," Carbonell grinned and nodded. "I

appreciate your assistance and understanding about how important Evangelina's freedom is for my people."

"Ramón indicated that plans and schedules have been delivered," Carter turned back to Lee, slighting Decker.

"Yes, yes, they are here," Lee motioned to the large conference table where several mounds of paper had been piled. As Decker, Carbonell and Carter headed toward the table, Lee went to a corner stand and poured himself a glass of dark, sweet rum. Carter noticed that the ex-General did not offer to pour a glass for anyone else in the room. They all needed to stay sharp.

Carter glared over to Lee as the old man sipped on his snifter. He was uneasy jumping into a plan that had already been half done, especially one most likely concocted by a reporter more interested in just another flashy story he could write. Risk in this case would need to be weighed with intense scrutiny. Carter preferred to work alone and did not care to be involved with a reporter's agenda. Lee made it clear he thought otherwise and that this prison break needed to be successful, he with reservations about Decker's impetuousness compromising the plan. Lee needed Carter involved. Carter capitulated to the joint effort, out of loyalty to Lee, and out of understanding the consequences of failure.

Arching his eyebrows, Lee terminated the non-verbal discussion, grinned and lifted of his snifter as if offering a toast.

"Prison plan," Decker stated matter-of-factly, pulling a large paper out from underneath the mounds. He dramatically slapped it down, flattened it, and then circled above it with his finger until he found his mark on the map. "As I have been told, Cisneros is in New Hall...here."

"What's over here?" Carter asked as he studied the map briefly.

"*La Casa.*" Decker said. "The whole area must have been a neighborhood before the Spaniards turned it into a prison."

"It was for rent. With the help of Consul Lee, I was able to secure it." Carbonell grinned proudly. "We can bridge across from here to the roof. It is a short span."

"And these are the list of guards, their rounds schedules, and available transport to get away," Decker added, listing the papers he had picked up from the pile and waved them triumphantly at Carter.

Carter thought as he skewered Decker with a sideward glance: *'What a pompous ass. If you recall, I got those.'*

"The guards are *not* the most diligent," Carbonell inserted. "They are there because the Spanish cannot use them in the jungle."

'That's a dangerous assumption,' Carter thought. He knew that many soldiers purposely bumbled to be assigned a safer city post. *'And your roundness is not a liability?'*

"I see," Carter responded, checking the schedules before refocusing on the map. With the facts understood, he walked through the plan in his head. The rented house next door would make this caper simpler. "How many in the room with her?"

"Eleven, at last count," Carbonell answered. Carter scrunched his face. "They are all rather 'nice' ladies. Not the kind a young girl should be with," he added, twitching his full eyebrows as his mouth twisted into a devilish grin.

"I can round up enough morphine to put a whole stable to sleep," Lee anticipated Carter's next question. He had propped his shoe-less feet on the desk and casually wiggled his toes as he milked his drink and puffed on a rather fat dark wrapped cigar.

"I'd rather use something else, but morphine will do for now," Carter mumbled.

"I have been able to bring small things to her," Carbonell added. "The guards usually do not search me."

"Does she know about this?" Carter noticed Decker's impatience.

"Yes, I sat with her last week," Carbonell said.

Carter looked over the guard schedule again, and then looked at his watch.

"Tomorrow night, then. Get the morphine to her this afternoon. Decker and I will go after her and then you can take her away in the carriage," Carter finished, pointing to Carbonell. All the heads around the table nodded. Lee grunted his agreement between draws on his cigar.

Kaiser Wilhelm was visibly disturbed by the dispatch he received from his ambassador to Madrid. His newly appointed foreign minister, Bernhard von Bülow, squirmed in his chair as he watched the Kaiser thoroughly read the document a second time.

"Insolence…!" Wilhelm spat. His forehead glowed red as he threw the document down onto his desk and slammed his fist onto it as if squashing a bug. "Yankee insolence," he growled at von Bülow.

"Sire, it is only conjecture that General Woodford will be delivering an ultimatum," von Bülow countered, rather sheepishly.

"This is an outrage. No one has the right to demand compliance." Wilhelm vaulted from his seat and started pacing about the room. "It is high time that we stand by Her Majesty and provide a concerted front against this blatant disrespect for our authority as monarchs. What Spain wishes to do in Cuba is her business and her business alone."

"May I propose caution, Sire. America does provide a very rich market for our exports," von Bülow started in an attempt to calm the Kaiser's volatility.

Wilhelm continued to march angrily in a circle about the room, his arms folded behind him, underneath each of the larger than life portraits of his father and his grandfather. He finally stopped, stomped his heels into the floor and turned toward his minister.

"That does not give them the right to snatch Cuba for herself!" he growled. "If not Spain, then I should have it! That has already been discussed."

Wilhelm knew that was not the complete truth. It was his desire to have Cuba, something that he had not directly discussed with Spain's Queen Regent. With Cánovas now out of the way, he should have little resistance in plying the pearl of the Caribbean from his European neighbor. Even if it took deception.

"May I suggest an indirect approach, Sire?" von Bülow

calmly offered. Wilhelm folded his arms in front of him, cocked his head, and assumed a listening posture. "I can test the conviction amongst the European monarchs with regard to a mutual stance in this matter. With caution I add that the concerted response shan't expose Germany as the one leading this charge."

"Who would you suggest?" Wilhelm mused as he tugged on his mustache.

"Perhaps Austria."

"Explain," Wilhelm demanded.

"Being the Queen Regent's birthplace, Austria should most willingly come to her aid, and take the lead in encouraging her to solicit the support of the other monarchies on her behalf." Wilhelm continued stroking the tips of his exaggerated handlebar mustache until a sly grin crept onto his face.

'*France would not be an issue, and Nicholas is so mired in his own debacles that he would be lukewarm to it but not opposed,*' Wilhelm calculated in his mind. '*England is the wild card.* He started back toward his expansive oak desk, gold leaf gleaming at the corners, then settled into his chair and stared up to the portraits.

"I agree," he conceded. "But assure Vienna that I will be ready to provide the most earnest consideration to any proposals which London or Paris provide."

"I will attend to this immediately, Sire," von Bülow said as he gathered his papers, folded them together and started back to his office.

As soon as the door had closed, Wilhelm unlocked the upper left file drawer at his desk, where he maintained his most sensitive files, and took out the plan that Admiral Tirpitz had recently returned to him. The details he had hoped his strategic confidant would add were there, clearly and meticulously printed in his bold, ornate script. He approved of the plan. It was brilliant.

Wilhelm turned the page and read over the requirements listed on the attached papers Tirpitz had titled "*Vorbedingung weiblich.*" As far as the Kaiser knew, the materiel he identified was on track. Tirpitz had won financial support from the Reichstag, and was now fathering the construction of the requisite dreadnaughts and battle cruisers in the Krupp shipbuilding factories.

Underwater vessels would come later. Tirpitz did not see the need for such a stealthy vessel, but Wilhelm knew better. Once Ziegler finished his reconnaissance for the invasion plans, he would assign him to investigate this Holland project the Americans were so secretive about. Once he had that information, he would have his own fleet of submarines. He filed the plans away, locked the drawer and recalled that he had heard little from his operatives in America. Those would be valuable pieces of information to affect his plan. An unwary McKinley, consumed by his struggle with Spain in the Caribbean fit well with his overall agenda. Ensuring the security of the plans, he rose from his desk and marched out toward the telegraphers' station with hopes of seeing Ziegler's reports.

Chapter 2

"If we are going to add anybody to this parade, I would prefer we add Domingo," Carter complained at Lee as he loaded the chamber of his Smith and Wesson revolver.

"Cain't do it," Lee responded, matter-of-factly. "Besides, Villaverde's been keepin' up with a whole stack of cables coming in from Madrid." Lee wagged his finger at a pile of yellow papers on his desk.

"Why?" Carter countered, Lee's response doing nothing to quell his disappointment.

"Just cain't risk it." Lee replied. Carter rolled his eyes and shook his head.

"Christ, Fitz. You're sending me out with a reporter, a banker and some Cuban which I've got no clue about and you expect me to do this without getting killed?" Carter finished loading his weapon and slipped it into a holster strapped underneath his armpit.

"Sam, you know as well as anyone, you git a dog that hunts, you don't race him and vice-versa," Lee shot back, his face growing red with anger. "Two things. We cain't afford to yank Domingo out of that palace right now and this here caper just gotta git done. So, quit your bellyaching and get on with it, boy!"

Carter bit his lip and grimaced. He unbuttoned his shirt, ensuring the opening allowed easy access to his weapon. He thought about refusing since Decker really didn't care for his intervention anyway, but he sensed the reporter might just fail without him.

"So tell me who this Hernandon is," Carter spoke.

"Ramon recommended him. He knows the streets better than you or me. You need someone like that."

"Great," Carter mumbled under his breath as he thought about the entire charade. If he refused to lead this cowboy-like stunt, and Decker got caught trying to pull it off, it was anybody's guess what he would spew out under interrogation. He and the whole of Lee's operation could be exposed. And if he were going to be fingered for anything, he would rather see it coming first hand rather than getting back-doored. In addition, to that end as well, he reckoned he would probably need to kill Decker if they all were caught.

Carter sighed deeply. It was not something he relished, but it was the grim reality of the times. He made one last check of his revolver then headed downstairs to the Herald offices where Decker, and Hernandon, the additional recruit, were waiting.

"Let's go!" Carter announced as he poked his head into the newspaper office. Decker and Hernandon scrambled to their feet, and the three men quickly disappeared into Havana's dark, back allies. The short, wiry, dark skinned Cuban made it clear from the start that he was well versed in the sordid alleyways that webbed between Havana's back streets. Enough so that Carter found it difficult to keep up. The three men converged at number One O'Farrill Street, the house that Carbonell had rented. Carter immediately noticed that as the map indicated, its bedroom window was positioned directly across from their quarry's indicated cell.

As far as Cuban autumn evenings had been, the weather was routine; hot, oppressive and thick. A weak breeze off the harbor struggled against the choking humid pall. Inside, the foyer where Carbonell had dumped the equipment, felt like a furnace. The three men hoisted the gear up the narrow center staircase of the abandoned house, then carefully staged the master bedroom and took their positions. Decker and Hernandon rested while Carter assumed the first shift at the window to watch for the signal. Carbonell had briefed the young lady to provide some indication that the morphine had taken its full effect.

Time passed slowly as he waited, and when his hour's watch was up, Carter relinquished the post to Decker. It was quiet. Quiet enough that as he melted into the wall, he thought he could hear sweat push out of his every pore and leave a water stain. He wondered if anyone back in Washington knew what they were up to. He then realized, right now that did not matter.

Midnight arrived. Everything remained still. Overcast skies provided adequate cover. Unable to nap, Carter joined Decker at the window and watched the cell, waiting. Carter checked his revolver, then secured it snugly back into his shoulder holster for ease of access.

Hands emerged from between bars of the narrow cell window. Tiny, delicate fingers deftly tied a white handkerchief to the center bar in the opening. It was the signal. From the darkness of the O'Farrill Street house, Carter hoisted his end of the ladder and with Hernandon's help, slipped it out the open second floor bedroom window, shimmied it into position across the alley, and set the far end on the flat roof of the *Casa de Recojidas* directly above the young lady's cell. As Carter monitored for activity below, Decker crawled across the bowing ladder, rung-by-rung in a prone, snake-like wriggle. He reached the end, and then swung his feet around acrobatically.

Carter saw Carbonell waiting near the entrance of the prison, hidden by the shadow of the thick waving palm tree fronds. Carter had assigned him an outlook position; keep a close eye on the lone outside guard who could stumble across their mission. Carbonell remained relaxed. No cigar. They were safe for now.

Carter threw a coiled, knotted rope over the alley to Decker's waiting hands, looked across the opening, eyeballing the sturdiness of the ladder that would carry him across. Quelling his private trepidation that he still harbored about the mission and the ability of the men he was dealing with, he moved steadily toward the prison roof. As he dismounted, he tethered the unsecured end of the rope on a vent stack and it down to the window ledge. He tugged on the lifeline, and satisfied, tapped Decker on his shoulder and handed him the line. Decker sprung as if a coiled snake, grasped the rope, and shimmied down with such agility, it appeared he was in free fall. As soon as his shoes clomped onto the ledge, the reporter extracted a hacksaw from a pouch in his pants and started filing away furiously at the bars. Carter maintained watch, his eyes bouncing between Decker as he hacked away at the bars, and Carbonell who paced patiently on the sidewalk. A gas-lit lamppost exposed a weak silhouette of the old banker, who paced slowly, back and forth, near a palm tree. Hernandon, still in the O'Farrill house, scanned repeatedly for reasons that might force them to abort the mission.

Carter listened to the chatter below him, Cisneros chirping in the night then hushing tones warning Decker to stop, followed by shushed begging him to continue more hurriedly. At the street level, Carbonell and the guards were silent.

The night continued to slip away. Carter reckoned that Decker had been sawing for at least two hours when he heard Decker's strokes slowing to a drawl. Carter glanced down and noticed a fatigued slump to the reporter's shoulders. *Gotta call it*, Carter thought as he yanked on the knotted rope to get Decker's attention, but the reporter continued, his pace further hampered by Evangelina's bleating. He double-checked the rope to be sure it was securely fastened on the vent stack, and then hopped down, catching each knot between his weathered boots until he reached the ledge. Decker finally looked up and Carter saw the gnarled, fatigued expression that conceded failure. The bar was only half cut through. Decker sighed as he bowed his head in defeat.

"We've got to leave. Now," Carter insisted.

"*No me dejan*," Evangelina cried. Tears rolled down her cheeks as she grabbed Carter's hand.

"*Bonita, es necesario que comprendas. No podemos terminar esta noche.*" Carter whispered. He glared directly into her deep, dark eyes as he held her hand. "*Mañana, lo prometo.*"

Evangelina whimpered softly as she closed her eyes.

Tilting her head back, she pressed Carter's rough hand to her forehead.

A woman's tear, Carter thought as he struggled emotionally to release Evangelina's hand. "*Mañana, lo prometo,*" he repeated.

"We must go, Evangelina." Decker spoke slowly and softly as he strained to stand and clutch the rope.

Evangelina relented. Sobbing, she finally released Carter's hand. The two men scurried back up the rope, then across the ladder. As Hernandon and Carter pulled back their makeshift bridge, Carbonell hurriedly lit his cigar.

"Down," Carter insisted. Gently to make little sound, they dropped the ladder onto the bedroom floor with a muffled thud. The guard who Carbonell had been watching emerged from the front of the building and peered into the alley. Decker meanwhile, stared across the alley with vacant eyes at Evangelina, still sobbing at the bars. Exhausted, Decker then slid lethargically to the floor, leaving a salty smear from his sweat soaked back against the wall.

Carl DeLauro, whose father had changed his Lithuanian family name to hide his ethnicity, believed that finally — today — he and his union brothers were going to make a difference. John Mitchell, the union boss, had chosen him to lead a march of close to four hundred men to one of the mines in support a newly formed United Mine Workers union in Lattimer. Mitchell had convinced him that joining this action would once and for all prove his and the other non-English speaking miners loyalty to their union brothers. Ever since they were all brought in as strikebreakers, out of ignorance rather than malice, they had been seen as company stoolies. He hated being taken advantage of by the company. He hated even more being called a scab.

Despite the camaraderie around him now, DeLauro was still not sure what to believe. He felt that he was following his grandfather's advice about working hard in this new country, but the rewards and wealth the old man promised were as elusive as his own happiness. A year ago he had been fired after a labor strike at the American Steel and Wire Company in Cleveland, even though the bosses said his work was adequate. Out of a job and running out of money, he picked up some carpentry work for a pair of well-dressed men. But when he tried to buy some potatoes with the money the men paid him with, the grocer had him tracked down and arrested for passing counterfeit bills. He didn't know. He didn't realize that he could be held responsible for what someone else was doing, either.

A man claiming to be a Treasury agent said he would stand up for him if he helped him find the counterfeiters. DeLauro agreed to that deal since he figured it was okay if it was a government man that made the offer. What he desperately needed was to clear his name so he could get back to work. So one night, he and the agent snuck down to the machine shop and broke in. When the agent started a fire near the money making machines, the two men appeared out of nowhere and started shooting. DeLauro ran as soon as the gunfire started and escaped, but realized he would be marked again as a stoolie. When he found out later that the Treasury agent was killed that night and the counterfeiters survived, he knew he had to leave town — and perhaps even change his name.

He stayed with some fellow Slavic immigrants outside of town who were planning to leave the area anyway since they were also looking for work. They told DeLauro that the coalmines in Pennsylvania were hiring. Together, they were able to hitch a ride on a boxcar, and when they got to Pennsylvania, the mine owners offered each of them a job digging coal. DeLauro didn't realize how harsh the work conditions would be, but it was work and it was money. The hours were long, the axes and shovels vibrated and splintered in their hands, and cave-ins and explosions seemed to happen every day. The work grew more grueling and dangerous daily, despite the promises the company bosses made. It was made worse by the threats made by comrades of the five old miners they had replaced. The bosses said they would protect them, but that was just another unfulfilled promise.

Despite keeping the bosses profits rolling in, no protection from daily beatings by the angry, returning miners was offered. The catcalls of scab and *bohunk* never subsided, even after he and the others joined their union. DeLauro continued to sour against the injustices that were the part of American society he experienced. Rich businessmen who owned and ran the shops and mines grew wealthier off the work he and his brethren did — using their lives to scrape out black gold from the tunnel walls. All the while his paltry savings dwindled under increased fees the company began charging them for tools and company supplied housing. Meanwhile the bosses' bankrolls grew fatter. He reckoned this growing inequity was the government itself, mired in a bloated aristocracy and tainted by the mine owner's wealth.

But today felt different for him. Today, DeLauro felt convinced that things were going to get better. As he marched in front of the crowd under a weak, early autumn sun, he reveled in the fact that the day was dry and warm, while the mine, below the earth was dank, cold and dark. Today he felt no fear from ceilings of fractured rock and coal collapsing on him or that a gas bubble would ignite by his candle and blow out his cramped workspace. He let the fresh air toss the tufts of his black hair back and felt warm sunlight bathe his face that was for once clean of coal grim. The quiet cool morning quickly turned to a warm afternoon.

"*März an, brüder!*" he proudly called out from the front of the pack as the comrade marchers rounded a bend in the dirt road. The dust remained close to the ground, still washed down from the previous two days of rain.

Stefan Pidulski looked up at Carl and smiled. Pidulski marched, more wobbly than straight, proudly carried an American flag, letting the breeze straighten the banner over the front lines of the crowd. Mining had been hard on Stefan, DeLauro thought, but Stefan stayed with him like a true brother. They had grown close in the few months DeLauro had been in Pennsylvania. When things got rough in the mine, Stefan stood up for him. When DeLauro had a bad day, Stefan would sit with him and know exactly what to say, or even what not to say. What little time they had off from work, they spent together, sometimes walking, sometimes eating, sometimes just playing cards.

Up the road about a quarter-mile, DeLauro noticed a group of navy blue uniforms of the local police lining the road, daring the strikers to continue. DeLauro felt a tingle crawl up his neck and stiffen his oily hair. As the strikers closed the distance, DeLauro caught a glimpse of the stern faces behind shotguns, at the ready, barrels still pointed at the sky.

"Do you think they use 'em?" Pidulski asked.

"They won't," DeLauro said at exactly the same time a faceless voice from the police line called out, "Disperse!"

"Your assembly is illegal," chastised a deputy.

"March on, brothers!" DeLauro commanded, and then repeated "*März an, brüder*", in German, the language the miners spoke to each other. Everyone kept marching. The police line split and let the marchers pass through the gauntlet without anything more than catcalls and grumbles. DeLauro felt relieved when the last marcher passed the police line. He glanced back at the battalion as the crowd moved on and watched the blue clad enforcers regroup and head off into the fields.

Jack Stiles was solidly built, just a hair shy of six feet tall. He looked every bit like he was raised in coal country, even though he was born and raised in Maine. His thinning brown hair, receding since the day he turned twenty, made him look older than he was. Lattimer though, was all too familiar to him. Since he had been assigned to the ongoing strikes even before he worked for the government; he was familiar with the many landmarks where angry emotions fueled contentious fiery, and at times, even deadly conflicts. Nothing it seemed in these hills ever remained buried or forgotten.

He also keenly understood how increasingly hostile the labor strikes had become since the economic depression. As a Pinkerton's detective during the 1886 Chicago Haymarket Riots, he barely escaped with his life when a makeshift bomb exploded and killed two fellow detectives directly in front of him. He was assigned whenever the agency was contracted out for peacekeeping at some strike about the country. He expected different when he signed on with the Treasury's new Secret Service. Even after ten years of service, Director Hazen would constantly tap him to investigate and evaluate the impact of those strikes.

The particulars of this assignment in Lattimer would be more like trying to find a needle in a haystack. Finding one union member among the hundreds, possibly thousands of coal-smudged faces might be next to impossible. He could not fathom why one man was so important to Director Hazen that it required him to place his life in the hands of thugs who were hired by the company to keep the peace. As ludicrous as it sounded though, Stiles headed directly to Lattimer crossroads when he arrived in town, the location local Sheriff Martin said would be the point of confrontation. Stiles remembered this as the location of the last bloody labor conflict.

He arrived at the same time that creaking wagons shuttling the Coal and Iron Police and their imported deputies from surrounding counties. Hooves slowed on the dusty road, then stopped. Men wearing bulky, double-breasted, blue tunics dribbled off the wagons to muster at the edge of the north road. Stiles approached Sergeant Adams at the head of the coalition of officers. Adams' face was mousy under his stiff brimmed cap.

"Sergeant Adams, I'm Jack Stiles, United States Treasury Service," he announced.

"Whatcha lookin' for, young fella," The old man grunted. He squinted as he peered back out toward the young officers under his purview, Stiles figured just for show. Having been in the shoes of these deputies before, he sensed their agitation.

"I am looking for Carl DeLauro," Stiles noted, thinking if he wanted DeLauro alive, he would need to keep the reason confidential, even if he did know.

"Who do you want?" asked Adams.

"Carl DeLauro. I need to ask him some questions."

"What kind of questions," Adams sneered as he turned toward Stiles, squinting and curling his lip.

"Can you make sure he's taken to the jail when this is all done," Stiles' realized he had little time for discussion as he saw the union crowd emerge over the hill on their approach to the crossroads. "Trump up a charge if you have to," Stiles noted, and then thought, *which you will probably do anyway.*

"Ya know all these *bohunks* look alike," the sergeant noted. "How am I supposed to know which one . . .?" Adams stopped as Stiles handed him a small sketch of DeLauro he retrieved from his pocket. The sergeant mumbled as he studied the sketch.

"Unless he's the leader, it'll be tough to tell where the hell he is," Adams said as he handed the sketch back.

"Will you do it?"

"I'll keep an eye out for him," Adams growled. "But he'd better not be some criminal, otherwise, well, you know." Adams then made a fist, extended his index finger. He then pulled back on his thumb. Stiles understood the signal. "I figure this ain't your first rodeo, is it, son?"

"Just take him and get him in the county jail over there and ice him. I'll be back to get him in the morning."

"And what are we supposed to tell Sheriff Martin?"

"Just do it." Stiles grew insistent.

"I won't promise ya a live body if the bastards get unruly. You know how those miners can get," Adams' voice was low and gravelly.

"Let me put it to you this way, Sergeant. I've been in your shoes before. I've been in theirs too. I know what some of your boys are scheming, and I know what they're thinking. Let's just say that it's **your** responsibility to follow orders delivered to you by a Federal agent. If you don't, we will be having an entirely different conversation if you catch my drift." Stiles glared at the sergeant, ensuring his eyes sent daggers toward Adams. He then turned and headed away as the marchers closed in.

Adams stepped toward the cadre of deputies, Coal and Iron Police, the company's own band of thugs, then directed them to assemble and wait for the marchers. Their wait was short as the miners reached the crossroads a few minutes later.

DeLauro was surprised the police line had reformed in order to prevent their moving ahead. Mitchell assured him there would be no trouble. DeLauro held his hand up and the marchers stopped in unison. The forces lined up before them were formidable — their uniforms dark and sinister, their arms at the ready.

Each line stood their ground unflinchingly. Catcalls were exchanged from both sides but no one moved. Finally, from the midst of the police line, Sergeant Adams and another, older, haggardly looking man, stepped out and took ten paces toward DeLauro.

"By decree of the town, you all are ordered to disperse! This is your only and final warning," Adams's stern voice boomed out over the crowd. His face was as rigid as stone. The deputies gripped their weapons.

"We will not, sir! We march for rights! UNION! YES!" DeLauro shouted directly into Adams' face. The sergeant chewed his lower lip for a moment, stepped sideways and stopped when he was face-to-face with Stefan Pidulski.

DeLauro placed his hand on Pidulski's shoulder. He could feel the old man tremble as Adams glowered at him. The sergeant then reached out and snatched the flagpole to rip it from Pidulski's hands.

"Leave him alone!" DeLauro yelled as he reached over to grapple with Adams.

"Worthless *bohunks*!" Adams yelled back, unable to wrest the flagpole from Stefan. He shoulder=butted DeLauro, who fell to the ground. The crowd surged forward. Two more officers charged DeLauro and then piled on top of him before he could get up and flailed kidney punches into his body. Marchers were transformed into an angry mob, flailing into the police line, armed with the same tools they used to feed their families — the tools of the mine they were forced to buy from the company — picks and shovels.

Gunshots rang out. Marchers froze. No one fell to the ground.

"Disperse!" Sheriff Martin demanded, having moved back to the center of the fray. His direction was followed by the clack-clack of shotguns reloading. Barrels dropped, level to the ground, now aimed at the bellies if the miners. Martin stepped back.

"Go to hell!" a faceless reply volleyed. The mob continued surging forward, arms raised. The miner's picks and shovels clanged as they waved above heads.

"Stand fast, men," DeLauro screamed from the ground, but his words were swallowed by the explosions of shotgun fire. Buckshot hit the ground, spraying dirt and gravel up into the marchers' legs. Tools fell hard, followed by pained screams announcing sharp, hard debris hit its mark. The crowd scattered from the melee, some retreating and some still attacking.

"Back off!" Adams ordered, but his command was swallowed by the frenzy. Shotguns racked in more rounds.

From his prone position, DeLauro saw pistols slide out of the thugs' hidden holsters. The miner's surge morphed into a scrambled flight away from the police line, but it was too late. Revolvers spit hot lead. Bodies fell, some screaming. The wet dirt looked like it oozed blood. More shots; more cries filled the frenetic Pennsylvania afternoon.

DeLauro was being manhandled by two deputies, but was still able to cover his head when the gunfire started. He saw Stefan crumble to the ground, still holding the American flag, tatters of blue and red. The gunfire finally ended. In the melee, Sheriff Martin had ended up on top of DeLauro, and now moved slowly from his knees to his feet. Martin yanked at DeLauro's arms, raising the beaten man to his feet, and began to bind his hands together. DeLauro took a quick swing and it landed on Martin's face. The Sheriff recovered quickly and kneed DeLauro in the groin, leaving the marcher unable to refuse further manhandling. Too sore and punch drunk from beating he had taken, DeLauro stumbled as Martin hauled him out from the sea of bodies and debris.

"Are you arresting me? You — not me responsible for these murders?" DeLauro stated a litany, head nodding to the still bodies that littered the road, among them his friend, Stefan.

"Not your concern. Not any of your concern," Sheriff Martin uttered. DeLauro frowned at Martin, and then squinted one eye shut. "Get moving," Martin barked as he pushed then hauled DeLauro through the line of deputies. When he passed Adams, he ordered, "Get this mess cleaned up."

The policemen fanned out to collect the wounded miners still writhing on the road. Everyone on the ground was stained by wet dirt and blood. Officer Flannery, who was part of a contingent brought in from Philadelphia to help manage the protests, approached one body that lay limp near the fallen American flag. He mused about how his boots would never come clean.

"Get up, you," he ordered at Stefan's body. He leaned over and grabbed the man's arm to flip him over on his back.

"Mary, Mother of God," he gasped, his thick brogue barely escaping his mouth. Stefan's blanched, bloodless face vacantly stared back at Flannery. Crimson ooze dripped from the front of his soaked shirt. Flannery had never killed a man before and never wanted to be sure that it was his that hit the miner. It did not matter to Stefan or the nineteen other miners who were also dead.

Carter had been trying to sleep most of the day but found the oppressive heat irritating and uncomfortable, even in only his boxer shorts. He would have rather spent some time near the harbor, cooling off near the water, perhaps catching a refreshing breeze at the Café Luz, but he knew he needed to be sharp for the coming night's challenge. He stumbled about the room, trying not to wake Hernandon and Decker. He navigated through the stench of his and the two other sweaty bodies that hung in the room until he reached the open window.

The evening's feeble breeze slipped through the open windows at O'Farrill Street, The evening was even more oppressively hot than the previous one, Carter thought. After a few minutes, Carbonell arrived at his position under the limp palm fronds. *It was time* he thought and turned away from the window to wake his colleagues. Carter squirmed as he slipped on his musty smelling dark shirt that now stuck to his skin.

Heavy clouds rolled across the sky as dusk turned into night, but as the three men started to set the ladder across the alleyway, the clouds vanished. The sky revealed a milky moon that bathed the rooftops in a chalky glow. A half block away, Carbonell started his pacing, stopping to rest each time he passed the carriage he had arranged to skirt their quarry away. Across the rooftop, Carter spotted a hand start to tie the white handkerchief to the bars, the signal from Evangelina that her cellmates had again been drugged asleep.

Hernandon was out the window as soon as the ladder had been set between the buildings. Carter followed, then Decker. But as Decker approached the roof, a fragile cornice broke off in his hand. His futile grab missed its mark as it tumbled just shy of his reach.

"Shit!" Decker's breathy voice shushed into the night just before the ceramic tile hit and shattered on the ground in the alleyway. He froze. Carbonell turned to the sound, then to the guard then frantically tried to light his cigar.

"Guard! Down!" Carter ordered in a hushed voice. Decker vaulted from the ladder onto the rooftop, joining Carter and Hernandon who were both pinned, flattened against the hot ceramic roof tiles. Carter's heart raced, pounding away in his sweat covered neck. He jammed his foot into the jagged edge of the cracked tile as he felt it start to slip. The drowsy guard poked his head around the corner, raising his lantern high enough that Carter saw ghostly shadows bathing his face. Carter held his breath when he thought that their eyes locked, but the guard quietly turned, meandered back and forth a few paces, then returning quietly to his post.

Carter released his breath only when he saw Carbonell grind out the cigar on a lamppost. Without hesitation, Decker slipped down the knotted rope and immediately started hacking at the same bar he had given up on the night before. Hernandon and Carter scanned the street and the alleyway as Decker's rhythmic sawing squealed at an ever-higher pitch. Carter knew it was close, even as time seemed not to pass. Fifteen minutes passed. The blade ground to a halt. It had jammed. Decker panicked He started frantically yanking at the saw, then pushing and pulling at the bar.

Kick it, Carted thought. *It's there.*

Decker leaned his weight into the bar. It snapped and sent him tumbling into the cell. He then bent the bar back toward him.

Carter glanced at Carbonell. Nothing. He then slid down the rope. Hernandon remained on watch. Small delicate hands emerged from the opening, followed by slender, bony arms. Then a tear smeared face appeared, her eyes dark and beautiful, struggling to stay open in the bright moonlight. Methodically, Carter and Decker finished the extraction of the lovely prisoner, gently pulling her out onto the windowsill. Evangelina fell into Decker's embrace, still sobbing while she clung to his sweat-laden shirt.

"Go." Carter ordered. He handed the rope to Decker and supported the weak, pale woman against his firm frame while he waited for Decker to shimmy up to the roof and take a position to help Evangelina manage the climb. Decker lay down on the roof and reached down as Carter released the girl and cupped his hands for a step.

Evangelina looked confused. *Jesus, don't freeze now*, Carter thought as he felt himself start to panic. "Step here." He shook his laced fingers at the young, quivering lady, and then rolled his eyes. "*Pisa aqui*," he repeated, but as he looked deeper into her tear-filled eyes, realized she was traumatized, unable to process the moment. He gently placed her hands on the rope, then reached down and placed her slippered foot into the palm of his hand.

"Reach . . . *llega en cuanto se puede*," he instructed, and then called up to Decker, "Show her your hands. She's stiff."

Evangelina was so petite and slender that he was able to raise her with only one hand while he supported her at the waist with the other. Decker snatched her outstretched hand and was able to lift her rest of the way to the roof.

A vile stench slapped at Carter's face that drew him to look back into the cell. The huge, filthy cage held eleven captive women in drugged stupor. All shades of skin — from deep ebony to pasty white — entwined in carnal positions, scantily clad, in lascivious embraces. Carter's sense of smell and chastity were deeply offended, disturbing him that the rescue may not have come in time to stave off the nightmare Evangelina must have endured. He simply wanted to vomit.

"Stay low and hold on tight. Move only one hand at a time. Watch him," Carter heard Decker coach Evangelina as Hernandon started across the ladder.

"*Mantenga la cabeza baja y agarra fuerte, mueva una mano a la vez y no miras hacia abajo, fijar la vista en mi*," Hernandon repeated in Spanish.

Carter shook off his queasiness and watched Evangelina as she started across, taken by the contrast between her and the inmates of the filthy cage. Her white dress, stained and torn in locations that betrayed the gropes of guards. It had clearly once been tied too tightly to accentuate her figure — now it hung more modestly and innocently. Her pitch-black hair flowed over her shoulders, mussed only enough as if slightly breeze blown. Moonlight graced the satiny, loose waves.

She's in. Carter looked down at Carbonell. The old banker was relaxed, leaning against the carriage. A smile had crept onto the man's face as he saw Hernandon help Evangelina inside. Decker slithered across. Once Decker had cleared, Carter scurried up the rope, balanced on his feet across the ladder, then leapt into a roll through the open window as he reached the house. Something skittered out from underneath his body as he regained his feet, but the room was too dark to see what it was.

Hernandon started to remove the ladder. "Leave it," Carter insisted as he regained his feet. "No time."

"We must. They will track Carbonell," Hernandon pushed back.

"Do it," Carter ordered. Hernandon complied.

Decker grabbed a cloak off the floor and draped it around Evangelina. "Keep this over your head," he warned and pulled the wide hood over the woman's beautiful hair.

"*Mantenga su cabeza cubierta*," Hernandon translated as he dropped the ladder's end to the floor, and then headed down the stairs.

He can't speak Spanish. Carter thought as he read smug victory in Decker's face. *The bastard can't speak Spanish and he still got the scoop he needed for his story line — "I saved the beauty from Butcher Weyler's prison."*

"And stay quiet." Decker flicked a tear from her cheek as he motioned to shush with his forefinger.

"Don't celebrate quite yet. Let's go," Carter warned as he headed toward the stairway toward the foyer. Evangelina and Decker followed, the latter practically whisking the thin young woman off her feet.

Carter cracked open the door and surveyed the area. The guard remained asleep in front of the prison, but Carbonell and the carriage were missing. Carter felt his heart race, but settled when Hernandon grabbed his shoulder and pointed the other way. The twin horse carriage approached and stopped in front of the house. Carbonell opened the door, grinned widely and waved.

The old paunchy Cuban tumbled out of the carriage, helped Evangelina up into the carriage, and then slid inside behind her. Even before the door closed, the carriage slowly lurched forward and as if defiantly, creaked past the prison, the sleeping guard, and toward the outskirts of the city.

Chapter 3

"Great to see you, Woody," Captain Charles D. Sigsbee said after crisply saluting his longtime friend. "I'm pleased you were able to port here for a bit."

"You're looking fit, Sigs," Captain John Woodward Philip, commander of the *USS Texas,* as he snapped off a smart salute then offered a return handshake as the two officers converged in front of the Officer's mess at the Norfolk Navy Yard. "Must be the sea air. Being a desk jockey never suited you much!"

Sigsbee cracked a knowing grin as he stepped ahead of Philip into the mess hall and led the way to a nearby table. *It had been a while*, he thought, settling at the table and pouring himself a cup of lukewarm coffee from the carafe. His time in Washington was not as bad as he thought it would be because he logged sea time on exploration vessels. Getting recognition for discovering the deepest trench in the Gulf of Mexico was an added bonus; pencil pushing clearly did not garner the same respect or satisfaction as was being the captain of a powerful warship.

"Where'd you go on your last leave, home?" Sigsbee prompted as he dropped some sugar into the cup, knowing this brew needed something to cut its edge.

"Yup. Just got back. It's all still the same old Albany we grew up in. Neighborhoods haven't changed a bit. Might as well put a fence between them all," Philip groused as he grabbed the carafe.

"How long before you get to ship out, Woody?" Sigsbee sipped on his coffee. His face responded immediately to the bitterness, his wide graying mustache hiding the curl on his lips.

"It's looking like a few more days." Philip slurped at the harsh coffee. "I expected to head right out when I got back, but they're still just finishing up on the telescopic turret sights. Sure will be nice to have those if we get into a scrap. What about you?"

"Shouldn't be long for me either," Sigsbee replied. He was anxious to get out of port but wasn't betrayed by his outer calm and immaculate demeanor. The *Maine* was his first official high seas military command, and he was convinced to make the best of it. As a machine, she was as advanced as the Navy had to offer; nimble enough to outmaneuver an adversary, yet powerful enough that she could hold her own in a one-on-one battle. In the yard, several keels had been laid for the expansion directed by Navy Secretary Roosevelt, several of them larger and more powerful vessels than his and his friend Philip's present charges. For the time being, his vessel and the *Texas*, the sisters with their oddly cater-cornered rotating gun turrets, were the pride and power of the American fleet. His crew already made him proud. They were as skilled as any in the Navy. His Exec, Lieutenant Commander Adolf Marix, was a young, bright officer who also worked at the Hydrographic Office. Sigsbee himself assembled his crew after scouring personnel and training records in Washington.

"Certainly hope this coal situation straightens out soon. Mixing in that volatile crap is just an accident waiting to happen, if you ask me," Philip set his coffee down.

"Just keep an eye on your temperature gauges, Woody," Sigsbee replied. "And as long as your firemen respond to the alarms and keep some steam handy if one of the bunkers does get too hot, you'll be fine."

"If the damned things really work," Philip grumbled. His coffee had cooled enough to take large mouthfuls. "Besides, that's just one more thing to worry about. These ships have no storage space that is safe for anything."

Sigsbee understood his friend's concern. The *Maine* had the advantage of having higher grade sensors and his had never been flooded out. The new fangled design gave his men occasional fits since they were overly sensitive. An unknown fire out on the ocean was not something he cared to have to deal with. Especially with the way ordinance and supplies were packed in the holds tighter than peas in a pod.

Movement from the hallway near the kitchen caught his attention. A signal corps messenger appeared and stopped. When the young sailor head saw the two captains, he raised a message in his hand and approached.

"Message from Washington, Captain," the ensign said. Both men looked up to the young man, who glanced at the epaulets, quickly realized his error, handed the message to Sigsbee and saluted smartly.

"As you were," Sigsbee mumbled, taking the paper. He took out his glasses and wrapped its curled wires around his ears before slipping the paper open and scanning the words. "Looks like I'll be headed out a bit sooner that I thought," he added, grinning.

"Something you can share?" Philip asked.

"Sure. In fact, you should know this," Sigsbee said quietly as he handed the paper to Philip. "Recon duty. Looks like Wainwright's picked up some intelligence about Kaiser Willy getting a little antsy."

Sigsbee bottom-upped his cup to finish the slurry of sugar and coffee as Philip read the message and nodded his agreement. "One advantage to heading out this early — we might even be home for Christmas." Sigsbee added as he stood and hand-pressed his tunic.

"I hope you are right, Sigs," Philip said as he handed the message back to Sigsbee. "Godspeed, Sigs and give 'em hell if you have to."

Sigsbee winked, offered his hand and after shaking his old friend's hand, marched out back to the docks and his new command.

United Mine Workers Union President John Mitchell

strutted into the Luzerne County jail and without hesitation, walked directly into Sherriff Martin's office. The small, cluttered corner room spoke of a man who was tired and stressed. Mitchell stopped at the open doorway, saw the Sheriff on the telephone, and decided to hand press his well-tailored pinstriped suit lapels while he eavesdropped.

"And I want those troops here tonight. This damned mob is getting out of hand." Martin demanded of the man on the other end of the telephone. He waited for a few minutes, obviously listening, and then replied, "Agreed. I appreciate this, Commander." Martin haphazardly set the receiver on the phone stand on the corner of his desk, lowered his head and sighed.

Mitchell cleared his throat. Sheriff Martin looked up slowly, his left eye swollen and starting to bruise. He recognized Mitchell from previous strikes when the well-dressed, well-spoken, lawyer-type posted bail for the instigators. Lately, with each strike growing more violent than the one before, Mitchell's arrival in town was again predictable. Before the strikes, he had never seen the union leader in person — only in newfangled ambrotypes.

Martin didn't much care for the union. It was the union that had wrested his county from its work-a-day bucolic nature. Gone were the peaceful days when quiet was interrupted only when some ne'er-do-well had a little too much tavern whiskey. Only recently he reluctantly succumbed to the reality that the old days of bullying dumb, immigrant coal miners were gone, replaced by useless verbal intercourse with well-educated lawyers like Mitchell who probably never had put a pick to a wall.

"You are holding one of my men illegally," Mitchell stated bluntly as he stepped toward the Sherriff's desk. Mitchell folded his arms across his chest and peered down to Martin, who glanced up and soured.

"You mean DeLauro? He was told the assembly was unlawful, but he kept on like a bull in a china shop."

"May I?" Mitchell asked as he pointed to a ladder-backed chair, but sat down even without Martin's response. *"May I?*

48

Hmm," Martin mimicked under his breath in disgust.

"I believe we followed all the rules for this march — your rules as I recall — and Mr. DeLauro assured me that all his marchers would be unarmed. They were unarmed, weren't they?" Mitchell arched his eyebrows.

"They had picks and shovels."

"Guns, Sheriff. Did they have guns?"

Martin cringed. "Your man is a criminal."

"I did not realize union activity was a crime in this country, Sherriff." Mitchell's comment was measured.

It should be. It's a curse on my county, mister, Martin thought, grunting. He fished through his papers as he suddenly remembering that Sergeant Adams said the Feds would be back looking for DeLauro. He had been tasked with keeping him on ice until they returned. He thought for a moment what other points he could argue with Mitchell, but since he did not have a winning track record at outwitting the polished man, he pulled out a paper from a disheveled pile and added, "He's got a rap sheet here. Did you know that?"

"Is this one of your fabrications?" asked Mitchell.

"I talked to the Sheriffs up in Ohio. He needs to be locked up." Martin then found the paper the Federal agent gave him and waved it at Mitchell.

"I am sure it is all just a misunderstanding — like this situation we have here." Mitchell declined to look at the papers and leaned back in the chair.

"Your boy is a thug," Martin dropped the paper and pointed to his face. "See here? I got him for assaulting an officer of the law. I didn't get this standing on any street corner, you know?" He stood and pointed to his eye again.

"I'm sure that is just another misunderstanding," Mitchell remained stiff, unflinching at the sheriff's theatrics. "My information indicates these fisticuffs were provoked by your men. But if you insist, how much is DeLauro's bail?"

Mitchell slipped his hand into his jacket and pulled out a folded paper and a fountain pen. He uncapped it and prepared to write.

"Didn't you see there are mobs out there, *Mister*

Mitchell?" Martin grumbled, maintaining a stare-down with Mitchell. "It's blown up into a God-damned war zone!"

"I understand your dilemma, and I'm sure there will be resolution forthcoming, but my concern at the moment is that you are holding a union member — perhaps even held without being charged with a legitimate offense."

"He started this riot and I'll be damned —"

"Mr. DeLauro is organizing those mobs from in here? From inside his cell?" Mitchell interrupted, smirking. "That is a tad incredulous, isn't it, *Sheriff*?"

"Put the check away," Martin grumbled, standing up. He grabbed a large set of keys and started toward the stairway that led to DeLauro's cell. Mitchell followed down the stairs and into the narrow, dank passageway. In the last cell, DeLauro sat head down, seated on a gerrymandered bed built out of clapboards. When Martin began fumbling the lock on the cell, DeLauro looked up with a vacant stare, revealing the bruises and scrapes all over his face and arms.

"Not completely unprovoked, I see," Mitchell sneered.

"Get out, and don't let the Feds catch up with you," Martin growled. DeLauro rose slowly, looking baffled. He said nothing as he slunk out of his incarcerations, briefly exchanging an angry glance at Martin as he passed him at the cell entrance. Mitchell escorted DeLauro to the stairs and in moments, they were both outside in the cool, sunny Pennsylvania morning.

"Thank you," DeLauro mumbled as he squinted in the bright sunlight.

"We have more work to do, Carl," Mitchell started as the pair walked along Lattimer's main street. "Your organizational skill impresses me. I'll need you to organize your brothers to help raise money for the provision of our lost brother's families."

DeLauro clenched his fists icily at Mitchell, spitting as he ranted, "Stefan did not have any family. I want that bastard, Martin! That bastard responsible for this —"

"I assure you, Carl. I promise we will prosecute this guy," Mitchell said. "But I need you to keep your nose clean and not get into any more fights. Martin will have you locked up in a snap if you do."

DeLauro looked up at Mitchell and tried to smile, but the bruises on his face did not allow his face to soften. '*No, this is more than just a local union issue,*' he thought. *My brothers are dead because the government wants to maintain this inequity in class structure.* He then looked up to Mitchell and mumbled, "I will hold you to that."

"Go home, clean up and get some rest, Carl," Mitchell said as he placed his hand onto DeLauro's shoulder. "I'll get a rally set up at the union hall for tomorrow. When your brothers see you there, it will cinch an agreement for us, I'm sure."

DeLauro turned away and headed to his room in the company-owned boarding house. He sensed a rally wasn't going to be enough. They needed more than a labor action. Someone needed to pay for this one if Martin wasn't going to.

John Elbert Wilkie melted into a red cloth, high-backed, overstuffed chair in the foyer of the Metropolitan Club, waiting for the concierge. He hadn't been inside this stylish institution in several years, being out of the country working as a liaison to the British railroad companies. He enjoyed London, but negotiating for American interests there had grown tedious and repetitive, unlike his newspaper reporter days, uncovering sordid facts that allowed him a satisfaction in making interviewees squirm.

He had received a letter from now Assistant Secretary of the Navy Theodore Roosevelt; it was more than just a routine business offer — it was Roosevelt's way. When Wilkie was working for the *Chicago Tribune*, he knew 'Teddy' as New York City Police Commissioner Roosevelt, who made the pompous pledge to eradicate corruption in the city's police force. His crusade was nationally newsworthy and intrigued Wilkie enough to join in the late night patrols on New York Streets. He uncovered more than just police corruption in the sordid neighborhoods where crime festered. He learned how the brash politician operated. His written letters only included enough information to capture interest and details, as if they were some secret to be maintained and the business could only be handled face-to-face. That was Roosevelt's way.

Wilkie drank in every detail of the foyer of the Metropolitan Club as he waited for Roosevelt's summons. Polished oak covered the walls, and in each corner, wooden trim had been handcrafted with ornate swirls. Every chandelier and lamp remained on, illuminating the room as if the sun had worked itself through the valence of heavy draperies. Crystal goblets spotted the room on each table, he thought oddly though since none of the glasses contained any fluid. 'Sophistication . . . no, arrogance is the lamination that oozed from every aspect of this room,' Wilkie thought.

He sensed a sudden presence behind him. His honed reporter senses had returned rapidly and effectively. Through the corner of his eye, he saw the tall, thin, well-dressed concierge approach quietly from behind drawn maroon curtains.

"Has the Secretary arrived?" Wilkie asked before the steward had a chance to address him.

"Mr. Roosevelt wants to meet with you in a private room. Please follow me, sir." The concierge's voice was low, measured and smooth. Wilkie rose and the two men walked down the hallway, past a large dining area and stopped at a smaller, more private room nearby.

"Mr. Wilkie, sir," the concierge announced into the room through the half-open door. Roosevelt stood and faced Wilkie. "Will there be anything else?" the concierge asked.

"Hold off on the menus for a bit, Charles. We have business first." Roosevelt replied as he stood. The concierge smiled, bowed politely, then turned and headed back toward the main dining room.

"John, it's good to see you!" Roosevelt said, almost shouting. He stomped toward the door with an open hand, while the half-smoked cigar clenched in his teeth remained stiff and parallel to the floor.

"A pleasure, Mr. Roosevelt," Wilkie answered. The Secretary's handshake was rather strong. Roosevelt grunted. His teeth clicked as he withdrew his cigar.

"TR is fine. Or Teddy. Have a seat, John." A frown wrinkled Roosevelt's forehead, but faded rapidly.

"I understand that you would like me to work for you?" Wilkie tapped the envelope he strategically placed to peek out from inside his jacket. He didn't care much for idle conversation, and knew Roosevelt couldn't abide it.

"Yes, yes," Roosevelt harrumphed and dropped into a chair next to Wilkie. As he forcefully cleared his throat, his cigar expelled a huge cloud of smoke, as if a boiler had backfired. "Well, first things first. I trust you are aware of what's going on up there in Pennsylvania?"

"Yes, sir. It has been rather raucous."

"More than that, John, it's a problem," Roosevelt's teeth clacked as he spoke behind a wide and toothy grin. "The mines are practically shut down, and very little, if any, coal is getting out. I need — well — *we* need to get the coal moving. I am sure you know that we can't flex muscle down south or anywhere for that matter without ships, and we can't run the ships without coal. The Navy runs on coal, John, but I know you know that."

Wilkie arched his eyebrows. He sensed Roosevelt had provided enough dots that he should be able to string together the man's plot and specifically where he fit, but at this point, the theme was all still obtuse.

"I have a gut feeling about all this bickering going on up there, John, but I just don't have the time to go and ferret out the information myself." Roosevelt stood in front of the fireplace, where inside, a few flames lapped around a single thick log, casting shadows as the Secretary started to pace. "Although I'd love to go up there and tan some hides, that just wouldn't look good right now," he added, smacking his fist into his open hand.

"So you want me to find out who's behind all this?" Wilkie crossed his legs and set his derby onto his open lap.

"No, no, I know who's behind it. Strikers and such, you know. What I need to know is if this is going to be resolved quickly or whether I need to belly up some personal heat like '*in the national interest*' or something like that. A Navy

Secretary doesn't have much control over this economic pissing contest unless I can drop that line, you know."

"How do I fit in, Mr. Secretary?" Wilkie asked.

"Resolve this damned issue, John. And it needs to be done quickly."

"I presume I am not going there as solely a negotiator?" Wilkie fished.

"I've worked out with Hazen that you will be up there as a Treasury appointee, John. Right now, they're chasing counterfeiters, bank robbers, two-bit thugs — that sort of thing. Not quite the way I would organize it, but I can't quite change that right now. I've got more imperative issues to resolve right now. This town needs some good old fashioned butt-kicking, but I figure you already know that." Roosevelt's toothy grin pushed his skin over the rims of his pince-nez.

"Treasury?" Wilkie prodded, feeling disillusioned.

"Well, that's the way this damned government is organized. There are more valuable things that can be done with these agents, but I'm getting ahead of myself. You, as a government agent, have within your purview the authority to mediate the negotiation between the unions and the company bosses so we can get this coal moving again. If they don't agree, then you have the authority to give them something they will have to agree on!"

"Like what?"

"Tell then I'll nationalize the whole kit and caboodle."

"And once that's done?" Wilkie asked as Roosevelt rose from his stuffed chair and started to strut about the room. *He thought better on his feet*, Wilkie remembered.

"I'm glad you asked that, John. I have been trying to convince that old stump McKinley that we need to expand our influence, but he hasn't budged one bit. I've got military intelligence but that's limited. I know he's got some operatives that sometimes leave the States, but there is no organization to it all. No real plan. It's haphazard at best."

'An organized civilian spy network?' Wilkie arched his eyebrows.

"I have inkling that there is some of this going on already.

That Lee fellow down in Cuba seems to have his fingers on the pulse of everything. I betcha he's got some snoops looking under the covers down there, if you know what I mean," Roosevelt winked.

"Spies?"

"Hell, we had better intelligence in the damned Civil War than what we have right now."

"Structure?"

"That's the ticket, John. I need someone like you to put some organization in all of that." Roosevelt clapped his hands as he cackled. "That way I figure after a few years, when I finally get the top job, you'll have it humming along like a well-oiled machine and I won't have to rely on these Navy snoops. They're not quite the cream of the crop you know."

Wilkie glanced around the room, wondering if anyone was secretly listening to Roosevelt's minor tantrum.

"You know, John, I bet you'll get it so that we know what color kerchief the Kaiser uses when he sneezes!"

Wilkie struggled to maintain his poker face as he calculated when Roosevelt could actually bid for the Presidency. McKinley had to know about this, and this concocted plan was very intriguing — a top job at the Treasury organizing an international network of trained operatives.

"But I need some way to get reliable information to work with now. Hypothetically, take Cuba for instance. I can't just send my naval officers in there snoop around right now. And I know you know how to get that information." Roosevelt completed a second pace along the length of the room before sitting back down in his cushioned chair. "So, what do you think?"

Wilkie swallowed hard. He would have to decide quickly with only the few facts that he had.

"I'll need to know about the people already deployed. Are they any good? Can they be trusted? Are they honest or are they just washed up cops? Hell, they might just be a bunch of washed up thugs," Wilkie rattled in Roosevelt-like fashion, stalling for time to decide.

"So you agree?" Roosevelt rapidly demanded.

Wilkie nodded, reflexively.

"Excellent!" Roosevelt grinned widely as he lifted his brandy snifter, still half full and then added. "Let's eat!"

I will need to be more careful around him, Wilkie thought, realizing Roosevelt spoke, moved, and acted as quickly as an auctioneer. His twitch said yes. Now he could not refuse.

Fitzhugh Lee paced near the window of the Consulate and looked out over the harbor while Carter brushed clean his revolver. More than two days had passed since Evangelina Cisneros had been freed, and the Spanish authorities finally relented from their hourly visits searching for her. The least difficult part of this particular mission was completed. The more dangerous part was ahead. Getting Cisneros off the island raised more concern than a young lady's life — it risked discovery of Consulate involvement, which would wreak havoc in international circles as well as political circles back home.

Lee usually reported his activities in code so that the State Department and McKinley would at least have some insight into what he had uncovered. He reserved comment on the more sensitive activities, since he preferred that his operations receive minimal scrutiny from the political winds of Washington. This scheme, Lee reckoned, was one of those on which he chose to remain silent and let the State Department puzzle together what had happened from intercepted Spanish transmissions. Lee could send a more secure, typed message with the ship's purser on the *Olivette,* but she had just left and would not return for a couple of days.

Lee didn't much care for the increasing oversight. He missed the days of the Confederacy where as a General, his leadership was respected enough that he was allowed decisions and choices as he saw fit. He had developed the most proficient scouts in all the Army of Northern Virginia, which served him well in every battle he engaged. The opportunity Cuba presented was the chance to develop his own little spy nest. He preferred the freedom that allowed him to apply his importance filter to the activity that occurred. Secretaries Sherman and Day were a bit slow on the uptake, and simply did not understand his need for rapid decision-making and some degree of independent thought in his dangerous chess game he played with the Spanish Governor-General.

Extracting a locally made cigar from his humidor, Lee sat back in his chair, fired up a match and lit the tip, all the while keeping his vigil keen on the street below. He was confident in Carter's abilities, and was convinced Decker's role as a lookout would be adequate. Their objective though concerned him greatly. Cisneros was a fledgling actress who craved public attention, and not his choice to poke at the Spanish junta. But since her incarceration was more a political statement by the Spanish Governor-General, her freedom could be just the same for the United States. Her willingness to keep low and stay out of the limelight long enough to get out of Havana was not something that sat secure in his mind.

"Anything?" he heard Carter call in from the other room.

"Not yet," Lee replied. He turned his attention to the American crews loading the *Seneca*. It was the perfect ruse —a stately passenger steamer destined for New York; the Spanish authorities would most likely be alert to a fishing boat or cockleshell as an escape pod for a young lady trying to flee. He had personally briefed Captain Frank Stevens, an old friend of his, about the special cargo. Stevens assured him that he had a couple of trusted men who could slip Cisneros through the Spanish authorities' cursory inspection on the docks.

Lee still knew he had little control over what the woman might do.

"Hernandon was sent to let them know the ship was here, right?" Carter asked as he slipped his Smith and Wesson into his belt. He joined Lee at the window.

"I see it," Lee's voice jumped an octave and leapt forward from his chair. As planned, the drapes on the approaching carriage were drawn in spite of the thick, mid-day tropical heat making the interior of the coach unimaginably oppressive. The carriage horses slowed, and then halted in front of the consulate. A short distance away, two policemen were patrolling on foot. Lee sensed trouble, knowing that Carbonell was careless at times. '*Perhaps it was that the old man was comfortable here*,' he reckoned. His let his thoughts about the Cuban banker being capable of following every detail of the orders pause his other thoughts.

"I'll get them," Carter noted as he scrambled out of the office and down the stairs to the front door.

"Don't go cowboy on me, son!" Lee said as Carter disappeared down the stairs headed for the front door. "I bet he didn't hear me," Lee added, mumbling as he shuffled back to the window to watch what was about to unfold.

Carter emerged from the building then sucked in a deep breath to gain enough composure to assume the role as a Consulate servant. When the policemen stopped to watch who was entering the Consulate, Carter felt for his loaded revolver.

Carbonell emerged, outfitted as had been suggested. The old Cuban then doted on his passenger, whose covered leg extended toward the cobblestone. The shoes were bland, the trousers loosely fit, a blue shirt and a large slouch hat. Carter knew it was Evangelina Cisneros, but her disguise of a young man appeared adequate. The butterfly tie around her collar was clearly Carbonell's touch. It would have to go, Carter thought as the pair started toward the Consulate gate, their heads down and eyes fixed on the ground.

"What a pity the police have seen us." Carbonell offered.

"Keep moving," Carter ordered brusquely as he grimaced and closed the gate behind the pair.

"I see our vessel has arrived?" Carbonell said in his broken English as he slowed and looked over his shoulder out toward the bay.

"Inside. Your papers ready," Carter mustered courtesy as he skirted the two up the stairway to the office where Lee greeted them.

"No sé cómo dar las gracias a usted y el Señor Carter ," Cisneros said to Lee in a soft, sincere voice. Lee understood she wanted to thank them, and just tipped his head politely. Carter watched Evangelina remove her hat, which freed her long, black hair. Her eyes remained moist, wide and alluring. Tactically, those could be problematic, Carter thought.

"I would like to offer you a splash of rum before you leave, but I see that we have little time." Lee smiled widely as he clasped Carbonell's hand. He turned to Cisneros, took her hand and planted on it a gentleman's kiss.

"*Papeles. Aqui*" Lee pointed to the forged papers identifying her as Juan Soladad. Her ticket and the other necessary documents for embarkation on the liner *Seneca* lay next to Juan Soledad's identification papers.

"The tie needs to go. Too much attention to the face," Carter whispered to Carbonell as he methodically inspected Evangelina's outfit.

Carbonell translated for Evangelina, and then asked Carter, "And Señor Decker?"

"He's at the dock," Carter said, pointing. "Are we all ready?"

Cisneros nodded.

"You will be walking alone toward the docks. I will be walking a short distance behind you. Mr. Decker will be at the Café Luz. If there is trouble, he will join us." Carter punctuated each sentence precisely, waiting for Carbonell to translate each one before starting the next. Carter sensed Evangelina's nervousness as she listened to Carbonell's cadence, repeating the sequence step-by-step.

"Once outside, head down." Carter finished.

Cisneros and Carbonell both nodded.

"The tie . . .?" Carter insisted. Carbonell removed it and left the top button of her shirt fastened. Evangelina sought Carter's approval with her wide eyes. Carter nodded. The young lady then folded her hair to fit under her large brimmed hat, and without another word, turned and started toward the door.

"It has been a pleasure working for you again, sir," Carter joked with Lee. He reckoned he would return very soon. The Cuban situation was not going away and Washington was sure to send him back soon.

Lee grabbed Carter by the shoulders and shook him slightly. "Godspeed, Mr. Carter."

Emerging from the Consulate alone, Cisneros walked with

feigned masculine strides toward the waterfront, casually puffing on a huge dark cigar. Carter followed, maintaining a consistent pace and distance, hand close to his revolver. The walk to the dock was short and the disguised young lady arrived at the small queue at the dock, and then calmly waited her turn to board. Carter hovered near the end of the line, maintaining a close eye on anyone close enough who might inadvertently reveal her identity, since the word of her escape on the streets had sky-rocketed her celebrity status. Decker, posted at the Café Luz, nursed a coffee as he scanned the people ambling close to the departure point.

Carter had additional concerns, though. The dock grew uncomfortably crowded with Spanish soldiers and officers. Two military inspectors at dockside were searching papers, and apparently with greater scrutiny than he expected. Carter locked eyes with the purser and pointed to his own hat. The purser surveyed the row, and then summoned Evangelina with a nod. The disguised young lady shuffled out and along the line opposite the Spanish authorities, hidden from their sight. The purser reached out and took her papers, and before the Spanish authorities could notice, faked a review and as he helped her into the launch.

Carter twitched. The Spanish officers started toward the purser, who waved them off. When the Spaniards stopped and returned to their mundane duties, Carter relaxed, eying Evangelina as she quietly settled onto the bench seat in the launch. A tiny smile wrinkled her face before she hid her whole face below the floppy brim of her hat. Even though the launch was not completely loaded with passengers and cargo, the purser raised his hand to stop loading. The Spanish officers took the cue and stepped to the front of the line to hold off the remaining passengers.

The boatswain then turned and yanked at the engine. It coughed but then stopped. He tried several more pulls, but the engine remained unresponsive and silent. Slamming his fist on the top of the engine, the boatswain burst into a litany of curses, fuming at the engine failure.

The commotion drew one inspector's attention. Carter

reached under his shirt and moved forward as the inspector headed toward the launch. Carter's pace quickened. He then saw Cisneros crane her neck to see what was going on. The frustrated boatswain yanked twice in rapid succession making the engine stammer, then purr with an irregular putter. Blue smoke spewed from the motor, thinning quickly to a whiter tint. The boatswain continued to tinker with links on the motor's casing until the arrhythmic clatter finally evened out.

"*Bueno*," the boatswain yelled out as he waved off the inspector before he could reach the launch.

Carter stopped his approach, then relaxed his still clenched grip around his revolver handle as the boatswain plopped the propeller under water. The Spanish officer backed off. The launch, with Cisneros aboard, swerved away from the dock. Only then did Carter sigh and stand down. He continued to monitor from the end of the dock as the launch chugged its way out toward the steamer *Seneca*, moored in the center of Havana harbor. He glanced back at Decker, still sitting at a table at Café Luz, and nodded. Confident now that Captain Stevens would handle the choreography on board until he arrived on the final ferry of the night, Carter headed to the Café and joined Decker in their wait. Cisneros would be ushered on board by Stevens himself then sequestered in a stateroom.

An hour later, as the gaslights illuminated the docks around the harbor, Carter and Decker joined the boatswain and the purser on the last ferry out to the *Seneca*. Shortly after they boarded, the steam ship sounded her departure whistle. Anchor up, the stacks of the *Seneca* billowed dark smoke into the evening twilight and commenced her escape. Swirling exhaust from the stacks eventually bent over and trailed the vessel as it gained speed, passed the imposing Castle Morro and then emerged out in the open ocean with Cisneros secretly stowed away in the safety of an American passenger liner.

The sea between Jamaica, Cuba and Haiti offered the prime observation point for Gervasio Sabio. His cockleshell, *Libre* weathered a number of storms over the years and had served him well whatever the sea and the sky chose to throw at him. His clever carpentry had fashioned a space for contraband storage under the main deck when her shuttled back and forth from Kingston to Santiago. It had passed muster several times when he had been boarded by Spanish authorities looking for the contraband. Today's voyage was meant solely for observation and relaxation.

Sabio was a Peninsular Spaniard by birth, coming to Cuba as a settler so many years ago that he had forgotten. He fell in love with the lush greenery that Cuba offered in contrast to the dry, desolate province in Spain where he had grown up, and now accepted the island as his home. When Colonial Governor Weyler unleashed his campaign to create a submissive colony, he chose loyalty to his new home rather than to Weyler and the crown. His heart galvanized in favor of Cuban liberty after being arrested following a scuffle with unruly Spaniards who had trespassed on his land. The scuffle removed a thumb from his right hand, retribution for raising his machete against the roguish Spanish soldiers; it stood as a reminder his new loyalty was not misguided. The severing of his thumb he found left him unable to farm effectively, so he left Cuba and moved to Jamaica at the urging of his friend, Gerasimo Lugo. He was able to meld into the fishing village outside of Kingston with his friend's help, and was soon able to acquire and refit *Libre*. Fishing provided him the additional guise to continue his support of the revolution.

This morning had been quiet. Even with a slight roll to the seas, the still surface mirrored *Libre's* gull-white hull. As he slowly maneuvered on his patrol, he followed a line of pelicans back into Kingston. The birds settled sentry-like postures atop the tall mooring posts spotted throughout the harbor. Sabio stowed his gear, rolled up his ragged leg trousers and waded to shore, feeling the cool water caress his legs. He slipped on his sandals and headed to the old Consulate building where he and Gerasimo Lugo established a makeshift base of operation. He climbed up the rickety, narrow stairs two at a time. The mid-day heat quickly reminded him to slow down. At the top landing, he rested for a moment then sauntered down to the office.

"Ah, Sabio . . . catch anything?" Lugo asked playfully. His wide, toothy grin and wild, white hair made him look of a vagabond rather than the head of a covert operation. He had been nursing a fat, black cigar for enough time that the saliva soaked wrapper stained his thin lips.

"German vessels from Port-au-Prince . . . one in, one out. I think Domingo and Garcia need to know," Sabio said as he melted into a chair near the table that had been covered with Cuban maps.

"Did you see where they were headed?" Lugo's voice betrayed his surprise.

"No. I can only suppose back to Germany," Sabio uttered cautiously.

"So they were passenger liners, no?"

"I do not believe so."

"Military vessels . . . ?"

Sabo nodded.

"Hmm," Lugo mumbled as he picked up a telegram he had been reading. "We need to keep vigilant on them, my friend, especially since we have an arrangement to prepare." He handed the telegram to Sabio, who read it quickly.

"Do you know who?" Sabio asked, setting the telegram down and glancing up at the ceiling.

"It says an American needs to meet with Garcia. I suspect it will be Samuel Carter."

"Ah, Carter. Little problem in. But Garcia is deep in Oriente. He and the Spain are moving. Getting him out may be a big problem."

"We will need to contact General Rios as well. He still controls the north." Lugo suggested.

"Across the island? That will not be easy."

"We cannot let Carter get captured by Spain. He is a good American. So, if that is what is required, then we need to have that ready."

"Nosotros asentimos . . . agreed."

"I will have the telegrams sent and also scouts to reconnoiter with Garcia. *Mí amigo*, you look like you need siesta."

Guntis Goncarovs

Chapter 4

The oddity of such warm late September weather in Washington gave the White House domestic staff the opportunity to open the heavy Victorian drapes and lace panels to let fresh air drift throughout the residence. Later in the day, the room would be clouded with stale cigar smoke. President William McKinley knew that today, as had been every day since he had been inaugurated, would be filled with meetings and cogitations, deliberation over domestic and international affairs with his staff while fighting off an increasingly hostile press corps. At least for these early morning moments he could relax, listen to finch song, calmly eat breakfast with his wife Ida, and gauge how much medical attention her infirmity would need.

'My dear Ida,' he thought to himself as he monitored her movements at the table. He grew concerned her condition had deteriorated and she needed monitoring. Her epileptic seizures made such monitoring a necessity, since his long days would afford him only brief moments with her. He knew he was fortunate though to have a man like Garrett Hobart as his Vice President, who volunteered to help him ensure Ida's comfort during the day and allow him to wrangle with his raucous Cabinet. Even with Garret's assistance, Ida's illness was chronic, which made him feel twinges of guilt as if he was abdicating his husbandly responsibilities. Their evening commitments had to be tailored to accommodate Ida's insistence that only she would function as the White House

hostess.

Today would be a good day, McKinley methodically concluded as Ida appeared more lucid than in the past weeks. She had a touch of color in her cheeks. He would not require frequent updates. He penned his customary note for Hobart to confer with him mid-day and following Ida's afternoon nap, thinking twice would be adequate. He reviewed the note, and then folded it over. He marked G.H. on the outside so a doting staff member could whisk it away. Finished with his morning ritual, McKinley assisted his wife from her chair, and then wished her a good day as she ambled back toward her sewing room. He followed briefly, and then slipped into the Yellow Oval Room for his first meeting of the day.

A bright morning sun poured in through the tall windows of the conference room as McKinley stepped through the open threshold. Heading directly for his desk, he slowed to take attendance with his penetrating eyes. He preferred smaller groups. Fewer people made for fewer streams of discourse, allowing him to maintain focus on topics without confusion. It also offered him the where-with-all to deal separately with the personalities. William Rufus Day sat in for State Secretary John Sherman, the latter his selection for the cabinet post because he was feeble, ancient and inept . . . it allowed McKinley his desired full control over foreign affairs. He knew William Day from his campaign and the elder statesman would continue to compliment his control.

Next to him around the large, Victorian table sat the aloof War Secretary Russell Alger, also selected for pliability. Across the table perched Navy Secretary John Long, a curmudgeon and one of Washington's elite. Next to John Long was the boisterous, very young by Washington standards Teddy Roosevelt, who McKinley felt pressured to appoint as Assistant Secretary of the Navy. The youth posed the only challenge to his authoritarian grip on the cabinet. Roosevelt was the only one of the cabinet that tended to be a rouge rather than work through political consensus to solve issues. As Roosevelt was the only rogue, McKinley felt able to contain him . . . he still needed to tap his talent and energy.

"Gentlemen, let us get this morning brief started," McKinley opened the discussion while settling into his swivel armchair. The posture amplified his smallish, five-foot-six frame. He peered over neatly stacked folders on his desk. "Is there a status from Ambassador Woodford?"

"Yes, Mr. President," William Day replied smugly. His appearance, rumpled as if he had slept in his suit, contrasted the dapper men in the room. Day's deep voice and controlled tone commandeered the respect his clothes couldn't. "We have confirmation from Mr. Woodford that he has met the new Prime Minister Sagasta in Madrid, and he has *tentatively* agreed to our requested concessions on the question of Cuba."

"*All* of the concessions?" McKinley leaned back in his chair, calculating responses as he fondled a fresh morning cigar wedged between his thin chiseled lips. There were no secrets around this table. McKinley knew Alger would welcome the news. He had no desire to plan for war. Roosevelt — on the other hand — would scoff at conciliatory news from Spain. McKinley knew that Teddy wanted to use the Cuban situation as an opportunity for the United States Navy to assert itself as a preeminent naval power. A quick, decisive strike against Spanish colonialism could make the clear statement that the United States was ready as a major player on the world stage. Long was a tough read for McKinley today — he tented his fingers and scanned the room, apparently for everyone else's reaction, save Roosevelt, who he had been coaching on meeting etiquette.

"Yes, sir, that is what Ambassador Woodford reports," Day confirmed.

"Have they also agreed to eliminate their re-concentration camps?" Long prodded.

". . . And will they finally release the Americans they're holding, or are we going to let some cowboy reporters spring them as well?" Roosevelt interjected.

McKinley recoiled, stung by Roosevelt's comment. He suffered personal and political damage because of Evangelina Cisneros' escape; his people in the State department had been working for months negotiating her release when some rogue newspapermen accomplished what his administration could not. As far as he was concerned, the Cisneros affair was now an issue he would personally and unofficially take up with the newspapermen Hearst and Pulitzer.

"That was part of the agreement, as I understand it," Day replied, glaring at Long.

"And you trust them?" Roosevelt grumbled.

"It is a new government, gentlemen. We need to let them get back on their feet after the Cánovas assassination and allow them time to validate their agreement," McKinley said as he thumbed through a neat stack of papers and pulled out his handwritten copy of the demands he sent with Woodford. He set it on top of the maroon bound books he had placed in front of him, then added, "If you would like, John, here is the text of the agreement."

Long declined. McKinley noticed the life-long New Englander flush and cringe, as if suddenly ill. He knew his Navy Secretary didn't tolerate Washington's climate well, and the recent heat wave did not seem to set well.

"Time? More time? I say they've had long enough." Roosevelt groused. "And what happens if the next penny-ante dictator changes his mind about this agreement? We've already lost a large investment on that island, Mr. President. As a businessman yourself, I am sure you need not be reminded those losses have yet to be repaid."

"We shall stand by our offer. Monetary retribution is secondary at the moment. When agreements bridge administrations consistently, I contend it nurtures lasting cooperation," McKinley pontificated.

"Patience, Mr. Roosevelt." Day replied, then under his breath added, "Something of which you have very little experience."

"I say we take action now," Roosevelt slammed his open hand on the table, clearly agitated with the conversation. "We've given them plenty of opportunities to come clean."

"We're in negotiation, Mr. Roosevelt. Negotiations take time," Day interjected.

"Tell that to the Cuban people. Haven't they suffered long

enough?"

"Gentlemen, we need to resolve these issues methodically," McKinley raised his open right hand to quell the discussion. "I insist that the lingering Japanese presence in Hawaii be fully settled first before we burst into Havana."

"The question of Hawaii has already been resolved," spouted Roosevelt. "We do not, and I repeat, *do not* have to ask permission about territory that is rightfully ours. The Monroe Doctrine states this clearly."

"Need I remind you, Mr. Roosevelt, that we did resolve that incursion with diplomacy," Day interrupted calmly, but in square measure with Roosevelt's fire. "Which I expect we will be able to do in Cuba as well."

"In the end sir, war is simply diplomacy by other means," Roosevelt sniped.

"Gentlemen, this is an informational meeting, not a declaration of war," McKinley used the tone of his voice and his intimidating stare to move the conversation back to workable proportion.

"And what do you propose for the debacle going on in Haiti?" Roosevelt erupted again, clicking his teeth as he slammed his fist on the table. "Are we supposed to ask the Germans to play nice while we debate the legitimacy of their claim? Shall we just let Willy just go ahead and ravage the damned island and perhaps pocket Cuba while he's at it?"

"Germans?" McKinley's mask-like face etched some surprise.

"This is the first I have heard of this," Day commented, quickly reviewing his notes.

"Read the packets, Gentlemen! This is not news." Roosevelt scoffed as he wagged his finger at Day. "If you and Sherman were competent . . ."

"Enough bickering!" McKinley shouted, vaulting up from his seat. He leaned over the smooth Victorian table and glowered. The room fell silent, all eyes trained on the President. His return stare seared his displeasure with everyone. "We shall be civilized in our discussions here. I will tolerate no less."

Roosevelt leaned back in his chair and wiped his mustache. His toothy grin peeked out from underneath. Day remained stolidly defiant, maintaining a disapproving frown toward Long and his assistant.

"The damned press is doing enough saber rattling out there on this Cuban situation," McKinley challenged, his face flushed red with anger as he returned his glare toward the table. "They're calling for war on a weekly basis while we try to negotiate peaceful solutions and delicately manage political impact caused by their roguish antics."

Silence mingled with the pall of cigar smoke the building humidity stopped from reaching the ceiling.

"These issues need reason, prudence, and resolution, not jingoism. We shan't be puppets of an emotional, headline mongering press. Provocative and potentially non-returnable actions will do nothing but play into the press's hands." McKinley began rolling a fountain pen in his right hand as his pallor returned. His stare grew blank again when he asked, "Perhaps you could enlighten us about this information you have concerning this German situation?"

"According to my sources, the Germans are already militarily engaged and are using highly experienced spies in other areas of the Caribbean," Roosevelt responded. "All of Hispañola appears to be their objective, not just a claim on Haiti. The unrest and resistance in Port-au-Prince is being quelled by force."

Silence re-captured the room, giving McKinley time to catch up. He distrusted most sources not under his direct control, especially military intelligence, since it had been egregiously incorrect before. He needed corroboration.

"What else," he asked.

"There are reports that the Germans have stepped up manufacturing and are moving more large war ships near Kiel," Long finally spoke up.

"I see." McKinley turned his head in Day's direction, who twitched his eyebrows before sliding his hand over his receded hairline. "William, I need you to look into this. ***Thoroughly.***"

Day nodded his affirmation.

"Will this change our timetable for Cuba? Two European countries infringing on our rights in the Caribbean is not a tenable situation," Roosevelt said. "If you ask my opinion, I think Kaiser Willy is schmoozing the Spanish queen in an attempt to get a foothold into Cuba. Perhaps even offer to take on the insurgency on her behest. This is a reckoning time — a bloody reckoning."

"I disagree. Despite what the press has to say, we need to look at these things independently," McKinley spoke directly to Long. "Can we can do something, non-provocative mind you, that would show Madrid that we want a finalization of our agreement sooner rather than later."

Day squirmed in his seat and leaned forward.

"What about maneuvers nearby?" Long suggested.

"Now that's the way to send a message!" Roosevelt leaned back into his chair.

McKinley remembered that the brash secretary had actually proposed an incursion plan to him while Long was on his extended summer vacation. The details did include moving the fleet already to the Florida Keys, and stand at the ready to take action within two days of war declaration.

"That sounds to be a viable option," McKinley mumbled as Long slid his thumb down the list of available cruisers.

"We are overdue for some drills in the Gulf of Mexico. The North Atlantic Fleet can muster in Key West and await orders." Long responded.

"I do not believe that meets your non-provocative criteria!" Alger gasped, as if finally awakened by the conversation. His lips pursed in outrage. "Why don't we just send our entire Navy to Havana and not waste any more time with this?"

"Now you're talking, Alger!" Roosevelt verbally sparred as he clacked his teeth and grinned.

"Gentlemen, I am not willing to accept that as truth. *And*, I am not so naïve to misunderstand the growing need for showing Madrid some muscle and putting some money where our mouth is." McKinley rose from his leather chair, folded his arms behind him and walked toward the thickly draped window, open to the late autumn air. He needed some time to sort out this new information. He could foresee the bickering between Roosevelt and Alger growing even more raucous if he did not intervene. He slowly turned back to the group and waved his open hand through the sunbeams slipping through the window. "I suggest we consider enjoying this day. It is not common that such nice weather blesses us this late in the year. Meeting adjourned."

Long and Roosevelt took the cue, rose from the table and headed out of the briefing room. As soon as he assured the two Navy Secretaries were out of earshot, McKinley sourly whispered, "Mr. Day. I need a minute with you."

As the Navy Secretaries emerged onto the north lawn facing Lafayette Park, Long noticed the thick morning dew had already evaporated into thickening humidity under a coalescing cloud cover. "We need some more information from down there," he said.

Roosevelt smiled smugly. His plan was moving forward exactly as he had hoped.

"We only have control over Naval Intelligence," Long stated.

"I've already arranged for Wainwright to be assigned to the *Maine*," Roosevelt noted, looking over his shoulder and through the window where he could see the argument raging between McKinley and Day. He fished into his jacket for a cigar, worked the end through his pursed lips before putting a match to the dry end. "Wainwright said he could tie up things in the office in a couple of days and that will give us a trusted and skilled eye closer to the fray."

"You've been busy while I have been away," Long's voice was tainted with mistrust as he stuffed his pipe full of tobacco.

"His forte is in the field, John, you know that," Roosevelt defended. "You'd have made the same decision. Besides, I can't think of a better man for this situation."

"Let me make sure I understand this. We'll send the *Maine* to Cuba so we can plant Wainwright in Havana? Were you planning to discuss that with me at some point or have you already conspired with McKinley about this?" Long arched his eyebrows.

"That is something I haven't quite worked out yet," Roosevelt answered matter-of-factly as he felt Long's stare spear him. "As long as she is headed to the Keys, she's headed in the right direction. I am sure something will happen to force a closer move."

"But what about McKinley?"

"We'll work something out," Roosevelt noted as he let out a blue-gray stream of smoke.

"This all still leaves us short on intelligence. Until we can get some incursion, friendly or otherwise, we still don't have anybody on the ground. And even if Wainwright does go to Havana, he may be a bit too obvious to poke around."

"As I recall, although he won't admit it, I am sure, Day does have some under cover action going on down there. Fitz Lee, if I recall correctly? An old Confederate war horse," Roosevelt replied, but then remained quiet, not willing to let on his plan with Wilkie under his wing.

"I do know that Hazen's got a boy down there. Carter. Sam Carter I believe is his name." Long offered.

"He has some ties with Garcia, if I am not mistaken," Roosevelt knowingly added. He had done his homework on Hazen's Secret Service branch personnel, men who should be his. He had already tied into Lee's cable route that detailed much of the activities in Havana.

"Before we put hobnails to the ground, we've got to know what we're getting into, TR. Going blindly into there is just a recipe for suicide."

"You know, I think Carter is back here in the States now. Perhaps we should offer to pay his way back down there, you know, a joint effort between the military and the government to get a bit more information."

"Are you asking or telling?" Long groused.

"Asking," Roosevelt capitulated.

"Then I would agree." Long noted. A smile cracked his lips.

"I will ensure Mr. Wainwright has a brief talk with Mr. Carter before he reports to the *Maine*." Roosevelt's eyes gleamed even more than sun off his spectacles.

Fitzhugh Lee considered his responses carefully. It was not often that a woman would come into the Consulate alone, and even more rare for one as stunningly beautiful as this one sitting in front of him. At the moment, she was pressing him for information.

"Miss McGeehan, what is it that leads you to believe . . ." Lee's words were slow and measured while he tried to remember anything that he may have on file about Annette McGeehan. He drew a blank.

"I have seen him come here often, General. To me, it logically follows that you would know who he is and what precisely he is doing," the young woman spoke with softness. Lee reckoned her accent was perhaps Georgia, but not as far west as Mississippi. He enjoyed watching her lean back in the overstuffed chair, tilting her head just so . . . just enough that loose strands of auburn hair that escaped from under her wide-brimmed hat caressed her shoulder.

"Mr. Carter does work for me," Lee replied with care and distraction. "He is one of my . . . ambassadors. I don't get out much and he does know Havana very well."

"Does this Mr. Carter have a first name?" Annette's stare appeared to thaw, just enough that Lee felt his concern dissipate.

"Samuel."

"Samuel Carter," Annette said under her breath. Her alluring green eyes drifted toward the high ceiling in the Consulate.

"So what is it that brings you to Havana, Miss McGeehan?" Lee asked, re-taking the offensive because from the time she strolled into the office, he felt he was at a distinct disadvantage.

"My father is Cornelius McGeehan, and his business is sugar, General," she replied. "Sugar brings him here. Travelling with him allows me an opportunity to continue my research."

"Research?" Lee asked patronizingly.

"I study birds, General," Annette continued, as if noticing Lee's quizzical expression. "Ravens, in particular. Do you realize they are quite intelligent? Some people even believe they are more intelligent than parrots."

"Ah, that is quite interesting. I do know there is quite a variety of tropical species on this island," he noted, then added, "And what is it that interests you about Mr. Carter?"

"Well, General, I have noticed him several times at the Café Luz, and I have seen him several times seemingly watching my father. As I have mentioned, I have also seen him coming here frequently. When I put all of that together, I begin to wonder if this Mr. Carter intends to do my father harm. Or perhaps he is under suspicion of something?"

"I can assure you that your conclusions have no bearing, Miss McGeehan," Lee said, smiling.

"My father is a very honest man, General. I assure you he offers no trouble at all."

"I do believe you, Miss McGeehan, but if you do not wish to believe me, speaking with Mr. Carter personally, I am afraid you will need to return at some other time — as he had some urgent business to attend back in the States."

"I see. Thank you, General." Annette nodded, stood, and then hand-pressed her dress. "Your words seem sincere, as I would expect for a Southern gentleman."

"My pleasure to be of service," Lee noted. Annette turned and started toward the door. The General fished under his desk for his shoes to slip on his hidden stocking feet, but when Annette stopped and looked back at him, he tipped his head and asked, "Is there something more I can help you with.

"Yes, sir, now that you ask, there is. I would indeed like to speak with Mr. Carter at some point. When, perchance, will he be arriving back to Cuba?"

Lee cleared his throat. "I believe he is scheduled to be back here in two weeks. I can have him meet you at your hotel, if you would like?" He lied, not knowing for sure when Carter was due back.

"I am afraid we will be headed back before that." Annette tipped her head and let a sly grin grace her soft looking face. "Perhaps I can see him back in the States. Where is it that you said this Mr. Carter had business?"

"My dear lady," Lee recoiled, but deftly realized his escape route. "Washington, of course."

"I see. Then perhaps I shall ask for him on a future visit here," Annette noted and turned back toward the door. As she exited, Lee sighed, believing his gamble had satisfied the young lady. As the door closed behind her, he ambled toward his files and worked through the names he had of registered businessmen. He extracted the one titled McGeehan, returned to his desk, and combed over the details.

"I knew it! Charleston," he grinned, tapping his finger on the paper that identified where Cornelius McGeehan lived in the States. He continued reading through the paper for any other information Carter may have collected on the man and the lady who claimed to be his daughter. What surprised him was that Carter made no mention of Annette in the file.

Rudolf Moser was deeply consumed in melancholy as he wandered through the dreary, gray mist, idly counting shoe worn cobblestones on the street. He knew that he had become a *persona non-grata* in Kaiser Wilhelm's secret service, left in the doldrums of Baltimore, far from the excitement he had once seen over the years in places like Europe, China, and the Caribbean. Here there was nothing more than merchant shipbuilding and laboring reconstruction of factories left disheveled by the Union forces during the American Civil War. Buildings after brick buildings now lined the streets, erected out of the rubble; fish markets and row houses, spewing out clouds of choking brown smoke that rained soot onto the streets. Ships built across the harbor, were nothing but mundane copies of trading ships; no dreadnaughts, no new innovations, no weaponry of consequence, nothing to uncover.

He knew his reports back to the Kaiser were ordinary and of little consequence. He felt marooned, unable to find anything of interest in a country that appeared interested in nothing more than pacifism. The abandonment allowed him time to think about where else he would rather be. He thought of leaving and heading south, to the city of Charleston. He knew an old friend, Gunter Rohlenheim, using the assumed name of Samuel Miller, reported an intriguing new weapon for the time — a submersible torpedo boat. But then the messages stopped. Or was he sent to China? He couldn't remember exactly, other than they had lost their connection. Moser reckoned several possibilities for his old friend to stop reporting from Charleston, but was never able to verify any of them. Moreover, that was so many years ago as well. Even being assigned to America these last ten years left him empty handed in the search for his old friend; no one wished to talk about this vessel, or the men who were associated with it. It was like as if both had simply vanished.

"Nothing but an insignificant old man," Moser mused to himself about himself as he shuffled toward the tavern where he was to meet another operative. Wilhelm Ziegler was a younger spy who had caught the Kaiser's favor, and seemed now more his director than his comrade. Moser resented that the Kaiser had grown a fondness for Ziegler over him. He had been loyal over the years — now it seemed he headed into obscurity.

"Ah, Rudolph," a voice startled Moser. He glanced over his shoulder and saw the young, brash Wilhelm Ziegler, thin and strapping, looking more a scientist than a spy. He was a bit taller than him, close to two meters tall, and his chiseled face sat behind week old stubble.

"You need to be more discreet. I heard you two blocks away." Rudolph lied. He figured Ziegler thought so as well as he tried to hide his relief.

"Do you know of the tavern up here? It has hearty dark lager," Ziegler announced.

"*Ya, ya*. Been there more than I care to admit." Moser grumbled. He shook his head and gazed at the filth that filled the cracks between the cobblestones. He wondered whose shit clung to the soles of his shoes.

"I have some information for you from his Excellency

which I am sure you will welcome," Ziegler noted discretely as the pair entered the tavern and headed directly to the far end of the raised bar. The young spy raised his hand for two lagers, to which the bartender responded quickly. Two froth headed mugs appeared, their thin foam spillage dribbling along the sides.

Moser waited until the bartender was out of earshot. "So . . . good news, *ya*?"

"Mmm," Ziegler noted as he buried his upper lip into the foam. He tapped Moser's leg with handful of bills. Without looking, Moser grabbed the money and buried it into his pocket.

"The Kaiser wants you to go to Haiti and monitor American activity."

Moser gulped at his beer. He had been to Haiti before. It was worse than being in Baltimore. Insufferably worse. At least here, he could get lost within some cultural distractions. Haiti offered nothing more than rain, mosquitoes, and French speaking natives. He hated French.

"I assume this is for travel?" Moser asked as he tabled his mug and tapped his pant leg.

"Mmm. Good lager," Ziegler swallowed and nodded as he scanned the room, as if looking for someone. "It may be costly since it is only fat, rich Americans that seem to go to the Caribbean."

Moser mulled over the information as he milked his beer. His plan to head south along the coast to Charleston, where he had hoped he might discover something of his old friend would now be delayed.

"There he is now," Ziegler noted as a disheveled sailor sauntered into the bar. "I understand he can get you there," he added as he nodded toward a sailor who was wolfishly viewing a table of women.

"I do not feel well," Moser lied. He bowed his head and feigned a sudden weakness. He briefly toyed with the idea of defecting so he could migrate to Charleston instead of assume a mission in Haiti.

"I'll arrange this," Ziegler patted Moser on his back,

slipped off his stool and approached the sailor. Moser watched closely as the younger spy interrupted the American sailor who was winning over the attentions of two older, coquettish women in the corner of the dining area. The discussion was minimal and then money moved from Ziegler's hands to the sailor's.

"All arranged. The *Albemarle* will take you to Jamaica. I will cable to locals to help get you to Port-au-Prince," Ziegler said quietly as he returned and settled behind his half-empty mug. "You will be able to send reports directly to Berlin from the Consulate."

"I see," Moser noted dolefully.

"I need to leave," Ziegler added then downed what was left of his drink.

"*Gutten tag*," Moser muttered as Ziegler dropped a few more bills onto the bar next to his empty mug and slipped out into the Baltimore evening.

"Lattimer," announced the feeble looking conductor, his sun-blanched blue tunic hanging loosely from his fragile frame. His craggy voice carried though the nearly vacant rail car as the train hissed to a stop. A screech of steam billowed up from underneath the carriages at the same moment the old man cried out, "All out for Lattimer."

John Wilkie checked his pocket watch then peered into the misty pall over the small Western Pennsylvania coal town through a sweat-smeared window. His ride from Washington crossed picturesque mountains and fog-blanketed valleys. That beauty had been replaced with a mural of desolation in the form of empty, silent coal cars snaking into a bleak-skied horizon. He rose from his seat, tucked his soft covered portfolio under his armpit, and then managed the aisle to the open door. Tipping his head to the conductor, he slipped outside and onto the station's worn, wooden planked platform.

Lattimer had devolved in the several years since Wilkie had come here to report on the miner strikes. The rail yards were bustling then, even during the wildcat strikes. Coal-dust blackened rail hands hopped on and off between the lines of coal cars like scurrying ravens hovering and pecking at piles of spilled grain. The men sounded off raucously when they screamed past squealing metal wheels and whistle blurts of the yard-machines that shuttled the black gold. This morning was cool, tolerable for this far north, although still dreary enough that Wilkie would rather have been inside. He checked his pocket watch, calculated the length of walk to the Union Hall and reckoned he had seven minutes. He would have to take care of the matter that Hazen needed settled after the meeting. Wilkie headed to the scheduled mediation meeting arranged between the Union and the coal company owners. He mused about how to quickly terminate this petty discussion and move to the more intriguing part of the Secretary's offer as he walked smartly through the town.

Wilkie took great pleasure in his punctual arrival. The mine owners congregated outside the building with cigar ashes smoldering, planning and plotting points of debate. They stopped their banter when they saw Wilkie.

"Jack Pardee," thundered a rather stout man with a heavily waxed handlebar mustache as he approached Wilkie with his open hand. '*His smile was insincere,*' thought Wilkie.

"We are sure glad you guys in Washington decided to help us out here," he added while still shaking Wilkie's hand.

'*Clueless stoats,*' Wilkie thought.

"Now we'll show those trolls we mean business," spoke a faceless voice whisper. Wilkie turned but could not identify which man had uttered the words.

"My time is limited. Very limited," Wilkie moved off the handshake and gestured the men to follow him through the building entrance, stopping finally at a rectangular wooden standing table dead center of the large room. The men followed him single file. In passing, Wilkie noticed that John Mitchell, the Union's leader, well dressed and clean-shaven, stood confidently behind his chair. They had met years ago when Mitchell was a young activist. He encouraged Wilkie to cover the developing unrest in the mines, figuring he would get favorable coverage. He respected Mitchell for that passion, especially since the stories in the *Tribune* gained him notoriety.

Nowadays, Mitchell was well-dressed and clean-shaven. Wilkie knowingly nodded as he passed, more out of protocol than respect, and immediately took his position at the head of the table. Mine owners lined on one side, union representatives on the other, Wilkie glanced down to the two stacks of papers in front of him before signaling for them all to sit.

"John Mitchell of the United Mine Workers. This is John Fahy and Sebastian Lietz," Mitchell introduced. Wilkie took mental note that Mitchell had developed a political polish that he could respect. His brethren appeared less so.

"Jack Pardee, Lattimer Mines. And these gentlemen are Corbin Jones, Benjamin White, Walter Hazard, and William Thomas." Each man nodded as Pardee introduced him.

"I have little time for bickering, so state your concerns clearly and concisely." Wilkie ordained that the mineworkers speak first and that each side would take it in turn. He folded his arms in front of his chest as if to challenge the men around the table. He squinted directly at Mitchell, wordlessly directing him to begin.

"The miners want safe working conditions, sir, not 'safer.' Housing costs must be reduced and indexed to wage scales. Wages need to significantly improve," Mitchell listed.

Wilkie turned to the owners and condescendingly arched his eyebrows.

"We do not have an issue with increased wages, sir," Pardee countered. "But the government needs to pay more for the product to offset that cost."

"Let me clarify this for you Mr. Pardee," Wilkie scowled and spoke with a measured tone. "Government offsets are *not* on the table and this meeting will move more expeditiously if we stick to those which are. Am I clear?"

Pardee and the other owners slunk back in their seats, raising their eyebrows at Wilkie.

"On the issue of safety," Mitchell took to the offensive. "Too many brothers have died down there, and there have been no improvements, despite our calls for better tunnel bracing."

"And the exposed bituminous veins require better ventilation to ensure against explosions," Lietz inserted.

"Bitumen is softer, making it easier to dig through. It is of lesser quality so we need more to keep the profit margin up," Pardee countered. Wilkie allowed the emotional bantering continue, despite his irritation, more because he knew it would eventually fatigue on both sides. Settling down to actual negotiations between the factions would be ineffective without a release valve opened up wide to get hostility, anger and name calling accusations out of the way. Wilkie knew this needed to happen and take as long as it needed, despite his impatience, since release itself was a cornerstone of successful mediation.

Wilkie fished out his pocket watch and glanced down to mark the time, deciding to allow only ten more minutes of debate. His experience negotiating between the English coal and peat miners versus the rail owners taught him that time was part of effective strategy, as was teasing out important names and incidents from angry oratory.

Senator Mark Hanna's name, a coalmine owner, was dropped several times. He knew that Hanna's colors in Washington flew in favor of big business. Wilkie continued to monitor the tempo and volume of all the voices, as well as listen for trigger words, which he knew to use as a cue to end the jabbering. When he heard Mitchell's voice grow louder and enunciate the phrase 'on the backs of the miners,' he knew it was time to interrupt and take over.

Ten minutes, Wilkie marked to himself, then sternly announced, "Enough!" He slammed his open hand onto the table. Both sides silenced immediately. Eyes locked on him with owl-like stares. "Do any of you understand the gravity of this situation?" Wilkie asked plaintively as he waved his bent finger about the room.

Silence remained.

"Number one, our country is quickly growing crippled as a result of your bickering." Wilkie chastised the inertia that forced Washington to send him to Lattimer in the first place; then he pulled strings of patriotism as hard as he could without stretching them by mentioning the brutality that brought the issue to this moment. "Initiatives vitally important to our foreign policy and pending White House military objectives depend on coal. As we speak, Kaiser Wilhelm has invited himself to sail into our ports, passing ships idled for want of coal, unable to hinder his invasion plans because you cannot come to some agreement? We need agreement, gentlemen. Coal production must get back underway. We are not now in a war, gentlemen, but the likelihood of war means that coal must be produced, shipped and available at all of our navy ports."

Wilkie stopped to let his words sink in. He could not believe he had spouted in a Roosevelt-like tantrum, but he sensed he needed to bring home the threat of war as part the reality and the importance it brings to the mediation table.

"Number two. Coal is necessary to heat homes and winter is on the way. I don't suppose you'll be bitching much when your lips are frozen shut."

Wilkie stopped again. Silence reigned.

"Third and last, the railroad is making headway, and can move coal from all parts of the country. I suspect this part of the country cannot afford to lose the income if the government buys from your competitors. If you all don't get your priorities straight and get your coal moving again, the mines out west and down south won't have a problem filling the critical void you'll be leaving."

"One last comment. If you continue this standoff and do not produce, Mr. Roosevelt has agreed to petition the President to nationalize the mines in the general interest of the country."

"That's preposterous!" Pardee grumbled, folding his arms over his extended belly.

"How well do you know Mr. Roosevelt, Mr. Pardee?" Wilkie fired back. The owners began to squirm in their seats as Wilkie continued.

"Senator Hanna . . ." Pardee started.

"I do not believe Mr. Roosevelt cares what Senator Hanna thinks," Wilkie cut off Pardee. "So, would one of you tell me what concessions you are willing to make to get this coal and the nation moving forward again? Or do I go back to Washington empty-handed and explain this behavior to Mr. Roosevelt?"

Their emotions skewered, the two sides reluctantly settled

into earnest negotiations. Wilkie moderated for another hour of discussions, which yielded a tentative agreement that the two sides could resolve their differences by the end of the week.

"Thank you gentlemen," Wilkie stood, satisfied. He stiffly walked toward the exit, but stopped just short of it and turned. "I will expect to hear from you shortly. You may send the details to me directly at the Treasury Department. Good day, gentlemen."

Without waiting for a response, Wilkie left and headed briskly toward the center of town. He regrouped for a moment, and then remembered he had some additional business with a counterfeiter Stiles had traced to Lattimer. Without stopping, he walked directly to the Sheriff's office and burst in without knocking. The area was strewn with papers. Sheriff Martin sat amidst it all, pouring over one of the many stacks that covered his desk.

"Can I help you?" Martin asked coldly. He peered up over his glasses.

"Wilkie. I work for Mr. Roosevelt."

"Roosevelt? Is that so?" Martin tipped his head, skeptically. "You got any proof?"

"If you insist," Wilkie stiffened his lips and snapped open his small portfolio. From the pocket, he took out an official looking paper that had Roosevelt's distinctive signature scrawled boldly on the bottom. He flashed it at Martin.

"I see. What is it that you need?" Martin asked, immediately stiff and complicit.

"I am looking for a Mr. Carl DeLauro. I had requested that he be held here until I arrived." Wilkie glared at the Sheriff with steely cold eyes.

"He —he was released." Martin swallowed hard. He quivered as he cocked his head, as if looking for a concealed weapon. After a moment to gather his wits, Martin added, "I had nothing that could stick. That Mitchell fellah from the miner's union sprung him. You gotta see him."

Wilkie winced and squeezed the bridge of his nose. "What about records. You must have records on him, yes?" he growled impatiently.

"Yes, sir," Martin fished through the piles, starting at the one closest to him. In the second pile, about halfway through, he stopped. His fingers trembled as he handed Wilkie the disheveled papers. "He started the fracas during that strike, you know."

Wilkie nodded at Martin, creased the papers then slipped them into his armpit.

"Hey, mister. You can't leave with those. They're official papers, you know."

"I am on official business, remember? And since you can't seem to hold some two-bit thug, well I guess I'll just have to go find him myself," Wilkie grinned, then turned, left the office and headed back to the train station, leaving Martin slack jawed.

DeLauro moped along the Baltimore docks, looking for a place to rest. This city was bigger and was laid out differently than his home town of Cleveland, which confused his navigation. He had heard about Baltimore from brothers in the mines who told him that work was plentiful. They told him it was easy to get a job at the mills; that didn't square with DeLauro's experience. He struggled to remember which of the factories he'd already sought out for work; he heard repeatedly that none were hiring without experience. Not even the enormous Maryland Steel factory at Sparrow's Point was interested. It was just another disappointment. Another hollow day of failure in a string of failures. He was starting to believe that his union activity followed him here and had marked him 'undesirable.'

Afternoon turned to evening. Exhausted and withered by heat of which he was unaccustomed, DeLauro crumbled onto an old, rusted metal bench, forming a heap on the soot-laden planks, and gazed across the bay's surface to the shipyard nestled in a safe inlet. Clanging on metal being forged and bent reverberated out from the yard as nearby brick-worked stacks grew, ring over ring toward the sky. These stacks would soon spew smoke from burned coal he had once mined, he mused. He'd try heading to that shipyard and ask for work tomorrow as a last resort, and if that failed, he dreaded he would have to consider going back to Lattimer and the mines.

DeLauro buried his head into his arms and let the breeze off the water tease his mussed, oil-laden black hair. Returning to Lattimer was not a good option. Even though the counterfeiting charges in Ohio were a matter of wrong place at the wrong time, he figured Sheriff Martin knew and was apt to come after him again. *After all, cops talked*, he thought. And if Martin had anything, even Mitchell might not be able to protect him.

He was too tired to let his frustration energize his growing anger. This land of opportunity as everyone called it seemed to escape him. Those like him had little chance at succeeding, even just survival. The same class society from Europe that his father had escaped seemed not to have been left behind.

"How's it going, fella," a voice surprised DeLauro. He popped his head up and looked at the square faced, bearded man standing next to him.

"It's not." DeLauro grunted as he studied the man's features. His cheekbones were high, making his eyes almond shaped. His wide shoulders fit tightly into the dark blue suit he wore that fit more like a uniform. It was soiled with hints of coal dust, DeLauro reckoned.

"Miner looking for work in the steel mills, I suppose?" The man arched his thick black eyebrows that hid behind his black-rimmed glasses. "Seen a lot of you guys lately. Kern's the name. Herman Kern." The man offered his hand.

"Carl DeLauro." DeLauro responded. Kern's accent was lightly European, like his father's. His vernacular though sounded like he had been in America for a while.

"Would have taken you for a Pole, or Hungarian," Kern cocked his head and contorted his face into an inquisitive stare. "Wouldn't have guessed Italian."

"Lithuanian," DeLauro revealed. "My father was Dilarentas, but he changed . . ."

"I see," Kern interrupted. "He did it so that you could blend in, get work and live a normal life. I understand, but I don't agree with doing that."

86

DeLauro bowed his head.

"So you from Lattimer?" Kern said as he sat down. DeLauro recoiled at first, but then nodded. "I heard the strikes were brutal up there," he added.

"Unbelievable. I don't believe what I saw and I was there," DeLauro rambled as he relived screams of agony, gunshots, and Stefan under the tattered flag. "Unbelievable. A massacre. Cops and sheriffs gunned down brothers and then just left them to die."

"Like this?" Kern handed DeLauro a leaflet.

DeLauro scanned the paper, skipping words his limited education couldn't manage. The author was Samuel Williams Cooper, a doctor from Philadelphia, and in it, Williams described Lattimer's police brutality exactly as DeLauro remembered. *As if he was there*, DeLauro thought.

"The deputies will probably be acquitted," Kern noted when DeLauro glanced up. "Let go. Freed."

"How? It was murder!" DeLauro's heart thumped as his face flushed. Mitchell promised him that Martin and his cronies would be held responsible.

"So tell me, do you think someone should be held accountable?"

DeLauro's eyes remained wide in disbelief. Kern's words struck a chord with DeLauro.

"We have been docile too long, my friend. We as workers need to take matters into our own hands. The mines, the mills, hell and even the government are owned by the rich men and we are no better off than serfs. Workers here are no better off now than they are in Europe."

DeLauro watched Kern closely as he shook his fists in the air. His words were oddly hypnotic as his eyes. DeLauro heard the name Johann Most and some ranting about propaganda of *the deed* in Kern's speech just before he vaulted to his feet and extended his hands.

"Come, Brother Carl. Let's go have some supper and we can talk more about a plan for change," Kern exulted.

The lure of supper was enough enticement for DeLauro, his cash running low and his stomach aching from hunger.

Chapter 5

Cold, driving rain had thoroughly soaked Sam Carter's overcoat by the time he entered the foyer of Washington's posh Army-Navy Club for his hastily arranged dinner appointment. Being wet didn't bother him — he had spent weeks in the Cuban jungle where rain fell in sheets day after day. Being cold didn't bother him much either — he had tracked several suspects through Chicago's brutal mid-winter bluster. Being wet and cold together though, nauseated him. It reminded him too much of the bitter winter that he and his mother had staggered through Mobile's cobbled streets after the Confederacy fell, homeless and hungry, begging for food scraps from the hoard of arrogant carpetbaggers that infested his home city like cockroaches.

When he arrived in Washington with Cisneros and Decker for a staged White House visit, the weather was bright, sunny, and warm. There was little warning that the clouds streaming in would quickly thicken, gray and sink lower until they had darkened the sky. By the time they boarded the return train back to New York, the rain started. Then it grew heavier and colder overnight and by morning, the north-easterlies started to gust. All day, sheets of wind driven rain scrubbed the Washington streets.

"Mr. Carter," a gravelly voice caught his attention. Commander Richard Wainwright, the Chief Investigator for the Office of Naval Intelligence emerged from the dining room. His straight-lipped smile amidst his bearded stubble was as cold as the rain outside, while his steel blue eyes began to inspect Carter. Shivering, Carter remained unsure whether protocol required a salute or a handshake.

"I am pleased you could come," Wainwright said reviewing Carter's condition. "I do apologize for the abominable weather. I understand it can be hard on you Southern types." His comment oozed condescension.

"It is a tad colder than the rain in Mobile this time of year, but nothin' I can't bear. I've dealt with it before." Carter emphasized his accent as he attempted a weak salute.

"I would suggest a firm handshake, Mr. Carter. Your salute lacks conviction," Wainwright icily offered his gloved hand.

"I will work on that, sir."

"Time's short. Hang up that overcoat and join me." Wainwright ordered as he pointed to an empty table in the corner of the busy, smoke-filled dining room, and marched off.

Assignments from the military made Carter uncomfortable, especially since he always sensed an underlying prejudice, in particular, as if it was directed toward his southern upbringing. Standing before Wainwright made him even more ill at ease. Nevertheless, as an agent with only five years tenure in the fledgling civilian secret service, a service growing closer to the military, he needed to grow and accept or at least tolerate it. The working interface between the Treasury and the military blurred with each passing month and more quickly now that the restlessness in Cuba blossomed into insurgent-like skirmishes.

Carter grabbed the collar of his long coat as it slid off his shoulders. He brushed off as much of the rain that he could, then hung it on the coat rack and carefully shuffling as he followed Wainwright.

"Sit down, Mr. Carter," Wainwright pointed to the chair opposite him. "Have some soup. It'll warm you up."

Carter glanced down to his chair as he pulled it out making sure nothing waited for him. Stiles had warned him that the Commander had a reputation as a habitual joker. The chair was empty, as was Wainwright's stare.

"Don't be concerned about me. I am not in a joking

mood." Wainwright carefully removed his gloves and laid them flat in his lap.

Carter cinched his way up to the table and considered letting his guard down. The commander pushed a bowl toward him. Steam bathed Carter's face.

"Bread?" Wainwright asked, ripping a chunk of warm bread from the small dark loaf.

Carter declined with a shake of his head. He spooned up some of the thin beef broth and let it trickle into his scratchy throat. "If I may be direct sir, what is it that you need from me? Director Hazen did not specify."

Wainwright scratched a word onto a small piece of paper and slipped it across the table, keeping his hand on the ragged edge. He waited until Carter acknowledged, then pulled it back and quickly crumpled it up.

'Garcia,' Carter thought as he tried to read Wainwright's expression. He had spent quite a bit of time with the insurgent Cuban General, and in fact had befriended the revolutionary in Miami a few years back. Carter thought his time with the General in the Cuban jungle was a discrete part of his past, but it seemed quite the opposite now. He learned much from Garcia about Cuba, the Spaniards and the Caribbean — information which was valuable for Lee and American interests on the island. Now it seemed the military was interested as well.

"I understand you know him?" Wainwright asked.

"Yes, sir, but not exactly where he is," Carter lied.

"We know. Eastern Cuba."

"What exactly do you need from him?"

"Information."

Carter bowed his head to focus on any specifics Wainwright was to offer.

"We need to know what he knows about troop strength — quality, condition, morale, officer character, sanitary conditions; anything about the Spaniards that will help us support him." Wainwright whispered.

"I see," Carter noted, and then added condescendingly, "Isn't that what your people are supposed to know?"

Wainwright's silence was an immediate affirmation for Carter. He knew the commander's operatives used brutal tactics, and since Wainwright now likely considered him a subordinate, would not admit it openly.

"Later," the commander then replied as his eyes grew large. "We need to know Spain's soft spots down there," he hissed through clenched teeth. "And Garcia needs to know we need a clear path."

"A clear path for what?"

"If he can't finish them off."

"Is Alger prepared for this war?"

"There is no war, Mr. Carter," Wainwright replied stiffly.

"Sound like we are fixin' to get into one." Carter spooned up some southern drawl with his soup, just to antagonize Wainwright this time.

"Secretary Alger has nothing to do with this."

"He is the War Secretary, is he not?"

"Nothing has been declared, so now there is no reason to involve him."

"But —"

"Let's just say that a Cuba free of Spain is highly desirable, especially if it is partial to the United States. We can't afford anything less. Whatever happens, when it happens, will mean we need to be ready to step in, if necessary to ensure the correct result. And we can't afford to be fighting Garcia as well. Trust me Carter, those who need to know are aware of this," Wainwright dismissed Carter's concern.

"How high?"

"McKinley specifically asked for you." Wainwright stabbed the fish on his plate.

"I presume then, a presidential endorsement leaves no room for refusal?" Carter thought Wainwright might have been lying, but he could not read the officer.

"You would be correct. Oh, and you should also find out what our friend may need in the form of support." Wainwright mused as he washed down the food with some water.

"Now, or if all hell breaks loose?"

"Now."

"What about my orders?"

"Can't risk it."

"What's at risk?"

"Christ, Carter, must you ask so many damned questions? Is an old fashioned 'yes, sir' in your vocabulary?" Wainwright snapped. He leaned forward and skewered Carter with a steely-eyed stare. "Listen, I don't like you guys in Hazen's agency almost as much as you guys don't like us in the military. And trust me, I would much rather use my own men. The point is, this 'excursion' can't look official in any way right now, and you are the closest that fits the bill. Understand?"

Carter swallowed, and then asked "When?"

"We've arranged passage on a rather indiscrete schooner early tomorrow." Wainwright slipped a ticket across the table.

Carter pushed it back. "I can go in through Havana."

"No you can't," Wainwright slipped the ticket back. "I understand you can't get to Garcia from the western end of the island."

"I believe I can. This seems like quite a huge production just to chat with an insurgent general."

"We've already determined it's the only way."

"I beg to differ. I can get this . . ."

"Listen, Carter, intelligence is our business in the military. We know what we can get and what we can't get. This is more than chasing a bunch of counterfeiters."

Carter leaned back and realized this was not meant to be a two-way discussion.

"This has already been arranged. Your train leaves for Baltimore at midnight, and Captain Aldrich knows you are coming. *Comprende?*"

"That's not much time." Carter realized everything he was wearing was wet.

"There isn't much time left," Wainwright quickly replied. "The situation is festering down there, and we need to get a handle on it quickly. The New York press has made an all-out frontal push to drive us into war. They're agog about Cisneros being freed, and the information they're getting from her is being twisted about, putting on more pressure for intervention."

Carter dabbed the corners of his mouth with the yellowed cloth napkin, then left it on the table.

"Then I shall ask your leave, sir. I have some things to take care of." Carter tipped his head toward Wainwright, slipped his chair back under the table and left.

Wilhelm Ziegler looked away from the train's rain streaked window to see his recruited accomplice asleep, slumped into the hard wooden seat beside his. He wondered how people in America slept on trains. DeLauro wasn't the first one he had seen. The tracks headed them back to Philadelphia, where he had wormed his way into an inner circle led by the world-known anarchist Samuel Cooper. It was the simplest way to get the explosives he needed to complete his mission meant to create disruption of the American Navy that in turn would ensure success for Tirpitz's plan.

He would have preferred to work alone, but Ziegler didn't hold enough confidence in his grasp of English yet, and he needed someone who could blend in. He knew DeLauro served that purpose. He was so dumb. Perhaps, just naïve. At least, he had the wherewithal to use Herman Kern as an alias. The downside of having DeLauro along was that he would need to be more discreet during his time at the consulate while delivering information back to the Fatherland. He would have preferred working with Moser who coped well with American vernacular. The Kaiser ordered otherwise, believing Moser's waning efficacy required phasing out.

Ziegler snapped open his pocket watch and checked the time. It was two o'clock. Back in Germany, the Kaiser would surely be reading his cabled message that Moser had been given the orders and that he was personally working his plan that included his own return to Baltimore. He had hinted that after seeing this city nestled inside the Chesapeake Bay, Tirpitz should consider Baltimore rather than Norfolk as a primary target for invasion. Access from the sea was better and strategically it was closer to Washington. Wilhelm would need more data to adjust his plans — more than just his opinion. DeLauro squirmed in his seat toward Ziegler. He could not discern whether his eyes cracked open or not.

"Another hour," Ziegler noted, although more to himself. DeLauro didn't respond. That suited him fine. It gave him more time to think. They would be in Philadelphia soon enough.

Carter ran through the wet Baltimore streets, worried he wouldn't make the dock in time. Slime grew thick and slimy between the uneven cobblestones making his hurried pace treacherous. He'd overslept. He never overslept. The Washington to Baltimore train had arrived late, so he had little time to rest. The cold morning made difficult any initiative he made to crawl out from under the covers. He had no time now to muse upon the growth that had reshaped the Baltimore he once knew— more people and more buildings. It hindered his double-time pace through the cold morning mist. He navigated turns into alleyways, street trash and new, too-tall redbrick warehouses that made the streets look narrow. The blocks of warehouses gave way to gleaming tin-roofed, block long steel mills. He tried not to slip as he raced through the open area that spread out at the head of the docks. He spotted one trail of men methodically loading a cargo of burlap sacks, working like army ants working a tropical rain forest. Each carried one sack at a time from the dock, across the rickety loading planks, and into the holds of an awaiting schooner.

The name *Albemarle* emblazoned the schooner on her brushed and slightly corroded copper plate. She stood a proud, large sailing ship lacking steam power refit — a remnant of a less complicated time — her three timber masts stood tall over a long, thin deck. The timbers were partly dressed with bleached canvas sails that hung precariously in rolls from each fully rigged yardarm. Her bowsprit angled proudly toward the sky, rigged with three jibs that lay in wait for open sea. In marine standards, she was now fading quickly into the shadow of an age driven by steam driven power.

Carter slowed as he stepped onto the heavy oak boarding planks. The wood waterlogged, his feet slipped as he struggled to save himself from falling into the water. He wasn't sure if he heard guffaws from the crew or if he simply imagined them. He moved more slowly and carefully up the rest of the wooden incline until his hobnail boots firmly met the main deck.

"Welcome aboard the *Albemarle*, a fine ship she be —" a well-seasoned and disheveled first officer greeted. ". . . Chief Seamus MacBride," the sailor added a shoddy salute, even worse than what Carter might muster.

"I apologize for being late. My name is Carter," he mumbled between breathless pants and politely nodded his head.

"No worries, Mr. Carter," MacBride replied. His face was unshaven, giving him a haggard appearance. A paunch ballooned under his dingy, tobacco stained rumpled blouse, straining button threads to their limit.

Carter grew concerned since the nature and secrecy of his mission as well as his personal safety may have been placed into the trust of this man. MacBride's slovenly dress elicited concern for maintaining confidence. For a fleeting moment, he wondered if this could be part of a plot by Wainwright to embarrass him. He broke eye contact, and then spotted the flag of the British Navy limp at the bow staff.

"White Ensign?" he asked.

"Can't fly Old Glory where we're passing by. They might think we'll stop and rough 'em up a bit," the middle-aged sailor winked and curled up one side of his mouth. "But I take it you knew that already — ain't you Wainwright's boy?"

'More like you're running guns for insurgents,' Carter thought as he smelled stale rum on MacBride's breath.

"Isn't this an American vessel?"

"Don't ye worry, son. Just ye, me and the Captain know." MacBride answered, winking his eye.

"Keep it that way," Carter said tersely.

MacBride continued his inspection of Carter, cocking his head as he glared at his face. "I was expectin' ye to be a bit more dark-skinned. Ya know, considerin' where you're headed," he noted.

"Skin color doesn't make as much difference there as it does here."

MacBride pursed his lips.

"No disrespect meant sir." Carter added as he cocked his head.

"None taken," MacBride frowned.

"I do think I'd feel a bit more comfortable if we all act like I'm just a simple, routine passenger." Carter stiffened his own lips to stress his point.

"You needn't worry your skinny little ass," MacBride whispered. "Just a sparse few take this old war horse to Jamaica."

"Jamaica?"

"We ain't a-goin' directly where you're a-going, son. Our cargo is not quite suited for our friend's liking, if you know what I mean," MacBride grinned. Carter noticed one of his front teeth was missing.

"How then —?" Carter started, but MacBride raised his dirty, calloused hand.

"Dinna know, but I assume the details of gettin' you where you want to go from there have already been a-fixed by your betters. But don't you worry, your secret's good with me." MacBride grinned while Carter studied his bloodshot eyes. The old sailor then pointed to the section of the ship behind the second mast. "Your cabin's below aft."

Carter concluded further discussion was pointless. Still perturbed with MacBride's foreknowledge, he turned and walked away. He stayed clear of any other crewmembers as he made his way over the mist-dampened planks. When he reached the stern, he dropped his satchel, backed into the rail and watched thick-necked crewmembers work. They wasted no time rigging chains to the side rails, then moving to their assigned stations at each of the masts, all the while their voices garbled sea shanties. Ropes flew to shore and aboard, sails dropped from their roosts, and then grew taut as they drank in the feeble morning breeze. Hands coiled the rigging onto shiny black posts, lashed precisely as the sails, luffing at first, slowly filled and bellied out.

The *Albemarle* slowly moved away from the dock planks, creaking as her hull kissed the long mooring posts goodbye. A sudden, stiff northwest breeze quickly filled her sail, urging the schooner past Sparrow's Point. The main mast sail holds chirped, brass rubbing hard against oak, as the deft crew adjusted their angle to the wind for a long, loping turn to the east.

Carter's senses heightened as the *Albemarle* picked up speed and again bellied to starboard. Newer steel mills on Sparrow's Point lined the shoreline, all spewing clouds from the already blackened brick stacks, streaking the sunlit sky cherry red and marbled thick, black smoke. The schooner tacked south and moved rapidly into the open waters of Chesapeake Bay. Exhausted, he turned his back on Baltimore with nothing left of interest for him, and then retired to his cabin to warm up, plan and most importantly, rest.

John Wilkie leaned back in the hard, ladder-backed chair as he waited for Roosevelt to enter the room. He slipped his finger beneath his collar to stretch out the stiff, starched ridge irritating his freshly shaven neck. He let his eyes take in the perfectly arranged seascapes and paintings of great naval sailing warships, each with tall, stately masts and gleaming hulls, cutting through the water at full speed under a bright blue, cloudless sky.

Those times were times of honor. Each battle followed a specific protocol and stayed within the confines of required calculations, proper execution, and the will of the wind and waves. Sea battles were *thinking men's* contests — like a chess match with organized possibilities and contingencies, shrewd adversaries, and multi-dimensional solutions — a synergy of experience and cunning of the combatants. Those days were now replaced with ones governed by blunt force, hardened steel, direct tactics, coal-tainted smoke spewing from huge stacks, and guns that spit shells in sheets of explosive rain.

Deception was part of a skill set lost from that time, Wilkie thought. The directness of steel ships that bore little regard for the whims of the sea obviated the need to plot furtive course and speed using only the sails. Wilkie felt fortunate that the line of work Roosevelt envisioned for him was more like the old days of sailing ships. Espionage commanded sharpness in order to remain two steps ahead of the quarry. His work as a journalist for the *Chicago Times* and the *Tribune* certainly prepared him well. He could glean usable facts and sort out the truth from fiction while rapidly discovering the connection. He was quite comfortable with Roosevelt's proposed plan to replace Hazen with him soon, so that he could mold the agency with his own vision.

"John, it is good to see you," Theodore Roosevelt announced as he threw open the door, commanding immediate attention with his presence. Wilkie silently and politely rose from his chair and faced the Secretary. "How are you?" the Secretary strutted past Wilkie, slapping him on his shoulder as he passed, then added without waiting for response, "Good, good. Glad to hear it."

"There'll be a resolution to the coal strike by weeks end," Wilkie reported.

"Good, good. You didn't have to do too much arm twisting, did you?" Roosevelt clicked his teeth as he smiled, clearly pleased with the good news.

"No, sir . . . The negotiations went smoothly — as planned," Wilkie passed off the Lattimer talks as passé, anxious to get on with what he envisioned as the furtiveness of espionage. "So, we have other ventures now?"

"Yes, we do." Roosevelt navigated around his oversized oak desk, and then settled into his high-backed leather chair. He pulled out a map from his top drawer and spread it out over the meticulously cleaned surface. He fished out his pince-nez and wedged them onto the bridge of his nose. Wilkie took the cue and leaned over to inspect the map, noticing some cryptic notes near Jamaica, Cuba and Haiti.

"Here," Roosevelt pointed to Haiti. "I have heard that the Germans are nosing around here. Have you?"

"Is this on or off the record, sir?"

Roosevelt leaned forward and let his arms straddle the map. The Secretary tipped his head just enough to look at Wilkie through the glass of his pince-nez. His message was clear.

"I do not have any definitive intelligence —" Wilkie stalled, struggling with the angst of his ill preparedness, thinking he understood Roosevelt's stare demanded response. "I honestly have not had time to evaluate the information."

"I don't care about official — you've been over there. You must know how they think. That's what I want to know."

"What I know is that the Kaiser wants in — in the Caribbean."

"He's sent people. Several — probably spies. What do you think they're looking for?"

Wilkie offered no response.

"Damn it, John, let me make myself clear. I want to know what you think. I really don't really care about official crap right now. Got it?" Wilkie felt Roosevelt's stare skewer him even sharper than his words.

"Reconnaissance is my best guess." Wilkie added with a nod.

"That is obvious, John. Elaborate," Roosevelt demanded. He tugged at his heavily waxed mustache allowing his gap-toothed grin to peek out from underneath.

"Bismarck may be gone, but people like him still run the show. Kaiser Wilhelm so wants expansion that he can taste it. More so than any of his predecessors," Wilkie grew comfortable counting on his time in England as a way to help him understand how the German emperor thought. He made a mental note to do more homework on Wilhelm.

"I thought so!" Roosevelt slammed his fist onto the desk and harrumphed. He began to pace in a circle behind his desk. He stopped at the window and looked out over the calm autumn day for a moment, stroking his full mustache.

"We can't have both Germany and Spain poised to nip at our underbelly at the same time. Not that it makes much of a difference, since I really don't care which ass we whoop-up on. Nevertheless, this does complicate our timeline.

"Has President McKinley reconsidered his time-table for Cuba?"

"He's stalling," Roosevelt growled as he stared out the window. "He sent Woodford to Spain to deliver our demands to their new Prime Minister, or whatever they are calling them now. I understand they promised to look closely at leaving Cuba, but that was just Woodford's opinion. And you know as well as I do, looking ain't doing, it's just stalling." Roosevelt's face was etched by concern.

"Spain will probably move quickly to save face," Wilkie mumbled, although he was not as sure what position Sagasta was going to take.

"Don't think so, John. Spain won't move until we push them out. I just wish McKinley would understand that simple fact." Roosevelt pruned his lips.

"So, how does this change affect us, Mr. Secretary?"

"It's imperative that we get things moving. I don't see Spain as a problem, but this German activity down there may make it complicated."

"Do I need to add this to my list of concerns?" Wilkie pointedly asked.

"Clearly — top of the list." Roosevelt's hands punctuated his words. "You know how much we need a tidy little war down there — quick in, quick out. It will shore up so many things both home and abroad. But if Germany is involved, I don't think we will lose, but I don't see how it can be tied up quickly."

Wilkie knew that Sam Carter had been directed to the Caribbean, but was not sure that Roosevelt knew that. He was not personally familiar with the young southerner; he inherited the recommendation that he be sent. Now he wasn't be sure he could find Carter if he was going deep into the jungle. A message through the Consulate might not get to him either. He was new to the organization, so Fitzhugh Lee would surely be cautious of him, especially disclosing any part of the operation. He could take care of that in due time. One thing he had heard about Carter was how very perceptive this southern boy was. If the Germans had people there, he'd sniff them out. Wilkie still needed assurance and information.

"Then I'll get started, Mr. Secretary," Wilkie stood.

"Glad to have you aboard, John," Roosevelt added, and then returned to the map on the table with focused concentration.

Wilkie didn't think Roosevelt even noticed him leaving the room.

Carter woke; surprised he had slept as long as he had. He dressed quickly, choosing his more city-like shirt and trousers rather than the bushwhacking ones he had slept in. The *Albemarle* had made good headway while he had slept. A stiff northwesterly wind filled her sail as the spit of the eastern shore of Maryland faded, now barely visible in their wake. He estimated the ship wasn't far from Hampton Roads at the mouth of the Chesapeake. That meant they'd be on open sea off the Carolina coast before nightfall.

He lit up the old short-stemmed pipe his stepfather had given him and savored the smoke. He tried to relax watching the small, early morning crab boats crawling up the Chesapeake coast. He knew Spain and the United States were as ready to ignite over Cuba like a bed of dry tinder on a hot summer's day. A state of war between Spain and the United States over Cuba would be disproportionate and wouldn't last long. At the end of it would be freedom for Cubans. The Spanish government was bloated with too many Generals, some petty, some more powerful, each vying for power.

As did the Cuban insurgency, Carter thought. Of deep concern were cautions voiced by his old friend, General Calixto Garcia. The rebel general led only one of the many factions competing for the vacuum that would be created by American intervention. Others waited in the wings, ready to swoop if the larger insurgency suffered decimation by the fight for freedom. The leaflet he found in Havana provided clarity that anarchists, some allegedly militant, were actively agitating in both the United States and in Spain as part of their bolstering strategies. These anarchists thrived on the press stirrings criticizing McKinley's administration, each with deadly, different reasons. He pondered upon the source of their support.

Then there was Arturo Colón, a renegade Cuban, as mercurial and unpredictable as coastal storms. He had sat with

Colón several times against the recommendation of Garcia and other generals. The young, pockmarked faced rebel was as ruthless as he appeared — no mercy afforded to anyone who would cross him, regardless of their affiliation. At times, his executions were doled out solely to send a message. Colón however, always had knowledge others did not, which made him valuable to Carter, but concerned everyone else.

Carter knew that the United States would look like the new bully on the world stage if they overtly intervened. He also knew General Garcia and it was clear that if his insurgency was successful, he would ensure relations between Cuba and the United States would be friendly. But if Garcia thought the Americans were looking to become a replacement occupier, it could all, including his present mission, be deemed as meddling, which could mean more than just losing Garcia's friendship.

"Your aloofness may be creating more interest in you than you want."

Carter was startled by the voice. He turned to see an older, bearded, wispy fellow, a few inches shorter than he was, and clearly fit for his age. His rugged square face was worn, weathered, and seemed oddly familiar.

"Never thought of it that way," Carter muttered while he sized up the stranger. The accent was odd, and his diction had a harsh quality. European, Carter concluded. "I don't find it necessary to socialize while I'm on business."

"You look familiar." the stranger then asked.

"Maybe a bar in Baltimore," Carter lied. He avoided bars when he could.

"Perhaps that's all it is. At my age, I may see in faces what I want to see." The stranger stopped for a moment, and then quietly continued, "After all, Samuel Miller would have to be in his seventies by now."

Carter felt suddenly undressed, disarmed when his birth father's name was mentioned. Samuel Miller died before he was born and very few people still alive would even know about his father. He knew that Miller was European, like this man, whose life and work was shrouded in secrecy. And now, a total stranger connected him with his father, based solely on physical resemblance.

"Should I know this Samuel Miller?" he fished. He wondered if it was all just an odd coincidence. It was a common name, after all.

"Maybe not," the stranger said, then added, "The man I once knew should be about seventy or seventy-five years old by now. If you know him, tell him I was looking for him," as he shuffled away

"And who should I tell him was asking — that is, if I do see him?"

"Rudolf Moser, an old friend." Moser tipped his head cordially, and then headed aft toward the cabins.

Carter remained at the rail to watch Moser disappear behind a bulkhead. He turned up his collar to stave the afternoon chill from his neck. His mother had met his real father in Mobile and had offered little else. Nor had anyone else. It seemed as if Samuel Miller appeared, then disappeared just as mysteriously.

Lieutenant William Alexander, who had become his stepfather, told him that Samuel Miller was an enigmatic foreigner, and that he highly respected his engineering skills. They were both associated with a secret Confederate project — a submarine. His own search led him from Mobile to school in Charleston to Richmond, and to Washington, where disheveled archived records revealed a few additional details. Only a handful of people even remembered individual sailors from any vessel, let alone admit to knowing details of the secret submarine. That time and place in history was a period everyone wanted to forget. Military records were sketchy as well, classified as 'secret' and sealed to even him as a non-military government agent.

Why Samuel Miller came was pure conjecture. Alexander avoided Sam's questions about his biological father, but he was unsure whether Alexander could not or would not answer them. Alexander did show him scratched group ambrotypes where his father's face hovered behind and in-between shoulders; small, imperceptible, almost as if stealth was being maintained.

Now this odd little man who called himself his father's friend appears out of nowhere. Sam's curiosity was piqued.

DeLauro sipped hot tea and felt warm. Outside, the Philadelphia morning started with a damp autumn chill. He sat at the simple table in the middle of Herman Kern's two-room flat. It had a table, a pair of ladder-backed chairs, a stool and a roll-up desk. There were also piles of books and papers that lined the walls where they weren't mounded high in the corners of the rooms.

"Ah, here it is," Kern tapped his forefinger on a single sheet he withdrew from a mass of strewn papers on the table. He added, ". . . something I have been working on for a while now."

DeLauro raised his head and listened closely as Kern started to read the details on the paper, sometimes turning it sideways to read the notes he had scribbled in the margins. Kern seemed to enjoy reading aloud, especially from these scientific papers. DeLauro did not mind, in fact he found his host's voice and topics very interesting.

"All bituminous coals exhibit a volatile ratio which may present a dust explosion hazard. It is important to note that both bituminous and anthracite coals can be involved in fires, but only bituminous coals can be involved in explosions. And if footprints are visible in coal dust on the floor or the coal dust is seen on the walls of a plant, then there is adequate material to propagate an explosion."

DeLauro listened closely as Kern read. He had heard the words for the types of coals before, but didn't pay close attention. He was paid in cents per load. More loads, more money. And more pain. It was simple.

"Without a match?" DeLauro asked, before he took a second sip of his tea.

Kern looked up to DeLauro, his eyes wide and a grin splitting his lips. "I am sure there needs to be some ignition source, or at least a heat source. I do know that piles of coal can absorb quite a bit of heat on their own."

"There was plenty of coal dust at Lattimer," DeLauro

noted as he set his cup down onto the table. "Is it that what caused the cave-ins?"

"I don't believe so. The coal from Lattimer was mostly anthracite, or at least that's what I know. Anthracite is much harder coal. Most of the bituminous coal is from other mines. Mines farther south. But I have heard there are veins that stretch up into that area."

"I see." DeLauro was surprised at how much Kern knew about the coal he had toiled over, but his information seemed disconnected. He recalled the coal he was digging before the strikes was the softer variety. He started to wonder if he was simply imagining that.

"It is easier to dig," Kern stared up to the ceiling. His eyes grew wide again. "So, here's what I think. I know that Dr. Most likes to use dynamite in his 'statements.' The problem is that dynamite is getting harder to obtain."

"And coal is everywhere," DeLauro added.

"Correct. If we get a some bitumen and mix it with an anthracite load, and have it delivered to some ship that will spend some time in the heat, like Florida, it should blow itself up."

"But wouldn't that be considered an accident?" DeLauro cocked his head. "How would they know it was us? How would they know it was us that were the ones mad at them?"

"Hmm," Kern rubbed his bearded chin, as if thinking. His evil grin returned. "*Ach*, I know. We ask Dr. Most release a statement to the press claiming responsibility for the 'deed.' *Ya, ya*. That would work, yes?"

DeLauro sipped his tea. He wanted everyone to know anything he did was payment for Lattimer and Stefan. He didn't know this Dr. Most except for what Kern had told him.

"Yes," DeLauro finally mumbled and continued sipping his tea while he mulled the possibilities.

Carter watched the shoreline as the *Albemarle* passed Hampton Roads, the last major port protected by the Delmar peninsula. A small pocket battle cruiser heading out to open water with her decks filled with white-clad sailors scurrying about, loading and unloading artillery supplies into their designated holds. Forward armament, unusual for battle cruisers, projected off to starboard, while her aft turret pointed to the port side. Carter recognized this unique design as the *USS Maine*, designed to outmaneuver any of those lumbering ocean plows in the shallower battlegrounds close to shore. In open sea, she would be easy prey to those foreign dreadnaughts. The cruiser was accompanied by a pair of large single-turret monitors, looking more like throwbacks to the Civil War, Carter thought. The low-slung, partly submerged vessels served to ward off any smaller ships venturing in for closer looks. Amidst all the traffic headed in and out of Hampton Roads, coal barges weighed low, wallowing about the harbor, and shuffling life-giving coal to the *Maine's* sister ships resting at the docks inside the protected waters.

"I'd bet she's the best in the fleet," Carter heard MacBride's voice brag behind him. Carter didn't respond. It was clear to him from their first encounter that this man was little more than a nosy, blow-hard that had left the real Navy before being summarily drummed out. Carter quietly watched the monitors veer off as smoke poured from the *Maine's* two huge mid-ship stacks and grew thick as they merged into a conical shape.

"She's a beauty, eh?" MacBride said like a lust-hungry sailor. Water frothed at the *Maine's* stern as her horn bellowed departure from the harbor. The field of white stars on blue background on her forward mast unfurled, as her cutwater knifed deeper below the surface, peeling sheets of water that curled at her sides. The cruiser swept starboard of the *Albemarle*, and with due haste, increased her pace toward the open ocean, her engines and crew fully engaged.

"I hear she's headed out to Tampa for some Gulf Coast duty," MacBride blabbered before letting a trail of tobacco juice fly over the rail and into the choppy gray waters below. "But I reckon that's a line of crap. I'll bet she'll be in Cuba afore long."

"Don't figure the Spaniards would cotton too kindly to that," Carter finally commented.

"Don't figure Roosevelt really cares a fig what the Spaniards think kindly of," MacBride replied half under his breath.

"It'd be presumptuous to think Roosevelt would be making gun-boat diplomacy moves without . . ." Carter stopped speaking when he spotted Moser at the starboard rail, attempting to monitor the *Maine's* progress. "What do you know about him," he asked in a hushed voice.

"Roosevelt? Well son, he's on a mission to bring glory back to the Navy and pride to America," MacBride clearly missed Carter's intention.

"Not Roosevelt, jackass," Carter spoke through clenched teeth, thinking McBride was as much a fool as he looked. He pointed to Moser. "Him."

McBride glanced over his shoulder and squinted. "Rudolf Moser. German, if I remember correctly. Doesn't say much and keeps pretty much to his self."

"Where's he headed?"

"I presume where we're headed. Jamaica."

"I mean after that?"

"Who the hell knows? I don't keep track of everybody's business who steps foot on this boat. We're headed to Jamaica, so I assume he's just headed to Jamaica."

"Any idea why?"

"He's probably making a deal for sugar or something. You know how those Germans like their sweets. I heard they import Cuban sugar to sweeten up their chocolate."

"Are you sure?"

"Ya know, if you're so damned curious about that fellow, why don't ye go ask him yourself. He seems harmless."

"Don't you think it odd?"

"Why would that be odd? You got money, you sail. And his friend had plenty. I figured what was the risk? He's a feeble old man that barely speaks our language."

Carter thought about explaining his question again, but backed off. MacBride was clearly a disengaged simpleton. He might have known everybody onboard, but it was clear there was little thought given to why they were on board. Carter realized in his position, he may have known more than an average sailor would, especially information such as German government interests in the Caribbean.

Only now did Carter start to appreciate the snippets that his immediate supervisor, Jack Stiles, gave him about the Kaiser's ambitions. Carter concentrated on Moser and thought more about this odd little man's interest in the *Maine.* He was worth watching out for more than just his personal curiosity about him knowing Samuel Miller.

Moser's eyes wandered toward Carter and MacBride for a moment, before they slowly retreated. He then remained at the rail for a moment, consuming a last bit of insight to the cruiser, and then moved away toward the cabins.

"Perhaps you are right," Carter mumbled although he was sure McBride was not.

Part Two
October 1897
In the Atlantic, Off the Carolina Coast

Chapter 6

Carter woke after a fitful night. It had nothing to do with the seas — there was calmness to the water he had never before experienced early in fall. The tropical storm that concerned Captain Aldrich earlier had veered westward toward the Gulf of Mexico, leaving the water a calm, gray satin sheet. He attributed his poor sleep more to the queer series of events, especially his gut nagging him about Moser. Carter couldn't put his finger on what specifically gnawed at him about this man. He seemed innocuous enough and MacBride's conjecture was plausible — an older German headed to the Caribbean on business — but it just didn't set well with him. Moser knew his birth father, saying only that Samuel Miller was an old friend. Carter mulled over what circumstances would be that a German man would know his birth father, he sensed something furtive in his story. His intuition hadn't failed him before and his years as a professional urged him to quantify it.

A strong shore breeze helped the *Albemarle* make very good time against a strong Gulf Stream current. They veered a few degrees east to avoid the storm, leaving the mainland visible as only a slim blue-gray line. A solitary pair of sea gulls floated above, twisting their stubby necks as if to inspect the deck as the vessel sailed through their flight path. They repeatedly pumped their wings as if to wave good-bye after each inspection. As the *Albemarle* neared the Bahamas, a wind shift stifled her progress, whittling it from swift to laborious. Carter understood this to be the demarcation of Cuban waters

— watery territory surrounding the troubled island, disputed between Spain and anyone who entered here. The Captain needed to maneuver carefully.

Carter took out a pamphlet from his satchel. It was written by José Martí, a poet martyred at the start of the insurgency in 1895. General Garcia provided him the tract so Carter could better understood the heart of Cuba's nationalistic zeal. It spoke to why Cuba needed to break free of Spanish colonialism; specifically describing prisons and labor camps they called *reconcentrados.* Martí described disturbing and vivid images of dismemberment, torture and rape that seared deeply in his mind. Sam's personal sense of humanity wouldn't let him detach and he felt caught up in its emotion. He knew if he grew empathetic, he might not be able to do the job he had been sent to do.

"Mr. Carter?" MacBride's gravelly voice accompanied a rap at the door, interrupting Carter just as he started reading. He set the pamphlet aside, went to the door, and cracked it open. "The Capt'n requests your presence on the bridge," MacBride barked. Carter noticed the old sailor was still wearing the same stained blouse as he had on the day before.

"Do you know why?"

"Didn't say." MacBride said bluntly

Carter realized probing further would be pointless. "Thank you," he said. McBride had already started walking away.

Carter obliged. The morning mist coated his arms as he maneuvered toward the bridge. He entered the pilothouse to see a highly polished helm. Captain Cornelius Aldrich, wearing a crisp uniform, looked to be an older gentleman. The uniform conformed to the Captain's wiry, six-foot frame. A white line of pencil-thin beard hugged his chin. He was facing the bow with arms crossed, and clenching a small-bowled pipe firmly between his teeth. Aldrich's appearance so sharply contrasted MacBride's that Carter could not help but wonder why the Captain chose him as his First Officer.

"Morning, Mr. Carter." Aldrich never turned his head. His gaze remained sharp and focused completely on a young sailor at his helm save swinging back his open hand, as if requesting silence and space. Carter stepped quietly onto the bridge, unsure whether or not protocol required him to ask permission to enter, but now was too late — the plane was already breached. "Well done, Ensign," Aldrich complimented the young sailor when he completed the navigational adjustment precisely.

"Thank you, sir." The ensign replied, sighing as if relieved of a great burden.

"I can take it from here," Aldrich added. "Go grab a coffee and a smoke." Aldrich's vocal tempo sounded more Northern than Southern, with a slight twinge of mountain Virginia, Carter thought.

"Aye, sir. Thank you, sir," the ensign exited for the mess.

"Need to wait a couple of hours before we try running the gut between Hispañola and Cuba. Timing and darkness will make all the difference." Aldrich said, maintaining his focus forward. He motioned Carter to come closer.

"Your prerogative, sir" Carter respectfully replied.

"I assume you know international maritime law. Even though we're flyin' a British flag, we'll still be subjected to search and scuttling if *our friends* feel we are trespassing . . ." Aldrich's eyes pointed south.

". . . or harboring materiel or human contraband," Carter finished Aldrich's sentence. "Not to be blunt, sir but are we at some added risk for what we have aboard?" Carter asked surmising he knew the answer.

Aldrich raised his eyebrows. "Mr. Carter, whether your question is official or unofficial, I believe you'll accept I can't answer that."

"Our little secret," Carter nodded. He had little doubt there was cargo eventually bound for Cuban rebels. "And I believe it was meant to be unofficial."

"If we play our cards right, we should be able to catch breezes off both shores and slip south before our friends even know we've been here." Aldrich ran his finger along the large depth chart to his right. He turned the wheel two revolutions to the right, checked his timepiece and the height of the sun behind him. "Do you believe in the Devil's Triangle, Carter?"

"To be honest, Sir, haven't given it much thought. My travels usually take me through the gulf."

"Just over there, if my bearings are correct," Aldrich pointed north. "We'd slip into the teeth of that beast if we veer just west-north-west of Hispañola. Some old sailors say it's alive — a sea monster waitin' to gobble up anyone who dares trespass."

"You don't believe the myth, do you, Sir?" Carter asked, wondering if the tremble in Aldrich's voice was real or conjured for effect.

"Whether I believe in it or not really doesn't matter. For all I know, it could be some natural phenomenon, but I'm not interested in taking chances I don't need to be taking."

"Sir, what do you know about the German fellow — Moser?"

Aldrich absently listened as he studied the twitching on his compass. "The devil's playing his game already."

"Sir?"

"Yes, the German. Moser. MacBride said he ran into him in Baltimore. He threw around plenty of money and didn't seem to be shy about pushin' it our way. He said he needed to get to Jamaica '*schnell*!' He's a peculiar sort, friendly enough, but I've got a hunch he's hiding something." Aldrich synthesized his impression and opinion while his head swiveled from port to starboard. Carter wanted more than just additional puzzle pieces about Moser, but it seemed that was all he was going to get.

"Come to think of it, MacBride said it was someone acting on his behalf that flashed the money, for whatever that means."

'*Acting on his behalf?*' Carter cogitated on Aldrich's words.

"I told MacBride to keep a close eye on him. So far he's been harmless." Aldrich glanced back at the map and sucked his expired pipe, out of habit, then pulled it out of his mouth and tapped the mouthpiece on Santo Domingo. "What's your gut tellin' you? Do you think he knows something about the Germans getting' agitated around here."

"What do you think he knows about me?" Carter asked,

and then realized he missed Aldrich's point.

"About you? This *is* getting' interesting," Aldrich arched his eyebrows. "MacBride tells me that he's been asking about you. You fellahs playing cat and mouse or something?"

"Whether your question is official or unofficial, I trust you will accept that I can't answer that," Carter joked, then asked, "MacBride didn't let anything out, did he?"

Aldrich shook his head once. "I know he looks a little rough about the edges, but MacBride's as loyal as they come," he noted, then nodded back toward the map. "We'll drift until nightfall, and then we'll run. Reports from Jamaica are promising —they haven't seen any of our friends patrolling this past week, but I still prefer using the night to cloak the run."

"I'll be ready, Sir," Carter replied and turned to exit. As he started out of the pilothouse, the young Ensign slipped through the bulkhead, clearly refreshed by his trip to the mess.

"Dang, son, wait a minute. I nearly forgot why I called you here. A message came in for you."

"From whom?" Carter asked.

"Wilkie. Doesn't ring a bell for me. D'you know him?"

Carter took the paper. He had heard something about a newspaperman by that name taking over the foreign interests of the administration — some deal between Roosevelt and Hazen as far as he had heard. Carter opened up and read it quickly, and then slipped it into his top pocket.

"Mr. Carter," the Captain started. "I understand only enough of what you are up to from Commander Wainwright. He authorized aid, and I'll provide whatever is in my power further as you request, if need be, whatever is in my power."

Carter looked through the pilothouse portals to the bridge. Things were lining up. Wilkie's message confirmed Carter's suspicion. His gut was correct. Moser had to be a spy.

"Aye, Sir. Thank you," Carter responded respectfully. When he stepped onto the deck, he spotted Moser starboard. Wilkie's words were in his thoughts. He reckoned this old man was wise enough never to admit he was a spy, but Carter needed to know, if for nothing more than personal reasons.

"Been in to see the Captain, I see . . . trouble ahead?"

Moser asked Carter, his accent unhidden and heavy.

"A course change, as I understand it. Planned." Carter replied with a persona of openness. "I'm sure we'll be in Jamaica tomorrow, perhaps a little behind schedule. I'm sure they will hold your room in Jamaica if it takes any longer." Carter added in order to study Moser's reaction. He sensed no haste to debarkation in Jamaica . . . no agitation. The pair quietly watched the horizon together.

"I apologize for my rudeness before. My name is Samuel Carter. My father's name *was* Sam Miller," Carter announced quietly, emphasizing the past tense. Moser's eyes grew wide. "I guess you just caught me a bit off guard."

"*Bitte* . . . ja . . . you are *sein sohn*." Moser spoke gently. "*Und* you have his first name only?"

"I know what he did," Carter needed this old man to fill in some gaps, and reckoned that disclosure would facilitate candor. "He died before I was born. I took my mother's name."

"I see." Moser continued his gaze out over the horizon. Carter sensed sadness in the old man hearing that his old friend was dead.

"Your father . . . he was a fine engineer," his words were tinged with solace. "*Und* that he was. *Bitte* . . . . please . . . how goes your Mutter, Samuel?" Carter recognized Moser's sincerity, and allowed his objectivity to fit the old man's sincerity in as a puzzle piece. He couldn't continue to let it divert him.

"In our business, we need to keep our personal lives separate from our work. It is something your father taught me, *und* it is a good lesson," offered Moser. "I am sorry," he added as he examined Carter's face.

Carter fished out the watch from his pocket. After a glance, he said, "It's late. So if you will excuse me."

"An item your father taught me, Samuel," Moser continued. "We can be associates as long as our adversary is common. *Und* as I see it for now, one of our adversaries is common. *Guten Abend.* We will see each other in Jamaica, *ya*?"

Carter nodded solemnly and warily for Moser's fishing.

'Until I can confirm we have a common enemy,' he thought to himself as he turned and walked slowly back to his cabin. He sat at the desk and laid his head down on folded arms. Moser's words were the same words his stepfather used to describe Samuel Miller and felt angry for not allowing himself the luxury to explore their simplicity. The old man confirmed knowledge of his father's work was spoken in the language of espionage. All he'd ever had were suspicions derived from unanswered questions. Samuel Miller, his father, worked as a German spy. Moser's words created doubt in the unanswered question that framed Sam's life — was his father dead, or had he created some elaborate deception to escape detection?

Roosevelt sat back in his office chair drawing self-confidently and deeply on his cigar, knowing that his plans were converging smartly. He'd convinced Secretary Long that their objectives were in lock step; Congress had just backed him with a huge appropriation to develop more diverse Navy assets, including his own favorite, the dreadnaught class battleships; and adding Wilkie to his network was a major coup for intelligence gathering and getting inside the State Department. Having confidants in every branch of the government would allow him the necessary control he believed he needed and deserved. Now was the time for implementation.

A knock on the door interrupted his thoughts. He checked the grandfather clock in the corner. *Twelve fifty-five*. Wilkie, never late, he reckoned. He got up from his overstuffed easy chair to open the door.

"Wilkie, I've been waiting for you," Roosevelt said, showing his famous gap toothed grin.

"Our appointment was for one o'clock," Wilkie's words were stilted. He entered the room and as he passed Roosevelt, saw the clock in the far corner. "It's twelve fifty-five."

"I like punctuality, Wilkie," Roosevelt clacked his teeth, satisfied that his boyish humor placed Wilkie on the defensive. He strutted around his large, oak desk and dropped into his leather chair. He quickly lit his half-smoked cigar and sent a blue-gray cloud toward the ceiling. "Now tell me all you know about Consul-General Fitzhugh Lee."

"Southern, polished, bit of a rouge," Wilkie provided.

"He's a tough nut to crack, but its better he's on our side than in some renegade Confederacy." Roosevelt tipped his head and revealed a smitten smirk. "What do you think about Confederate boys running these spy shows without any direct supervision?" Roosevelt prodded, knowing Wilkie despised small talk. He was using the primary Harvard debate tactic: keep your opponent on the defensive and remain in control. Besides, he was having a bit of fun keeping Wilkie alert.

"That was a long time ago, sir."

"Not that long ago, especially for some good ol' boys," Roosevelt uttered. "So tell me about this secret 'network' in Havana? What do you know?"

"I have evidence Lee may have been responsible, at least in part, for the Cisneros escape. Lee wouldn't admit that or anything else directly. Moreover, Carter was most likely involved."

"It was a rather brash operation and certainly got into McKinley's knickers," Roosevelt barred his teeth, pinching the end of his cigar between them. He then asked, "Carter works for you now, correct?"

"Through Jack Stiles, but ultimately, yes."

"Stiles. Another good man. We've had dealings. Sounds like you have a whole stable of good men, Wilkie." Roosevelt clacked his teeth as he rose from his chair to march around the room. He stopped at the large window and as he peered outside, added, "There's a lot going on, Wilkie, and I expect big things from you and your people. I would expect that you or Stiles keep close contact with Carter so we all know what is going on down there. I like what General Lee's boys are up to, but it'll be more advantageous for us to know what he knows and what he's doing —especially what he is sending up to Secretary Day."

"I'll do whatever it takes, sir," Wilkie affirmed.

The *Albemarle* docked at the port of Kingston on Jamaica's south shore at precisely nine in the morning. After the schooner moored, the crew made quick work emptying the cargo before the passengers could even assemble and reconnoiter at the rails. Carter caught a glimpse of the last few sacks being removed. It left no doubt when he saw the cargo offloaded — Aldrich was delivering guns and ammunition bound for Cuban rebels.

Carter chose to remain apart from the line of passengers gathering near the departure gate. He spotted Moser over the hats and bonnets and monitored him as he jockeyed for position in the departure line. The older man's comments sparked more questions than they had answered. From his viewpoint, Carter watched Moser wind through the passenger's queue on the gangplank and be greeted by a small enclave of welcoming Jamaicans. The old German melded into anonymity among the crowd that was dressed like European visitors. Moser would no doubt find his way to Hispañola, if Wilkie had been correct and that was where he was headed. Carter turned his attention to Captain Aldrich and Chief MacBride who were directing the *Albemarle* crew to prepare the ship for a short turnaround.

"Could you send a message back to the States?" Carter whispered to the Captain as soon as MacBride left earshot. Aldrich acknowledged. "'Senior operational contact confirmed.' That should do it."

"Moser?" Aldrich asked. After Carter nodded, he added, "Son-of-a-bitch," under his breath.

"Thank you, sir." Carter noted when he left Aldrich to debark the ship toting his small cloth satchel slung over his shoulder. When he reached the dock, he noticed that the cargo, now buried in several wagons was headed north. He reckoned he'd see the cargo again soon enough.

Carter navigated toward the center of Kingston, much the same as he had remembered, having been here just before the electric train lines were being laid in. Swaying palm trees lined the main thoroughfare, King Street; their trunks swaddled with emerald leaved Mandevilla vines, spotted with crimson and yellow blossoms. Sweet aromas, coconuts and melons melded with the floral fragrance and drifted on the light breeze through the city streets. Nearby, the new centerpiece of the city, Kingston's Botanical Gardens had opened.

He meandered along the street, passing pleasant locals wearing their colorful shirts that reminded him of a quiet and relaxing tropical vacation. He pined for a Jamaican run, but with so little time to dawdle, could only promise himself that diversion for a different time. Lugo's office stood near the American Consulate, he remembered and continued meandering his way toward the west side of the city.

"Señor Carter?" Carter turned to the meek voice behind him. A grizzled old cane farmer spoke with a toothless grin inside the shadow of a wide-brimmed straw hat. "Señor Lugo sends his regards."

"¿Usted ha visto a Martí?" Carter gave this phrase as the signal.

"Bueno, la Rosa Blanco," answered the old man.

Carter tipped his head.

"Arriba?" The farmer tipped his head upward.

Carter glanced up. He managed the narrow steps leading to the front door and waited inside the musty foyer for his farmer escort to hobble up the rickety flight of stairs. He spotted a door cracked open partway down the hallway. The old man soon caught up with him, and Sam deferred to his lead through the door.

"Samuel, it is good to see you again," a croaky voice announced in broken English when the door was opened. Although he engendered friendships with several revolutionaries, he was uncomfortable that so many people knew when he arrived. "I was very pleased when I heard you were coming to see us."

Carter asked, rather sheepishly. "I thought my arrival was a closely held secret?"

The old square-shouldered soldier let a wily grin slip onto his face. "Ah, Samuel, Amigo, you know we also have our ways." Gerasimo Lugo looked up from his stooped position over a map spread out on the center table. His rugged face had pushed out a week's worth of stubble; his thick, white hair uncombed and wildly out of control. A fat cigar stub sat wedged in the corner of his mouth, pushed his lips apart enough to show his tobacco stained teeth. When his eyes met Carter's, he smiled, Lugo's teeth gripping harder on the cigar.

Lugo aged considerably since they last met in Miami a few months ago. As he studied Lugo's eyes, he noticed they were hooded with dark half-moons sagging and bulging underneath. Carter looked past him to four soldiers pouring over a ratty map of Cuba spread out open on a large mahogany table.

The four huddled soldiers were as old as Lugo but more deeply sun-darkened, as if they had just came in from the cane fields. Rounded shoulders and hollow eyes evidenced recent struggles, working side-by-side with Lugo for the insurgency from his self-imposed exile in Jamaica. They each worked separately for a common goal, helping Generals Garcia and Gomez to galvanize and renew nationalist enthusiasm across the Caribbean.

"I have something you'll like, Samuel," Lugo growled playfully, gesturing at three tall bottles of deep amber colored rum that sat unceremoniously on a small wooden table.

"*Gracias*." Carter's grin split his face.

"It'll put color in that pale face of yours," Lugo laughed aloud. "And I think we should have enough time for a relaxing smoke as well."

"Thank you." Carter approached the table and filled two small, dirty glasses. As soon as the amber liquor splashed, it released an aroma that wafted up to his nose; the smell coaxed him to savor it before he took his sip. It numbed his lips, and then his tongue before the prickly sensation moved into his throat. Sam felt warmth spread through his chest.

"Come. I've been working on a plan to get you past the Spaniards and to the General," Lugo grinned and coaxed Carter to look at the map. "Getting you past the Spaniards will not be an easy venture, but it is possible. We have a route that has proven successful. Much of our supplies are taken this way."

Carter saw the grizzled cane famer who revealed the building tug Lugo's shirtsleeve. After a moment, Lugo looked back at Carter with wide eyes and said, "Raul reminded me of

Sabio's discovery. Germans are moving from Dominica, what you call Hispañola. We will need to take extra precautions in the water."

Carter stiffened. '*First Moser, now ships.*' He was now convinced he knew where Moser would be headed, but that point was immaterial. Lugo stationed himself at the map, tracing out his proposed route for Sam. His finger crossed the narrow straight between the islands along the northern end of Jamaica and then moved to the south shore of Cuba near Santiago. Carter saw it wasn't the shortest route, but most likely the safest. Lugo continued to trace a tortuous path through where he remembered were mountains until he stopped and tapped out a location near the eastern shore.

"Here. He should be here."

"I should be able to navigate," Carter said as slid the map in his direction.

Lugo stopped him. "I believe you, Samuel, but I will give you two trusted comrades."

"You know I've worked alone here before, Gerasimo."

"Perhaps before you could, but not now. It is different. I would not welcome any harm befall you."

"At the risk of —?"

"I insist. Perhaps you would better accept if I say I follow General Garcia's orders." Lugo put his open hands over his ears.

"Then I have no choice," Carter knew his stealthy friend he referred to as the 'old fox' survived because of the man's caution. And if Garcia was adamant about escort, there was certainly a clear reason for his concern.

"*¡Es aqui!*" A lookout at the small window interrupted.

"Perhaps I was mistaken about the smoke," Lugo shook his head as he reached into a humidor, pulled out a cigar and handed it to Carter. Lugo's eyes looked worrisome and tired. "Perhaps you can enjoy this on the ride. Good luck, Samuel."

"I will do what I can," Carter said as Lugo grabbed him by the shoulders and bear-hugged him briefly. Two men in peasant clothes hustled Carter down stairs to a waiting carriage. Carter felt as if he had been stuffed through the open door just as the driver snapped his reins. Horses jolted forward, smearing Carter into the wooden seat, and the carriage moved furiously out of Kingston.

Carter took out one of the cigars as then rolled one end in his mouth to soften the wrapper. He chomped the tip, and then clenched the cigar between his teeth. He lit the end and inhaled a mouthful of sweetened smoke. It was as smooth as he remembered. He craned his neck to see through the small coach window and watched as they moved past the small enclaves of grass and bamboo huts spotted along Spanish Town Road. The carriage flew by the wide leafed trees being strangled by thick shaggy barked vines lining the road. Eyes and faces under wide brimmed grass hats gazed at him from front stoops. Half way through the cigar — Carter reckoned about four miles — the carriage halted suddenly.

A man with eyes wide enough to reveal blood streaked whites opened the carriage door. He was dressed much like the grizzled old cane farmers, baggy trousers pulled up to expose his ankles and bare feet.

"Señor Carter?" he asked.

"*Sí*," Carter responded.

"We move you to another carriage now."

Carter complied and emerged. He spotted another waiting cart one hundred feet away from the edge of the jungle with its curtains closed. The drawn curtains would create an oppressively hot and steamy atmosphere inside the carriage. This was not a time to protest. Carter stubbed out his cigar and mashed the ashes into the ground. A minute later, the new carriage started moving. Carter squirmed near the open window to catch as much breeze as the small opening allowed. He watched the mountain ridge backbone of the island pass by before they veered north again, toward the blue waters of the Caribbean at St. Ann's Bay. They reached the water's edge by sunset, and after a short, slower pace along the shoreline, the carriage stopped at a remote railway station.

The station was quiet as was the road. Back toward the slope of the cut in the mountain range appeared a group of men, moving like an ebony wave. Carter grew uneasy. Friendly locals? Did the Spanish uncover his mission and put Jamaican officers on his trail? Just as he began to calculate his odds of escaping, an old, coal-black skinned fellow, moved toward the carriage with his hands full.

"Ah-lo!" the old man announced with a toothy grin. Carter didn't need to run. The small, frail man held a roasted chicken in one hand and two bottles of ale pinched between craggy fingers. Carter's stomach growled when he caught a whiff.

"Much appreciated — *gracias*," Carter obliged as he opened the carriage door.

"Welcome to *our island*, white man with red hair. Here . . . gifts for you. We celebrate getting the Spaniard bastards on our sister island."

Carter caught and understood only a word or two of the old man's rapid-fire patois, but the meal offering generously sufficed. While the old man babbled, he noticed that two fresh horses had been exchanged and hitched to his carriage.

"Much appreciated," Carter repeated. Anything more said would simply be wasted.

"I am happy I can do this for your welcome," the man said, handing Carter the food with both hands.

This driver wouldn't wait. He'd finished hitching the horses and before Carter could savor his first bites of sustenance. The driver cracked his whip.

"Good-bye, *Uncle!*" Carter shouted as the wobbly door slammed shut. As the carriage raced along the shoreline, Carter wolfed down the tasty chicken. When he finished sucking the juice from the grizzle, Carter looked out and realized they had reached the camouflage of the tropical forest, whose beauty and intrigue wore brilliantly at night. The insect world was flittering, tiny lights swallowed by twilight. Island glow-worms turned on their phosphorescent lights to flood the forest floor. He imagined he was traversing a veritable fairyland.

The food and drink in combination with the hammered rhythm of the horses' hooves helped Carter doze. A shrill whistle abruptly pierced the darkness and woke him. The carriage stopped. A band of men carrying rifles and knives appeared as suddenly as if they had sprung from the ground and surrounded the wagon. Carter listened to the whispered patois between his driver and the leader of the armed patrol. The driver's singsong voice kept its calmness while the patrol leader sounded like a barking dog. Their conference was short. The patrol receded quickly. The journey continued, following the shoreline, but Carter could not rest now, feeling his heart race and head pound. The carriage traveled another hour through the glowworm spotted darkness when it stopped in front of a one-story brick house. The carriage door swung open and a tall, wiry, determined-looking man with a fierce mustache peered into the coach.

"*Buenas noches*, Señor Carter. I am Gervasio Sabio," the man said. "Come, dinner waits."

Carter grasped Sabio's hand and shook strongly. He noticed the old man's right thumb was missing. Sabio's eyes mirrored nobility, and who Carter immediately felt trust. Sam wanted to hear the story behind the missing thumb, but kept that desire available for later. "A pleasure to meet you, Señor Sabio," Carter replied. He stepped out of the carriage and thanked the driver, who left without acknowledgement.

"Jamaican rum?" Sabio offered.

"Lugo has betrayed my vice?" Carter followed Sabio into the modest home. Sabio whistled sharply as they stepped through the threshold into a dimly lit room with a low, flat ceiling. A small, friendly servant appeared with a tall glass filled with welcome amber sweetness.

"We'll talk, drink and rest before we eat, Samuel."

Carter melted into a cane chair. His sides felt the cane comfortable. He reckoned that his journey covered nearly seventy jaw-rattling miles.

Sabio waved to a rather smallish man with straight black hair. "This is Manuel, who will assist us in our journey on Cuba," Manuel nodded politely before disappearing back into the house. "These other men will be helping us get to the launch."

"We travel tonight?" Carter asked. He knew the opportunity to slip through the Spanish controlled waters would be a limited to a few dark hours.

"Yes, tonight. Miguel went ahead to prepare the boat. The sea is calm, so there is opportunity."

A hobbled old man came behind Sabio to gain his attention. After a brief exchange of whispers, Sabio said, "Finish your rum, Samuel. We must eat quickly before Raul's fare grows cold."

Carter found the dinner filling. The spiced pork and rice laced with habañeros made for a fine final meal. He knew hot meals were to be savored and stored, since in the coming days, any fare might well be very limited.

Chapter 7

Jack Stiles sat in the Washington office building and stared through the cracked open window behind his new boss, John Wilkie, as the wiry, dark-suited man milked his tea. The city was busy; hooves clomped constantly as carriages on large steel framed wooden wheels creaked; bearded businessmen wearing high collared white shirts under long, dark suit coats strutted on cut stone sidewalks; young ladies in long, bustled dresses glided past sporting parasols.

Wilkie's cup clinked into his saucer while his other hand rustled papers. Stiles didn't care much for Wilkie's appointment, but he was comfortable where he was. Positions higher up in the growing bureaucracy would move him further away from the fieldwork which he enjoyed. Stiles maintained a dignified profile — "duty first" — when he enlisted in the Philadelphia Police force, continued it when serving as a Pinkerton detective and maintained that attitude when he joined the Treasury's young Secret Service. He maintained that principle even if those in authority inserted someone above him — even a newspaperman with a reputation for skullduggery. He was duty bound.

"Carl DeLauro," Wilkie finally spoke rather bluntly. His steely-eyed stare pricked at Stiles.

"The coal striker in Lattimer?" Stiles turned back to his new boss.

"Same one. I am convinced there is more to him than his record indicates," Wilkie noted as he took out a paper from his jacket pocket, unfolded it and began musing aloud. "Little stuff to start — fist fights, petty theft, general hooliganism. But each ensuing charge increases in violence."

"Martin didn't hold him?" Stiles noted. Wilkie's eyes provided enough of a response.

"And there is this counterfeiting charge in Ohio. Combine that with an incident in the same town with a Sheriff being killed — the Sheriff that charged him — well, it's more than just coincidence, I say."

"Where am I going?" Stiles asked, rhetorically, assuming that was the purpose for the meeting. Wilkie hesitated for a moment, looking over the rims of his round glasses. He couldn't read the man as well as he read Director Hazen's. He would need to learn how to pierce Wilkie's coldness, if for nothing else, survival.

"They didn't hold him like we had asked, so I put a trace on him. When he left Lattimer, we followed him to Scranton, Baltimore, and now Philadelphia. There was another man he's been spotted with in Baltimore. Wilhelm Ziegler, using the alias Herman Kern."

"Ziegler? Don't recall the name." Stiles asked as he looked at his tea-colored water, hoping his stomach could stave off getting sick from it.

"The agency does not have anything on him, but my hunch is that he is involved with Dr. Most."

"The anarchist? So he's involved in random bombings as well, yes?" Stiles asked, combing through his mind for more on Ziegler and coming up empty. He sensed there was something more about Ziegler that Wilkie knew but was not telling him.

"Correct. DeLauro's probably the easiest to locate, and if we find DeLauro, we may break into that entire group." Wilkie stiffened his back and sat straight.

"I understand. Philadelphia, then," Stiles noted.

"Start there. They may have taken a train out of town, but in any case, I need you to track them and report back to me what they are targeting. It would be real beneficial if you can catch them red-handed and we can bring them both in."

Stiles nodded. He knew it would take him some time to

find DeLauro, but once he did, he was confident he would be able to fulfill his charge.

"Dismissed?" Stiles asked Wilkie, who had quickly buried himself in the stack of files on his desk. The glance up from the desk was all the brusque answer Stiles needed, and without further delay, he headed out of Wilkie's office and took the first train to Philadelphia.

In the island's darkness, Sabio led Carter and Manuel from his modest home and headed north into a split in the cane field along the dirt road. Manuel used a small machete to cut a small, curved opening where Sabio and Carter could follow without being cut by the tall barbed canes. The three men tramped in silence for what seemed about a mile until the cane field ended and a coconut grove began. Through the weaving trunks of the swaying palms, Carter saw a rock and sand shoreline on the other side, and a tiny bay of rippled sea.

"There," Sabio whispered as he emerged from the grove. He pointed to a flash of light about fifty yards off shore. He dug through his satchel and pulled out a shuttered lantern, with which he immediately answered with several flashes. "We wait now," he said then looked around until he found a large rock on which to sit.

Carter preferred to stand and watch the fruit bats acrobatically flit through the coconut trees, darting in and out of the palm fronds, their flapping wings sounding like the small waves surging onto the shore. Faint sloshing in the water behind Carter gradually overtook the wing beats. He noticed Miguel emerge from the water wearing his trousers rolled up above the swirling and foaming sea at his knees. Miguel wrapped his carried rope loosely around a rock then anchored the end to the trunk of a coconut tree and started back out into the water.

"Take hold of the line, Samuel. Follow us out." Sabio directed and headed out, following Miguel and Manuel. Carter complied and slogged into the bay under the darkness of the night. Warm water inched higher as he moved further out into the bay, until finally, when the depth of the water had reached his thighs and engulfing his hips with gentle swells, they came upon a rather odd shaped cockleshell. Sabio deftly slipped into the boat, lifting himself by pushing up on the gunwales. Carter followed him and rolled into the bottom of the boat.

"Rest now, Samuel. We are headed to see Garcia!" Sabio whispered, pointing to the hold. Carter slipped into the small space below the main deck, as it was, until he felt the boulders used for ballast push into his back. Other oblong bundles next to the rocks creaked under his weight. He weaseled his way near the center between the cargo and boulder ballast. Within minutes, Sam understood that the carriage rides might have been the most comfortable part of this journey.

From his vantage point, Carter watched Manuel push off sideways to turn the boat seaward as his comrade, Miguel started to paddle. Sabio whistled twice, took his position at the tiller, and began to skull the vessel seaward as well. Carter sat up from his prone position. There wasn't room enough for him to stretch out, just to curl into an awkward turtle-like position around the boulders and covered cargo. The late summer's soupy air added to his discomfort. His head tingled and throbbed from the rum and fatigue.

"Can I help?" Carter offered.

"No, no. You need to stay hidden. Spaniards don't care about fishermen. You, my friend, are a different story. You can't pass for Jamaican if we are stopped."

Carter acknowledged Sabio's prudence. The grizzled old man's calmness had matured over the years of navigating these waters. Sam needed the rest anyway. Reckoning further discussion pointless, he curled back in his nest between the boulders and cargo and listened as Sabio commenced barking commands to Miguel and Manuel. The moonless night provided sanctuary from detection, Carter thought as he listened to the singsong banter between his comrades as they progressed. A hundred miles north were the shores of Cuba, patrolled by Spanish light-draft vessels armed with small caliber pivot and machine guns. Carter knew what would happen . . . no one on board would survive if one of those patrols boarded them. No one carried papers. No one would know any different. No one would be missed. Whatever remained of the Spaniards rage would be left to the mercies of tropical sun and wandering sharks. At this point, he was as much a liability to these men as the contraband weapons in the hold.

Carter understood Sabio's plan. The voyage would keep them out in the open ocean through the night and most of the day. They'd arrive just outside the Cuban three-mile limit at next sunset; much depended upon how rapidly the men rowed and found a spit of friendly coral reef in which to float safely until daybreak. A light breeze danced across Carter's sweaty face. Sabio ordered the men to raise the ship's two small sails. Miguel and Manuel responded immediately, removing their oars from the water and scrambling to the center mast. In minutes, the force of the gentle winds nudged the boat forward and toward open waters. The night should be uneventful.

Jack Stiles knew Philadelphia well. He had grown up in the area, spent time as a foot patrolman in the city before he moved on to detective work. He knew all the taverns and could get information on anyone. The docks near the Delaware River were rife with the riffraff that fed off the more sordid elements of the anarchist movement. Starting there made sense.

"Ale, Charlie," Stiles crowed as he stepped into *The Bull's Head Inn*. Charlie Buxton, the owner and bartender, was an old friend — rugged, middle-aged, and Philadelphia born. Buxton had a brief stint in the boxing ring before a well-placed right hand broke his nose so badly he had to retire. When he took over *The Bull's Head Inn* he had plenty of fights to break up, but his presence scared the brawlers off to the taverns on the other side of town.

"Coming right up, Jack!" Buxton turned from his business at the small sink full of steaming, sudsy water, and flashed Stiles a grin. He motioned for his young helper to pour up a beer for Stiles while he rubbed his hands dry. The young man set the beer stein on the bar then relieved Buxton at the soapy sink.

"How ya been, Jack," Buxton asked. He nodded and

winked at a table near the wide front window. Stiles looked over his shoulder and spotted the women Buxton wanted him to notice.

"I'm here on business, Charlie," Stiles said, but still could not resist a second look at the low cut blouses that revealed rather ample chests. He flashed them a smile, then turned back to the bar.

"New?"

"From New York," Buxton offered. He twitched his eyebrows twice.

"Actually looking for someone else, Charlie," Stiles leaned forward. Buxton did the same until the two men were face to face. "I hear 'Dyna-Most' might have a new protégé."

Buxton recoiled and glared, as if concerned that someone may have heard Stiles.

"About my age, maybe a bit younger . . . came down from the coal mines." Stiles added in a subdued voice.

"Those people don't come here, Jack. You know that," Buxton whispered.

"Carl DeLauro is the name," Stiles said. Buxton turned away, grabbed an empty glass and started nervously wiping at it, working his way from the rim to the inside. "And some guy by the name of Ziegler — might be going by Kern. Supposedly has been here for a while, but the name's new to me."

"I told you Jack. They don't come here." Buxton grew agitated.

"Yeah, yeah, I know, Charlie, but have you heard anyone talk about this guy? Dark hair, dark eyes, and a bit of a wild-eyed look. Ya know, just the type that Dr. Most would want to suck in and proselytize."

Buxton went silent, his eyes locked on Stiles. He shook his head slowly and then dropped his chin to his chest. "Chester's tavern burned down the other night and the cops are thinkin' it was one of 'em," he mumbled.

"Any leads?"

". . . Just the usual. They're snoopin' around Walnut Street," Buxton pursed his lips tight enough that the scar on his left cheek bulged and stared at Stiles with wide eyes. "I ain't afraid of much, Jack, you know that. But let me tell you, those bastards scare everybody. Even me. Nobody knows what the hell they're up to and who's next on their list. If you and your boys can roust them out of here, I won't be the only shop keeper breathing easier."

"I'll do what I can, Charlie. I'll be around for a bit and I'll drop in often. Just let me know if you hear anything," Stiles grinned and guzzled the last of his ale, upturning his glass. "I think I know where to start," he added, wiping his lips clean of the froth with his sleeve. Stiles dropped two coins on the bar and stood.

"Goo' night, Charlie," Stiles said as he started toward the door. He glanced at the two ladies near the window, smiled, and then exited the tavern heading toward the dock area streets. After two right turns through slime covered alley streets, he emerged on the west side of Walnut Street, and walked until he arrived at row house number seven-hundred. It was the last location that he remembered Dr. Most held several rooms that he handed out to his 'disciples' as Stiles knew them. He verified the address before he left Washington. Stiles used a lumbered gait — slow enough to notice if there was any movement on the second floor. Even after three passes along the street, he had seen nothing.

When he stopped pacing midway between two of the gas lit streetlights to let his eyes acclimate to the darkness, he peered across the street again. Still nothing. He thought it odd that the flat would be empty at this hour. He surveyed the street quickly, then crossed and quietly moved up the stoop to the door. He slipped the skeleton key he had kept from his beat policeman days into the lock, jiggled it open and snaked inside the building. Navigating the stairway on his tiptoes, he stole down the hallway to the flat he had been watching. At the door, he knocked, and then waited for a moment. No answer. He knocked again. Same response. He used his skeleton key again, jiggled the lock open and slipped inside.

Scanning the room quickly, he saw that he was alone. In the center of the room was a rather simple table, covered with papers, books and some black rocks. After a closer look, he realized that the rocks were actually coal nuggets, two different kinds. He glanced at the papers nearest the coal, which described the differences between anthracite and bituminous coals, and the explosive nature of the latter. Everything else in the flat was neatly stacked, or otherwise set aside in organized piles. Whoever was here had not left for good. They would be back, he thought,

Stiles realized that Philadelphia would need to be his home base again at least for a few days so he could work on the row houses. Checking his pocket watch, he realized it was too late in the night to catch up with any other of his old friends, so he turned and headed back to *The Bull's Head Inn.* Charlie Buxton would know where he might find a flop for the night. As he maneuvered over the slippery cobblestoned alleys, he started wondering about Ziegler. He sensed there was something more about him that he should know that Wilkie wasn't telling him.

His thoughts though were derailed when he stopped in front of *The Bull's Head Inn,* and through the window, the young ladies, still at their table, winked at him.

Fitzhugh Lee stood out on the Captain's walk, an allowance his friend Captain Cyrus McManus offered to only a handful of civilians, watching the tugboats belly out and close the distance in their direction. Opaque smoke belched from the stubby stacks on the tugs as they finally kissed the *Olivette*'s port side and started pushing her toward the pier at Tampa Bay. He turned and congratulated the Captain with a tip of his gray brushed derby. In short order, the *Olivette* came to rest at the pier, and amidst the small contingent of passengers, Lee debarked and headed directly to the Tampa Bay Hotel.

"Welcome home, General Lee," the uniformed doorman said as he opened the wide double-door entrance of relatively new and opulently posh hotel that was a short walk from the docks.

"Thank you, son," Lee tipped his derby and dropped a small coin into the doorman's hand. He enjoyed these return trips to the States and Tampa, now grown from a small fishing village to a bustling port on the Gulf. This little town had become a surrogate for him, yet despite all her wonderful attributes, Tampa still ranked a distant second to his Virginia hills. The fact was that for him, nothing would ever compare to Richmond.

Lee stopped inside the carpeted foyer for a moment to marvel at the ambiance this modern hotel offered. A wide staircase covered in deep red carpet, opened up in front of him, leading up to the guest rooms, each of them opening up to the balcony that encircled the dining area. In the distance, the *Olivette* sounded her horn, signaling she was headed back out to sea.

"I will have your bags taken to your room, General," the concierge noted as he placed Lee's canvas bag onto a squat, four-wheeled cart. "And a message for you, General," the concierge handed him a folded note.

"Much appreciated," Lee replied, slipping the concierge a small coin, understanding he would again have his customary suite. He hand-brushed his long-coat's tails, stiffened his back into a regal posture and peered around the dining area. He then unfolded the letter, quickly read through the hand-written note, and then scowled as he looked up to the far corner of the dining area. As the note indicated, a thin, well-dressed man in a rather plain black suit was situated at the corner table.

"Must be this Mr. Wilkie," he mumbled to himself, then strutted with feigned help from his carved, mahogany walking stick. He knew of Wilkie as a newspaperman from Chicago, but he had also heard that this rat-faced Yankee had wormed his way into a government position. *A cordial welcome was still appropriate*, Lee surmised, not willing to let politics dictate his manners.

"Good Day, Mr. Wilkie," Lee announced as he approached the younger man. Wilkie looked up; his face was expressionless, except for the frost that chilled his stare. Lee pulled back his hand when Wilkie didn't return the courtesy.

"Sit down, Consul," Wilkie icily stated then boorishly sipped at his tea.

"General is preferred," Lee grunted. He sat down slowly,

eyeing the rude man before him. Wilkie did not respond to him, instead simply placed his teacup directly in the center of the delicate saucer and snapped his fingers toward the waiter.

The boy needs schooling, Lee thought to himself.

"Coffee or tea, General?" the waiter asked.

"Coffee, son, with just a hint of sugar, please," Lee replied. The waiter bowed slightly and headed back to the kitchen.

Wilkie's eyes searched the room, including a glance up toward the balcony before he leaned forward and tented his fingers in front of his lips. "I know that you are involved in a special network of activities."

"Perhaps Secretary Day can provide you the details of my position," Lee responded in a measured tone, stifling his urge to counsel the directness of this weasel-faced man.

"The State Department is responsible for matters of the state; diplomacy and the like. I am more concerned about your other activities."

"I believe *I* know my job, sir."

"I have little time for foreplay, Consul." Wilkie's words seethed out from between his teeth. "To be blunt, I know of the Cisneros escapade, the raid on the Spanish armory, and the connections you have with the insurgency. I believe those actions are outside the bounds of normal diplomacy."

"Rather than being subjected to an inquisition sir, shall we begin with some enlightenment on the purpose of this discussion?" Lee asked, feeling his ire begin a slow simmer.

"I am now responsible for all foreign intelligence and covert actions outside the U. S. boundaries proper," Wilkie responded coldly. "You need to brief me on all the activities you are involved in, including those you are planning."

"Are you military, sir? I do not believe we have an active civilian espionage service, if that is what you are implying," Lee countered.

"What I am in charge of is a *non-military* government organization," Wilkie hissed back.

"I keep Secretary Day informed," Lee pushed back, feeling his irritation blossoming into full-blown anger. "When I have the opportunity," he sternly added.

"You WILL brief me BEFORE you take actions which could be remotely considered covert," Wilkie stopped to scan the room, then leaned forward and whispered, "Espionage is now in MY purview."

"Things occur at a rapid pace down there, son. I am not inclined to cable back anything I deem trivial or sensitive. I believe that is why President McKinley retained me in his administration . . ."

"Perhaps you did not understand me, Consul," Wilkie spoke through clenched teeth.

"I reckon what I said was clear, Mr. Wilkie," Lee fired back. He felt his anger boil.

"I am now responsible for your activities," Wilkie wagged his finger at Lee. "And if I am held responsible, I need to know. That includes plans, details, execution, and an exacting evaluation afterward."

Both men silenced when the waiter returned and set the coffee in front of Lee.

"Nothing more at this time, thank you," Lee bluntly responded to the waiter's inquisitive gesture then watched the young man as he turned and headed back to his station.

"Have I made myself clear," Wilkie finished.

"Yes, sir, you have." Lee glared. '*This damned Yankee is meddling and needs to be taught a lesson*', he growled under his breath. "But you sir, need to understand how extremely volatile an area this is. Things happen — sometimes rather abruptly. When they do, I need to respond quickly. I *do not* require nor do I request permission to act."

"Keep in mind, Consul. I can have your credentials pulled at any time if you feel you cannot comply with my directives."

"Is that so?" Lee fired back. He reached into his inside jacket pocket, pulled out a bulging envelope and slammed it on the table. "Here they are, Mr. Wilkie."

Wilkie sipped at his tea, stared back at Lee, and then calmly slid the envelope back. "This tirade is unnecessary, Consul, unless of course, you are capitulating."

Lee seethed. His veins strained at his necktie. He knew his

weakness was a poor poker face. His emotions were for all to see, especially from someone who clearly enjoyed skullduggery.

"You needn't have come here for this, Mr. Wilkie. I believe you could have more efficiently sent me a simple cable informing me of your *coup d'état* of the State Department."

"On the contrary, Consul. This is face-to-face business. I wanted you to understand several points, and I wanted be certain you understood them. One: I know what you are doing. Two: things are a little different in Washington now. Being an ex-field General, I am sure you recognize chain of command."

"I do, sir. My chain of command runs through the State Department," Lee was now subdued, more to control and hide his emotion rather than to show agreement.

"Three: Your covert activities, including your people like Carter run through me. I believe it is that simple, Consul."

Lee closed his eyes and brushed his handlebar mustache with his fingers.

"Enjoy your breakfast, Consul," Wilkie noted as he stood and waved the waiter over to the table. He drew out a bill from his pocket, dropped the money onto the table, and then leered down at Lee who remained silent and seated. Wilkie carefully slid his high backed chair back underneath the table before stiffly strutting toward the exit and disappearing into the Florida morning. Lee sucked in a deep breath and looked at the envelope still sitting on the table. 'This relationship was going to be difficult *at best*,' he mused.

"Would you like some breakfast now, sir," the waiter asked politely as he approached.

"That I would, son," Lee growled, then sucked in a cleansing breath as he slipped his papers back into his jacket pocket. "The usual — biscuits with a pat of butter each; eggs, lightly scrambled, and thick slab of ham smothered with red-eye gravy. And would you have some fresh orange juice?"

"Yes, General. Squeezed this morning."

"Son, you are making an old man very happy." Lee smiled. Despite Mr. Wilkie's interruption, he resolved to enjoy his stay back in the states.

Except for the lull of small waves sloshing and rocking the hull of the boat, the night passed quietly and uneventfully. Carter chose not to rise with the early morning sun since his night was fitful, edging the ballast boulders with each roll of his muscles. Each time he turned over onto the cloaked cargo sacks, metal gouged his skin. Rather than battle the discomfort, he wormed his way to the main deck where he was sure, deliciously cool air waited.

"¡*Lanchas*!" Sabio shouted as Carter's head popped above the deck. Carter spotted two headed directly toward them. The signal sent Miguel and Manuel scrambling to arm themselves with long fishing poles stored inside the gunwales. Their lines flew out port and starboard with precise choreography, as fluidly as if the men were suddenly alerted to a great school of tuna.

"Samuel, get below!" Sabio ordered, concern carving his face. He secured the tiller to keep the boat parallel to the Jamaican coast.

"Any pistols down there?" Carter scrambled toward the cargo.

"No! Leave them. We cannot outrun them. We cannot outgun them. Soldiers have Mausers," Sabio's words spilled out rapid-fire. He leaned over, relaxed on the handle of the tiller, keeping the boat's nose parallel with the Jamaican shore. Carter glanced back at the approaching patrol boats.

"¡*Vayase*!" Sabio insisted. "You are too pale, Samuel. We must make them believe we are only Jamaican fishermen. Then they will not board us. It is the only way. ¡*Vayase*!"

Carter slipped back into the hold and squeezed deeply into the cargo, and then underneath a suffocating canvas tarp. In the shredded light that seeped through the tarp's pinholes, he blindly fished around and found an old pistol in the bags of contraband. He thumbed the hammer. It didn't move. He felt rust flake off onto his hand. The mechanism finally budged, but only slightly. It would be of no value now, but he slipped it into his belt anyway and assumed a prone position.

The patrol boats closed in, their blunt bows chopping into

the slight wave crests. Sabio mumbled brief but precisely
ordered movements to his men like a director would for actors.
Chatter on deck grew faster with a practiced, melodic tone.
Sabio encouraged more seasoning with a touch of patois. The
motors on the patrol boats slowed.

"*¿Se captura cualquier cosa ?*" Carter heard a young
voice announce.

"No, mon. Two hours and nothing," Sabio whined. His
accent oozed as smoothly as if he were still in a Kingston alley.

"Fish not biting this morning!" Manuel voiced his part.

"Miserable feesh!" Miguel added, groggily. "Miserable,
smelly feesh."

"Be mindful where you are, old man," Carter heard a
different patrol officer warn in broken English, followed by a
boisterous laugh. "We might need to search you if you drift too
far away from your little island."

"Aye, mon. Nothin' but leetle feesh here. Smelly bait."
Sabio replied in a submissive tone, then added something what
Carter understood as shark food to Miguel and Manuel. The
Spaniards giggled.

"No problems here, Captain," Carter heard the younger
voice report back. Still no boots on the deck. He wanted to
know what was happening, but Sabio's warning was clear.
More chatter. Sabio and his men mumbled briskly. Then a
lower, more decisive voice from the patrol boat ordered
something that was washed out by their wake slopping onto the
cockleshell's hull. Motors revved up, then turned and faded.
Carter let loose his held breath.

"*Buenas dias, perros,*" Sabio cursed at the Spaniards as
his sandals clomped onto the wooden deck just above Carter.
After unraveling himself from his nest, Carter poked his head
out from below. Sabio's grin spoke volumes. "If the Señor is
tired and wants sleep up here, he can now indulge himself more
comfortably. I think the danger is past," Sabio added.

"*Gracias, Sabio,*" Carter reached into his shirt pocket,
pulled out one of cigars that Lugo had given him, and offered it
up. Sabio took the roll, immediately slipped it into his mouth,
and then widely smiled as Carter retreated below deck for some

more sleep.

If anything else had occurred that morning, it left Carter undisturbed until his tolerance limit was met for the slow broiling oven which the tropical sun made of the below deck. Still partly asleep, he groped his way back to the main deck, gained his bearings, and once fully above the gunwales, felt the steady, hot southern wind and blinding sun whisk away his sweat.

Sabio remained jovial at the tiller, joking with his crew and still savoring the cigar Carter had given to him the night before. Behind Sabio, Jamaica was all aglow, like a jewel in a setting of emerald. The turquoise sky above was cloudless and the northern green slopes of the island were blocked off in large squares, showing to great advantage the light green of the cane fields alternating with the deeper hue of the forests. It was a magnificently splendid picture.

Carter glanced north and saw nothing behind an immense bank of swirling clouds that enshrouded Cuba. He stumbled back toward Sabio on weary sea legs, and stubbed his toe on a crate where he could sit and watch their approach. As if the wind at their backs had finally pushed hard enough to whisk away the clouds, the shroud around Cuba fizzled away, revealing their treasure, the majestic Sierra Maestra. Carter remembered this as the most unique part of Cuba, and for that matter, anywhere in the world — an eight thousand foot tall mountain range standing so close to the sea, its summits clothed in napped verdure that extended for miles. It was like drawing the curtain aside to reveal an unrivaled painting by an extraordinary artist, one who masterfully blended color, mass, mountain, land and sea.

"*Buenas tardes*, Samuel," Sabio announced.

"How — how close," Carter eked out scratchy words, squinting as he struggled to peer through the thinning cloud cover.

"Closer than I thought," Sabio's sleepy voice registered enough alarm to scramble his crew to the sails. "The reef. We must stop and wait for darkness."

"*¡Abajo!*" Sabio called out, keeping hold of his tiny jib sheet. Miguel and Manuel sprang to life, dropping and roping the main sails together, leaving oddly bent masts stark naked as if it were a blighted pine tree. With a flick of his hand, Sabio directed the men to the cargo hold to begin their examination of their secret contraband.

Carter followed the crew into the cramped hold and even in the dim light, could see frightfully rusted rifles — most no better than the Smith and Wesson he had extracted for his own protection. Caked on rust would need to be chipped away from the barrels and the firing mechanisms would need several layers of oil just to get them to move. Carter hoped the opportunity for their need would never exist out here, but also realized that with each roll of the water toward the shore, the potential for their need grew that much greater. Although more than one shot would be doubtful without further work, it was one shot more than what they presently had available. With nightfall at least about an hour away, Carter chose to work on the revolver that he was sure he could rejuvenate. When four rifles were completed, they all headed topside.

"Except for the night and the reef, we have nothing but enemies here," Sabio noted as indigo darkness crept in now minute-by-minute, sunset an hour past.

"We land tonight?" Carter asked Sabio as an old stolen Mauser flew toward Sabio. The old man caught the rifle's mid-section without flinching, and then slung the webbed strap over his head.

"No Samuel. We need to be just inside the reef. *Lanchas* draft deep — they cannot pass here. We will have a chance to survive until Garcia's men arrive over there in the morning," Sabio said as he pointed to an area of water just inside an odd, green stripe of sea. The grizzled old rebel then directed the men into prone, defensive positions; bow and port with Carter to starboard. Sabio then raised the jib sheet and rigged the end to the tiller for one-handed operation while he positioned himself to the stern. Then they drifted laboriously toward the shore.

Hours passed. No *lanchas*. Sabio finally released the jib

sheet and directed Manuel to sound the shallow water with his oar. A timely roller gave the boat a final lift and shoved the small craft into the waters of a hidden peaceful bay.

"Reef!" Manuel announced. He dropped his oar to the deck, and then slung a tethered grapple over the side.

"Shouldn't we just slip in and land tonight?" Carter asked Sabio.

"We have enemies both ashore and afloat, Samuel. It is better that we drift into the mangroves where we can stay hidden. We have no friends on shore tonight. Garcia's men will not be here until morning. Our only friends tonight are the reef, the mangroves and the darkness."

"Then we wait until morning?"

"Ah, Samuel, you understand. Morning."

Chapter 8

"*El Turquino, Señor* — the Tutor," Sabio said, his voice hushed and reverent.

Sam Carter woke to the voice and then wiped salty crust from his eyes. A tropical, mist-like morning haze hanging at the meeting of the sea and sky lifted lazily, as if drop by drop, divulging a gnarled mass of tangled mangrove roots blanched from air exposure. Thorn-set trees mixed with them at water's edge, where colors melded like a wet painter's palette; emerald to grape, grape to gray, and then gray back to green. Then as the dawn grew brighter and the sun burned off the mist, the marvel of the rocky southern fringe of a single mountain edifice seemingly more than a mile high appeared, leaving its peak still shrouded in clouds.

Miguel tested the cove's depth with an oar, and satisfied, rolled over the gunwales into hip-deep water. The wispy Cuban retrieved the anchor rope and began slogging toward shore as Manuel repacked the sack of weapons and their rusted parts.

"I have yet to see a more enchanting view," Carter whispered, fully captivated by the view. "Night's candles are burnt out and a jocund day stands tiptoe on the misty mountain tops," he mumbled, reciting a poem, which Lugo had once read to him while Sabio tapped the cove's bottom with a short, thin pole.

"Now, we go," Sabio said and stowed the pole on-board. Carter estimated they were fifty feet from the beach. "No *lanchas* here. Patrols passed last night," he added.

Manuel immediately cinched up one burlap sack, and then slipped over the side. Holding the sack above his head, he headed directly to the dark, narrow opening in the mangrove thicket where Miguel had disappeared moments before. Sabio then rolled into the knee-deep water. Carter followed then slogged at the tail of the file headed toward a hidden piece of shoreline.

"Quickly, Señor. Sand sharks hide in here," Sabio said over his shoulder, as if sensing Carter looking at the water froth around his trousers. Carter complied with a more deliberate pace and the foursome emerged onto the shore, through the straw-like breathing tubes the mangroves sent up from the sandy muck. They all dragged the boat from the water, finished unloading their secret cargo, then removed the boulders from the boat, before ditching it, overturned and hidden in a small jungle estuary.

Carter plodded back to their landing spot, working his way through the sand, small rocks and shells on the beach to ensure their footprints were obliterated. He glanced back from his task and noticed Sabio along the edge of the jungle's thickness, as if searching, while his charges displayed an odd but obviously practiced ritual of arranging the sacked gear into four piles.

"*Aqui*," Sabio whispered as he poked his machete into the smooth, mottled bark of a particular mahogany tree where a barely perceptible trail nearby entered but was immediately engulfed by vegetation. Sabio's men responded, dragging and dropping the supply piles to the mouth of the path.

Sabio whistled a quick series of tweets.

"They are coming to us?" Carter asked.

"Shh," Sabio motioning for silence. The old man whistled again, inter-mingling a series of clicks this time, and then tiptoed across the beach to the farthest path. Two more guttural clicks. Silence. Carter heard twigs snap. He stiffened. Sabio jerked his head toward the sounds, and then motioned everyone down with his hand.

Huge heart-shaped leaves parted. From the opening, Carter watched five ragged men emerge, their rifles level with the ground. *Natives,* he reckoned from their skin color and the scarred bulging pink streaks on their naked arms; the healed remnants tracks Mauser bullet flesh wounds. One rebel, a rather short, light-skinned fellow, wore a black patch to cover his missing eye.

Sabio rose from his haunches first. The jungle rebels' dour rapidly faded, replaced by blossoming smiles. The guerillas slung their rifles over onto their backs, stepped toward Sabio's crew and greeted them all warmly.

Carter felt different. There was skepticism in the five sets of camouflaged eyes locked on the twists of his curled red hair escaping from under his slouch hat. Sabio interceded. Carter heard only a few of the Spanish words that Sabio whispered to the leader of the guerillas, but when their faces melted and grew more cordial, Carter understood. There was very little more debate. The guerillas relaxed again as Sabio and his men loaded themselves with the materiel delivery, and then like army ants, all filed into the shoreline reaches of the jungle, heading west.

Machetes swung back and forth as the group bushwhacked their way through the thick undergrowth. Thin rays of sunlight that seeped through the thick forest canopy bounced off juice-moistened blades that swooshed through the low growth. Carter and Sabio carried up the rear of the group, unarmed save Carter's rusted pistol, following the winding path opened before them.

Carter felt the humidity start irritating his lungs, as if he were aspirating water with each breath he inhaled. His calves and thighs painfully rebelled as the march started an upward climb. He grabbed his trousers and leaned forward, resting for a moment, but when he glanced up, realized he had fallen far behind the human machines working their way up the mountain.

"We can rest shortly. We need to keep them in sight," Sabio noted. Carter understood the urging, stood on his rubbery legs, and continued the ascent with his old friend. He realized his work in the cities had whittled away his fitness. His breaths grew shallower and his strides shorter as they climbed ever higher along the mountain range. A glance at his companions, who were smaller and he thought, less fit, revealed his miscalculation. They all continued to extend their distance from him. Sabio and Carter continued their exhausting chase of the nimble jungle trained men and by mid-morning, reached a large, level clearing where the line of wanderers had stopped to wait. Despite Sabio insisting that this was where they would meet General Garcia, Carter saw nothing but forest around them. Desperately needing a rest, Carter melted onto a broken stump, closed his eyes and dropped his pounding head into his open hands.

"Samuel!" A familiar voice perked Carter. He looked up and noticed a pair of khaki clad soldiers with wide brimmed jungle hats just as they parted to reveal the older, rather paunch-shaped General Calixto Garcia. The old man brought a smile to Carter's face.

"General." Carter stood up and examined his old friend approaching, his gait stiffened by his high horseman's boots. A welcoming smile grew under his large, frayed white handlebar mustache that sat starkly in contrast on his sun-darkened face. The pair extended their arms and solidly belly-bumped. Dullness in Garcia's deeply set brown eyes set Carter to wonder if it was age or the revolution that was taking its due. The brightness he knew from years back was faded. Hints of sun-damaged skin sagged underneath.

"Whatever happened to Calixto, Samuel? We are still friends, no?" Garcia tipped his head and let his infectious smile spread through the gathering. Carter sensed the smile was feigned.

"It is good to see you are well, Calixto," Carter lied. The General looked worn. He wanted to be more cordial, but the circumstances stifled his intentions.

"So, Samuel, I understand you are on government business this time," Garcia's welcoming expression faded as he swiveled his head like an owl and shooed away his bodyguards.

'Is your insurgency making progress? Are your men surviving the movement? How is your son? Has age dulled the one I once knew as the old fox?' Carter wanted to ask as he gazed into the General's eyes, but "Yes, sir," was all he could

push past his lips.

"Has it been that long, Samuel. Have you already forgotten you must pace yourself in this jungle?" Garcia wagged his finger at Carter, who was clearly exhausted and in pain. "Follow me. I will move slowly for you," he added, chuckling.

Undergrowth tugged at Carter's weary legs as he tried to keep up with Garcia. After only a few minutes, they emerged at the edge of the well-hidden encampment. Carter stumbled toward the half-circle of stumps and makeshift trail chairs, sat down and collapsed as Garcia veered off.

"I believe we should be able to help get what you need," Carter said as Garcia returned and sat down next to him. An aide brought them both canteens full of fresh, cold water. "But we need to know your exact situation, General."

"What should I tell you which you do not already know?" Garcia said rhetorically while Carter took a mouthful of the clear mountain water.

"I have seen your supplies," Carter nodded back toward the cache of weapons his men were now mulling over with Sabio. "You will need better. Much better."

"I am growing tired of all this trouble, Samuel. We make one advance, and then we lose ground somewhere else. I must admit, there are some days that I would like this to just be done and over with. But you know, I must be true to my heart and persevere."

"How long can you hold this part of the country," Carter said, bluntly. "How soon do you need . . .?"

"No, no, Samuel. Your military needs to keep its distance," Garcia warned, waving his hands in front of him. "Your intervention would be a big mistake — some would see this as just a prelude to another takeover. No, Samuel, we Cubans need to do this for ourselves. That way our countries remain friends."

"But can you defeat the Spaniards alone?"

"You still do not understand, Samuel?" Garcia grew immediately agitated. "We must first consolidate our insurgency. Several factions are fighting the Spaniards. These groups must be brought together under one person. One leader. That was General Cisneros' vision."

"But an intervention could —"

"Listen to me, Samuel," Garcia wagged his finger as he continued his lecture. "If your country is the one to defeat the Spaniards, how will they chose which of the Generals are to be the new leader? Would you choose me? Perhaps Gomez? And what then about others like Arturo? Do you believe he would relent to one of us? No, Samuel, you must tell whoever is planning to take on our burden, which is to fight the Spaniards until they are bloodied enough to leave, that their intervention is unwise. We may not be able to defeat the Spaniards directly, but . . ."

"General," a young uniformed aide interrupted Garcia, waving a small paper as he approached.

"Excuse me, Samuel," Garcia noted after reading the message. "This is something I fear I must personally attend," he added as he stood and walked away. Carter drank more of the refreshing water from the sweating canteen as he watched Garcia stop at the forest's edge and regard the message. The General bowed his head, slowly shook it from side to side, then looked up toward the sky and sighed. After a moment of contemplation, he returned.

"You will need to excuse me, Samuel. I have some business I need to tend to personally."

"I should come," Carter started, hoping to get a first-hand look at the Spaniards.

"I shall leave you in good hands until I return." Garcia's terseness and glower was a clear response. The General then waved toward a younger officer, and as the figure moved closer, Carter recognized the face.

"Samuel, this is Colonel Garcia."

"Carlos?" Carter considered the younger Garcia, who was about ten years younger than he was. He was no longer a gawky teenager, having grown solidly into his once willowy build. His dark hair and thin mustache poorly camouflaged the resemblance to his father.

"Carlos will stay here with you. I need to take care of this little business." Garcia said, and then continued to speak to Carlos with only his eyes.

"I understand," Carter agreed, reluctantly.

"And you should have something to eat and rest. I trust that you understand you still have a very long trek ahead of you. Getting out of here will not be quite as easy as you have found in the past." The General grasped Carter's shoulders.

"That I do understand, Calixto," Carter noted as Garcia released him.

"We will talk more when I return. I am sure Carlos can provide you some of the information you seek," Garcia added as he marched off with deliberateness. The General rallied together several of his staff officers, and in minutes, headed out on horseback at a speed Carter thought dangerous for the narrow forest trails.

"It has been a long time, Carlos," Carter said as the older Garcia and his entourage disappeared.

"Yes it has, Señor Carter," Carlos said. Carter saw hollowness in the young Garcia's eyes rather than the life and vigor he once remembered from years before.

"The war is draining on your father, is it not?" Carter prompted, walking toward the makeshift chairs. The young Garcia joined Carter at the stumps, dropping onto the chopped mahogany and rested his head in his hands.

"The war has taken much out of Papa. It has taken much out of all of us. Perhaps you should not listen to my father's pride and suggest to your government that intervention *is* the just action."

Carter mulled the young Garcia's words for a moment, choosing to hold his response and let the young man pontificate further.

"And perhaps you could tell your people that it would be wise to select Papa or Gomez to lead the country once the Spaniards are eradicated," Garcia dropped his head into his open palms. It was clear to Carter that the General's emotions were clouding the undesirable truth that a strong enemy, regardless of how much passion stood against it, was inexorable.

"Carlos, look at me," Carter insisted. The young Garcia complied. His eyes were wide with concern for his father. "If the message I bring back results in the United States intervening, will your father consider me less a friend and more an enemy of his heart?"

"That I do not know," Garcia pushed himself up and slowly paced in a circle, arms folded behind his back, face lifted toward the sky. When he stopped pacing, he turned toward Carter and tipped his head. "I do know that Papa trusts you and believes you will do the right thing."

Carter bit his lip, concerned he now believed an American intervention was necessary had become the right move in his mind, but he still wanted General Garcia to believe that as well.

"He respects that you will provide the correct message to your President," Carlos continued. "Most of us know McKinley is trying to avoid a war, but we see daily it is becoming unavoidable. Our dream of freedom from Spanish rule slipping slowly through our hands, like sand does through weary fingers."

"Have you told our father this?" Carter asked.

"Yes. Several times. Others as well," Garcia lowered his head again. "But I do not believe he is listening to anything but his pride and his heart. The Spaniards are stubborn and proud. And fatigue has sapped our strength, Samuel.'"

Carter understood. At least he thought he did.

Lieutenant Commander Richard Wainwright stepped through the watertight doors along the under-deck of the *USS Maine*, bending forward as he thrust his long left leg through the portal. He had seen too many officers suffer embarrassment rather than injury because they forgot their indoctrination on these newer Navy battle cruisers and rapped their head on the crest of the now smaller opening. Once through, unscathed, he inspected the seal on the watertight doors to ensure they would serve their designed function — to hold back water from a simple mistake like an open sea-water valve, like what happened on their sister ship, *Texas*. Satisfied, he continued his rounds on the below decks portals and headed toward the coalbunkers.

Since slipping out of the Navy Yard nestled within Chesapeake Bay, the *Maine* had maintained full speed and a full head of steam until they had attained the outer reaches of U.S. waters. At that point, Wainwright convinced Captain Sigsbee that a slower, more lumbering speed in a southerly heading would allow added visual surveillance over the open ocean along the Eastern Seaboard. Further out also gave his "ears," Ensign Simpson, the advantage of focused listening eastward for telegraphic activity without the chatter and chaff that usually spewed from the ports along the shore. Whether Sigsbee knew or not, part of Wainwright's mission was to monitor activity in the Atlantic, especially German activity headed to and sculling around Hispañola. Their reduced speed would still get them to the Keys by early December — plenty of time for their scheduled Christmas liberty in Tampa.

"Morning, Commander," Charles Lohman, a coal passer stopped his shoveling to stiffen and salute as Wainwright stepped out from a bulkhead and into the coal rooms.

"As you were, sailor," Wainwright replied in kind, snapping off a crisp reply. He stepped back to give the passer room to swing his shovel. Lohman resumed where he left off, and continued filling the cart he used to shuffle coal from the bunkers to the boilers.

"Where are the temperature logs, sailor?" Wainwright asked, thinking it archaic that with all the technology designed into this particular warship, she lacked a mechanized way to feed the fires.

"Over yonder, sir. I'll get them in a jiffy." Lohman dropped his wide-mouthed shovel into the cart scurried along the passageway to retrieve the log. As he handed the clipboard to Wainwright, he grumbled, "Ya know, those damned sensors in A-16 are a bit touchy, sir. Seems like they're always popping off for no reason. Makes it tough on us to keep the feed rate up when we're chasing ghosts."

"Better that not working at all." Wainwright scanned the logged temperatures. All of the numbers looked normal. "I know plenty of boys that would have rather chased ghosts than fight fires out at sea."

"Good point, sir," Lohman agreed reluctantly and continued to shovel.

Wainwright had made a career of studying coal and its properties; proper portions of volatility to a margin of safety, an engine's maximum power per ton, the risk of fires, loading patterns. Coal's volatile nature was definitely a problem on board if not controlled. Keeping it from igniting or even exploding in bunkers near engine rooms where typical temperatures were close to combustible was a challenge. Smoldering fires were not preventable, so the temperature surveillances were important. Wainwright lobbied for installed instruments, and even if the newer models were a bit sensitive, his resolve for their importance was solidified following his investigations of the fires aboard the *Oregon*, *Cincinnati*, and *Brooklyn*.

Wainwright flipped the log sheet and ran his finger down the coal inventory. It did not surprise him that it was being used up quickly, since this load was almost purely anthracite. Although the harder coal they typically used was much safer, he knew that a load of bitumen might give them the extra kick they would need if called to action, and perhaps even stretch out the usage somewhat. 'Bit', as they called the coal, was risky though, since the coal bunkers on the *Maine*, and in particular A-16, were situated so close to the shell and magazine storage.

'Battles were never won when the tactics used were entirely conservative and fail-safe,' he mused as he made a mental note of the inventory, reckoning he would true up the supply requirements later that day. Tampa typically stored bitumen he remembered, then returned the log to its location and finished his inspection of the lower deck. Lunch with the Captain would come soon, and then he could get back to his surveillance of the open Atlantic.

Carter stumbled to his feet, startled awake out from a deep, sweaty sleep by the thunder pounding of horse's hooves. He scrambled to the front flap, drew his repaired sidearm and crouched in a defensive position. Peeking out into the encampment, he tried to focus through the thin film that had coalesced over his eyes while he slept, but all he could see was a deep green and brown blur of the forest.

"No Spaniards out here, Señor Carter," Colonel Garcia's guttural belly laugh rattled as he lay prone on his cot. He tipped his wide-brimmed hat away from his face. "Just Papa returning."

"How can you tell?" Carter sheepishly returned the rusty Smith and Wesson to his holster, rose to his feet and brushed himself off.

"Spaniards don't ride quickly through here. Our territory is foreign to them," the young Garcia stated as Carter watched General Garcia emerge from the forest trail, his troupe in tow at a slightly slower gait. A handful of youthful handlers converged on the band of rebels as they slowed to a trot, each one of the horses halting precisely in accordance with the General's quick hand signal. Carter stepped out of the tent as the General turned and dismounted. A more vibrant expression now beamed from the old man's face.

"Ah, Samuel," Garcia noted as he slung a newly acquired Mauser over his shoulder. "You look to have had a good siesta?"

"I have had some long days recently, but I am sure yours have been more eventful."

"Change is a tortuous and tiring road, my friend," the General directed Carter to sit on a stump just outside his tent. "I can only hope that he may live to see this change come to my Cuba," the General added as he noticed his son emerge from the tent.

"I am sure with your conviction and efforts, it will be so, Calixto," Carter said as the trio sat down together.

Garcia sighed deeply as he rummaged through his small leather satchel and pulled out a pair of cigars. He offered one to Carter, and then added, "You would have been better staying in Havana, Samuel."

"I was offered little choice," Carter noted as he tapped his breast pocket, which contained maps he drew of the Spanish positions in the Oriente Province after talking with Carlos.

"I see," Garcia blew gray smoke out through his nostrils He leaned back as if thinking while he savored the aroma. "What was wrong with the way we communicated before?"

"Things have changed. Besides, I needed to give you information I believe you need," Carter offered as he lit his cigar.

"Such as —" Garcia's eyes grew wide open as he tipped his head.

"German warships are maneuvering nearby."

"Haiti? I have heard there have been some movements off Dominica. You do know Lugo, yes? He does keep me well informed." Garcia blew a cloud of smoke toward the sky.

"Perhaps not just Haiti. Several large warships are being produced in Germany. I have heard they may also be forming an alliance with the Spaniards." Carter whispered so that only Garcia could hear. The words clearly disturbed the General. He squeezed his forehead in his hand as a pair of boys approached carrying large leathery leaves mounded high with sliced fruit and cured pork.

"*Gracias*," Garcia looked up, took the leaves and gave the boys a fatherly smile. He then turned to Carter, offered one and added, "It is not much, but this is all we have, Samuel."

"If that happens, can you manage that alone?" Carter asked as he started on a mango slice. Juice dribbled onto his chin.

"That I do not know," Garcia offered as he slurped on a pineapple slice. "That does add an element of which we may not be prepared to handle. Perhaps we should discuss this matter further . . ."

Garcia stopped when a young aide approached. He waved him closer and the boy, clearly not more than fifteen, leaned over and whispered into the old man's ear.

"I apologize, Samuel, but you will need to leave tonight," Garcia sighed heavily. "I have news that we have started the incursion which should lead to breaking the Spaniards' backs. Unfortunately for you, the only road we control leading to the northern coast and our connection with a trusted man, General

Rios, will need to be sacrificed for the time being for this incursion to be successful."

"I can go back south — with Sabio, no?" Carter offered as he lit his cigar.

"No, Samuel, you cannot. He has left. His travel is at the mercy of Spanish shore patrols."

"Then can I wait here until you return."

"Unwise."

"This area is safe enough, is it not?"

"We will break camp here."

"I see." Carter said.

"I have trusted officers that I need to send to assist General Rios. You may travel safely with them."

"I have travelled that road before, Calixto. I believe . . ."

"Samuel," Garcia interrupted, his tone turning condescending. "For your own good, you need to listen to me. Many things have changed on this island since you were here last."

"But —"

"No Samuel. Again, I insist," Garcia waved off Carter. He blew a tight stream of tobacco smoke skyward. "I must be moving. We may have delayed you too long already, but we cannot change what we have done."

"I understand," Carter relented.

"You will find my men useful. They have spent their lives with me in Cuba, and are trained and tried through the pathways you must take. The sum of their particular capacities will answer any additional questions you would likely propose. And when you see General Rios, he can provide you any more of the information you need," Garcia cracked a grin that spread quickly across his broad face.

"Tell me at least one thing. What is it that you think you need the most, Calixto?"

"Medicine," Garcia responded without hesitation. "Yellow fever is rampant from the mosquitoes. That is what I see as the most important. Doctor Vieta can give you more detail."

"Arms?"

"*Sí*. My men need arms, especially artillery," Garcia let

155

his eyes drift up. "The cannon must be mobile so we can penetrate the blockhouses the Spaniards have built."

"I see," Carter took mental notes. "The guns Sabio brought? Is that what you are using?"

"Yes, and we are also very short in ammunition. We have so many different rifles it is difficult to ensure an ample supply."

"Perhaps it would be better to re-arm with American rifles in order to simplify that question," Carter noted.

"Perhaps. But listen to me, Samuel," Garcia warned. His eyes were wide saucers. "I need your government to understand that it cannot come in here and take over this war from us."

"Despite the Germans?"

"Yes, despite the Germans."

"I understand, Calixto."

"You, I believe. Your government, I do not have the same conviction. That is the most important thing for you to bring back. You must let us win this without bringing soldiers here. Anything except soldiers would be helpful." Garcia stood up from his stool and waved in three men. His gaze at Carter required a response. "This cancer which the Spanish have spread has agitated those who wish anarchy. We need a strong Cuba without that intervention."

"I understand, Calixto." Carter said.

"*Bueno*. We are settled then. Paco!" A man with a harsh, gruff looking face approached. Like Garcia, he wore a white tunic that bulged at his hip where his sidearm pushed out. "This is Colonel Hernandez. He will lead the party," Garcia added.

Hernandez forced a smile on his harsh face, then tipped his hat and stared at Carter. "Señor Carter."

"Hernandez knows all of what we have. He has fought on the front lines with our men and has seen the fight in their eyes. He has seen the Spanish camps, and knows how they think. I trust him. I ask him for the best way to avoid the Spaniards. I will have you know, Samuel, Colonel Hernandez jungle skills have been honed by leading guerillas on spot attacks of the Spanish."

"If the supplies are already in Florida, I will ensure they are sent as soon as it can be arranged, Calixto." Carter said.

"Your journey north will be much longer that your trip here, Samuel," General Garcia continued. "I know of a small secure clearing a few miles north of here. I will have some horses sent there. Hernandez knows. We will be moving this camp shortly after you leave. Such is our existence."

"Thank you, Calixto. I promise that we will soon be together again," Carter replied with one last glance into the General's and his son's eyes.

With Hernandez in the lead, ten insurgents and Carter left camp on foot, headed toward the looming Sierra Maestra ridge before them. An hour out of the main camp, the line of soldiers plunged into the rainforest underneath the protective canopy of wide, leather leaf filled boughs as the island's daily thunderstorm rumbled in from the west. Rain hammered onto the leaves, lightning flashed and cracked nearby, and wind whooshed through the trees. Undaunted, the line continued its meandering march, hunkered within the shield of the forest's awning. As if it was a leaking roof, the torturous path between the overlapping leaves allowed some of the rain to worm its way through and drip onto Carter's slouch hat. It was his own perspiration though, that had soaked his clothes more than the rain from the flash storm.

Hernandez stopped the entourage as the storm subsided and the rains moved on to the south. Lightning in the distance illuminated the sky behind the training clouds as he tapped two scouts to move forward and investigate the small clearing in front of them. The scouts carefully moved forward, rifles level to the ground, stepping sideways as they swung the barrels from one side to the other. Minutes passed. Then three whistles. The colonel signaled the group to move forward.

Carter stood back and watched as the soldiers set up camp, working as if their individual tasks had been choreographed; wood was collected, sentries assumed perimeter posts, small fires appeared, and hammocks webbed out in a protected circle amidst a stand of mahogany trees. With what seemed only minutes having passed, Carter and the soldiers converged and decompressed near the fires. Mentally and physically exhausted though, Carter moved away and slogged toward his assigned hammock.

Carter stopped when he noticed one of the sentries questioning a pair of ragged men he did not remember. He approached Vieta, the physician Garcia had insisted join the group, and asked," Who are they?"

"Deserters," Vieta replied rather calmly as he watched Colonel Hernandez converge with the sentry and begin a rather intense interrogation. "We see many of these stragglers out here. Some are isolated countrymen; others are defectors from the Spanish army. They all come to us for food, complaining of harsh treatment by their officers. We can get some needed intelligence for a few scraps of food."

'And you just accept that?' Carter thought, remaining suspicious as he considered the men closely. Their faces did not look as drawn as he would have expected for someone mistreated or malnourished. The shorter deserter appeared to be scanning the encampment as Hernandez questioned him, but froze when Carter sensed their stares engage.

"Does Hernandez question all of them?" Carter asked. His neck prickled.

"Personally. Standard protocol. Hernandez can tell if the man is truly deserting or if he is a spy." Vieta leaned back and started his torpedo shaped cigar. "We will give them some food anyway. It shows — humanity."

"Hernandez will keep them under close surveillance?" Carter asked, still struggling to accept the situation.

"I am sure." Vieta added and sent a stream of smoke into the fading fire light as the guards escorted the stragglers off to a location near the forest edge. Carter's neck continued to tingle as he maintained a vigil on the men as he retreated to his hammock. Melting into the hanging mesh, Carter closed his eyes and dozed.

An hour passed. Carter dozed off and on as he tossed in his hammock, unable to fall asleep. The oppressive humidity left in the wake of the afternoon storm had yet to subside, leaving him with pools of sweat lying on his skin. The thick air reminded him of mid-summer in Mobile, when he would steal out to the docks to sleep under the sky, hoping for a breeze off the water.

Snap.

Carter startled awake. He swiveled his head as if he were a bird dog locating a quail to flush. Nothing.

"Stop!" a voice broke the night's silence.

Crack.

A bullet twanged off a tree nearby as he spotted the muzzle flash through the corner of his eye.

The stragglers, Carter thought. He slid from his hammock to the ground, then rolled to his left and crouched in a three-point stance, back against a tree trunk, weapon drawn, hammer cocked.

"*Donde?*" he heard, followed by moans. He turned to the sound, and then thought he saw something nearby. A machete blade whooshed directly in front of him, just missing his shoulder. His neck veins pulsed. He sucked in a deep breath as he aimed in the direction of the noise, widening his eyes to see any movement.

"Bastard!" Carter heard followed by agonized scream emanated near him. He pulled his arms to his chest but still maintained his weapon's aim toward the commotion. Boots hammered on the hard jungle floor, approaching him from behind. Lights from lanterns bounced as the soldiers, he reckoned, ran toward him. One of the lights swept the ground until it passed over, then returned and fixed on a writhing body next to him on the ground. The soldiers and the remaining lanterns converged, revealing an armless man on the ground with crimson blood spurting out from his shoulder, splattering on the dried rubber tree leaves around him.

"Explain this!" Hernandez demanded as he placed his revolver barrel in the center of the deserter's forehead.

"*Voy a morrir al Americano sí Juan no escapó,*" the deserter admitted. Carter noticed blood frothing at the corner of his mouth.

"*¡Mierda de perro!*" Hernandez pulled his gun back and

motioned to one of the sentries.

"Wait!" Carter yelled, but before he could scramble to his feet, the guard's rifle discharged and obliterated the deserter's face.

"Throw that shit in the woods!" Hernandez kicked the suddenly limp body hard in the ribs. He holstered his revolver, then turned and asked, "The other one?"

"Dead," another sentry admitted.

"Throw that garbage out as well. Cockroaches!" Hernandez growled, then turned and stomped back in the direction of his own hammock. Carter followed.

"Colonel, I — " Carter started as he caught up to Hernandez.

"Horses and saddles will not be available until late tomorrow." Hernandez said as he held up his hand to interrupt Carter. "Garcia is on the move. Once he has completed that incursion, we will have saddles."

"But if I head off alone, or with one or two guides," Carter started.

"No guides."

"Then I don't need guides."

"When was the last time you walked the forest, Carter?" Hernandez laughed.

"I am not here as a tourist, Colonel." Carter grew agitated with his restriction.

"And that is precisely the issue, Carter. The risk to us is too great. We cannot have you fall into Spanish hands. "

"Perhaps the risk of —"

"Keep this in mind, Señor Carter. It would be better for you to be killed than captured because of what you know now. I am ready to do my duty if necessary." Carter glared at Hernandez as he spoke and realized that the truth was as icily cruel as he stated. "I will hear nothing more of separation."

A scowl etched Hernandez's face. Carter nodded his agreement.

"I was ordered to get you to Rios, and that is what I will do. I will maintain my honor with Garcia. End of discussion." Hernandez added, his arm flailing ended and crossed them over his chest.

Carter realized argument would only further aggravate Hernandez. Accepting the reality, he headed back to his hammock, poured himself into the hanging strings and watched the glowworms start their eerie greenish light show in the tropical soup. Too tired to fight with his heavy eyelids, he started to drift off to an agitated, uncomfortable sleep.

Chapter 9

Rudolf Moser waited at the café near the dock for the ship that would take him back to Germany. Haiti was a wretched island, he thought, and Port-au-Prince was the epitome of the filth and squalor that seemed typical of this island exile. He enjoyed warmth, but the weather here was intolerable; an endless succession of hot, steamy days followed by torrential rains in the afternoons, and then by oppressively humid nights, all of which made him as miserable as he was uncomfortable. Both the native Haitians; black-skinned locals, years ago inoculated with French civilization, as weak-minded as their former colonial rulers, as well as the transplanted, integrated Germans were insufferable. The guidance from the Fatherland as what he remembered the Kaiser calling it, was nothing more than an arrogant, self-serving, imperialistic rule virtually ignored by the indigenous.

Moser sipped at his morning coffee, an odd tasting brew, thinner that he liked, laced heavily with sugar, and stared out over the harbor's blue water. It was the only thing that seemed clean in this city. He could not help but wonder why he or anyone should even be here, no less expecting to see anything other than a weak anarchy. He sensed no passion here for anything but hedonistic drunkenness and lethargy. Nothing that he had seen in the past few days was any different from what the Kaiser already knew. The French were gone, the English had no interest in this seemingly God-forsaken island, and the

Spaniards, their hands already bloodied by repressing a recalcitrant population in Cuba, would certainly not want to deal with another indigenous, ungrateful population.

In addition, there were no Americans intermingled with the indigenous. Moser reckoned they had already recognized and then abandoned hope for any limited value this island might offer. Haiti was just Haiti, nothing more, nothing less — a desolate island in the Caribbean — nothing more than a geographical bump in the pathway of tropical storms and hurricanes. Haiti was just an insufferable steam bath with a local population that believed the next in the long line of interceders would eventually capitulate to their political *laissez faire* attitude, and just leave.

Moser slurped another mouthful of his black drink. He would have preferred a strong breakfast tea, even taken bitter, but his choices were limited. The symbolism for him being here was not lost. The political winds back home made him feel increasingly more a vestige than an asset. He had been loyal to Otto von Bismarck for several years before Wilhelm rose to power, but ever since the younger Kaiser Wilhelm had pushed the old man out of power, he felt more like lingering extra baggage from years gone by.

'The vigor of the youthful leaders always seemed to discount the wisdom learned from age and experience,' Moser thought. He was now in his early sixties, and wondered whether the disloyal, nagging twinges he felt may have sprouted from what he had seen to be the treatment of Old Otto. Like Bismarck, he had dedicated himself to his work at the expense of a family. He had no wife or children. His parents had died several years back. He wondered if he could even survive alone, shivering during another cold winter in Germany, one in which he may be disenfranchised, a result not improbable since there were no stunning revelations to be uncovered in Haiti.

Moser could not fathom another taste of the sickeningly sweet coffee. As he pushed it away, he looked up and saw a large glistening white passenger steamer work its way into the harbor channel and toward the docks. It was his passage home.

The Imperial German flag flapped at the bow and stern masts. Perhaps. He dropped a coin onto the small weathered wooden table and started toward the loading station nearby. After two steps, a horse drawn cab creaked to stop at the curb in front of the café. Moser stopped and stared at the carriage for a moment.

"Do you know where the American Embassy is?" Moser asked as he looked up to the coal-black skinned driver who responded with a wide smile.

"Yes. American Embassy, yes." The driver nodded agreement. His white teeth gleamed behind his dark-skinned face. "You go there?"

Moser glanced toward the German passenger steamer, now plowing slowly into the harbor. He struggled for a moment, then bit his lip, grabbed the door handle, slipped quietly into the carriage, and closed the door behind him.

"American Embassy," he said. His heart thumped as he listened to the horse's hooves tap at first, then quicken to a steady, rhythmic clomp along the cobblestoned street. He tried to settle his whirling thoughts as he worked through what he could offer of value to the Americans, but the carriage stopped before he had a salient thought. He kept thinking as he emerged carefully from the carriage and walked slowly toward the large plantation-like mansion, hoping some semblance of order would come settle in his mind.

"I would like to speak to the Ambassador," Moser announced to a young man sitting in the cavernous, sparsely furnished foyer.

"Ambassador Powell has not arrived yet this morning," the young man responded tersely without looking up.

"Soon?"

"Yes, sir. I believe so."

"Then I shall wait," Moser sighed and found a solitary soft chair in which to rest. He mulled over what he knew and what might convince this Ambassador William Powell that he was sincerely considering defection. '*Would the Americans be interested in what he knew about the Kaiser's plans for China, Africa and South America? Perhaps the shipbuilding in Kiel would interest them? Or would they would be interested in how Admiral Tirpitz had revised submarine plans the Kaiser had acquired years back from an odd Englishmen by the name of James McClintock.'*

James McClintock. The name struck a familiar chord. That was the same man that his old friend Gunter developed a keen respect, enough that he had followed the man to the States in pursuit of developing that vessel. He remembered Gunter used the alias of Samuel Miller. The vague image of Samuel Carter emerged. The young man he happened across on his way here said he was Gunter's son. Perhaps . . .

"Good morning, Mr. Moser. I am Ambassador William F. Powell." A deep, steady voice interrupted his thoughts. Moser quickly rose to his feet and offered his hand to the smartly dressed ambassador. "My clerk indicates you would like to speak to me?"

"Sir, I would like to discuss something that may be of great importance to you and your country." Moser replied. He arched his eyebrows and tried to read through Powell's deeply set blue eyes and inquisitive face. *'No, he is skeptical.'* Moser thought.

"Please come in then," Powell offered, leading Moser through a pair of tall, double doors with etched glass panes.

Carter's body ached with a soreness he had not felt since sleeping in Sabio's cockleshell. He rolled out of his hammock, dropping to the ground before fully waking up. He untied the mesh from the mahogany trees, and then balled it up enough to stuff into his satchel. The forest around him was already awake with screeches, trills and warbling bird song; the softer, more docile nocturnal overture had gone to sleep with the sunrise. He stretched his arms skyward and groaned, noticing the morning sun peek through the forest canopy. The light seeping through allowed a glimpse of a trail that led away from the clearing and headed up along the backbone of the ridge for some distance. It then vanished, consumed by a thick, lush undergrowth of vines and roots.

'Perhaps Garcia was right,' he thought, reckoning he had

not remembered this wilderness being as overgrown and complex as what he saw now. Combined with the tortuous windings, he would surely have become lost, or worse, fall into the hands of wandering Spanish patrols. He stumbled on stiff legs toward one of the small fires, now nothing more than glowing embers, wisps of smoke and paper-thin ashes meandering into the morning air. He stretched again to work out knots that twitched through his back before he rekindled the fire to boil up water for some coffee to wash down hard tack rations. There seemed a calm confidence in these insurgents, Carter thought, as one-by-one they joined him around the tiny fire. As a group, the men passed hard tack and boiled beef, took their ration, and then passed on the fare as it settled.

Mid-morning, a column of horses appeared where Carter could not see any useable trail. In the lead was a huge, coal-black faced Cuban. Despite the ubiquitous mosquito swarms, the man wore a threadbare shirt, sleeves purposefully ripped away to leave his well-defined muscles on each of his arms exposed. Once the man was clear of the brush, he sheathed his two-foot long machete, dismounted, and coached the horses toward Hernandez.

"I see General Rios has sent Lieutenant Dionisio Lopez," Vieta relayed to Carter, as the insurgents responded to a quick thrust of Colonel Hernandez's hand to break camp. "You will see he is particularly adept at travel through the forest. He wields his machete as skillfully as any surgeon does. Some even say he senses pathways as easily as you and I would see broad high roads."

"Not someone I would wish to cross," Carter noted as he carefully watched Lopez march directly toward Hernandez. The men talked briefly, and then parted. In what seemed only minutes, the soldiers packed their gear, mounted the horses, and formed into a single file behind Lopez. Hernandez motioned for Carter and Vieta to mount as well, and the file slipped quietly into the lush undergrowth and for all practical purposes, disappeared.

Carter worked his way close to the front of the file, close

enough to monitor the centaur-like Lopez tirelessly carve a pathway through the jungle. Networks of vines fell before his steady strokes right and left; thickly closed spaces became openings, and tangled growth dropped, shredded into harmless stubs that could only stroke feebly at their legs as they rode by. As the canopy and undergrowth thinned and the angle of the climb slowed, the top of the rocky ridge, barren in spots, opened. Their pace hastened as the sun passed overhead and beat mercilessly from the west on their uncovered heads and naked arms. Sweat poured down Carter's face, unabated by the cloth sweatband encircling his head. He wondered how much more of the tropical sun, unchecked by the openness of the ridge, he could endure.

His answer arrived as soon as he thought it. Lopez, several lengths ahead of the pack, turned his glistening steed away from the rocky divide and into the brush, commencing a descent of the eastern slope. With each switchback the marchers encountered, the trail widened on this side of the range, having clearly been used frequently and recently. A welcomed, slight breeze followed them all the way down to where the trail bottomed out near a meandering river. Appointed sentries fanned out as each canteen was filled with life-preserving water. Carter followed the lead of the soldiers and rinsed his face with the cool water as well, dribbling the refreshing wetness down his face. He soaked his hat in the stream then plopped it onto his head. Steam rose where the water hit his skin.

The brief rest was completed much too soon for Carter's liking, but that was the least of Lopez' concern. The afternoon slipped into evening, and the march turned away from the river and into the outer reaches of the rather disheveled town. After what seemed only a few minutes, Carter noticed a motley group of bare-chested and shoe-less children playing with a rather ragged ball and being monitored by a single, bent and prune skinned, white-haired old man. Hernandez halted the procession for a moment as if not to frighten the boys, and with Lopez, moved forward to speak with them. The children froze in their positions, and then cautiously approached Lopez until

the soldier's broad smiles invited the children to stroke his
massive horse's rippled shoulders and flanks. Lopez accepted
the adulation as a gentle giant to the children; his wide, bright
smile cracking through his otherwise chiseled face. A few more
words passed between the bent patriarch and Hernandez before
the children looked up and pointed back to Carter.

"¡*Viva Delegado americano!*" shouted one of the ill-clad
youngsters as he pointed to his head.

"¡*Viva Cuba libre!*" shouted another.

Carter found it comforting that he was being viewed as an
ally, but also felt disconcerted that the secret of his presence
was clearly compromised. He wondered if these villagers'
knowledge endangered or secured him, but could only hope
that their acceptance of Hernandez's band maintained him as
an unattainable target for the Spaniards. Instead of dwelling on
the loss of secrecy, all that mattered to him was that he had
made an otherwise destitute old man and a crowd of little
children happier.

The troupe moved on, still skirting the village, which
provided some solace to Carter that interactions would be
limited. The sparsely wooded road meandered along the fields
until a series of chest-high stonewalls emerged. As if passing
through hallowed ground, the patrol stopped and gazed upon
the walls. Some bowed their heads in prayer while others let
their eyes drift skyward. Carter moved closer to the walls,
which appeared to have been cobbled together using sharp
edged stone broken after being carried down from the hills and
mixed with rounded field and river stone. Behind the walls that
snaked for yards were trenches, two or three feet deep. The
entire vista reminded Carter of the redoubts he had seen at
Manassas and Gettysburg.

"This is Yara," Hernandez noted. "Where our revolution
began."

"And Martí? Is this where he joined the revolt?" Carter
asked.

"You know our history very well, Señor Carter,"
Hernandez raised one of his bushy white eyebrows. "Yes, this
is where we say the first demands for liberty emerged."

"And the walls?" Carter asked.

"Fortification to defend this gorge. No Spaniards have dared challenge us in the ten years we have held this area."

Carter noticed the brilliant hues streaked across the sky. Since he had been a forest creature for several days, he had almost forgotten how majestically the sun painted the autumn sky at sunset. Their travels done for the day, Hernandez ordered respite, hammocks unfolded, and guards assigned vigil through the night. Despite the heat and humidity, no one, including Carter, had problems sleeping that night.

"This will be the last time any nation is going to insult the German people," Kaiser Wilhelm fumed as he stormed about his office, livid over the report that two German missionaries had been murdered in China. The Kaiser stomped from one side of the vast room to the other like an angry and caged animal, mulling over what his specific demands would be in response for the insolence.

Bernhard von Bülow, the Kaiser's trusted foreign minister, burst through the door into Wilhelm's office, then stopped mid-stride, as if suddenly frozen. He gasped, catching his breath before saying, "I came as fast as I could, sir," then cringed, expecting the Kaiser's rage to explode.

"Did you see this?" Wilhelm shook a paper above his head. His eyes bulged in fury. "Two missionaries, *missionaries mind you*, are now dead. We should have been swift in Hangkow last week."

"I am sure this is just some misunderstanding, sir —"

"Silence! I will not accept that excuse, Bernhard." Wilhelm slammed the report to his desk then pounded it angrily with his fist. "There is no misunderstanding here. This was deliberate — a deliberate act of violence. This time we will respond."

Von Bülow remained close to the door, since an immediate escape would be warranted if the Kaiser's tantrum included hurling objects about the room. His eyes remained trained on the pickelhaube atop Wilhelm's imperial helmet and the storming Emperor circling the room.

"Should not we consider some diplomacy first before sending troops so far from the Fatherland," von Bülow offered.

"I have already dispatched the Asiatic squadron to the scene. Diedrichs understands. I am thoroughly resolved to show these Chinese at last that Germany does not allow itself to be toyed with." Wilhelm clenched his fist, extended his index finger and waved it above his head. "And they will incur my wrath for such insolence. They will be handled with full severity and with the most brutal regard."

"My counsel, Sire, is that we still need to resolve the Haitian issues before we take on this second front, sir," von Bülow countered.

"These are acts of insolence, Bernhard, not battle fronts," Wilhelm squeezed the words through his clenched teeth. Wilhelm's mercurial emotions appeared to relent as he settled at his desk and set his hobnailed boots up onto his desk.

"Sire, the foreign ministry has already started negotiations with the Haitians on this very issue," von Bülow said calmly, attempting to soothe the Kaiser.

"That contemptible crowd of Negros will also be taught respect for the German people is an expectation," Wilhelm's head tilted toward the ceiling as he reached over and stroked the bill of his battle helmet. "Our people, Minister von Schwerin, Lüders, and anyone else in this fray with a drop of German blood will be vindicated. Mark my words, those rogue officials on that island will be deposed, and an appropriate rule of law will be established over that island."

"As you wish, Sire," Von Bülow atoned as he cautiously moved deeper into the room and settled into one of the cushioned chairs facing Wilhelm. He remained cautious, having experienced the Kaiser's volatility on a regular frequency.

"Public executions would send a much clearer message, don't you think, Bernhard?" Wilhelm grinned as he lit up a cigar and invited von Bülow to take one as well.

"I do not believe that would be necessary, Sire."

"Now that you mention it, Bernhard, we do need to renegotiate this flaccid policy of the Foreign Ministry. I believe you understand me, Bernhard, but those people over there clearly do not understand my desire to move their culture forward — more in line with the rest of the civilized world, which I have repeatedly, and I emphasize, repeatedly presented them over the recent years."

"And going in with an armed force will provide that diplomacy?"

"Sometimes, Bernhard that is all these insolents understand. I have already commissioned my school ships, the *Stein* and the *Charlotte*, to set sail for the Indies. Even manned only by boys, they will teach the islanders manners."

"And do you think the Americans will take to this lightly?" von Bülow asked cautiously.

"They have no right to dictate my actions." Wilhelm said then leaned forward, grimaced, and added, "I dare them to interfere with our destiny."

An uncharacteristically chilly tropical morning relented as the sun rose, promising another arduous tedious day for Hernandez, Carter and the entourage. Coffee and hardtack devoured, the encampment transformed into a nomadic file of horses, men and gear, while leaving nothing perceptible behind. The ascent along a spur of mountains projecting northward along the east bank of a meandering river grew steep quickly, but Hernandez insisted the higher road be taken for safety despite its ruggedness. No one questioned his expertise and knowledge that the Spaniards never chose the harder path.

Carter struggled as the heat and thinner air rapidly sapped his energy. Once the pack broke the tree line, rocky, eroded ridges of the mountain range emerged, evidence of battering by hurricanes that had tried and failed over the years to scale the mountains on their initial assault from the open Atlantic. The narrow trail eventually flattened out and widened once they entered a misty cloud layer that hovered atop the ridge, finally relieving the torturous climb over narrow and dangerous outcroppings. It was only a momentary relief. The westward switchback resumed, plunging the column of travelers into a series of vicissitudes across the streams with vertical banks that at first glance appeared to Carter as impassable.

Lopez and Hernandez halted the procession only briefly while they scouted the possible ways to travel, and then signaled the grueling trek to carry on. As each traveler headed down into deep gulches, where muddy, vertical edifices stood cut by rapidly flowing streams, Carter watched, appalled at the cruelty and punishment meted out on the horses as they balked at traversing down to the bottom, through the stream, and then out again. The animals' resistance only heightened the intensity of the whipping, beating and yanking at their muzzles.

The column finally emerged from beneath a forest canopy that seemed to have cloaked them since their first descent that morning and stopped, exhausted and parched. Carter saw in front of them gently rolling hills, their texture a patchwork of tall and wide cornfields, reminiscent of autumn in the Midwestern United States. With the moment's rest, Carter shared in the collective sigh that the hardest day of riding that not only him, but also all of them had ever experienced and endured. Even Lopez, as fit as any man Carter had ever known, appeared completely and totally drained.

The rest for a drink was short, too short, Carter thought, but in the open, the band of soldiers would be an easy target. Hernandez ordered the column to enter the field, and the men moved forward, swallowed by the maze of tall stalks rising around them like green walls with wide leaves reaching out to brush along the shoulders of the horses. Hidden from everything but the sun and the field, the band plodded at a relaxed pace until they emerged from amidst the stalks and fanned out in a wide clearing. As if a mirage appeared before them, a remarkably long, grass-roofed hut stood from which smoke seeped out from a center chimney. A very distinct aroma wafted in their direction.

"We rest here for the night," Hernandez announced.

"Who are these people?" Carter felt skeptical. His scan of the area revealed a motley band of half-dressed men milling about and feasting loudly.

"General Rios is the leader up here — the General of the Coasts. As you will see, Rios is a very generous man."

"That I can see," Carter noted.

"At least for those who are with the revolution," Hernandez added. A sly grin etched his face. "For the Spaniards, the greeting is much different. That I assure you."

Carter nodded. The parade, now wide rather than narrow, had moved toward troughs of water and grain where the horses were secured in front of their just reward. The band dismounted then headed into the door less shack. As Carter entered, the wide smile of a cook busily preparing slabs of beef over an open pit greeted him. Behind the old man, a freshly slaughtered steer hung from the rafters. Next to the hanging beef, a large sack of cassava bread had been dropped on the table, several of the loaves spilled out to the column's delight.

Carter joined the festive clamoring around the generous portions laid out before them. His stomach ached as it growled for anything but the hard tack and boiled beef it had been provided the past week. But as soon as he placed his hands onto a dripping slab of beef, the dirt floor began to quiver.

Horses, Carter thought. He anxiously scanned the room but quickly realized his fear was not shared by anyone else in the room. Instead, the patrol headed back toward the door amidst a great commotion of voices to greet the intruders.

Whoops and hollers greeted the lone rider that emerged from the corn patch. Atop a muscular, chestnut-haired steed sat a well-dressed officer.

"Viva Castillo! Viva Rios!" chanted the patrol as they threw their slouch hats into the air.

"Señor Carter!" the officer announced as he abruptly halted his horse, kicking up a thick cloud of amber dust.

Carter stepped forward. Colonel Demetrio Castillo dismounted and presented himself to Carter with all the grace of a well-heeled officer. He hand brushed his white tunic and saluted Carter, all the while, beaming a toothy welcome grin.

"On behalf of the General of the Coasts, General Rios, we celebrate your assistance in our fight for liberty. The honorable general will personally greet you in the morning. For now, enjoy the feast."

Castillo then dropped his salute and extended his hand to

Carter amidst the clamor of the patrol. Then as deftly as he had dismounted, he re-mounted his steed with an athletic spring and put spurs to the horse's flanks. He leaned forward and held on tightly as his mount reared up, tipped his wide brimmed hat to the crowd, and galloped into the cornfield and disappeared.

Without further delay, the patrol rolled like a human wave back into the shack and continued with their welcomed bountiful meal. Carter knew they were at least two days away from the coast, and those promised to be both long and tedious.

Chapter 10

"I believe we have waited long enough, Mr. Wilkie," Roosevelt groused as he stared out his Washington office window.

"Aren't you being premature?" Wilkie asked, squirming in his hard, ladder-backed chair.

"He should have cabled us by now." Roosevelt straightened his posture.

"He's only been in Cuba for a week."

"That's my point. It has been a week. If he hasn't returned by now, we must assume he is a casualty," Roosevelt said bluntly without turning around.

Casualty. The word stunned Wilkie. That meant *he* was responsible. He was not ready to accept that. It was too early in this new career to accept accountability. '*No,*' he thought, '*Roosevelt just didn't understand how long reconnaissance took. It was like researching a story. Or not. Maybe it was him that didn't understand and Roosevelt did.*'

"It's not like you to be quiet, John," Roosevelt prodded as he turned around and fixed his eyes onto Wilkie's.

"There had to be another explanation."

"It's reality, John, cold reality." Roosevelt clicked his teeth and grimaced. "Let me lay out the big picture for you. If we have not heard from Carter by now, he's either dead or worse, captured. If he's dead, we have some explaining to do, but it won't be too tough. If he's been captured . . . well, your mission may be compromised. If your mission is compromised,

I had better get some asses moving and do something. Understand?"

"My mission?"

"You know this can't be government sanctioned, John." Wilkie swallowed hard.

"It was a risk you took, and you guessed wrong. That's the way it goes. What's done is done. Accept the cold facts and move on. Now, what do you know about these German vessels cranking up their boilers to head this way?"

Wilkie didn't want to make up information, and what he had was sparse at best. "I believe you would have more information on them, sir," he started, but Roosevelt's glare said his response was unacceptable. "What I know is that two warships are gearing up for a trans-Atlantic sail. Training ships," he finished.

"That's just what I thought — his prelude. The Kaiser's getting frisky." Roosevelt started a rooster-like strut around the room, his head swiveling about as circled, maintaining one eye focused on Wilkie. "Do you know anything about war?"

Wilkie remained quiet, still stunned by how quickly Roosevelt passed off his accountability for the life of one of his men. He started to think about what he would have to say to Carter's family, but then realized he had not researched into whether there even was a family to console.

"You need to get a bit savvier in the ways of the world, John," Roosevelt broke into his thoughts as the Secretary unrolled a map of the Atlantic. He then pulled out a handful of coins from his trouser pocket and placed two at the Western tip of Haiti, then two more at the Northern shoreline of Germany. "And I don't mean the business side, either. Step up here and let me lay it out for you."

Wilkie warily stood up from his chair and joined Roosevelt at the map.

"Mr. Kaiser — over here — is itching to show that he has the best Navy out there. He's sending his scout ships to Haiti as a jumping point for his troops. There isn't crap in Haiti, so that's all that he could be doing. Personally, I think he's itching to make his way into Cuba."

As Roosevelt ranted about his war plans, Wilkie fumbled with a message in his pocket he had received an hour earlier from Ambassador Powell in Haiti. He reckoned now there may be something he needed to know from this German defector, especially since the information gleaned could engender him more with Roosevelt.

"You see, what Mr. Kaiser doesn't know at this point is that we haven't been sitting on our hands while he and the Spaniards have been scheming behind our backs." Roosevelt conniving smile parted his lips as he danced around the map-covered desk. "We've got some ships now — some real ships, you know — big ones. And I intend to make sure everybody knows we're not afraid to use them."

"So you know the Germans are plotting with Spain?" Wilkie furrowed his brow.

"If they do, well, that'll be just fine, if you ask me. We'll take them both on if we have to and run them both back from where they came." Roosevelt dropped a handful of the tokens onto the map in the area of Norfolk. "This is what I'm talking about, John. We have more ships and they're better equipped than those bathtubs those guys over there are using," he pounded his thick finger into the map.

"We can't just sail out of Norfolk and hope to get there in time," Wilkie offered.

"Here," Roosevelt pointed to the southern part of Florida. "I've already sent them to Tampa and the Keys under the guise of maneuvers out in the Gulf. We'll be just a stone's throw from Havana — glide right in at a moment's notice."

"If I remember correctly sir, the coal supply is thin down south."

Roosevelt harrumphed. "You made the deal with those fellows up in Pennsylvania. Get them to ante up some carloads and send them down to Tampa right away. If they aren't ready, get some from further south. We've got a rendezvous with destiny down there and we need to get some ships ready to go."

"Yes, sir," Wilkie replied as he stood and exited the room. He emerged into the bright Washington morning under a clear blue sky and thought about the list of questions he needed to ask Moser. He needed to beat Roosevelt to the punch line on what the Kaiser was planning on doing.

Carter watched as dark fingers crept across the afternoon sky and over the spit of land along the Cuban northern coast that the insurgents tenuously controlled. As evening melded into the night, thunder rumbled in the distance while behind the clouds in the eastern sky, haunting images illuminated, morphed and dimmed before flashing to life again. He hunkered down in the shelter near the shoreline and listened to the winds build rapidly from wispy whooshes to sustained louder howling. He had endured tropical storms in the States before, and the winds that now rolled down the mountain range preceding this one carried that same distinct tang. Even the feasting mosquitoes and blood-sucking gnats had vanished, as if hunkered down to survive this blow.

"Nothing more than a typical evening storm," Vieta noted casually. Carter knew different. This was more than just an afternoon rain so joining the others in a vain attempt to stay dry, he moved as far as he could away from the opening deeper inside the haphazard shelter. Wind-driven rain penetrated every open error in the lean-to's construction. A streak of lightning sizzled nearby, exploding as it seared through a mahogany tree. The sweet smell of electric discharge drifted past Carter's nose just as the sky released an even heavier deluge of warm, drenching rain, as if a dam had released a stored reservoir. Froth grew as mushrooms out of the salt-laden sandy loam as the rain drilled between the grains, then took flight, before splatting onto anything that dared stand in the way. Wind whipped stronger yet, more vicious by the minute, building to a sustained howl as it shredded tropical fronds and hardwood leaves into unrecognizable pieces of green and white.

Carter felt fortunate, sensing that he was close to the end of this mission. Hernandez, Castillo and Rios had fulfilled their promise to him and duty to Garcia over two days. Or was it three? They had successfully travelled across the heart of the Spanish controlled region on this side of the island, without being detected, even as they were close enough to hear the jingle of horse's trappings and rattling of short, sheathed sabers. Once Carter and a handful of men were settled in this lean-to, Rios and his hundred strong guerilla force escort broke off in order to create the diversion needed to let him safely take to the water and begin the last leg home.

"Once the rain ends, the patrols soon resume. Move deftly, Señor Carter. You will have little time to get out to sea," Hernandez said over his shoulder as he stood at the front of the shelter. Carter watched the Colonel from his haunches and reckoned he was calculating when they would be able to make their move. Then as suddenly as the storm had started, it ceased, as if simply turned off and hastily swept off to the north. The time had come.

Hernandez turned and looked back into the lean-to and with only a stare, set the men into action. Not a second was wasted — they all understood the escape window would be short-lived. Carter studied the bottle shaped bay to the narrow channel at the north end as Hernandez directed traffic. A handful of men scurried toward a sparse coconut grove and removed huge palm fronds that lay atop a hidden cockleshell, stored on its side. Another handful scampered back to the shelter for necessary supplies while the first detachment dragged the round bottomed hull toward the water. The Spaniards would certainly have this patrolled, if not armed with shoreline cannon to protect from incursions as well as prevent escape, Carter thought. Despite all he had gone through, he knew this, the final escape, was the most dangerous part of this mission. One step ahead was all they needed to be.

"We will do what we can to divert the patrols so you may attain passage out the mouth, Señor Carter," Hernandez mumbled as Carter watched two barebacked men rig up gunnysacks and piece them together for sails on the limited capacity fishing boat. Hernandez then pointed out to the spit where the land formed the bottle shaped outlet. "Surviving that, you are at the mercy of the *lanchas* and the sea."

"Needs be when the devil drives, my friend." Carter feigned a sloppy salute. He smiled at Vieta then headed toward the rickety craft where three men were already rigging the boat for running.

Even as the storm had passed in the sky, its anger remained virulent in the fiercely rolling water spanking along the bay's shoreline. Carter examined the flimsy craft that he was about to entrust his life, and wondered how much more brutal the open ocean may be. But waiting for calmer seas any longer simply beckoned danger. Under a dark, cloud filled sky, Carter and three Cuban guerillas paddled out into the bay. The height of the tide told him that lurking behind the clouds was a bright full moon, leaving only a hope that the trailing clouds of the passing gale would resist dissipating long enough to conceal their escape.

Sitting precariously low in the water, the cockleshell strained under the weight of four grown men. Above, ragged clouds rushed like mad animals on a chase across the face of the moon, alternately hiding and disclosing the tiny craft as the men tugged together at the oars as quietly as they could. The distance to the channel was closing, but under the cloak of darkness, Carter could not see where the land narrowed. He could only imagine the picture of frowning muzzles of guns trained on them, waiting for a glimpse of their escape pod. He expected at any moment that the cannon would explode and a shell would scream by them. Nevertheless, the small craft, reeled and tossed like an eggshell on the verge of capsizing, escaped the bay and slipped out into the trackless green ocean. A breeze finally picked up as did the current, perhaps on the fringe of the gale, and the gunnysack sails bulged full.

Carter stopped his rowing enough to rest his weary arms and exhausted mettle. The rolling waves continued to lift and lower the boat in a monotonous ride from crest to crest, occasionally sending a spray of stinging salt onto his sunburned forearms. He leaned back against the gunwale and drifted back to sleep, but no sooner than he did, an immense wave crashed over the side, drenching him. Suddenly awake, Carter joined the scramble to save them from capsizing. Adrenaline surged through tired veins. Buckets, scoops and even hands flailed away, feverishly bailing water from the already low riding vessel. Even Raul, the man on the tiller, after tying the control stick securely in place, joined the rush for their lives. Sopping with stinging brine, weary and worn, they all bailed for their lives as the flimsy boat bobbed a mere foot away from being swamped again.

Admiral William Sampson stood proudly at the bow of *USS Iowa*, the flagship of the newly formed North Atlantic Fleet, and let the sea breeze slip through his long thick white beard. She had done well in the drills off the coast of Virginia, where her big guns moved meticulously through their paces, impressing Navy Secretary Roosevelt with her range and span of influence. Sampson, an expert on ordnance, had selected specific pieces to use for greatest visual effect. The noise from the guns was equally extraordinary, booming loud enough that some of the glass portals on board now required replacement when they docked in Key West.

Behind her, stretching back for several miles, were ten additional cruisers and battleships in two-by-two formation. The Admiral glanced up and noted that the smoke plume spewing out from the boilers had a brownish-yellow taint. *Bituminous*, he thought, but worried little about its volatility since the *Iowa's* coal bunkers were specifically designed to contain the more volatile fuel.

The maneuver he was leading had unfolded exactly as the contingency plan he and a handful of officers had developed in case war with Spain was imminent. They would berth at Key West in a week or two, send out scouting missions with the smaller destroyers, and be at the ready for any change in status. The only deviation from the plan was that the *Maine* was still off on her own, moving at a slower pace than the fleet, scouring the eastern coastline for German vessels.

There was something going on there that concerned him. Captain Charles Sigsbee had command of the vessel, and Commander Wainwright, who had been the head of the Naval Intelligence office just prior, had been assigned as his executive officer. That had all the signs of some internal investigation to Sampson. Moreover, since 'Sigs' was one of his best students at Annapolis, it just didn't add up that he would have done anything to warrant an internal investigation from the Navy.

"Message from Washington, Admiral," a corpsman announced, interrupting his thoughts. Sampson thought about buttoning the flap on his tunic, but decided otherwise. It was a quiet day, he reasoned, and the night promised to be the same. There would be other times to maintain formality. He turned and the corpsman stiffened into immediate attention with a sharp salute.

"As you were, son," Sampson returned the salute sharply, and then offered his open hand for the message. The corpsman obliged. "Thank you, son. Dismissed."

Sampson turned back to the open ocean, where the sun was now sinking into the horizon, painting a masterpiece he had not seen since the last time he was out to sea. The trails of magenta and red clouds training as far south as he could see refreshed his memory — a gale was blowing down near the Caribbean. It would be off into the Gulf, perhaps even lashing out on the Mexican coast before his squadron made the Keys.

"Why the hell they do this is beyond me," he mumbled as he slipped his finger into the envelope and extracted the message. "They don't need to be sealed out here."

"*Fishing vessel with possible American interests aboard may be near your pathway. If encountered, recover and notify Olivette to provide transport from Keys to Tampa.*" He read the words methodically, looked back up to the bow and stared back at the cloud formation. '*They must have been in one hell of a gale coming off the island,* he reckoned. *They'd be lucky if they didn't sink with the first wave that washed over their gunwales.*'

Sampson made a mental note to send the message onto the rest of the fleet to keep their eyes open, and continued his relaxed view over the open ocean. "Never could quite understand how those boys could take those rickety old tubs into the open ocean,"

Carter woke at sunrise, still queasy from the incessant ocean roll, but at least the urge to vomit had subsided. Over the grey-blue water, the sun began its ascent and peered through the haze on the horizon. He adjusted his floppy brimmed, brine soaked hat to shade his prickled, sunburned face and stared northward.

'*Something's there*,' he thought, wiping his eyes clean of crusty discharge. He worried his imagination was now conjuring what he wanted to see.

"*Un vapor, Señores!*" Raul then yelled from the rear of the boat. Carter's heart started to race. Everyone stopped bailing and stared.

"*Dos vapores, tres vapores, Caramba! Doce vapores*!" Raul chirped from the front of the boat, his high-pitched voice cracking. Carter scrambled to the front of the cockleshell and stared, but the lumbering images were just out of discernible range.

"*Telescopio*," Carter asked. The pilot shoulder shrugged. '*I know there's one*,' Carter thought, and worked his way back on his hands and knees to the center of the boat. Under what looked like two inches of water, he saw it and fished it out. He wiped it down with the tail of his now ragged shirt, inspected for broken lenses — it was sound — then kneeled to steady his fatigued body to peer out through the tube.

"Can't see shit," he spat, but continued to adjust the focus.

"*Americanos?*" was all Carter could understand from the babble his three shipmates carried on. A water trail tracked down through his view, but the image was clear enough.

"*Sí, Americanos*," he confirmed. He counted ten vessels in all, headed perpendicular to them, at full steam. Old Glory flags flapping on the main masts convinced him. "American ships, comrades," he added.

"*Viva!*" the crew chanted.

'*They're moving too fast. They'll never see us*,' Carter thought, but quickly realized that unless they had some signal that could get the vessel's attention, hope was slim that they would be seen. The bright sun, a tiny, ratty old cockleshell on a vast ocean, and everything they had stowed below soaked by the swamping conspired against them.

Unfazed by the reality that Carter had already resolved

that they were, for all practical purposes invisible to the war ships, Raul and Alberto continued chanting and hopping about the boat as if the ships miles away would hear them. The enjoyment, elation and for that matter, even the presence of the ships however, did not make any difference to the water still seeping through the hull of the cockleshell. And if Spanish gunboats still patrolled the waters, and their belabored progress was still slow and for all practical purposes, directionless, Carter realized danger remained perched on their bow.

The steel-hulled vessels continued off to the west, and as quickly as they had appeared, faded into the distance, leaving only occluded and dissipating vapors in their wake. The angst with their enemy and friend, the sea, continued through the day and into the night. Night fell on four of the most tired men that ever lived, Carter thought, worn out, sunburned and beyond fatigue. He rested only long enough to consume a few strands of the shredded, boiled beef they had stuffed away in their sacks. But as darkness grew indigo and then black, a minimal moon brought back a building wind. With the wind came taller and more angry waves and with the waves, the toil of bailing would surely be the order to keep the little vessel afloat at least for one more night.

John Wilkie sipped at his morning tea as he poured over the information that seemed to have accumulated overnight on his rather small, four legged office table. Large, pompous desks wee wasteful, he believed, opting for a more efficient looking modest piece of furniture. He set the tea cup onto its saucer that sat on a separate six inch square metal stand beside his desk, and then continued working through the 'domestic issues' stack of papers.

Coal was on the move again as Roosevelt had demanded; lines of rail cars were headed to Mobile and New Orleans to fill colliers designated for the Keys. Episodes of counterfeiting continued to increase, leaving his boss, Director Hazen, in a very tenuous position with McKinley. Wilkie reckoned that Hazen might not survive this scandal, a second since McKinley took office. Worse yet, the President had originally disapproved of this particular money issue since it appeared so easily copied. A few more cases like this and the President would have no choice but to make a change, Wilkie thought. Smitten, he knew he was now positioned as the best clear choice to replace Hazen.

Wilkie sipped more tea then turned his attention to the foreign cables. *"All quiet. Nothing to report,"* read Fitzhugh Lee's typically stilted and short cable. He needed to get Consul Lee to be more open with his information since he was sure there was more going on in Havana than Lee was willing to share. A fleeting thought crossed his mind that Lee might know what had happened to Carter. Remembering Roosevelt's coaching on cold reality iced that thought, instead.

His agent in Spain reported that the Queen Regent and Prime Minister were still cogitating over Ambassador Woodford's ultimatum over Cuba. The issue of Cuba could become quite interesting, perhaps even volatile once Roosevelt's armada passed by Cuba on their way to the Keys, Wilkie resolved.

There was also a cable from his operative in Germany. Kaiser Wilhelm was continuing to build his fleet and two, possibly three vessels were already headed from Germany to the Caribbean. The defector Moser had indicated he could provide some insight to the Kaiser's plans, but Wilkie was not sure if it could be trusted. He never did trust Germans or defectors, and this old man was both, which by default, made him a liar. There was also a question of how current this defector's information was. It could also be just a convoluted ruse — a ploy to get into the United States. But he had no way to validate.

"Mr. Wilkie," the door burst open in front of him. Jack Stiles rushed in, breathing hard as if he had run all the way from across town.

"Stiles — I assume this is valuable information?" Wilkie scowled at the interruption.

"Yes, sir. It's from the squadron. They spotted a cockleshell — drifting east toward the Bahamas."

Wilkie set his pince-nez down on the papers and glared up

to Stiles as a quizzical expression etched his face.

"Even money it's Carter." Stiles dropped the official Navy cable onto the desk. Wilkie picked it up and scanned it cursorily. He wiggled his small, brush-like mustache for a moment, rose slowly from his seat and stepped toward a wall map of the North Atlantic. Stiles followed.

"Brits. I would suspect they will be incarcerating anyone they even suspect to be coming in from Cuba." Wilkie looked at Stiles with a rather bland expression then back to the map. "The Brits are deathly afraid of the yellow fever epidemic running through Cuba."

"The Bahamas," Stiles flicked his finger at the islands on the map. "I'm sure I can catch a steamer there."

Wilkie pruned his lips as he studied the map while mulling over the information Stiles had blurted out. He then realized that Moser specifically mentioned that he knew Carter. It was his chance at corroboration.

"Go," Wilkie said.

Stiles, already halfway to the door, replied, "On the way."

Carter regained consciousness. He didn't believe he could consider his exhausted rest from bailing as sleep, nor did he feel he could consider that he was now as awake. He felt even as he was lying on death's doorstep, the Grim Reaper did not see him as worthy. His shoulders burned inside and out as he picked up his pail and feebly scooped and moved the water from the inside to the outside of the boat. His stomach roiled with the undulating motion of the vessel, complaining bitterly for the want of anything but the stringy boiled beef. Pail after pail he continued returning the sea from where it came, only to watch it return.

He stopped and tried to work out the stiffness that had settled in at his shoulders. He opened his eyes as his face pointed skyward, then startled when he spotted a flock of pelicans skimming low near the sea surface, swooping in their direction. They approached from the east, then turned and soared over the boat. Carter scrambled to fetch the spyglass, then glanced at the birds and followed the horizon in their direction.

"Land. I see land!" Carter shouted.

"Bahamas?" Carter heard Raul mutter. The shirtless Cuban crawled up from the tiller.

"Bahamas?" Alberto repeated as Carter melted into the mast. The Cubans scrambled to the gunwales, giving up their bailing for the moment to catch a glimpse of Carter's discovery. With nothing but elation driving them, Carter and his comrades began a frantic paddle while the ratty gunnysack sails luffed weakly. After only a few minutes, Carter's efforts waned as he spotted a small steam ship off to the north, and rapidly closing on their position.

"We are out of Spanish waters, Señor Carter," Raul noted, continuing to skull the bobbing cockleshell with the tiller with what remaining strength he had. "Not *lanchas*."

Carter retrieved the spyglass again, twisted the rusty crust formed at its joints, and then focused on the white vessel as it grew larger and closed the gap between them.

"It's a Jack," Carter announced. "It's British!" he added as the ship continued to close the distance, slowing and turning as it moved within voice range. Carter could not quite discern features of the man now cupping his hands around his mouth, other than his beard and his very clean uniform.

"Heave to! Prepare to be boarded," the man demanded.

"*Qué dice?*" Raul asked. His grasp of English was minimal. His eyes were wide with fear.

"*No es nada. Son amigos,*" Carter noted. Although not absolutely sure the vessel was friendly, he knew at least, they were not Spanish. He stood as best his wobbly legs could manage, waving his arms over his head as the vessel drew alongside the cockleshell. Two towlines flew from the steam ship. Two officers in white uniforms emerged on the Captain's walk surrounding the raised bridge.

"Lash the lines to your bow," one of the officers called down. Carter motioned for Alberto, in front, to comply.

"¡*Señor*!" Raul shouted, pointing out toward the sea opposite the British patrol boat, where a massive rolling wave headed toward them. Carter grabbed hold of the mast as the leading trough sucked the cockleshell's stern down and tipped the bow skyward.

"Hold on!" Carter heard the officer call out to his men as the oncoming wave broke, slamming onto the deck of the little craft. Raul and Alberto cursed. The breaking wave hammered his nose into the mast. Water rushed by his ears. He felt his grip slipping as froths and salt washed over him.

"Men overboard! Life rings to port!" Carter heard just as he pulled his head above the surface. The cockleshell then capsized and dragged him under the water again. He released his grip, and then struggled, flailing away from the sinking craft.

"The rings! Grab the rings!" Commands emanated from the vessel, between garbled calls for help from his Cuban comrades. Carter thrashed about, his shoulders stinging, his thighs burning. He skulled himself around and saw that Raul had already grabbed a ring and clutching to the life-line, was now being pulled on board the rescue ship. Carter spotted one more of the Cubans splashing frantically in the water, and started in his direction, dragging the ring with him.

"Leave him be!" Carter heard an officer from the rescue ship call out as he swam toward his comrade. Once close enough, Carter threw the ring. Alberto clutched onto the ring and the crew began hauling him toward the boat as Carter spotted another ring fly out toward him and splash not more than ten feet away. Carter breast stroked his way to the life preserver, slipped his arms around the orange ring and withered into the stiffness. He could feel he was being pulled. All he had to do was hold on, he thought as he thought he felt something scrape against his leg as water continued to flow over his back.

"Give me your hand!" Carter heard. He opened his eyes and realized he must have blacked out and had been pulled all the way to the rescue boat. He tried to reach up, but his arms felt locked on the ring, unable to move.

"Can't," Carter bowed his head.

"He's good. Get him up now," the officer directed. Carter felt pulling on his arms, and then the rest of him extracted from the water. He tightened his arms to be sure he did not slip off.

Finally, he was onboard. He then exhaled, exhausted, and melted into the deck.

"I suspect you are American?" Carter heard the blunt voice but he could not respond.

"Take him below and warm him up," he then heard and felt his body being hoisted and moved. He could not resist.

"He's moving, Captain." Carter heard the accent of a young British sailor.

"You got a name?" Carter opened his eyes and it was now the Captain of the boat addressing him.

"Yes sir. I am," was all Carter could muster. He looked around the small room and noticed only two others. "Carter. American," he pushed out.

"And these black skins with you — Cuban?"

Carter didn't directly respond. His colleagues remained huddled in the corner of the cell, clearly not sure of the officers intentions. The third guerilla must have drowned.

"So then you were in Cuba?"

Carter nodded.

"Adjust bearing for Hog," The captain directed his first officer, a young lieutenant, who nodded a "yes, sir." and headed back to the main deck. "We'll need some hot antiseptic when we get back," he then muttered and turned away.

"Sir, if you would let me explain," Carter pushed out. His throat seared with pain as he spoke.

"Make it quick," the captain stopped but did not turn around to face Carter. "I can already feel the fever creeping in."

"I am Samuel Carter, an American. I will willingly go to the camp as long as you contact the Consul General and let him know where I am."

"I do not believe you are in a position to negotiate, Mr. Carter."

"Perhaps, sir. But if you do not do as I ask," Carter fought through the scraping in his throat. He held back a cough that lingered in his tight chest. "This could be considered impressing a United States citizen. And right about now I do not think either of our governments would want to get into that fray."

"And why should I believe you?" The captain finally turned back to Carter. "You have no papers to prove that."

"So, why do you think we don't have papers? An American with a couple of Cubans," Carter tossed out.

The officer crossed his arms in front of him and studied Carter.

"Escaped prisoners," the officer's eyes darted between Carter and the other men.

"Political or criminal?"

The officer bit his lip and backed away. He glared at the Cubans, then back to Carter.

"Is that too much to ask?" Carter poked again.

"My standing orders are to get any refugees coming from that hell hole over to Hog and that is exactly what I plan to do. You should have been aware that yellow fever is rampant over there."

The officer said nothing more, turned sharply and headed back up to the pilothouse.

Part Three
November 1897
Washington, DC

Chapter 11

Sam Carter fidgeted as he sat in the foyer of the Department of the Navy building, waiting to be escorted to Navy Secretary Long's office for his debriefing. He felt the chill in the morning air; a welcomed change from waking up day after day over the past month to steamy humidity. The clean, gray suit, which Jack Stiles arranged to have waiting for him in his Washington hotel room, was a bit stiff for his liking. Especially the tie and raised white collared shirt. They chaffed at his sunburned neck and shoulders. However, it looked to be a rather fine fit on him, and the suit was certainly more presentable that what he had been wearing.

He was, in contrast, quite comfortable with the information he would be providing, the real purpose he was in Washington. He was concerned that the maps and notes he compiled in Cuba, still not adequately dried after his watery rescue, had become unreadable, but he understood enough that he could redraw the details on a new map if necessary.

Two Navy officers marched by, inspecting Carter with stone faces as they passed. Their voices volleyed between hushed tones and whispers, leaving Carter to wonder what secrets exchanged their lips. He also wondered what had evolved here and in Havana that warranted such a large convoy on the open seas; a convoy that just a month ago seemed a very remote possibility. Stiles revealed some things on the voyage back from his quarantine on Hog Island, but there seemed to be much transpiring.

"Mr. Carter?" A young voice snapped him out of his thoughts. A sharply dressed Marine stood near the end of the long hallway. "Secretary Roosevelt will speak with you now."

"Roosevelt?" Carter balked as he rose. "I understood that I was to see Secretary Long?"

The soldier responded only with a crisp hand signal for Carter to follow him before he turned and marched away. Half way down the hallway, the soldier abruptly turned again down another passageway. Carter followed, his turns more relaxed than the soldier's were as they continued to the end of the corridor. The soldier stopped at a closed office door, rapped on it twice, then stood patiently at attention.

"Enter!" a gruff voice emanated from behind the door. Carter heard the distinct clacking of hobnailed boots. The soldier opened the door and politely insisted that Carter enter.

"Sam Carter! Glad to see you! Thought you were a goner, son," Theodore Roosevelt greeted, exuberantly extending his hand as he approached. A wide, toothy grin that looked more like a grimace creased his face. His pince-nez was a bit dusty and smudged at the corners, but clean enough that sunlight still glimmered off the ground glass. The pictures Carter had seen of the notoriously cantankerous man did his robustness no justice.

"Welcome home. I understand you had quite an adventure." Roosevelt said as he briskly shook Carter's hand. The Secretary's eyes worked over every thread of his suit.

"That I have, Mr. Secretary," Carter took out the maps from his pocket and surrendered the flimsy, damp papers. Roosevelt released his grip and gingerly peeled at the corners of the wet maps. "Pardon me, sir, but I thought I was to meet with Secretary Long? Carter added."

"Long asked me to take this meeting. We've got full agendas up here that keep all of us hopping like frogs in a rainstorm," Roosevelt absently grumbled as he turned and headed toward his desk. Carter sensed insincerity on the Secretary's demeanor. "Please, have a seat," Roosevelt added, still fumbling at the mess in his hands.

Carter obliged, stiffly walking into the office. Sitting at

the long, oak conference table in the center of the room was a rather thin, well-dressed dark-haired man. Carter thought about introducing himself, but shied away when the man's steely-eyed scowl and arrogantly tipped head skewered him. The standoff was icily mutual as Carter cautiously took a seat opposite him.

Roosevelt plopped the maps with a splat on the one tiny open spot on his desk, hovered at his high-backed chair, and looked over his neatly stacked notes. After wiping his hands clean of the paper pills from the map, he stretched over the mounds of paper and extracted a fat cigar from his glass humidor. He scratched a match across his desk and lit the cigar with the stick's sparkling life before blowing a stream of smoke toward the lingering smoky cloud already hovering at the ceiling before parking himself in his chair with an audible humph.

"Wilkie," the man at the table bluntly announced without as much as an offered handshake.

"Sam Carter," Carter responded with a polite nod, not knowing what else to say. He had never personally met the man who was now his boss. Jack Stiles had warned him of some of Wilkie's quirks — a rather cold man, calculating with a surly demeanor, and clearly someone not to cross for concern of his reputation for vicious retribution — but had not pictured him as the poker faced, relatively small man who was now apparently studying him.

"So tell me, Mr. Carter, how long can they hold on before we muster up some troops?" Roosevelt cut the thickness in the air asked as he absently picked at the moist papers, carefully laying each fold flat on his desk as he peeled it free from the mat.

"Troops? Sir, I was under the impression that there were already enough Cuban volunteers in Florida," Carter questioned. He noticed that Wilkie raised his eyebrows at him.

"Two, three months?" Roosevelt grunted as he moved his finger over the papers he had laid out piecemeal. "Are these blotches here Spanish or belligerent locations?"

"Insurgents, sir. The X's are Spanish strongholds."

"X's? My word man, those are X's?" Roosevelt chuckled. Wilkie remained cold and silent.

"General Garcia stated that he needs medicine, arms, and supplies. Yellow fever has taken a toll on both sides, sir."

"Looks like Santiago and the eastern side of the island should be doable," Roosevelt absently mumbled, still studying the map. "We can get there from either approach.

"The General was very clear about his concern against interference, in fact, he was insistent . . ."

"You need to stop thinking about policy, Carter," Wilkie's words were abrupt and gruff. "Your responsibility was to collect information. You did your job. Others, such as Secretary Roosevelt here, are responsible for making decisions based on that information."

Carter recoiled, not clear as to how to read Wilkie's brusqueness. The twelve warships that he had seen in the Caribbean headed west and the troops massed in Tampa were obvious signs to him that something was already in the works.

"If I may be so blunt, sir, has a decision to send troops already been made then?" Carter fished, looking directly at Roosevelt. From the corner of his eye he could see Wilkie's face sour. Roosevelt squirmed in his seat before glancing up and drawing deeply through his cigar. The room remained deafeningly quiet as the Navy Secretary exhaled and sent more smoke to the ceiling. He cleared his throat as he leaned forward. Wilkie remained stiff scowled prudishly.

"Mr. Carter, I do not believe the President has not made any decisions yet. Decisions imply actions, and we, as interested parties in the progress toward an independent Cuba, have done nothing overt at this time."

"It was our fleet that I saw headed . . ."

"To the Keys. Simple maneuvers." Roosevelt interrupted. "Intended as a nudge."

"You might still be driftwood if they didn't find you, Carter," Wilkie interjected.

"Spain is deeply invested down there, Carter," Roosevelt continued. "Do you really believe they will leave just because we asked them?"

Carter remained silent, measuring Roosevelt directly and Wilkie through the corner of his eye.

"I didn't think so," Roosevelt responded, clacking his teeth. He stood and slowly marched to the window and peered in the direction of a reflecting pool in front of the recently completed obelisk in honor of the first president. "And I am sure you are aware that the Kaiser has decided to start acting a bit impetuous down there, to say the least. I'd say the Haitians are pushing him to his limit."

The parts of this strange puzzle were starting to come together as Carter listened carefully to Roosevelt's soliloquy. His encounter with Moser was now clearly more than a mere coincidence.

"I am sure you recognize that across the years, liberty was never attained through diplomacy alone. As well, there has been no successful revolution without some outside help," Roosevelt pontificated. "You do remember that the press is saber rattling — saying that we have waited too long to teach Spain a lesson."

"Yes, sir." Carter noticed that Wilkie was consumed in his own thoughts.

"Medicine for yellow fever, arms and ammunition for an insurgent army of a couple thousand, canned food stuffs for same. Tents, boots, cotton clothing —" Roosevelt recited, as if he had been next to him while Garcia rattled off what he needed. The Secretary turned around from the window and grinned as he strutted back to his desk. "You know as well as I do these things are not a problem for us, but it doesn't guarantee he will win. Our boots on the ground can, and we need to kick the Spanish asses all the way back to Europe!"

The room fell silent as Roosevelt dropped into his chair, clacked his teeth, and swiveled his gaze between Carter and Wilkie.

"Now, I would say we would need some reparation for our assistance," Roosevelt started in a more subdued tone. "After all, there is a cost for all of these. What do you think he is willing to give up in exchange for arms?"

"I cannot speak for the General, sir," Carter grew

uncomfortable. "Nor is he guaranteed to be . . ."

"Nothing big. Perhaps just a port city," Roosevelt continued, stroking his chin. He leaned forward again, this time close enough that Carter grew even more uneasy. "A small one. Guantanamo, perhaps. And a buffer zone around the port. Do you think he would go for that?"

"Again, I can not say for sure."

"He does realize that the Kaiser is saber rattling next door?" Roosevelt's tone tempered to a furtive hush as he tapped the opened map on his desk.

"I did provide him that information."

"He's already taken a chunk of China, you know, and I've heard from some very reliable sources that he's posturing for something down there, perhaps even Cuba for himself. Now, Mr. Carter, does Garcia know enough of the Kaiser to think he'll stop at just one little island?"

"There certainly isn't enough on that God-forsaken island to satisfy anyone's needs." Wilkie quipped.

Carter leaned back in his chair, exasperated. He wondered if McKinley was even aware of what was progressing, potentially outside of his own influence.

"You're an intelligent man, Mr. Carter," Roosevelt leaned forward again and squinted. As he smiled, his teeth clicked twice. "Put two and two together. If that happens, Garcia will have more to deal with than some penny-ante Spanish dictator. If we act now, quick in, quick out, things will run much smoother, and Wilhelm can go play with his toys in Asia." The Secretary sunk back in his chair and blew smoke rings spiraling upward.

"I believe you and Wainwright have the information which you had asked for," Carter respectfully, yet curtly responded. He glanced across to Wilkie, who was motioning that they needed to meet outside.

"Yes, I believe I have most of it. If I have any further questions, I believe I can address them through Director Wilkie."

"Yes, Mr. Secretary," Wilkie confirmed. Carter stood as Wilkie responded, which drew a frosty glare.

"By the way, Carter," Roosevelt said as he stood to wish Carter good-bye. Shaking Carter's hand, he added, "You may wish to consider a career in politics once this war is over. You look mighty dapper in that suit."

"Thank you, sir," Carter said coldly. It was all he could think of saying. He sent a wary glance Wilkie's way as he exited and then walked with measured steps down the corridor. Confusion surrounded the disconcerting revelations he had just absorbed. He was clear several plots were in motion, perhaps concerted. He wondered if Garcia, his friend, realized the hope he desired, a self-supporting insurgency evolving into independence, was lost. Carter turned the corner and started down the long corridor.

"Carter," Wilkie called out as he emerged from Roosevelt's office. Carter stopped, turned around and waited.

"Yes, sir," Carter replied as Wilkie drew closer.

"You were discourteous to Mr. Roosevelt in there. I need you to understand that is behavior of which I have a very low tolerance," Wilkie hooded his eyes.

"I believe I was simply asking questions, sir."

"As long as you report to me, you will be more respectful of authority. Do I make myself clear?" Wilkie folded his arms on his chest.

"Yes, sir," Carter growled.

"I am glad we understand each other." Wilkie fished into his jacket pocket and handed an envelope to Carter. "I would like you to investigate something before you head back to Cuba."

"Yes, sir." Carter politely acknowledged, though he would have preferred to refuse.

"I have arranged for you to meet someone in Charleston."

"And what information should I extract from him?"

"I need you to verify the information . . ."

"An informant?" Carter grew curious.

". . . And if he knows anything else that may help us stay one step ahead of the Germans."

"A German defector?"

"His message was cryptic. He did also ask for you

specifically. It sounds to me like he's got some useful information. Use the phrases here to verify he is who he says he is, and then find out what he knows."

Carter fondled the envelope. He thought about opening the letter at that point, but decided against it, thinking it would be better to wait until he was alone. "Is there anything else, sir?" he then asked hesitantly, slipping the envelope into his jacket pocket.

"Yes there is, Carter. Welcome home," Wilkie said as he hand pressed his jacket and forced a rather weak, insincere smile. "But don't get too comfortable. I need you back in Cuba as soon as practicable."

With that, Wilkie put his stiff black derby on his head and walked away. Carter stood still, feeling a myriad of conflicting thoughts. His stomach roiled as if he was at sea again, reliving the nausea. His head spun as thoughts whizzed by. With the envelope in his hand, he grew concerned that events in Havana may have already spiraled out of control and he, along with everyone else here, was about to be sucked into them.

Commander Chester O'Neill relaxed in his office aboard the docked *USS Marblehead*, taking afternoon tea with his officers. He would have preferred to be at sea, but after several long, cross-Atlantic assignments, his ship had been driven to her limits and was in dire need of maintenance. He and his vessel had already been in the Annapolis Navy yard for two weeks and most of the refit equipment his light, unarmored cruiser needed was completed with the exception of the one repair she desperately needed; replacement boiler tubes. Without that repair, the *Marblehead* would be sentenced to half her normal engine power. He had lobbied for a full boiler refit, but the combination of inadequate materials and lack of labor here, resultant from a Roosevelt order for all out focus on building heavy new armored cruisers and battleships, left O'Neill and the *Marblehead* wanting.

At least the weather is decent, O'Neill thought as he listened to the progress reports from his shipboard staff. Brass plugs for the leaking boiler tubes were in progress, as was a regulation coat of paint above the waterline. The guns had been greased, gearing worked through, ammunition stored and secured. Coalbunkers had been cleared, cleaned, and half refilled.

"Half-capacity?" he asked the Engine room Chief, hoping he heard incorrectly.

"That's all the bastards rationed us, sir," the Chief replied. O'Neill made a mental note to ensure the quartermaster lined up a refuel stop in Charleston. They would not be refused coal once they were on patrol, he reckoned.

"Continue," O'Neill encouraged, but just as the quartermaster started his report, an impatient clack started on the mechanical phone that sat precariously on the edge of his small desk.

"O'Neill!" he answered. The officers around the small table went silent and focused their attention on him. As he listened to the message, his eyebrows arched enough to toggle his stiff brimmed cap. "Send it up," he then growled, hung up the phone and turned back to his officers with a stern expression.

"Sir?" Lieutenant Henry Boyd, his executive officer prodded.

"Gentlemen, how soon can we make steam?" was O'Neill's reply. The mood in the cabin suddenly improved. Boyd took out his small notepad and ran a finger down his list. The others followed suit as O'Neill stood and met the messenger himself at his portal. He took the message, snapped off a quick salute and dismissed the young sailor.

"An hour sir, but without new tubes, we'll only be able to make ten knots, fifteen if the plugs hold," Boyd finally responded, regaining his Captain's attention.

"It'll have to do," O'Neill snapped a finger against the yellow paper message. "Screw the paint job. We have orders to steam to Haiti as soon as we can. Looks like the Kaiser decided to create some chaos down there and the Haitians are asking for our help."

A reserved silence was the only response the commander received. O'Neill knew that during their last patrol along the

European coast most of his officers had been duly impressed by the size and strength of the German warships. Each of those vessels were heavily armed and armored, and clearly an overmatch for their vessel. The *Marblehead's* advantage of being small and nimble had been vaporized with the boiler problems. The Captain knew if they were going up against one of those vessels, he and his officers would need to personally belly-up some strong leadership to muster his crew's courage in the face of what was sure to be insurmountable odds.

"We've got our orders, men. Let's tidy up this old girl and get her out to sea," O'Neill ordered. With that, the crew of the *Marblehead* snapped to attention, saluted their Captain, and filed out of his quarters to ready their vessel. As he had been promised, in just less than an hour, O'Neill watched the *Marblehead*'s stacks spew brownish-black smoke into the cloudless sky over Annapolis. He rang up one-third power on the Engine Room ringer, took the wheel and announced for all to hear that she was ready for departure to points south.

The grandeur of Charleston, which Carter remembered from before the 1888 earthquake, was being methodically rebuilt stone by stone. Twenty years had been spent puzzle-piecing together the destruction laid onto it by the North's bombardments and Sherman's rage, but only hours to rattle the buildings back into rubble. Even so, with what seemed a recurring, ravaging turmoil through the nineteenth century, it seemed remarkable to Carter that Charleston was flourishing again, now at the cusp of the new century.

Carter meandered along Market Street at dusk, a stroll that was familiar to him from his Citadel days. Scarlet-lipped buds, peeking out in the camellia hedges filled the street-side gardens. Stately palmettos swayed above them, their fronds swishing in the light evening breeze slipping out to sea. Browned oak leaves, still clinging to thick, stately branches, rustled in the salt-tainted air. A cooler morning would be coming, but for now, the warmth and fragrance was fresh and clean.

He had grown to like Charleston, enough that it was here

he wished to eventually settle. His first memory of Charleston was when his stepfather orchestrated his appointment in the first class to attend the Citadel, reopened almost twenty years after the Civil War had closed it down. During his time at the military school, he spent hours, sometimes days strolling along the Battery and visiting the various battle sites spotted throughout the area. He graduated near the top of his class, and dutifully served his conscripted two years teaching in the local free schools before moving back to Mobile.

The earthquake though, brought him back. He felt it his duty to help at least start the rebuilding this wondrous city. He started with work crews along the Battery then moved inland along Market Street. Carpetbaggers converged on Charleston, weaseling and conniving their way through bank accounts of every shop owner, leaving them with only empty promises of assistance. He joined the government service at that point to help end that thievery. Carter's work now, even as he enjoyed it for the most part, maintained a more vagabond nature to it, and it was the most apparent conspirator to thwarting the hints of desire to make a home in Charleston. He reached the intersection of Meeting and Market Streets, where the white spires St. Michael's Church marked the turn toward Sullivan's Tavern where he was to meet the defector as Wilkie had called him.

The tavern was as he had remembered — dimly lit on the inside, yet vibrant and well attended. Once he worked his way through the patrons moving in and out, he stepped and noticed two young ladies at the same time they noticed him. Their ample breasts bulged from their low cut blouses, as if beckoning him for earthly pleasure. Their hair, coquettishly strewn about their face, and their inviting smiles, left no doubt in Carter's mind that their intentions were. It had been a long time, Carter thought as he eyed the trollops, but despite an urge to delve into their proposed pleasure, he realized that now was not the time for such a wonton diversion.

"Maybe later," Carter mumbled to himself as he passed the girls, slipping an undisciplined leer their way, and headed to the opposite side of the bar. He pulled up a tall stool and ordered a lager.

"Two, sir," a raspy, vaguely familiar voice said from behind Carter.

"Moser?" Carter mouthed the name. He glanced around and saw Moser angling toward him.

"Holland has fine tulips, don't you think," Moser said as he settled in next to Carter.

"I do prefer roses, though," Carter replied. The bartender served up lagers to both of the men, then shuffled back to the girls, his only other customers at the bar.

"Your father enjoyed lager, Samuel. Did you know that?" Moser said as he took a drink. A wry grin cracked his face. "Perhaps you are more like him than you wish to admit."

"You never did fully answer how it is that you know my father?"

Moser appeared to mull over the comment, swirling his beer while he glanced up to the pall of expelled, stale cigar smoke that hovered at the ceiling. Carter recognized that Moser's years had been hard on him. His face was thin and drawn under his scraggly mustache. His posture was poor enough that he needed to support his hunched shoulders with his elbows on the edge of the bar.

"Gunter Rohlenheim was his true name. Whether you know it or not, he was an operative for Bismarck. In fact, both of us worked for him. I would presume you had learned about Bismarck in your studies, yes?"

Carter agreed with a nod, personally accepting that he had nothing to hide at this point.

"Your father was a good man, Samuel. Not all spies are evil, you know," Moser cocked his head and squinted in Carter's direction, hiding the vacancy in his eyes. "You don't mind me calling him your father do you?"

"No, sir," Carter replied pensively. Very few people talked to him about his father despite his desire to know more. Moser was the first person that willingly offered details of the man who was at the center of his personal quest. The short time he had with Moser as they headed to Jamaica whetted his appetite for what he so wanted to know.

"We talked about many things. I learned many things from him," Moser stopped to take a mouthful of beer. Carter noticed a tear well in the corner of his eye. "Your father enjoyed music as I did. Real music. The delicate, intricate melodies of Brahms and Chopin, not the raucous cacophony of Bruckner. He said that music helped him think clearly while he worked on his personal engineering projects."

Carter listened carefully as the old German mused.

"And he was a very skilled engineer. I do not believe he understood that he had ideas years ahead of his time. *Ach*, but he was modest enough not to be pompous and proud. Did you know he was involved with developing a German submarine years before he came here?"

"Why did he come here?" Carter asked.

"He was sent here to investigate your . . . oh, the name escapes me. Ships made of iron instead of wood."

"Ironclads," Carter offered, mesmerized by Moser's words. He sipped at his beer, trying to picture his father from the faded image from the single photograph his mother owned.

"*Ya, ya*, ironclads. You know America was years ahead with those vessels? Indestructible. Something Bismarck wanted so dearly back then."

Carter still struggled to accept the fact that his father was a spy, and only by happenstance had become involved with his mother. Nevertheless, it did resolve a number of questions that had nagged Carter as long as he could remember.

"Do not get me wrong, Samuel. You don't mind me calling you Samuel?"

"No, that is fine," Carter noted as he mulled a swallow of beer.

"Your father was a good man — an intelligent man. I for one am very saddened now knowing of his death so many years ago."

"But I do not suppose he is the reason you are here now?" Carter noted as Moser looked up. His eyes were glassed over, and tears had spilled onto the stubble on his cheeks. Over Moser's shoulder he noticed that a trio of well-dressed men had entered the tavern and had gravitated toward the women at the other end of the bar.

Moser eyed the action at the end of the bar through a sideward glance, and then turned back to Carter. "Perhaps we should go down to . . . the place along the shore."

"The Battery?"

"*Ya, ya*, the battery. It is quiet there, no? I would prefer only you hear what I have to offer." Moser took another mouthful of his beer.

Carter nodded agreement. He glanced down for a moment to reach into his pocket for a couple of coins to pay for the drinks, but clinks on the wooden bar told him he was too slow. Moser had already dropped two coins onto the bar, stood and had started toward the door. Carter followed, slowing down as he passed the women to get a better view of their wares. His glance though, was met by the suits' possessive glares, and he moved on.

Once outside, Carter needed little effort to catch up to Moser, thirty years his elder. The pair of men looked more like father and son than counterparts as they walked over the brick and cobblestone sidewalk, especially since they remained silent, plodding toward the Battery. The series of gaslights that lined the walkway had already sparked to life and although they cut the edge of darkness, still only provided minimal light. The walk was short, and the pair settled onto one of the benches overlooking Charleston Bay, where the surf rolled rather than frothed as it crept in toward the seawall.

"Do you know how my father died?" Carter started as he leaned back on the wooden back slats on the concrete bench. A flock of pelicans drifted in from the bay and perched on the pylons near the seawall.

"No. If you recall, I did not know he had died until you told me," Moser admitted. "But I did suspect something unfortunate had happened to him when I had lost contact with him. The nature of our business is what I assumed."

"So you do know what he was doing here?" Carter fished.

"Yes, he was investigating the weapon development which your Confederacy, I believe it was called, was involved in."

"Like the Hunley?" Carter asked.

Moser fell silent as a couple, arms wrapped around each other, strolled close by. Carter watched his dull, sunken eyes follow the pair until they passed.

"Hunley?"

"Yes, that was the name of the submarine," Carter responded.

"That name sounds familiar, but I do not recall from where," Moser stroked his wiry beard, then shrugged his shoulders. "It seems during the testing of this underwater machine, one of your generals became a bit annoyed at the pace that the engineers were taking. Has your step-father talked about James McClintock?"

"Briefly. I vaguely recall the name," Carter lied. Alexander had spoken about an engineering partner many times, including a confrontation with General Beauregard, but never revealed the name.

"Well it appears he left for England soon thereafter with his own copy of the plans for this underwater machine."

"And you were able to obtain them?"

"I did sit with him for a bit before he was killed in an unfortunate accident. They were crude. He had scribbled some notes on the plans for items he wanted to change, but they were unreadable. I was sure there were also some additional improvements made while it was being built that did not appear on those diagrams. When I probed he revealed that he had heard the vessel was lost."

Carter watched the rolling waves wash upon the shoreline. Thirty years ago his father, his real father, went out there. As far as he knew, his remains were still out there, somewhere.

"These things are not important, Samuel. What is important is that the concept, the idea of a submersible war ship, one which cannot be seen, is being shared between the Kaiser and Spain."

"Are they building one?" Carter asked. He knew the Navy had commissioned the Holland project in New York, but was far enough removed at this point that he did not know how far along the work had progressed.

"I know that Wilhelm has charged some trusted Navy officers to design such a weapon," Moser noted, then added, "Perhaps even steal your Holland project?"

Carter considered the information. More appropriately, he considered the source. It seemed improbable, but so many technological advancements, once thought improbable, were now occurring, it seemed, on a daily basis. Carriages with engines, some steam powered, some fueled by gasoline, were being produced with the promise that one day they would replace horse drawn ones. Steel had already replaced wood on seagoing vessels, and the time to travel from one shore to another had been reduced as a result of turbine driven propellers rather than the old piston driven engines.

"I have seen a drawing of this vessel, and I believe Spain is building one in their port, Rhoda. This vessel looks quite like this Plunger your Navy has built." Moser broke the silence.

"Seems a bit farfetched." Carter said, but knew otherwise. He was aware that several countries, including Germany were keenly aware of the Holland project, and were looking to build one of their own.

"Perhaps. But I know that the Spaniards realize they are no match in conventional arms. And when a nation is desperate and seemingly headed into a war, farfetched ideas tend to be the ones that are usually developed."

"Why should I believe you?"

"I am no longer needed in Germany. I find myself in the autumn of my life, Samuel. I have grown weary of this youthful game your father and I embarked upon so many years ago, and you engage in presently. When Bismarck was our leader, we were the envy of the world. Oh, not just the mighty ones, but the merciful ones as well. We were the engineers and the artists that everyone would look up to, respectfully. But now, the Kaiser is unraveling all of what we had accomplished for his personal gain. He takes everything, keeps what he wants, and discards what no longer suits him."

Moser stopped his soliloquy as his eyes grew teary. He stared out onto the water, now growing choppy as the land drew in the cooler blanket that lay over the ripples. The old

German sniffled for a moment, drew out a handkerchief and rubbed it over his nose. He sighed heavily, glanced up to the darkening sky and exhaled noisily.

"I find myself discarded, Samuel. I am of no use to Wilhelm," Moser continued as Carter listened intently. "And Germany is too cold for old men, Samuel. It can be very cold there, you know. I was sent to Haiti to die, Samuel. Charleston is a much better place for this old man to spend his final years."

Carter pieced the story together. He is deserting his old country because he felt he was no longer needed. At a loss for words, Carter simply listened to Moser's rattling breaths.

"I caution you Samuel. You must be very careful with this information. I am but an old man, but the Kaiser has others, younger men in your country."

"Where?" Carter prodded.

"I do not know where he is, but the Kaiser's most dangerous is a man by the name of Ziegler."

"Do you know where Ziegler is?" Carter took note. He would need to pass on the name.

"No, no. He is very mobile. The last I knew he was in Baltimore." Moser said as he fished out his pocket watch. He nervously flipped it open, and added, "It is getting a bit late, isn't it?"

"That it is," Carter agreed as Moser stood and tipped his hat.

"Your father was a good man, Samuel," Moser added as he took hold of Carter's shoulders and pressed as hard as his weary arms allowed. He then smiled, turned and hobbled his way back toward town. "And I now know he had a good son."

Carter remained alone at the Battery, sitting on the bench in the moonlit night. As he looked out over the water, his view occasionally interrupted by couples tied together by held hands or wrapped arms, he wondered where beneath the shimmering water lay the remains of his father and the crew of the submarine that they sailed into history. He dwelled on that thought for a bit longer, then returned to the tavern for another drink before retiring for the night.

Chapter 12

Carl DeLauro adjusted the sack of coal dust he carried on his shoulder, following the man he knew as Herman Kern through Philadelphia's back alleys. The quiet night was cold enough that the few people who ventured along the city streets would not have considered them odd, lugging a sack of something that most probably had been scavenged to be used for heat. They turned onto Walnut Street for a few blocks, then finally into a narrow cobblestoned alley that split two and three story brick edifices. Rickety metal fire escapes, zigzagged stairs and straight ladders, cascaded down from each of the buildings, narrowing the alley so much only a single file could pass. Kern stopped at the foot of one the rusted metal waterfalls and inspected the four-story building. The scraggly-bearded enigma then swiveled his head as if to ensure no one watched them before deftly spidering his way up the metal stairs, stopping only briefly at each landing before scampering up to the next floor. From the top landing, he waved for DeLauro to follow.

Bethlehem Steel Company, DeLauro recalled the massive copper letters on the nameplate on the front of the building. This was the conglomerate that owned the coalmines that had enslaved him for hours on end. *'This would be adequate vindication,'* he thought as he started up the flimsy stairs, struggling under the coal dust and uncrushed chips shifting on his shoulder with each of his steps.

"Hurry!" Kern encouraged from the top landing.

DeLauro's thighs burned and cold air stung at his lungs as sucked in replenishment. He maintained a methodical plodding climb.

"In there," Kern called down as he pointed into the small open window at the fourth landing. As DeLauro reached the top, he bent over and breathed deeply, trying in vain to slow his dizzying panting. "The boiler's running," Kern added.

"We drop sack there and wait?" DeLauro pushed out the words as reached the landing and slid the sack down onto the metal grate landing. He peered inside then asked, "How long?"

"It all depends on how close the sack hits, how quickly the dust fills the room and how much gets sucked in," Kern said, his eyes darting about the room as if surveying until he stopped and pointed. "There. You see that boiler over there?"

DeLauro peered deeper into the room. "I see."

"Throw it as close to this side of the boiler that you can," Kern indicated, then grabbed the long, thin ripcord attached to the top of coal sack. "I'll pull this when it's in there, and we're done. Then all we need to do is get the hell away from the building and wait."

"How long?"

"Could be minutes, could be hours. It all depends on how much that boiler is cycling."

"Cycling?" DeLauro asked quietly, beginning to worry that Kern would think him stupid for asking so many questions.

"Cycling. You know, starting up and shutting down — like a machine turning on and off," Kern said.

DeLauro studied Kern's face, which looked rather ghoulish in the milky moonlight, looking for reaction to his question but there was none. DeLauro decided he should ask his other questions later.

"When the dust is drawn into the box — boom — it will go," Kern finished his explanation, pantomiming the debacle with his hands.

"Tonight, it is cold. It should be quick, yes?" DeLauro asked as he moved closer to the open window. Kern assisted as he groaned while lifting the bag up over his head.

"Got it," Kern confirmed. He wrapped his hands with

strips of cloth then grabbed the thin rope. With a huge grunt, DeLauro heaved the sack through the open window across the room. It landed close to where Kern had pointed earlier, a foot away from the base of the boiler.

"*Ach, gut!*" Kern pulled the string back hand over hand until it was taught, then yanked twice. He stumbled briefly as it released as DeLauro watched the powdered coal began to pour out of the bag and started a swirling gray-black dust cloud. Kern regained his footing and peered inside as well.

"*Macht schnell!*" Kern said as he dropped the string. DeLauro was stunned by the German words, having not heard them since he left the mines. Kern grabbed the straight metal ladder, deftly vaulted over the railing and began sliding down toward the cobblestones. In seconds, he reached the ground, looked up and again yelled, "Move! Go quickly!"

DeLauro complied, scrambling down the wobbly steps, two at a time, sometimes three, and in less than a minute, he also reached the brick and cobble-stoned street before chasing Kern out from the alley. They turned the corner onto Walnut Street just as the building erupted behind them. Stopping briefly, DeLauro turned and watched bricks crumble, tumbling into piles on top of the metal fire escapes that screeched as they twisted toward the ground under the weight. Black smoke poured into the sky, chased by a fireball of orange-red flame. Fire alarms clanged, but were quickly drowned out by additional explosions.

He looked at Kern and grinned. It unfolded exactly as the man said it would. DeLauro finally felt he had made a statement — he had exacted his revenge.

Commander Chester O'Neill paced in his quarters, agitated with his ship's lumbering pace. Clearing the Chesapeake's Cape Charles had taken so long that his crew rotated two shifts before the *Marblehead* was finally free to navigate in the open waters off the Carolina coast. He now lamented that he did not insist that the boiler tubes at least be sleeved before heading out rather than live with the inefficiency, but it was too late to recant.

Rapping on his metal door drew his attention. Through the small round portal window he saw Lieutenant Boyd and waved him in.

"We'd be better off with sails, sir," Boyd said as he stepped into the cabin. His sullenness was a shared expression. "She's as slow as molasses in January. Hell, it'll be Christmas afore we get to Haiti," he groused, melting into the small-armed steel chair against the bulkhead.

"We can't get down on the old girl, Boyd, especially in front of the enlisted. You know that's conceding defeat even before we face the Kaiser's boats."

"You think we will?" Boyd poured up a cup of tea for himself.

"Excuse me sir," a signalman interrupted. O'Neill feigned a bright expression when he looked up. "Captain Sigsbee sends his regards and looks forward to seeing you."

"Dismissed, sailor," O'Neill added a salute to his order. Once the messenger spun around and his footfalls dissipated along the metal-decked passageway, the Captain glanced back to Boyd and asked, "How soon before we meet up with the *Maine*?"

"At this rate, could be . . ." the sailor started, but stopped when O'Neill's scowl iced him. "Half-hour sir"

"Tell the engine room to push it." O'Neill ordered.

"I'll try to squeeze out another knot or two, sir," Boyd popped up from his seat and saluted rather sloppily.

"Remember what I said, Boyd. Tighten up," O'Neill stood and snapped off a crisp salute to his executive officer. "You know Sigsbee's boys will be ragging on them."

Boyd nodded and exited, leaving O'Neill alone in his quarters with only the rumble of his ship's engines and his now cold Earl Gray tea to keep him company. He respected Sigsbee as a sailor's captain. He felt it was a travesty of naval justice that after Sigsbee's huge navigational accomplishment, when he completed a detailed hydrographic tour of the western Gulf of Mexico, a mission that discovered a canyon over three miles deep off the coast of Mexico, he was assigned to teach at the Naval Academy. Sigs took it better than he would have,

O'Neill thought, but that was the unflappable Sigs. The old bird had always been astute enough to work the politics, as raw as they could be to his favor.

The last time that he saw Sigs was when he had finally worked his way back to a captaincy. The sight of his old friend's beaming face on the deck of the spankin' new *Maine* as she departed was something O'Neill found pleasing, even though he had secretly hoped that Sigsbee would've requested him to join his handpicked crew. He would not have minded being reduced to an executive officer to be with his old friend, but the Navy had other ideas. Captains were still a rare breed, and O'Neill understood it was his duty to remain with the *Marblehead* for at least another year.

"We've got the *Maine* in sight, sir," Lieutenant Boyd poked his head into O'Neill's cabin.

"Be there shortly, Boyd," O'Neill squeezed his eyes closed as he stood up from behind his small wooden table. *Guess I drifted off*, he thought as he slurped down the rest of his tea and quickly hand pressed his tunic. He clanked up the grated metal stairs to topside, and as he emerged, saw the *Maine* had already started a turn to port. O'Neill watched carefully as Boyd directed his crew to bring the *Marblehead* starboard, and then carefully maneuver a broadside approach up to the *Maine*.

The Captains made eye contact, although Sigsbee's focus was clearly on his vessel's oddly situated turret, a spot where the smaller *Marblehead* could ride up and cause havoc for them both. Boyd's commands were meticulously followed, dispelling concerns and making the rendezvous flawless.

"Permission to come aboard?" O'Neill chuckled as he called through the megaphone.

"Permission granted," Sigsbee called back then saluted.

"She's a beauty, Sigs," O'Neill commented as he carefully boarded the *Maine* over a quickly positioned gangplank. Sigsbee simply smiled and urged O'Neill to head to the stern. "Glad to see you back out here where you belong," O'Neill added.

"Nice to be back out here, Chet," Sigsbee said as his tall,

lanky executive officer approached. "Have you met Commander Wainwright? My XO?"

"Captain." Wainwright smartly saluted. "My compliments to your pilot."

"Boyd's a good sailor," O'Neill replied stiffly as he eyed Wainwright. "You boys find anything?"

"Just some recon about two vessels on the way. Cadet ships, they say. There's some other movement out of Kiel, but nothing else headed our way at this time." Wainwright provided.

"Nothing to worry about, Chet," Sigsbee winked and twitched one corner of his mouth into a grin. "You can handle them," he added, under his breath.

"My boys will be relieved, for sure." O'Neill said as he regarded Wainwright. It baffled him why the Chief of Naval Intelligence was aboard a cruiser headed for the Caribbean, which is where he understood the *Maine* was headed. O'Neill recognized he had only one small piece of the overall game plan.

"Stay for tea, Chet?" Sigsbee offered as Wainwright excused himself and headed back to the bridge.

"Don't think I can Sigs."

"Are you sure? I remember the old *Marblehead* as a pretty quick vessel. You should be able to beat the Germans into Haiti from here."

"At one time maybe, but not right now. She's a little slow — lost some boiler tubes coming out of Europe. Knowing you were in the area though, I had to at least divert to say hello."

"Well, it is always good to see you, Chet. Hold on for a few and I can have my navigator rustle up what we've seen so far." Sigsbee noted as the pair walked casually back to the boarding plank.

"Thanks. That will help. Once around your girl then while I wait?" O'Neill asked.

Sigsbee happily complied and the two officers took one lap around the upper deck, the *Maine*'s Captain pointing out to his old friend the features of his new charge. The intelligence Sigsbee promised was waiting for O'Neill when he returned to the gangplank, and he then headed back to his own vessel. As soon as the *Marblehead*'s Captain stepped onto his home deck, the boarding rail was retracted and smoke poured out from her stacks. Engines willingly engaged, she pulled away from her brightly painted big sister, blew her horn, and resumed her track south.

John Wilkie turned up the collar of his long coat, and then slipped his hands under the pocket flaps as he headed to the Navy offices. The bitterness in the air reminded him of Chicago rather than Washington, a place where he had grown accustomed to warmer weather. Fortunately, the walk from his office to Roosevelt's was short enough that he could quell his shivering before it was time for their meeting. He checked his watch again as he walked toward the Navy Department to ensure he would be exactly five minutes early. Being punctual was something he thought important, and the extra five minutes would be useful to organize the rather discontinuous notes that Carter had relayed from his meeting with Rudolf Moser. He carefully climbed the icy granite steps, entered the building, and then headed directly to the reception desk.

"John Wilkie," he quickly flashed his credentials to the marine stationed at the desk.

"Third office on the left," the marine said as he pointed down the hallway. Wilkie thought fleetingly about thanking the marine, but he was just doing his job. Instead, he started down the hallway toward Roosevelt's office when he heard the distinct sound of hobnailed boots stomping at a determined pace down the hallway.

"John, follow me," Roosevelt ordered and marched by before Wilkie could turn around. Perturbed, Wilkie hastened his pace down the corridor and stepped into the open office door, where the Secretary had already situated himself at his large oak desk where he meticulously shuffled through the piles of papers in front of him.

Wilkie noticed the stout, sour-faced Commander Richardson Clover seated at the conference table in front of Roosevelt's desk. His uniform was crisp and well decorated with two lines of ribbons. The Navy Secretary had just appointed Clover to replace Richard Wainwright as the Navy's Chief Intelligence Officer, the Navy's position comparable to his. Clover's eyes moved toward Wilkie and a cordial, short-lived grin broke through his dour before his eyes attended to Roosevelt.

"Commander," Wilkie tipped his head slightly, but offered no handshake.

"John, have a seat. This is Commander Richardson Clover. I believe you've both met."

"Correct, sir." Wilkie coolly noted as he sat down. Years ago, he had met Clover but the situation never grew contentious. When he was with the Chicago Tribune, Wilkie took an assignment to rummage over Clover's seemingly rapid rise through the ranks, looking for something to expose, but Clover was practically spotless — not even a drunken brawl as a teenager. Since then, Clover had fallen off Wilkie's own personal list of people he needed to monitor. That had now changed.

"I see." Roosevelt set his papers down and focused on Wilkie. "Let's all be very clear here. Bygones are bygones and we are all now working together."

Clover and Wilkie nodded tentatively.

"Good, good." Roosevelt clacked his teeth in a Cheshire cat like grin. He turned toward Wilkie and asked, "I understand your agent got one hell of a story from this Moser character. Do you think he was leading us on?"

"Whether that submarine story is true or not, the Spaniards are clearly making efforts to bolster their Navy." Wilkie replied. "We've tracked contracts for at least two dreadnaughts."

"My agents confirm. They are soliciting both Britain and Brazil." Clover blurted. Wilkie arched his eyebrows as he considered the man he now suspected to be his competition. He made a mental note that despite the lack of what he found before, he would need to dig up something, or fabricate some plausible indiscretion in this odd fellow's background so he could regain an upper hand.

"What about Hispañola. Did he get any information about what the Germans are thinking?" Roosevelt then asked.

"There is a bit of unrest there concerning a German national. Looks like they are more focused on maintaining control over the island than moving any further west," Wilkie offered.

"I doubt that," Roosevelt brooded a bit before reaching into his humidor. He inserted a cigar and used it as a pacifier rather than light it. He leaned back, sent a sideward glance at Clover then asked, "Perhaps the Commander has more pertinent information?"

"My agents overseas indicate they are building up for a major incursion on that island, and perhaps even provide some assistance to the Spanish in Cuba. Like they did over there in China," Clover said matter-of-factly.

"Okay, fellahs. I think we can all agree we have two issues to deal with here, one more insidious than the other," Roosevelt gazed at the ceiling. "Clover has agents over in Europe, so he can keep track of those developments. John, I need you to be a little more invasive down in Cuba."

"Three issues, sir," Wilkie added. "Moser indicated one of the Kaiser's most trusted spies is now over here." Clover recoiled. Wilkie fired off a spirited glare that was icily returned.

"Here as in — Havana?" Roosevelt wormed in his seat.

"No, sir. Last report was Philadelphia," Wilkie responded.

"You've got eyes on him?" Roosevelt asked.

"Yes, sir. We have him under surveillance now." Wilkie lied.

"Don't let him get too close to our bases at this point. I want him neutralized."

"Yes, sir," Wilkie made a mental note that Stiles would need to make better progress on finding Ziegler. Roosevelt smiled, finally lighting the cigar he had worked into the corner of his mouth. He expelled an aromatic cloud of whitish smoke into the air where the currents in the room coaxed it to swirl away from the Secretary's face.

"I would suggest some increased security on the Holland

project, as well," Wilkie added. His sideward glance to Clover was frigid. Clover's head spun around he glared at Wilkie like an owl that had spotted a field mouse.

"Good point, John," Roosevelt noted. "Clover, get an extra detail of Marines on that thing. I may not like it, but we can't let anyone else have it, either."

"Yes, sir," Clover's words were measured; his stare never wavering off Wilkie.

"Now, this contract thing intrigues me," Roosevelt said. "What do you think about buying those ships right out from underneath 'em. Money talks, agree?"

"I do not believe we need to exact those extraordinary measures, sir. Even if Spain obtains those ships, they would still be overmatched." Clover said.

"Do they realize that?" Wilkie questioned.

"Yes, I believe they do. They're just too arrogant to accept it," Clover responded. "If I may add, I see the more troubling question being what to do with Cuba once we run the Spaniards out."

"That is not our concern, gentlemen" Roosevelt jumped in. He wagged his finger threateningly but not specifically directed toward either man. "Once we clear the island, it is the State Department's issue. We'll hold on for a while, just to maintain the peace, you know, but once the petty dictators are cleaned up, Cuba is Sherman's headache, not ours. The more important fact is that Spain is still in this hemisphere and they need to be eradicated. And if this is the opportunity for us to do so, then it needs to happen now." Roosevelt punctuated his comment with a fist bump on his desk.

"Would it not be true that if we move in unprovoked, there would certainly be political consternation against the administration? Perhaps even you specifically," Wilkie questioned.

"I believe the inhumane treatment of Cubans right now is provocative enough. It is only a matter of when is the right time," Clover commented.

"The public is clamoring for us to do something. As I see it, we need to draw a line in the sand and send a message — a strong one. Not this namby-pamby crap that Day and Woodford keep prancing around with," Roosevelt slammed his fist to the table then glared directly at Wilkie. "You aren't getting soft on me John, are you?"

Wilkie took a breath as he calculated his response. Clover glared at him as well. "No, sir," he finally said after a few seconds, which to Wilkie felt like an hour. That should buy him some time, he thought.

"We have some maneuvers planned in the Caribbean, sir," Clover noted. "We can move them closer — to the eastern side of the Keys. That might shake things up some."

"And I understand the *Marblehead* has been dispatched to Haiti to keep an eye on the Kaiser's shenanigans," Roosevelt noted. "I know all that, Clover. "What would you think about sending a warship right into Havana harbor right now?"

"My predecessor has been assigned to the *Maine*. That position would make her the most advantageous, from both covert and overt perspectives," Clover said in a hushed tone.

"Where's is she now?" Roosevelt asked. Wilkie noted that the Secretary's tone was rhetorical. *He knew*, Wilkie thought. He was just toying with Clover, who was shuffling feverishly through his papers that noted the positions of each of the Navy's active warships. He ran his finger down the list until he stopped and tapped the paper twice. "She is scheduled to join the maneuvers planned for January off Key West."

"Where is she now?" Roosevelt repeated, leaning forward and clacking his teeth.

Clover hesitated. Sweat beaded up on his wide forehead and channeled along his grayed temples. "North of Cuba," he offered.

"Hmm. What if we send her directly to Havana instead? Once she gets into the harbor, it is sure to show them we mean business." Roosevelt offered.

Clover nodded, sheepishly. Wilkie recognized Roosevelt's tactic, having seen him bully his way through the New York City Police Department. He realized he would need to stay clear of the shrapnel that would soon be spread in Clover's direction.

"Sounds like we're in agreement. Let me work on McKinley so we can get the *Maine* in Havana harbor before the New Year comes. Gentlemen, I believe 1898 will be a very good year for us." Roosevelt grinned, propped his boots on his desk and relit his cigar.

A warm dark evening crept in over the decks of the *Maine* as she methodically plowed west toward the Florida Keys. Captain Sigsbee had ordered one-third speed and round the clock stations as they traversed north of Cuba through the Caribbean Sea, concerned with Wainwright's confirmed sighting of two German cadet ships headed in their general direction. He assumed Haiti, but he still preferred to have confirmation of their direction. Radio silence ordered once he passed Charleston though, obviated obtaining that confirmation.

Sigsbee retired to his cabin after evening dinner in the officer's mess to review his weekly letter home to his wife. Wainwright could have cleared the letter but he preferred words with his wife remain between him and her. He used the separation in time between writing it and reviewing it to be sure he did not reveal any sensitive particulars of his multi-faceted mission. The only part close to breaching secrecy was that he confirmed his hunch that when he left the Navy Yards, he would most likely be spending Christmas at sea again. No positions were revealed. He was satisfied.

It was better this way, he thought as he rose from the small teak wood desk that his small captain's cabin afforded him. Since the letter would be sent out of the Keys when they arrived, it would give her ample notice to arrange spending the holiday with her parents in Saratoga. They were on in their years, did not travel well, and would anyway need someone to help with the chores the brutal upstate New York winters required.

He wrapped the metal wire curls of his round eyeglass frames over his ears before stepping outside his cabin for his nightly walk. He had taken to a meandering once-around in the last four weeks as a means to clear his head so he could relax and get a good night's sleep. As he had discovered years before, when tensions built like a rumbling volcano, he needed a good rest to keep his mind sharp enough and body fit enough to respond properly to whatever the sea may throw at him.

Clean, crisp air enveloped his vessel's deck — more comfortable than he expected for the tropics. He reckoned the last hurricane that passed through here in October, the last of the season, must have dragged the humidity up north with it. A slow pace was warranted, he thought. He reached the poop deck, stepped up and stared out behind his rumbling ship, water churning behind her propellers, surging to the surface a trail of phosphorescent green algae in a trail behind him. Port side was Cuba, starboard was home. Until he reached the Keys, he knew he would be the first and only response for Consulate-General Fitzhugh Lee, if he deemed conditions needed some muscle in Havana. He was sure the rest of the Great White Fleet, as Roosevelt called it, had already docked in Keys.

Sigsbee settled into the metal chair on the poop deck, crossed his legs, stared south toward Cuba, and thought about the interesting fellow that he felt Lee to be. He had the chance to talk with the ex-Confederate several times when he returned to Washington for report and respite. When he and Lee had the chance for a few drinks, they reminisced about how different Sigsbee's attack on Fort Fischer would have been if Lee commanded the North Carolina fort during the Great Civil War. He grew to respect the old General, and once the hatchet was buried, he and Lee consummated a strong friendship.

"Evening, Captain," a deep voice greeted. Sigsbee recognized it as his Executive Officer's before he caught the wiry, six-foot officer through a sideward glance. Commander Richard Wainwright approached the stern with his customary long loping strides and his straight-stemmed pipe clenched in the corner of his mouth, exactly parallel to the deck. Having the former Navy Chief Intelligence Officer as his Executive Officer was just another twist in this entire convolution of events, Sigsbee mused. The replacement of his former XO, Commander Adolph Marix, was not his choice, and as far as Sigsbee could determine, not Wainwright's either. Sigsbee had heard that Roosevelt himself insisted that Marix was needed as a Captain, since he was expanding the fleet, and would personally provide a suitable replacement. To this point, Wainwright had been just that, but Sigsbee could not extricate the sense there was another, more furtive purpose for the lanky spy to be on his vessel.

"Any word from Fitz?" Sigsbee asked.

"No, sir. Not a peep. Perhaps things have settling down a bit." Wainwright worked his way to the rail. A thin wisp of smoke curled up from his pipe.

"This has got to be pissing Roosevelt off, don't you think." Sigsbee noted. He knew that the conditions in Havana were as tense as they had ever been and the Spanish colonial government seemed to have lost their grip on control. He could read the concern in Consul-General Lee's eyes the last time he had talked — when they set up a special message to be sent if all hell broke loose.

"Sir?"

"All this waiting around. I don't recall Roosevelt ever wanting to sit back and wait. I figured he would rather jump in, take control, and just be done with it."

"I agree he has never shown much patience," Wainwright now stood next to Sigsbee and stared out at the same glowing algae trail. "However, sir, I do believe he fully understands the implications which this Cuban situation holds. And I am sure that he recognizes even if some of those sugar traders on the island might be crooks, they are still Americans, and potentially still in danger."

Sigsbee felt his calves tighten up, a sure sign of his anxiety. Waiting for a signal from Lee, anything but radio silence, was simply adding to it. He mulled over the black-powder they had stowed for saluting. Ever since the *Cincinnati* caught fire a few months back, he worried his vessel's storage facilities were inadequate for black-powder and the bituminous blend of coal the now had to use. His Executive Officer however, was one of the principle investigators of that fire, and clearly would ensure his vessel would remain in safe condition.

"When the time comes, we will need to make the right

choice," Sigsbee mumbled, loud enough that he was sure Wainwright heard.

"Yes, sir. When the time comes."

"Who has the watch tonight?"

"Lieutenant Hood, sir."

"Insist that he checks the temperatures in the coal bunkers," Sigsbee sighed, then stood, turned and headed back to his cabin. Over his shoulder he mumbled, "Have him wake me if there is any word,"

"Sir?" Wainwright called out. Sigsbee stopped and turned back to his Executive Officer. "I want you to know I will support your decision."

"Thank you, Mr. Wainwright." Sigsbee replied. That comment alone relieved Sigsbee a tad.

Sam Carter could not understand why Gerasimo Lugo asked him to meet him in Miami. The message was rather cryptic, and it took the circuitous safe route by courier out of Cuba aboard the *Olivette*, through Tampa and by special delivery to the boarding house where he routinely stayed in North Charleston. Just the fact that Lugo was in Florida was not odd, since Carter knew that a handful of Americans partial to the revolutionaries were running arms and ammunition out of the fledgling city, similar to what the blockade runners had done during the Civil War. Nor was it odd for Lugo to contact him from time to time when he was in Florida. The tenor of the note was the oddity that baffled Carter.

He cobbled together his trip on a series of trains that traveled along the coast from Charleston through Georgia and into Florida. As the last train arrived at the small, decrepit station of Miami, now a community with a growing Cuban refugee population, Carter racked his mind for what could have been so urgent that Lugo risked the secrecy of his shipment being discovered by American authorities, but could not fathom one solid reason. The train slowed as it arrived at the station, which fortuitously was close enough to the docks that Carter could walk to them in minutes. As dusk settled in, he departed the train and headed down to the docks.

The docks were eerily quiet tonight, Carter thought, save the echoes of crickets and peepers as he walked by the haphazardly built storage barns. He stepped around a corner near the dock he knew Lugo favored — still nothing.

Whack. A thick board thwacked him across his stomach, doubling him over. He fell to his knees and tried to recover his wits as he caught his breath. Despite the pain, phrases of what he had to say to keep from being punished further ran through his mind. He felt a hard-soled shoe press heavily into the small of his back.

"Lugo. I am here to see Lugo," Carter pushed the words out his mouth, the heavy boot pushing even deeper into his back, stifling hope to suck in any more air.

"*¿Cómo sé?*" a faceless voice growled.

"Go ask him," Carter's voice whistled. He drew in enough air to catch his breath. "Tell him it's Carter."

Silence. Carter sensed he might have staved off execution. He was not sure.

"*Desea verle, Julio,*" a different, deeper voice directed.

'*I am not about to go anywhere,*' Carter thought as he chose not to move. For all he knew, Julio, or whoever it was, had a gun trained on his head, and any wrong move on his part would surely convince him to use it. Even if Carter wanted to vault up and pummel his adversary, the initial attack had sapped his energy and left him still gasping for air.

"Señor Carter!" Carter recognized Lugo's voice. Footfalls on the wooden docks drew closer.

"I think you have your answer, Julio," Carter said. The pain in his gut had subsided, but still stung enough to keep his attention.

"*Con el fin de dejarle levantarse,*" Carter heard Lugo's voice.

"Get up," Julio barked in clear English. Carter complied. He rose to his feet, still more crumpled than straight. When he looked up, even though dusk had moved into evening darkness, he recognized Lugo's scruffy gray beard and wild white hair just a few steps in front of him.

"You do have quite a way of welcoming me, Gerasimo.

You ask me to come here then beat the crap out of me."

"Chances are something I cannot take. I am sure you understand that, Samuel," Lugo offered in his broken English. The pair embraced very briefly.

"I could use that rum you offered me back in Jamaica about now, Gerasimo."

"*Sí, Señor*. Before leaving Kingston, I received word that two German warships were headed toward Jamaica. I would suspect they are headed toward Hispañola, but I am not for sure."

"Do you know if they arrived?" Carter asked then thought to himself, '*This is what was so urgent?*'

"I would suspect so. As we were headed north, we spotted the vessels. They were perhaps a few miles out. We did not dare approach, since we were not, *cómo se dice*, legal?"

"Did you tell Garcia? He needs to know this."

"Sabio spoke to him before he left Guantanamo. But, Señor Carter, we grow concerned that Spain and Germany have allied. Do you know?"

"No, I do not have that information, but I am sure someone in Washington knows."

"General Garcia had a message for you. *'Ahora. Comprendo, hacer lo que tengas que hacer.'*"

Carter arched his eyebrows, understanding that General Garcia had concluded he could not win his fight alone. "*Comprendo*," Carter confirmed.

Julio had been creeping up the dock and appeared, as if from nowhere and inserted his rugged face between Carter and Lugo. His eyes narrowed, his head twitched back toward the mist working its way in from the sea. Lugo's eyes widened.

"We must leave now, Samuel," Lugo grabbed Carter by the shoulders and embraced him tightly as Julio slinked back in the direction of the vessel. "Perhaps I will see you in Jamaica soon, yes?"

"You owe me some of that rum. I intend to collect," Carter noted as he watched Lugo hustle down the dock, a humorous sight since he ran more like a stork than a man.

Things were getting much more complex than Carter ever

imagined.

Chapter 13

"I came up as soon as I saw you come in, Mr. Carter," Mrs. Johnston, Carter's raven-haired landlady handed him a cablegram. "It's from Washington. It's important enough that they made me sign for it."

"Thank you, Miss Johnston." Carter said, rolling his eyes as he took the letter. The official Department of Treasury, Special Operations script on the edge told him all he needed to know. He expected assignment back to Cuba, but did not think it would be this urgent.

He slipped his finger under the flap and opened it.

Cuba. Meet Lee, was all it said. Three words, nothing else.

He would have preferred a bit more detail, but he was starting to recognize Wilkie's stilted, brief cables. Moreover, as was his boss's expectation, arrangements to get there was his own responsibility. Only if he ran into problems was he to contact Wilkie to have special travel arrangements made.

"You are heading out of town again, ain't ya?"

Carter wasn't listening. He was already thinking through the most convenient means to get to Havana. There was a schooner scheduled for Miami, due to sail this evening. He could then take a train to Tampa and then get passage to Havana on the *Olivette.* He could not remember the exact days the *Olivette* sailed for Havana, but this one time it did not matter. If he missed one, there would be another two days later.

"And your young lady friend stopped by while you were gone. I told her you were out of town on business. That was alright that I did that, wasn't it."

"Lady friend?"

"Yes, that sweet young lady from Charleston proper —
Miss McGeehan? She has the nicest auburn hair and the most
darling complexion."

'McGeehan. That name is not familiar,' Carter thought,
trying to recall any woman he had met with auburn hair.

"Oh, I apologize, Mr. Carter," Mrs. Johnston hunched
over and grew an impish grin, obviously reading Carter's
confusion. "It is a secret, isn't it? I see. I won't tell anyone."
The woman held her finger to her lips and shushed. "But if you
ask me, you won't do much better than her," she finished,
turned and headed back down the stairs to her part of the house.

Still baffled at who this Miss McGeehan was, Carter
stuffed the message into his jacket pocket then absently
checked his pocket watch.

"Damn!" The watch reminded him that he was to have
dinner with Moser and his mother in town in an hour and he
still needed to pack to catch the schooner. He had already
resigned himself to the fact that his Thanksgiving, and most
likely Christmas would be in Havana rather than in Mobile, but
at least this year brought for him a rarity. His mother and
stepfather were visiting friends in Charleston early, and he was
pleased he had time, although brief, to see them.

Carter haphazardly packed his cloth satchel with some
fresh clothes, and then headed down the stairs. As was his
custom, he slipped his tagged door key under Mrs. Johnston's
apartment door, which signaled her that he would be out of
town again. Once outside, he grabbed the cable car that ran
along North Market Street, arriving at the intersection of East
Bay as the gas lamps along the street came to life.

He stepped off the trolley, and started down the cross
street, but found himself slowing to drink in the swaying dance
of the palmetto fronds, coaxed on by the early evening sea
breeze. He felt himself urged on toward the bistro by that
breeze until he reached his favorite open-air restaurant in town,
now partly enclosed for the coming winter. As he had arranged,
Rudolf Moser was ready to meet him, sitting alone at a table

near the center of the outer dining area.

"I am glad you could make it, Rudolf," Carter said as he settled into a seat at the table. Moser looked up and smiled with his cavernous eyes.

"Good evening, Samuel. I trust you are well."

"Yes, very well." Carter searched the sidewalk.

"I must say this weather is more appealing to my withered bones than Berlin can be this time of year."

"It can be, Rudolf," Carter spotted an older couple sauntering toward the bistro. Anticipation blossomed in his chest and he felt his heart flutter, though briefly. The woman he saw leaned slightly on the square-faced man's arm that she held tightly more for warmth than support. The white-bearded man walked stiffly and steadily, as if marching in slow motion. No, it was simply the English gentlemanly manners that caused him to strut like he did, Carter thought. His mother, now Adrianne Alexander, having taken his stepfather's name, had aged gracefully in the years following Reconstruction, when rearing him would have most accurately been described as a series of acts of desperation and survival. Despite the cruelty they had encountered in those years, she had not grown bent and sickly like many of her friends who, like her, had been widowed by the Great Civil War. Her red hair had blanched and thinned, yet enough of its body remained for it to rest in waves underneath her floppy wide brimmed hat. Her strides were more deliberate than he remembered — they remained loyal to the grace of her traditional Southernism.

William Alexander, his stepfather, had been faithful and considerate to her as well as him. The old man had nurtured him in studies and responsibility beyond what he had seen to be customary for many of his companion urchins, as the carpetbaggers had referred to them. At the time, Carter remembered thinking Alexander as prudish, but as he grew and time passed, Carter learned to respect the man's wisdom. It was this man's encouragement and tutoring, after all, and perhaps connections he had which Carter never realized in his youth, which cut for him a safer road to his own adulthood than other young southern children experienced.

"I can see what kept Gunter here," Rudolf Moser commented, more under his breath than aloud.

"Gunter?" Carter asked.

"*Ya*, your father's given name. Gunter Rohlenheim. Sam Miller was his operating name." Moser reminded Carter as Adrianne released her grip on Alexander's arm and opened her arms to greet her son.

"Momma, I am pleased you are well," Carter whispered as they embraced for a moment, heads on each other's shoulder.

"William Alexander," Carter heard the older man introduce himself. He glanced over his shoulder and saw the two men shaking hands.

"I am Rudolf Moser, sir," Moser responded.

"Samuel tells me that you knew his father?" Alexander said. Carter saw a quizzical expression etch both their faces.

"That is correct, sir. Gunter — you know him as Samuel — he was a counterpart of mine many years ago. I believe you and I encountered each other as well many years ago."

"That I do not remember." Alexander replied, aloof yet polite.

"In London," Moser noted as Carter and Adrianne approached.

"Rudolf, I would like you to meet my mother." The German stared into Adrianne's eyes, now faded from green to a haunting steely gray, and then lowered his lips to her hand.

"Samuel tells me that you knew my Mr. Miller?" she asked as Carter moved behind her and politely slipped the high backed chair underneath her. She glanced over her shoulder and visually thanked her son.

"Did you know that his given name was Gunter?" Moser perched his eyebrows as he sat down with the others, almost in unison.

"Yes, but we spoke very little of that," Adrianne admitted. Carter slackened his jaw, surprised. Adrianne clearly noticed her son's astonishment. She tweaked her lips into a smile, and said, "Some things, Samuel, are simply meant to be left as they are. I trust you have learned that."

"Would you all care for some hot tea?" a waiter stated as

he stood over the foursome. "It is frightfully cold out here for this time of year."

"Certainly," Alexander nodded as a ship's horn bellowed nearby. Carter fished out his pocket watch and glanced at the timepiece.

"You will need to excuse me. It seems I have miscalculated how much time I had before the ship was leaving," Carter mentioned as he stood. He circled the table and leaned over his mother's shoulder.

"I understand that you cannot talk about this voyage you are taking, but please be careful. I hear things are getting a bit testy down there," she whispered in Carter's ear.

"I will try, momma," Carter whispered back as he kissed her rosy cheek. "Perhaps you and Rudolf can talk about father. I am sure Mr. Alexander will understand."

"I am sure he will," Adrianne smiled briefly as she gripped her son's hand. "Be careful," she added as Carter turned and slipped out onto East Bay Street.

In less than a half-hour, with Carter aboard, the schooner's boiler valves were opened to start the screw, and the vessel steamed out Charleston Bay, past Fort Sumter and into the open Atlantic.

"As I understand your report here, Ambassador, two war ships have anchored off Port-au-Prince this morning?" Secretary of State John Sherman expelled a lung full, not completely convinced in the validity of the Haitian minister's statements. He could believe routine passenger vessels, but characterizing what he thought was a routine diplomatic visit as an act of war was outlandish. Sherman felt his hand start to twitch, and reckoned that a quick shot from his hip flask would most likely help, but protocol prevented his "medicine" at this point. When William Day arrived, which he had indicated would be soon, he could more easily render himself a secret dose.

"That is correct sir," Jacques Nicolas Leger, the Haitian minister to Washington was clearly growing impatient with Sherman's stalling. Leger was a frail looking man, very dark skinned and balding. His suit hung rumpled and loose over his narrow shoulders, oversized for his stature. "As I indicate there, in that report, the ships are the *Charlotte* and the *Stein*. We have confirmed they are warships."

"What's this about warships?" William Day's voice cracked as he stomped into the room, his rumpled appearance mirroring Sherman's. He cleared his throat rather loudly, hawking up phlegm that he spit into the brass spittoon holding the office door open.

"And this here is the demand from the Kaiser, delivered by Captain Theile." Leger's voice trembled as he handed over that official letter. His eyes were so wide that white rings surrounded his pupils, accentuated even more by his black skin. Sherman took the letter, stared at it with a glazed look, and then passed it to the stiff huffing Day.

"We must pay indemnity of twenty thousand dollars along with a formal apology to the Kaiser. And we are required to readmit the criminal Lüders," Leger rattled.

"Lüders? Who is Lüders?" Sherman asked, looking at Day.

"German national — caused some fracas over one of his drunken hostlers and was thrown off the island," Day said under his breath, his stare skewering Sherman.

"They can't demand that!" Sherman spewed, and then looked over to Day as if to ask for concurrence. Day melted into the chair at the round conference table, shaking his head.

"And if this does not occur?" Day asked, his tone exasperated, his head propped upon his open hands.

"We have until one o'clock to respond positively. If we do not, they have warned that all our ships will be sunk in the harbor, the Palais National destroyed, and the city bombarded. They are warships, Mr. Secretary."

"They are bluffing. I understand these are school ships!" Sherman said.

"Then tell me why they would make such a threat," Leger squeaked.

"Wait a moment," Day's head popped back up. "Haven't we dispatched a ship to Haiti? The *Marblehead*, is it not? That should deter them."

"The weather is a bit rough in the Atlantic and she's at least a week out," Sherman's tone was disparaging. "I have already telegraphed Ambassador Powell that we cannot provide aid in time."

"So, my recommendation to my president shall be that America — the same America that claims to be the champions of freedom — cannot protect us?" Leger's eyes darted between Sherman, who was now rubbing his eyes, and Day, who sat in his chair, stupefied.

"I am afraid that is all we can offer, Ambassador," Day dropped his head, embarrassed as he shook no.

"I see," Leger quivered then vaulted up from his chair, ripped the papers from Sherman's trembling hands, hand pressed his suit and headed out the room. "This is a dark day for our people," he muttered as he stepped out of the room and into the hallway.

Sherman took the opportunity to take a quick drink off his hip flask.

"Damn it!" Day spat as he leaned forward. He then pushed himself up from the chair and marched back to the window behind Sherman. He crossed his arms behind him and stared out the window.

"We need to tell McKinley," Sherman said in a hushed tone.

"How did we miss this? How the hell did we miss this one?" Day groused as he stomped around the room, pounding his fist into his hand.

"I thought that Ambassador Powell was just being overly cautious." Sherman noted as he cleared his throat.

"Excuse me? You knew about this?"

Sherman lowered his head and focused squarely on an empty spot on his desk.

"How long has he been warning us about this?"

"A week, maybe a week and a half."

"A week? We could have done something in a week! I am sure Roosevelt would have gladly given us something more that some old decrepit bathtub." Day growled.

"McKinley needs to know," Sherman repeated, his words beginning to slur.

"So we are supposed to go into McKinley's office and tell him that we just gave Haiti to the Germans while he's presenting a message to those war hawks in Congress that everything is working as planned down there?" Day hammered the desk with his fists. After three slams of flesh on wood, he looked up to Sherman, his eyes bloodshot from lack of sleep. "Even worse, this makes Roosevelt look like a prognosticating genius that nobody listened to."

"We can tell McKinley that we never received the messages," Sherman offered.

"You think he doesn't know? Damn it, John. If the *Marblehead* was sent over a week ago, Roosevelt had to know something. He makes it his business to know what every damned boat is doing. And if Roosevelt knows, you can be damned sure that he's already groused to McKinley."

"Look at all these papers, William. We can always say it got lost," Sherman rationalized.

"No, we've got to tell him the truth. It may be politically suicidal, but he has to know." Day said, exasperatedly.

President McKinley returned to his office, exhausted from delivering his annual message to Congress. Wilting into his high-backed leather chair, he slipped his finger underneath his collar and popped open his top button. Although he publicly voiced that his policy was vindicated — a plan that emphasized some latitude for the Spanish reforms to work — he was not sure that he believed it any more. The agreed to autonomy plan included suspension of their re-concentration policy, a declared amnesty for political prisoners, and the release of Americans still being held in Cuban jails. Spain had also relinquished a greater domestic rule for the Cubans, but still maintained control over the military and foreign affairs. It was much less than he had hoped for based on what Ambassador Woodford initially demanded, but it was at least a starting point.

McKinley was keenly aware that Spain felt recess with honor was not possible and maintaining that attitude would ultimately lead to inevitable conflict, but he claimed conviction to use continued diplomatic pressure would resolve the issue of Cuba. If not, at least it would give his administration more time. He dodged addressing the building German crisis in Haiti, since he had yet to obtain any additional intelligence from Day or Sherman. Outside of sending one small ship to Haiti, there was nothing more that was needed, he thought. The lid on Haiti remained in place at least for the time during the speech, but he sensed it might not be long before that would also devolve into something ugly.

"You seemed a bit tentative," Garret Hobart, McKinley's Vice-President, commented as he appeared in the doorway.

"How is Ida doing?" McKinley asked without looking up. Hobart was a rather stout man, but not overly short, with a straight, honest face. He was direct and business-like whether the topic was prostitution, the crippled economy or even foreign affairs. Although McKinley knew little of him before they were elected to office, he had grown to recognize Hobart as a wise beyond his years, valuable confidant.

"She's fine, now," Hobart noted. McKinley glanced up to Hobart with a dull vacant expression. "Jennie got her settled after the little problem this morning. She's keeping busy — crocheting some more slippers."

"Thank you Gus," McKinley rolled his head to loosen his neck stiffness.

"I'm not so sure the Democratic Caucus will support your assertion that Spain will relent, Hobart noted as he sat down in a stiff-backed chair.

"That's the least of my worries at this point, Gus," McKinley admitted. "I know they assert that for all practical purposes, a state of war exists on the island. You know I had to clearly state that we were against Cuban belligerency, even though we need to support the Cubans. But with the Kaiser rattling sabers down there . . . well, you know, Gus. We just need to be a bit more veiled about where we stick our noses."

"You said what you had to say." Hobart whispered as leaned forward in his chair, locking stares with McKinley. "There will come a time, I suspect sooner than later, when

Spain will blunder. Then and only then will you have just cause to intervene. Stepping in now cannot truly be justified, despite what the war hawks spout."

"I hope you are correct, Gus." McKinley replied as Roosevelt stepped into the room. Hobart gave the Secretary a sideward glance. McKinley's voice quelled to a whisper. "Keep a close eye on Day and Sherman. It's too touchy right now to have them blunder their way through diplomacy."

"We can talk later." Hobart winked, turned and shuffled by Roosevelt, cordially tipping his head as he passed. Roosevelt continued into the room, hovered briefly, then sat in what had become his assigned seat, directly left of McKinley.

McKinley peered up to the Navy Secretary with hooded eyes. "Is Long still out of town?" he asked.

"Yes, sir," Roosevelt replied briskly. McKinley twitched his eyebrows and scowled as Secretaries Sherman, Day and Alger entered the Yellow Oval Room and sat at the opposite side of the table.

"I certainly hope he recovers soon," McKinley muttered under his breath as the three other men took their seats at the oak conference table across from the Navy Secretary. McKinley pursed his lips, not completely convinced Roosevelt's stated reason for Long's extended absence was valid.

"Gentlemen," McKinley greeted, revising his tone to be more cordial. He sucked in a lung full of fresh air, surveyed the long table, and made eye contact with each of his cabinet members. They knew what he was looking for, he thought.

"You delivered a very appropriate message," State Secretary Sherman started.

"Yes, sir. Well put." Alger added.

"Appropriate?" Roosevelt humphed. "The words were received in the spirit of intense hostility from the whole of Congress, not just the Democrats. How much longer are we going to sit on our butts and watch this butchery go on?"

"Mr. Roosevelt, did you even listen? They have capitulated Cuba." Sherman's voice quivered.

"Bull!" Roosevelt slammed his fist on the table. "They

have capitulated nothing. You know as well as I do that nothing has changed on the island. Saying they would release our people was nothing more than the rhetorical pacifier."

"Negotiations take time," Sherman responded, rather timidly.

"I don't see any boats headed this way, do you?" Roosevelt pointed out toward the window as he clacked his teeth in an open, rather devious grin.

"We should let this play itself out . . ."

"Have you lost your mind?" Roosevelt interrupted, barking back. "Weren't you the one that told us about Havana's Bishop appealing for food? And I emphasize, *appeal* not request. We are obligated to do something."

"Enough!" McKinley said. He waited for the combatants to disengage and lean back from the table before he continued. "I realize the overall plan is moving slowly, but as I see it, we have few options but to let it work. We can put increasing pressure on them by upping the ante incrementally."

"We do have options, Mr. President," Roosevelt spoke up. "We have naval maneuvers planned for the Caribbean at this point. We must break off one of the vessels and send her to Havana. That should provide enough of a message."

"Provocative and unwarranted." Sherman replied, vaulting up from his chair.

"I say the best diplomacy is a big stick." Roosevelt grinned. "Perhaps if you were a bit more diligent in Haiti, we wouldn't have that mess to deal with."

Sherman and McKinley were both stung by Roosevelt's comment.

"One crisis at a time, gentlemen," McKinley felt Roosevelt's comment sting. He was not certain how far the news from Haiti had travelled — now he was certain. "We can discuss that issue a bit later," he added, hoping to defuse the brewing storm in his office.

Roosevelt grunted, flashing a toothy sneer toward Sherman, who sat back down.

"I still believe we should let diplomacy work, but I also somewhat agree with Secretary Roosevelt," McKinley leaned back in his chair again and sighed. "What precautions can we take, as non-provocative as we can I do caution, that would at least show Spain that we are committed to an independent Cuba?"

Roosevelt leaned back in his chair and let slip a Cheshire cat-like grin.

"We can move the maneuvers closer, east of Key West instead of in the Gulf." Roosevelt glanced down at his notes. "Close enough to see them from Havana," he then added.

"That may be too much. What about just one vessel?" McKinley then offered.

"The *Maine* has already arrived at Key West," Roosevelt responded. "She is stationed for response if Ambassador Lee feels he needs to escape the chaos."

"Mr. President, I believe that to be unwise," Sherman protested.

"How do you know that?" Day's eyes grew as wide as saucers.

"She may be small, but she's one of our best. Formidable. Agile." Roosevelt continued, clearly ignoring Day.

"It could be seen as a threat," Day added.

"And the damned German warships down there aren't!" Roosevelt glared back at Sherman. "And if I'm not mistaken, the Kaiser and his boys are preparing armored cruisers to steam toward Haiti even as we speak!"

"You offered the *Marblehead* to face that challenge, if I remember correctly?" Sherman cut in.

"After *you* rejected sending the *Maine*!" Roosevelt countered. He wagged his finger at Sherman as he shot a sneer toward a rather aloof Alger.

McKinley rose, momentarily interrupting the bickering. He slowly and silently walked toward the window, his hands folded behind his back. He didn't want to believe it, but the time had come for something to be done proactively before his hand was forced. He lost the confidence that the Spanish government had enough control over their army that had now nested in Cuba, and that it possibly had no intentions of leaving. Nor did he have the confidence that the Cubans would relent for anything less than unilateral withdrawal. Asking Congress to declare war on Spain at this point, only weeks before Christmas, could be tantamount to starting impeachment proceedings, even if they were growing more hostile by the day. But doing nothing could result in the same demise.

McKinley slowly turned around and glanced at the ceiling, then drifted down to the stiff lipped portrait of James Madison, fixing on the Virginian's deep-set eyes. Eighteen-twelve. The world was crumbling down around him. McKinley pondered how Madison must have felt as the British, gaining victory after punishing victory, began their approach on Washington. The situation he found himself in now was like that critical time. '*No, Washington was not threatened from the outside*,' he thought. The threat was more internal this time — perhaps more brought on by his inaction. He sucked in a deep breath, turned to his staff then cleared his throat.

"Gentlemen, these are trying times. We must, and I emphasize, we *must* work together in order for everything to work the way we all would like it to." McKinley stepped toward his desk, but remained standing. He leaned forward, rested on his fists, and scanned each of the faces before him. "Mr. Day. Inform the Sagasta government that we will be sending a small battleship into Havana harbor. Please add that in the interest of good relations, we will wait for their response."

"But sir," Sherman interrupted. McKinley immediate raised his hand.

"Make sure they are aware that this is a gesture of concern about the safety of our people still in Cuba, since we see that they are still struggling with the Cuban insurgency."

Roosevelt smugly leaned back his chair.

"You may continue the maneuvers, on the western side of the Keys, Mr. Roosevelt," McKinley turned his attention to the be-speckled Secretary. "There are to be no aggressive moves toward the island or any of the Spanish fleet,"

"What if they make the first move?" Roosevelt countered.

"There will be no cowboy diplomacy here," McKinley glared directly at Roosevelt. "There will be no action against the Spanish unless I personally order it. Is that clear, Mr. Roosevelt?"

"Understood, sir." Roosevelt replied staring at McKinley.

"And you will provide me the names of your second class warships and the records of their Captains tomorrow. I will make the decision on which vessel to send."

"Yes, sir," Roosevelt responded.

"Then, gentlemen, we have nothing more to discuss." McKinley announced. He sat back down in his chair and as his Cabinet quietly filed out of the room, he stared at the papers neatly piled on his desk. Even with the room empty, he began reviewing the papers in earnest — the walls continued to echo the bickering men's voices.

He started with the special message that Hobart had received for him while he was providing his speech to Congress. He mused for a moment as to whether he wanted to open it, reckoning what more bad news might be inside. Nevertheless, it was his position, for better or for worse, and everyone in the country was looking to him for leadership through these trying times. He reached over his desk, grabbed the letter opener and carefully slipped the envelope open.

The letter was from the American minister to Haiti, William F Powell. Before reading, the President sucked in a deep breath and braced himself for the additional details that Powell always seemed to belabor. As McKinley read the letter, he imagined the Palais National in Port-au-Prince as more an overly huge plantation house. Powell's description of the lowering of the Haitian colors and the raising of the German flag over Hispañola disturbed him. Powell went on to describe the weeping by the local dignitaries as the Haitian Navy Band played the German National Anthem. With the event staged to be a gay gathering for all who were German, it seemed there was a great loss for the freedom of another West Indies archipelago.

"This is the first time in my life that I have ever had cause to be ashamed of being an American, or have to blush for the flag that protects us," McKinley read aloud so he could feel the dispassionate sense that must have consumed Powell. That epitaph stuck in McKinley's craw as he laid his head into his arms on his desk and rested.

"Cut engines to one-third," Captain O'Neill ordered down to the *Marblehead*'s engine room. He rolled his eyes, realizing his order was reflex — his vessel had only mustered a true one-third the entire course down.

"One-third, aye." The response echoed up the voice tube.

The wide western approach to the harbor surrounding Port-au-Prince did not require him to slow down, but O'Neill wanted time to reconnoiter the entire harbor before steaming in. He pulled out his spyglass, more to confirm personally what his perched lookouts would report than anything else.

"Captain, you need to see this!" Boyd announced from his position in front of the bridge. "Their damned warships are already here."

O'Neill swung his view toward the front of the bridge to look for himself. He quickly inspected the German vessels and quickly confirmed what Sigsbee had told him — they were schooling ships, most likely on training runs. He adjusted his focus onto the decks to evaluate the gunnery each had. *Two, maybe four gun mounts*, he thought. *And they look pretty relaxed*.

"Message from Washington, sir," a signalman clomped across the steel decking with his hobnailed boots. O'Neill looked down to the signalman's shoes and frowned. He had missed that on his inspections.

"Thank you," he noted, pointing to the signalman's shoes. "Those won't work aboard a ship that might get some water on the deck, son. I don't care what the marines are telling you, but I would rather you have bare feet than have those on. Got it?"

"Yes, sir," the signalman responded, then sheepishly, turned and headed back out the portal with much quieter steps.

O'Neill turned his attention back to the message and read it. The final line was rather disconcerting.

ONI has confirmed SMS Geier has left Kiel for ports south. Godspeed, Marblehead.

Two more warships. That was news O'Neill did not want

to hear let alone share with his crew.

Chapter 14

Wilhelm Ziegler knew that the element of surprise was an essential piece to Admiral Tirpitz's invasion plans for Norfolk. He also knew that the only place he would be able to obtain the materiel he needed for his next step would be an active military yard, which the only one nearby was Norfolk, Virginia. He was not sure whether it was wise to let DeLauro assist him with his reconnaissance of the Navy Yard, but he knew he would not be able to carry everything he needed to steal without an extra set of hands. And since to this point DeLauro had not indicated he was smart enough to piece together what Ziegler's intentions, he reasoned he was safe enough.

Shortly after midnight, Ziegler with DeLauro in tow, slipped through the back gates of the Navy Yard and moved toward the building that Ziegler assumed would be the munitions factory. At the rear of the machine shop, where DeLauro happened across an unlocked sliding door, the two men slipped inside. Together they tiptoed through the aisles of idle machines and presses that lined this long brick building, searching for anything that could be useful. As Ziegler poked through he piles of metal and wood detritus for fragments, he noticed DeLauro scanning the machines for unfinished artillery shells that would hold enough black power and guncotton for the bombs he planned to make. He carefully watched the ex-coal miner rummage through scrap, collect a few thin, cup-shaped pieces and slip them into a burlap sack.

"Some shells," DeLauro noted as he approached like a cat

with a mouse, proudly showing the shell fragments to Ziegler.

"I see," Ziegler absently noted, his attention drawn to an open window into the night's darkness. Another two-story brick building stood just outside, closer to the river's edge, overlooking what appeared to him to be partly completed vessels. *'That building was someplace to reconnoiter,'* he thought, *'and that excursion was one he had to make alone.'* Without the confidence that DeLauro would be able to keep up with him on his next incursion, he then suggested, "You take the materiel back to the rooming house. I need to see what's over there."

DeLauro agreed. Ziegler was relieved he didn't refuse. He monitored DeLauro closely as he slipped out of the building then clumsily zigzagged his way out of the yard, back toward town. Feeling freer to navigate, Ziegler wormed through a small open window, scampered across the narrow footbridge connecting the two red brick buildings then slipped through a cracked open window. He maneuvered through the desks along the first floor, looking for diagrams or plans that would give him any details of the ships and hulls that were lined up in the dry-docks below. He moved from desk to desk, hoping that at least one engineer had been sloppy enough to have left his prints out on his desk.

Nothing.

Frustrated, Ziegler scurried up the stairwell to the second floor. He noticed a window at the end of the hallway, positioned precisely overlooking the docks. As he peered down to the water, he took out his small box camera and took pictures — they would be crude and the lighting would be problematic, but he wasn't sure Wilhelm would believe him if he did not have the first hand evidence. He identified five completed vessels that were close to ready, two of them were large dreadnaught-type battle ships. They were at least seaworthy if not battle ready. He counted another five hulls being fitted out. There was also a very intriguing, low-slung vessel sandwiched, almost hidden by several other hulls. It was more than a simple monitor, he thought, squinting to get better focus on the vessel. Eleven additional ships and no inkling on what tactics the Americans might use for deployment. Whether they were for here or elsewhere, Ziegler reckoned, the Kaiser needed to know. A naval invasion here would most certainly not be met with the assumed absence of resistance.

Ziegler heard footsteps clomp up the stairwell at the end of the hallway.

"That moron came back," he fumed. Slipping his hand over his Mauser C-96, he stepped back toward the stairwell. He peered through the open metal grated stairwell and saw a figure headed in his direction.

It was not DeLauro. Of that, he was sure. Stepping back into the expansive room, he scanned quickly for an alternate escape route. Nothing up, no skylights. He quietly moved to the window and looked down. Directly underneath him was a narrow strip of ground next to the lapping water of the inlet, water in which he knew would be too cold to survive. The footsteps stopped. First landing he assumed. He looked down again and estimated his fall. Two stories. The footsteps resumed.

'No choice,' Ziegler reckoned. He grabbed the top ledge of the window, swung his legs out, and briefly sat on the windowsill. He rolled to his stomach, then slipped down and let his hands grip the windowsill as he dangled his legs along the brick wall. *Story and a half*, he thought. He had done that before. A slight breeze picked up, swirling in his ears enough that he could not hear if who approached was still moving.

Keeping his knees bent, he let go. His legs buckled as his feet sunk into the marshy soil. He quickly wormed his feet out, then hustled out of the compound and started back to the rooming house.

Jack Stiles reached the top of the steps and drew his Smith and Wesson revolver, assured that the man he saw scamper across the compound had slipped into this building. As each of the doors along the hallway remained open, he realized that by himself, this would be a tedious and most likely fruitless search. He held his breath as he stopped at each door, positioning his ear to listen inside for breathing while he continued surveillance down the hall. When he finally reached the end of the hallway, he saw the open window.

'*Too late*,' he shook his head as he thought. He carefully walked to the window and looked out. No splashing in the water, but along the brick face of the building was a strip of ground. '*Enough ground for a skilled burglar — or a spy*,' he thought. There were impact marks. He holstered his sidearm, and then hurried out the building and to the area that was underneath the open second story window. At the scene, it was clear that his objective had slipped him — the imprints in the muck and tracks headed between the buildings clearly revealed someone had dropped out of the window and headed off out of the compound.

'*The bastard*,' Stiles knew it had to be Ziegler. The bastard had slipped him again. Wilkie was going to be furious.

"Well, well. How did TR weasel this," Captain Chester O'Neill spouted as he looked west from his mooring in the harbor at Port-au-Prince. Lieutenant Boyd turned and startled at the sight, almost spilling his morning tea onto the *Marblehead's* poop deck. Heading into the harbor was the *USS Wilmington*, one of the Navy's newest gunboats, its white paint so fresh it was glistening in the morning sun. The sight of reinforcements brought a smile to O'Neill's face. He had seen the plans for this class of gunboat —heavily armed with guns and torpedoes, a full three-sixty range of attack, and a triple expansion steam power plant geared tightly enough that it could spin the screw with enough torque to lift her bow right out of the water at flank speed.

"Anything on the telegraph?" O'Neill asked.

"Right on it, sir," Boyd responded, launching into a scramble back toward the bridge. O'Neill remained at the stern, watching the *Wilmington* slow and turn ten degrees to port. He racked his brain for a moment until he finally remembered who had been assigned to the new vessel. Commander Chapman Todd.

"Nothing on the telegraph," Boyd returned, breathless from running the length of the Marblehead. "But I've got the signaler in tow."

"Good, good," O'Neill said. As soon as he did, his signalman stumbled forward and onto the raised poop deck, lugging the portable Aldis lamp. He deftly set up the tripod and started flashing in semaphore toward the *Wilmington*.

"Cap'n. I'm thinkin' trouble to starboard." Boyd pointed to the German training ships. O'Neill saw that the *Charlotte* had started moving out to sea, directly toward the incoming *Wilmington*.

"Tell *Wilmington* 'Hold fire,' " O'Neill ordered his signaler as he retrieved his telescope and surveyed the deck of the German ship.

"Sir?" Boyd stared at his Captain in disbelief.

"It's a trap, Boyd," O'Neill said as he continued studying the *Charlotte*'s crew. He swept back toward the *Stein* and reviewed its crew as well. "They know we aren't positioned to cover the *Wilmington* or make a run at the *Stein*. He's baiting them to start something." O'Neill then ordered, "Tell *Wilmington* — '*Charlotte* rigged to run, not fight'. That should settle Todd some."

"*Wilmington* says 'Understand,' sir," the signalman translated the flashes for O'Neill.

Stand fast, Todd. They're baiting you, O'Neill thought, biting his lower lip, convinced in his assumption as he watched the *Charlotte* close ranks toward the *Wilmington*. O'Neill lifted his telescope again and scanned the German vessel's deck, homing in on the Captain, who was standing at the bow of the ship with another officer, their glares directed at the *Wilmington*. None of the guns were manned. They were simply studying the gunboat.

"Tell *Wilmington* — 'turn to port, show 'em your ass.'" O'Neill ordered.

"Sir?"

"Moon the bastards! They're window shopping," O'Neill crowed. He waited for the signal to be sent then watched for Todd to take heed of his advice. He did. The *Wilmington* bent their approach even more to port, slowing to a standstill to avoid an approach to the shoreline. As O'Neill thought, the *Charlotte* veered away to starboard and sped up, headed out to sea.

O'Neill sighed. He took out the notepad he carried in his overcoat pocket, scratched out a message, and handed it to the signalman. "Get back to the telegraph and sent this to Key West."

"Sir, the Germans would surely intercept," the signalman balked as he took the message.

"I'm counting on that, sailor." O'Neill folded his arms across his chest and watched the stern of the *Charlotte* disappear in to the western horizon.

Kaiser Wilhelm mulled over the cable from Ziegler as his naval confidant, the long fork-bearded Admiral Tirpitz, leaned over his oak table and studied the map of the Atlantic Ocean. The imposingly large Admiral fondled the small blue markers along the American seaboard, and then turned his attention to the black markers, which designated his own fleet.

Wilhelm strutted to the large window overlooking the courtyard of his palace, slapped his riding crop into his armpit then folded his hands together in the small of his back and gazed out to the swirling scattered snow showers spitting down from the gray overcast. A chill shivered down through this neck and back. '*It would be winter in Germany soon,*' he thought. '*. . . And this would be a fine time of the year to be in Havana.*' His empire needed a place in the sun for this time of year. Haiti was a wasteland. He needed something more. '*Cuba, Florida, perhaps even Virginia, as Ziegler had described,*' he mused.

"Eight battle ships," Tirpitz growled as he read the details provided by Ziegler. His eyes grew hooded as an arrogant frown creased his face.

"The Americans?" Wilhelm turned and strutted back to the table. "I thought Ziegler indicated that ten ships were either floating or ready to be floated."

"I need eight battleships," Tirpitz clarified. "I would not worry about the Americans, your Excellency. They have small ships. That is all they have built. Tactically, they are only suited for defense or blockades in shallow water."

Wilhelm returned to his large desk and melted into his chair while Tirpitz remained at the map, moving the tokens around. "How does this change your plan?"

"We will need to wait until they clear the yard," Tirpitz noted as he looked up to the Kaiser and tilted his head enough that the dim light in the office gleamed off his bald head. His steel blue eyes were trained directly at Wilhelm. "Our Imperial Fleet can make quick work of them. But if we are to bring the world to its knees, I will need eight battleships."

"I would like a warm port for this time of year, Alfred." Wilhelm mused as he turned his head and glanced back out the large window. Frost had started to creep up the glass from the sill. "An Emperor of my stature deserves a place in the sun."

"As I have provided, Sire, Cuba and the West Indies will be ours once we reduce the Americans to a more submissive status. The plan —"

"Intercepted message, sire," the Kaiser's personal messenger scrambled into the room, interrupting Tirpitz in mid-thought. The Admiral glared angrily at the young soldier. "My apologies," he added, genuflecting toward Tirpitz as he handed the translated cable to Wilhelm.

"We have them," Wilhelm quickly read the cable, grinned and handed the message to Tirpitz. The Admiral stroked one side of his beard as he perused the message. He nodded his head in agreement. "They believe we are running from them," the Kaiser added.

"We should send the *Kiel* now," Tirpitz pursed his lips.

Wilhelm took out a prepared message from his desk, which on the outside he had scrawled "Ziegler" and handed it to the messenger as Tirpitz returned to perusing over the map, rearranging the tokens seemingly in random fashion. The messenger bent toward Wilhelm, snapped his heels, and scurried out to deliver the message.

'*This will be grand*,' the Kaiser thought.

Fitzhugh Lee watched in surprise from the Consulate window as the *Charlotte* steamed past the ramparts of Castle Morro and into Havana harbor. Through his spyglass, he monitored the large German national training ship as it slowed and waited for the harbor tugs to maneuver it into an open mooring.

"Would you look at that," Sam Carter noted as he stepped up next to Lee. "Looks like we've got someone else to worry about now."

"This is not good," Lee grumbled as he slogged away from the window and dropped into the high backed leather chair at his desk. He took out some paper, uncapped his pen then began mouthing the end of it in thought.

"Have we heard from Domingo?" Carter asked as he turned away from the window.

"No. Nothing," Lee said curtly as he mulled over what to relay in his message. He was disappointed that he was caught unaware of the German vessel coming. He was also concerned that his own pleas for a naval vessel to be positioned in the harbor had gone unheeded. He debated sending the signal to the *Maine* as he had worked out with Captain Sigsbee, but prudence reminded him this was not a clear threat. After all, it was just a training ship sliding into the harbor.

"Is it possible that Governor Blanco does not know about this then?" Carter asked as Lee's telegrapher busted into the office, his face blanched.

"Sir, Key West says that *Marblehead* reports a German training ship was headed out to sea a day ago."

"Well son, if the Kaiser is looking for it, you can let them know we found it," Lee noted sarcastically.

"They also said O'Neill added 'Tricky Dickey Pearce' in his transmission." Lee's eyes widened as he blankly stared at the messenger before the meaning of the code word finally registered. "Understood, son." he added with a brief grin.

As the telegrapher left the room, Carter cocked his head and asked, "That's a new one on me. Care to share what that was all about?"

"Baseball, son," Lee leaned back in his chair. "You know anything about baseball."

"I'm afraid not," Carter admitted.

"Baseball is an American sport, Samuel. Neither the

Kaiser or Blanco would know what we're talking about if they intercepted the transmission."

"Alright, why is this Pearce fellow so important?"

"Dickey Pearce was a ball player that invented a play that bluffed everybody — a bunt," Lee blew smoke toward the ceiling. "You know where the fielders play, son?"

"Yes sir."

"Well, the bunt used to be called the tricky hit, best used when the other team is sitting back and not expecting it. That message tells me that is what O'Neill thinks the Kaiser is doing. He thinks the Kaiser is moving his ships around to rattle McKinley's cage — to make them come closer for some reason."

"To see if McKinley will back down?"

"Or show his cards, if you follow me, kinda like poker. But that does not mean we need to let our guard down. I still think we should up the ante and bring a ship into Havana, and that's just what I am recommending. We can't let the Kaiser think we will not make a single comment on his move. If the *Wilmington* or *Marblehead* are no longer needed in Port-au-Prince, well they could very well make a statement by at least stopping off here on their way to Key West."

"I see."

"Let me finish this message up so you can get it sent back with the *Olivette*. If the Germans are listening, which both O'Neill and I think they are, we can't risk uncoded messages being intercepted.

Carter nodded. He understood and prepared the envelope to be sent back with McManus and Ames.

Part Four
January 1898
Havana. Cuba

Chapter 15

Sam Carter re-read the cryptic, scribbled message, wary that it could be a trap. He did not recall ever meeting Javier Polenta before, but Ramón at the Café Luz insisted this newspaperman was loyal to the cause. If what Polenta identified was true, the risk of set-up was well worth taking, Carter reckoned.

Dawn was less than an hour away when he slipped out the rear door of the Consulate about a half-hour before dawn and snaked through Havana's web of back alleys that Hernandon had revealed to him. These trash strewn, rat infested narrow passageways were highways for the underground insurgency, safe ways that seemed unknown to the Spanish soldiers, and now that he knew of them, valuable for Carter's freedom of movement. He slipped through the slime-covered cobblestone in the alley that led to the rear of the newspaper office, all the while nervously snapping his head side-to-side to be sure no one had caught a glimpse of him before he plunged deeper into the darkness. He felt his way along the cool, damp, slime covered block walls that seemed to go on forever, quietly shuffling his feet to assure he did not wake anything that might lay sleeping in his way. The only thing he stirred up was a thicket of lethargic flies. When he finally felt the building's corner, he followed the edge and inched his way to the door.

Carter's eyes wandered around to ensure nobody was watching him. The alley, the street in front, and the building all remained quiet. Spanish night patrol officers would have already relinquished control to Cuban patrol officers, and already headed back to the station for early relief. Carter turned back to the window on the door and peered inside, hoping his eyes would acclimate quickly, then knocked softly three times on the door, waited a few seconds, then knocked twice more, precisely as the message instructed. Movement. Seconds later, the door slowly cracked open, revealing Javier's candle lit round face, twisted and etched as if terrified.

"Señor Carter," Javier whispered, ushering him into the building. "Come in, please." Carter complied. Javier closed the door behind him, and then slipped a letter into his hand. "We found a letter that we are sure you would be very interested in."

"Gracias." Carter realized now was not the time to ask for clarification or even attempt to read the letter. Authentication would have to wait until he had some space and back at the Consulate. He slipped it deep inside a pocket he had sewn into his trouser pocket.

"We are certain it is in de Lôme's handwriting." Polenta revealed. Carter considered the importance of that revelation, especially that Dupay de Lôme, the Spanish minister to the United States, allegedly maintained a network of spies in Washington. He was certain that this letter would.

Carter nodded in appreciation then exited out toward the main boulevard. The street was still empty, but he sensed it would not be for long. Even though he had been inside only a few short minutes, the sun peeked over the horizon and had brightened the morning considerably. A speedy retreat at this point was more useful than stealth, he figured, so he double-timed across the boulevard and oriented himself back toward the Consulate but after only two steps, he froze. Two patrol officers had turned the corner a block in front of him. He thought through the curfews he was aware of, but realized at this point it was simply too late and too obvious to change his path. Instead of attracting attention by bolting, he just dipped his head, hid his face under his wide brimmed panama hat, and continued walking.

Carter mumbled "*buenos dias*" in rapid-fire Spanish to the police officers he passed them. Nothing happened. They did not stop him. He let out a deep breath, and maintained his pace. Once out of sight of the Cuban patrol officers, he quick-stepped back to the Consulate, a short walk from the newspaper office, and instead of using the front, more visible entrance, he slipped around the compound and entered through the rear.

"Well, I see we're up quite early this morning," Lee said, surprising Carter as he finished climbing the stairs and entered the office.

"A friend had to give me something." Carter did not want to admit Lee had scared the tar out of him.

"Considering what time it is, it must be illegal, immoral or something that implicates the Spanish," Lee joked. "It's not that McGeehan lady now, is it?"

"It is a letter," Carter noted without hearing Lee's last comment. "I'm pretty certain it's from de Lôme, but I need to authenticate that."

"The Spanish Minister? What does it say?" Lee asked, suddenly more interested.

"I haven't had a chance . . ."

"Down with autonomy! Down with autonomy!" A sudden burst of chanting in English shouted from the street below interrupted Carter before he could extract the letter from his pocket. He rushed to the window, followed by Lee and witnessed that in front of the newspaper office, where it had been placidly quiet when Carter had been only a few moments earlier, an unruly mob had swelled and collectively grew angry.

"*Yanquis*, go home," The crowd chanted, still in clear English. Carter spotted several uniformed men oddly mixed amidst well-dressed civilians. He could not help but assume they were loyal to the Spanish colonial government. Carter retrieved the spyglass that Lee had resting on the desk and focused on the growing chaos. Spanish military uniforms. His sighting confirmed his thought. The soldier's faces were also quite youthful, but it was clear that it was their egging on which incited the unruly mob into a pitched fever. The mass surged toward the newspaper office where violent beating concentrated on the door. The door briefly held off the pounding until one final surge of humanity shattered it free of the casing, collapsing it inward. Heinous shouts at their victory replaced the chants. A swarm spilled into the building.

"My God, it has started," Lee mumbled as he stood quietly at the window, helpless, his face blanched and long.

"Down with autonomy. Americans must go!" the chanting continued. Windows shattered as pieces from broken desks flew out through them and into the street. Typewriters followed, attracting the growing mob to attack the machines with the broken desk and chair legs.

Carter grew concerned in his silence as he thought about his confidant Javier's safety. As he watched the debacle spiral out of control, Lee gathered up some paper and hustled out of the office toward the radio room. Rotating the crank on the dynamo to charge the telegraph's battery, he scribbled down a message, worked through the translation into code, stretched his fingers and started tapping furiously at the single key.

"If this isn't enough to get a damned ship here, nothing will," Lee seethed as he hammered away on the telegraph key.

"Bastards," Carter hissed under his breath as he finally saw Polenta dragged out of the building and into the street. He counted five young men converge on the newspaperman, including one in uniform, and start kicking at the curled up body. Polenta's pleas for the beating to stop could be heard even in the Consulate, but the mob would not relent.

Carter heard gunshots. Further down the street, a line of Cuban patrol officers emerged and marched purposefully toward the crowd, their clubs raised in attack posture, arms locked to form a wall. The flank officer's weapon was drawn and raised toward the sky. Carter surmised he had been the one who fired the warning shot as the police officers marched closer. Another volley of gunfire. Carter saw that had finally attracted the now quieting crowd's attention. The riot fell flaccid. Spanish officers poked their heads out the door, and then disappeared. Back door, Carter reckoned. They were heading into the same alleys he used to head back to their garrison. The crowd's chaotic frenzy dissipated, retreating away from Polenta and the office, which now lay strewn about the street. As the mass of Cuban police passed the wounded man on the street in pursuit of the retreating crowd, one officer broke off to assist.

Carter zoomed onto Polenta's face as the officer turned him over. His face was bloodied and bruised; his body lay limp. A dutiful urge raced up Carter's spine. He dropped the spyglass on the desk and bolted toward the door.

"Where the hell are you going, son?" he heard Lee's voice raise an octave as he started out the door. Carter complied, turning around to face Lee. "What in God's name do you think you're doing, son?"

"The man needs help."

"And they want our heads." Lee's voice had jumped an octave.

"Right now, sir, I don't give a damn. If you are so concerned, just back me up," Carter spit back, then rushed out of the Consulate and headed into the street to help his new friend.

"I need to see him," Carter pushed by an officer groping to hold him back when he arrived at the scene. He broke free and kneeled next to Polenta. Blood dribbled onto Carter's hand. "Why?" Why did they do this?"

"The editorials —." Polenta pushed the words out through a bloody froth. "The letter —"

Carter remembered Polenta's paper had run several pieces supporting true autonomy for Cuba, scathingly attacking the agreement Spain and the United States had resolved. They had also accused the present government which Sagasta had formed was not much different from the 'Butcher' maintained prior to his forced resignation.

"The letter — get letter to America . . ." The words dropped out of Polenta's swollen, trembling lips just as he fell silent. Carter dropped his head.

"You should not be here, American," a police officer whispered. Carter looked up as the patrol officer gripped his shoulder. His eyes betrayed his loyalty. It was not for Spain. "This not a place for you right now. You may be next," the officer said, nodding his head toward Polenta.

Carter stared at the policeman as several of his

subordinates stooped to remove Polenta from the street. His warning registered. It was the simple truth. Rather than debating, Carter rose, watched the officers set Polenta's limp body into a horse-drawn cart, and head away. As the cart turned the corner and disappeared into the suddenly quiet morning, Carter heeded the officer's advice and headed back to the Consulate.

"Mr. Wainwright, meet me in the radio room right away," Captain Sigsbee's voice echoed through the narrow communications tube that connected the cabins on the *Maine*. Wainwright set aside the logs he was reviewing, shored up his tunic, and started fastening his buttons, but two knocks on his door announced the Captain passing by. He stepped out into the corridor and followed Sigsbee toward the tiny communications room adjacent to the bridge.

"Two dollars, sir," the signalman announced as Wainwright bent his gangly frame to enter.

"Are you certain that was all?" Sigsbee asked, standing next to the ensign, fidgeting with his jacket buttons.

"That was all sir. Two dollars."

"Fitz?" Wainwright asked.

"Yes, sir. It came from Consul Lee."

"Looks like it's blowing open," Sigsbee turned toward his command post but Wainwright stopped him at the open portal.

"Put the ship on full alert." Sigsbee sucked in a deep breath, tilted his head back, and blew out his breath slowly as if he were releasing a stream of cigar smoke. "We'll need to be ready for full steam in two hours."

"Yes, sir. Ready for full steam in two hours," Wainwright agreed. As Sigsbee skirted by him, headed for the bridge, he stepped toward the signalman and slipped him a paper scrap. "Send Roosevelt a request further instruction. Tell him we received two dollars. Code it appropriately."

"Yes sir," the sailor replied, turning back to his telegraph.

"Confidential. Only the Captain and I see the response. Is that clear?"

"Yes sir, right away sir." After cranking the dynamo, the

sailor flexed his fingers then started tapping on the round, worn black key.

Wainwright caught up with Sigsbee as the Captain detoured into the map room. The officers had prepared several potential routes over the past two weeks since they last had contact with Lee, but reviewing the course once more might find a few more minutes to shave off. The helmsman extracted a map of the Western Caribbean, dropped the roll onto the long, narrow table then headed to the set of weather instruments Sigsbee had insisted be installed.

Wainwright unrolled the dog-eared map, flattening it out with his open palms, and then secured the corners with large, rust tainted nuts. Wasting no time, Sigsbee traced the route with his finger. The helmsman handed the weather data to Wainwright then grabbed a straight edge and followed Sigsbee's finger, measuring the angle and scribbling numbers at the edge of the map.

"Bearing — two-zero-five degrees, south-south west once we get to open water," Sigsbee read off the map.

"Agreed, sir, nothing but open sea. Weather Bureau reports show calm seas," Wainwright replied as he glanced up from the reports and through the south facing portals.

"Plot the course and relay it to the bridge," Sigsbee ordered. "I will meet you there."

As the Captain exited, the helmsman scribbled down the plot coordinates off the map. "Keep me informed of the weather reports, sailor. Things change rather quickly down here," Wainwright ordered as he took the paper from the helmsman and strutted on his long legs along the battle gray bulkheads toward the bridge, delivering directives to eager crew chiefs mustered along the way. Coal passers scattered off to the coal bins, firefighters headed to the boilers and oilers fanned out to position the steam valves about the engine room and ready the twin screws for travel. Gunners jumped as Wainwright ordered, "Defensive status," then scrambled toward the armory to prepare the artillery and their big turret guns.

Wainwright snapped to attention, saluting Sigsbee as he

entered the bridge and handing him the coordinates. "The crew is at full alert, sir. She will be ready for full steam in two hours."

"Bearing two-zero-five, south-south-west when we are free to maneuver, Commander," Sigsbee read off to his coxswain.

"Aye, sir," First Class Oskar Anderson replied, stiffening at the controls.

"I hope this is not pre-mature," Sigsbee whispered as he pressed the snaps on his tunic together and adjusted his cap. Wainwright sensed trepidation in the Captain's voice. He knew that Sigsbee loathed waiting at full alert. It was nerve-wracking for everyone on board. He also knew that the situation in Cuba was not about to relent either, and if Lee had made his first call, the second, more urgent call was more than likely not long in coming.

Wainwright's stomach growled. He checked the time on his pocket-watch. Eight fifteen. He would normally have already eaten breakfast by now, his usual oatmeal, biscuit, apple and coffee. Just like Sigsbee. But this was no longer a normal morning. His stomach would have to wait. "I've got the walk-about," he noted.

Sigsbee nodded agreement. Wainwright stepped out and headed to the center stairwell, clomping along the steel platform that led to the center of the ship, before plunging down the stairwell to check on the boilers. He knew the most embarrassing condition for a vessel would be a lack of power when headed into battle. His boots clinked on the metal grated stairs until he reached the *Maine's* heart — the engine rooms, then worked his way through consecutive three-foot tall portals until a blast of heat greeted him at the entrance to two watertight fire-rooms.

"XO on deck!" Chief Engineer Patrick Howell announced as Wainwright stepped into the first fire-room. Everyone in the room snapped to attention and saluted.

"As you were, men," Wainwright quickly dismissed the salute. "Let's focus on our work rather than slapping at our foreheads. As far as I am concerned, no salutes at full alert. The

Captain is in concurrence. Just a 'yes sir' and get the damned job done! Do I make myself clear?"

"Yes, sir," the room erupted with a hurrah and buzzed into action. Passers shuffled coal from the bunkers to the firemen, firemen loaded the furnaces, and the engineers tended to the condensers. Large, round gauges moved as pressure built in the system. Satisfied, Wainwright exited, working his way through the second fire-room, and further on to the coal bunkers, where he spotted Assistant Engineer Frederick Bowers fussing again with the temperature indicators in coal bunker A-16.

"Problem, Bowers?" Wainwright prodded.

"Not a big problem, sir," Bowers quickly replied as he monitored and tapped at the gauges. "Just these damned temperature sensors seem to be poppin' off like lightnin' bugs in the summertime again."

"Better than not sensitive enough, don't you think?" Wainwright replied. "We talked about this before."

"Just saying, sir, that I'm afraid I'm going to miss the real one after all these false alarms."

Wainwright didn't think he needed to lecture the sailor again on what he had seen in his investigations of coal fires on other, less fortunate vessels. He remained silent and let Bowers work through his frustration.

"I suppose so, sir," Bowers finally relented.

"Just make sure this coal stays cool, and we won't have to worry about it lighting up on us. Carry on, Bowers." Wainwright said as he turned and proceeded back to the bridge. He detoured into the officer's mess and ordered up breakfast for him and the Captain — coffee and biscuits. He stopped off in the communications room and verified his message had been sent.

"The *Maine* is ready for departure, sir," Wainwright announced as he stepped into the bridge. To his surprise, a small table had been set near the front window with two steaming cups and a plate of biscuits. Sigsbee's face was already beaming.

"Coffee, black. I think Cookie said it was Cuban. And he brought up some fresh biscuits as well." Sigsbee said as he picked up one of the cups and sipped. Wainwright joined him. Bitter and stout — precisely the way the Captain liked his coffee.

"Thank you, Mr. Wainwright." Sigsbee mumbled as he sunk his teeth into the soft bread. "Now, we wait."

Commander Richardson Clover sat in the foyer of the White House's Oval Room, nervously waiting for Secretaries Roosevelt and Long to arrive for the hastily arranged Cabinet meeting. He fretted that his two-month tenure as the Chief Naval Intelligence Officer left him more a liability than an asset, more so now that a crisis appeared to be festering in Cuba. He wasn't as versed in the nuances of war precursors, nor was he as battle hardened as Wainwright. His tour of duty in the Northern Pacific paled in comparison to the storied Civil War legacy of his predecessor. Nevertheless, Roosevelt selected him to succeed Wainwright over several others with more impressive backgrounds, and he reckoned, that should be enough a vote of confidence in him.

Clover regarded the message from Wainwright as exactly what Roosevelt hoped to hear — Fitzhugh Lee's call for assistance would surely edge President McKinley closer to conclude that war with Spain was necessary and imminent. If General-Consul Lee feared enough for his life that he signaled the *Maine* for help, in code no less, then the Cuban situation must have decomposed and spiraled downward. '*Add the Germans to the mix, and paramount action on the Caribbean scene was surely now required*,' he surmised.

"Are you daft, man?" Long's voice bristled echoing in the chamber. Clover looked up to see the two Navy Secretaries marching with a determined pace down the hallway.

"No, sir, I am serious. Dead serious," Roosevelt responded.

"You're going to abandon everything here, including your family, just so that you can go bushwhacking against the Spaniards while Cuban mosquitoes feast on you?"

"We'll talk later, sir," Roosevelt harrumphed as Clover noticed his eye contact. The pair continued closing, but without saying another word.

"Good Morning, Commander." Roosevelt said, almost shouting as he neared.

"Good morning, sir." Clover vaulted to his feet.

"No time for frivolities, son," Roosevelt chastised as he stomped by, tugging on Clover's jacket sleeve. Clover grabbed his notes and hurried to catch up. "Follow my lead, Clover. Keep your chin up, back erect and exude confidence. Don't say anything to embarrass me," Roosevelt added.

"Yes, sir," Clover reflexively responded.

"And don't wait to be invited. Just walk in with us. We're a team now, you know, so we act like it," Roosevelt continued as the trio passed through the threshold into the briefing room where inside, McKinley appeared to have just entered through his rear entrance himself.

"Gentlemen," McKinley greeted as he set an armful of papers down on his desk. "Please sit down."

"Where is Sherman?" Long questioned, noticing the State Department's side of the table was empty. "He should be here."

McKinley's sour expression provided enough of a response for everyone.

"Let's get down to business, then," Roosevelt stated abruptly as he slung his suit coat onto his straight-backed chair and shoved his shirtsleeves up to his elbows. "It's going to hell in a hand basket down there and Fitz is looking for help. Will you authorize the *Maine* to steam into Havana now?"

"I cannot authorize that at this time," McKinley said. His eyes were hooded and his voice was atypically passive.

"We can't let the Germans just roll their warships in there without some sort of message that we're keen to their backroom deals?" Roosevelt clacked his teeth together. "What does Ambassador White have to say about what Wilhelm is trying to do?"

"Ambassador White is just that, Mr. Roosevelt. An Ambassador, not a spy!" Secretary Day defended. "And as for Spain, we do not yet have word from Day concerning the Spanish response to our request."

"We requested allowance? Are you kidding me?"

Roosevelt's tone was condescending.

"Isn't the word from Fitz answer enough?" Long asked.

"I would say provocative enough," Roosevelt groused.

"Mr. Clover. What facts do you have?" McKinley ignored Roosevelt.

"Lee has sent the designated 'pre-amble to distress' signal to Sigsbee, as I recall." Clover swallowed hard, feeling as if he had been purposely put on the spot by McKinley. Moving only his eyes, he glanced down to his notes. "The signal was not the one he agreed to use when danger was imminent."

Roosevelt glared at Clover with an expression that confirmed they would talk later. The Secretary was too polished to disrespect his own people in public.

"And what facts do you have about the Germans?" Roosevelt rattled in his chair. He clicked his teeth in an open, rather straight grin.

"I do not have any information about the German warship now in Havana harbor," Clover noted sheepishly.

"So your spies have nothing either?" Day injected, impishly.

"But they now have five — count them five warships at Port-au-Prince," Roosevelt growled back.

"That, sir, is a fact," Clover tried to save some face.

"And they could move at any time," Roosevelt continued his grilling.

"That would be more conjecture on what the Kaiser is planning to do," Clover responded, his voice low, his words chosen carefully. McKinley clearly monitored the grilling of Clover, grateful that Roosevelt appeared to have a new target.

"May I suggest then a compromise, sir," Long then interrupted.

"I would like to hear those thoughts John?" McKinley sat back in his chair, receptive.

"We have the *Texas* steaming toward Key West right now," Long countered. "She is due to dock in Key West by the twenty-third. We can telegraph ahead and have her head for Cuba at that point. That delay should buy Secretary Day the time he needs to convince the Spaniards our intentions are purposeful. Alternatively, if all hell breaks loose, we can send word for the *Texas* to veer off to Havana. Would you agree?"

McKinley rose from his chair and walked slowly to the frost-covered window. He folded his hands behind his back, clearly mulling over Long's suggestion. After a moment, he turned back toward the room. "There is no way we are getting out of this, are we?" he asked.

Clover recognized that Roosevelt finally had the answer he wanted.

Chapter 16

Alabama felt strange and foreign to Carl DeLauro. In stark contrast to what he had grown accustomed to for January, the weather here was rather mild. His long-sleeved flannel shirt adequately staved off what little chill tainted the air. Snow was absent from the ground — though through the broken slats on the boxcar, the fields that spread out were spotted with rows of scraggly, wilted shrubs on which tufts of creamy white clung to their branches. He reckoned these must be the cotton fields he had heard about that were as much money in the south as coal was up north. He wondered if there was work for him here.

A sharp pain stung him at his waist — he had to urinate. He was hungry too. Save the couple of hard tack biscuits he and Kern had scrounged that morning, he had not eaten the entire day. He hoped that they would travel through a town that had at least some small tavern or bistro where they could hop off and get something a bit more substantial. Another pang doubled him over. He had to go. He gathered himself as the train whistle sounded several whistle peeps in succession, and strained to stand up without spotting his pants. He then stiffly stumbled toward the cracked open door.

The train whistle sounded a couple more times as he unbuttoned his pants. He grasped the door with one hand and started to relieve himself. The stream piddled out, stinging as it passed, then bending toward the rear of the train. Out in front of him, there was nothing but a wide-open field as far as he could see, browned and broken, only stubble left to be turned over in the spring. The pain intensified. He clenched his teeth and squeezed his eyes shut to manage the pain while he pushed out a couple last, weak squirts.

The train suddenly jerked. DeLauro staggered.

"Kern!" he called out as he lost balance and fell forward out of the open doorway. He twisted his body to recover, but when his shoe slipped on a crusted over cow pile, his knees buckled and his chest thumped onto the floor. His grip on the door slipped. His legs, now outside the rail, dangled precariously close the moving ground. Rusted steel on the door rail chaffed at his chin as he struggled to pull his legs in and avoid catching his feet on the railroad ties passing rapidly underneath.

"*HELP!*" DeLauro bleated. His hands slipped again. He saw Kern turn over and sit up as the train jerked once more. Its brakes squealed. DeLauro's fingers lost the tenuous grip on the cracks between the floorboards. Kern moved, but when a sprawling sumac whacked him on his back, he realized Kern would not reach him.

Ziegler looked over the edge through the open door and watched DeLauro's body hit the rail in front of squealing metal wheels then disintegrate into bloody, dismembered body parts along the metal track. A tight-lipped smile cracked his lips. Since the excursion into the Navy yard, he had wondered how he was going to get rid of DeLauro. Fate had just served him his solution. He returned to his corner and went back to sleep.

Ziegler woke an hour later and watched out the open door of the boxcar as the train slowed and started a sharp westerly bend, the location that he reconnoitered would be closest to his next objective. He scanned briefly for a soft landing spot, and when he spotted an adequate location, jumped off, tucked his satchel of tools into his belly, and then barrel-rolled into a patch of scrub along the track. He recovered quickly before orienting himself in the direction of the mines and headed out. After another hour of traipsing near open, rolling fields of oddly tufted scraggy brush, he noticed a rutted road headed off toward the north. He chose the pathway and continued until he spotted a series of small, run down wooden shacks where several black-skinned men milled about.

"Coal mines?" Ziegler asked as he approached. The men silently inspected every inch of Ziegler. "Mines?" he repeated, swinging his arms as if he were using a pickaxe.

The tallest man, standing close to six feet tall, twisted his eyebrows and grimaced before slowly raising his arm and pointing further to the west. Ziegler nodded a thank you and headed in the direction he had been given, glancing back at the gathering over his shoulder to be sure they weren't following him. It wasn't so much he felt that he couldn't take them all — each one seemed sinewy and weak. It was more he just didn't want to deal with it. As the black men faded from his view in the distance, he plotted though how he was to get to the colliers destined to fuel the Navy ships, which he had recently determined were mustering in the Keys.

Sam Carter thought winter cold was his least concern since he had convinced Director Wilkie to meet him in Florida rather than Washington. The weather though, chose not to cooperate. Tampa was miserably cold, even for January, he thought as he managed the brisk walk between the dock and the Tampa Bay Hotel. The only solace today was that cold winter rains were holding off.

The commute from Havana on the *Olivette* was eventless and Captain McManus had once again deftly plied his mastery of the choppy Western Caribbean, arriving in Tampa ten minutes ahead of schedule. Carter thought it a quiet trip excepting a nosy sugar baron that dogged him the entire voyage from Havana. He wondered how many of these portly, well-heeled men should be watched more closely for their activity, but that was no longer his primary focus. He stopped for a moment and mused at the relatively new hotel Consul Lee recommended for any excursion back to Tampa. On the outside, it was as ornate as any hotel he had seen in Washington, excepting what seemed to be throngs of soldiers and officers milling about the grounds. He drew little attention

269

as he slipped by the men and into the posh entrance and foyer. Once the door closed behind him, he took a moment to thaw out. Nervously, he re-checked his trousers, as he had done his entire trip from the island, to assure the letter Polenta insisted be presented to American authorities was still in his possession. It was.

Before he left Havana, Lee authenticated the letter to be from Spanish Minister de Lôme. It was clearly not meant to be seen by American authorities, since the incendiary tone was as Polenta had implicated. Indirectly, the letter confirmed the delay tactics the Spanish government had been using during negotiations were intentional, used primarily to show a total lack of respect for a weak willed McKinley.

Carter melted into an overstuffed chair sitting in the reception area off the foyer. Many of the businessmen that had travelled with him from Havana on the *Olivette* had already checked in, breezed through the dining area and headed directly toward the bar. A sparse few gathered in the far corner and separated from officers who had chosen to take an early dinner. Four o'clock, Carter heard the large grandfather clock in the foyer chime. Wilkie was due to arrive at six, but he still scanned the room to assure Wilkie had still not arrived. He hadn't. All the better for him, he thought, reckoning that two hours should provide him enough time to bathe and clean up enough that Wilkie would not badger him about his hygiene.

'If the man had spent a bit more time in field operations, he might be a bit more understanding,' Carter thought. He pushed himself up from the chair, acquired a room, and headed up to his room to bathe and warm up. Once he dropped his personal anchor near the sofa in his room, he wasted little time in drawing a bath, stripping and slipping into the hot water even before it had covered the bottom of the tub. It had been a week since he had taken the time to clean off crusted sweat and dust accumulated on him while he weaved through the chaotic whirlwind that Havana had become. He leaned back, draped his arms over the edges of the tub and let the pain ease out of his muscles, then closed his eyes and let the warmth penetrate through his skin.

A sharp knocking on the door startled Carter.

"Who is it," he startled, realizing that he must have dozed off. He stepped out of the claw-foot tub, quickly dabbed himself dry, then groped into his satchel for a fresh pair of trousers.

"Mr. Carter? There is a Mr. Wilkie here to see you," the gentleman's voice announced.

"Son-of-a-bitch, he's early. It's only five-thirty," Carter muttered, seething as he glanced down to his pocket watch. He grabbed an unworn shirt and punched his arms through the sleeves. "Tell him I will meet him in the lobby. Ten minutes."

"Yes, Mr. Carter," the voice replied. Footsteps headed away from the door. Carter finished dressing, slipped the de Lôme letter into his pants pocket, and then sauntered out onto the balcony overlooking the posh dining area. He spotted Wilkie sitting in a corner, fondling his cigar. Carter proceeded across the balcony to the stairs and descended into the dining area, waving off the concierge as he headed directly toward Wilkie.

"Good evening, sir." Carter said as he pulled out his chair and sat. The goblet of water before him had the color of weak tea. He chose not to take a sip.

"What do you have that is so urgent?" Wilkie groused and adjusted his thin wire-rimmed glasses. Carter recoiled at Wilkie's "I'm a busy man, let's get on with it" expression before taking out the letter and slipping across the table.

"Are you sure this is de Lôme's handwriting?" Wilkie said as he impatiently flipped open the envelope and unfolded the letter. His eyes bulged and a devilish grin cracked open his mouth as soon as he started reading. The short-lived smile decomposed to a scowl.

"General Lee and I confirmed it with some other letters we had on file.

"Who knows about this?" Wilkie's eyes skewered Carter.

"I am not sure, sir, but —" Carter held back his conjecture, remembering Wilkie's response the last time he provided his opinion to the man.

"This is excellent work, Carter," Wilkie sat back for a

moment mulling over the letter. He was clearly enjoying the moment of having the letter in his possession. "Excellent work."

Carter thanked the waiter when he appeared with his drink and quickly took a swallow. Once the waiter left, he asked, "Do you know if the supplies have been shipped to Garcia?"

"That is not your concern, Carter," Wilkie's mercuric and icy cold response stunned Carter. "We will make sure that Garcia gets what he needs."

"I see," Carter felt chilled. This letter now provided a reason, although a weak one he thought, for the United States to threaten invasion into Cuba.

"You appear as if you have something more to add, Mr. Carter?" Wilkie leaned forward and tented his fingers in front of his lips. Carter felt penetrated by his stare.

"Yes, sir," Carter recognized an opening. "There is anti-American sentiment festering in Havana, as it is in the other cities which the Spaniards tightly control. Anarchists are actively agitating as well — they're slipping in from the other islands."

"I'm aware of all of that," Wilkie said. He leaned back and slipped the letter into his jacket breast pocket. "You have more?"

"There are loyalist factions — Weylerites. Havana is spiraling out of control," Carter whispered.

"Noted, Mr. Carter," Wilkie said bluntly, and then cursorily glanced at his pocket watch before snapping it shut. "My train leaves for Washington in an hour, and you need to get back to Havana right away," he added as he vaulted up from his chair and hand pressed his suit.

Before Carter could respond, Wilkie surveyed the room for a moment, then turned back and leaned into the table. "Monitor the Spaniards — and what preparations they are making toward conflict. I need daily reports."

"The General already provides all that to Secretary Day," Carter protested, although mildly.

"It is *Consul* Lee. The war is over, Mr. Carter," Wilkie scowled and peered over his glasses with wide eyes that shouted disapproval with Carter's questions. "Secretary Day works for the State Department, as does *Consul* Lee. I work for Roosevelt. You work for me. I thought we had all of that squared away. Day and Roosevelt spar with the information from all over the world. In addition, I need to have the same intelligence that Day is receiving so I can keep Roosevelt briefed. It's the way Washington works, get it?"

"So you want me to spy on Lee?" Carter prodded.

"No, you imbecile. You are spying on the Spaniards, the Cubans, and for that matter, the Germans — they are down there as well, if you didn't know."

'I believe I gave you that information,' Carter stewed under his breath. For the first time in his short career, he wondered if he really wanted to continue.

"I need you down there right away — to keep me informed." Wilkie's soft delivery contrasted his dour stare.

"The *Olivette* has already left and won't return for two days," Carter noted.

"Key West ferry — travels tonight. If you hurry, you should be able to make it. Once there, get onto the *Maine*. It will be heading to Havana shortly," Wilkie said under his breath.

'Havana — the Maine?' That revelation stunned Carter. "A Navy vessel? They will allow me to board —"

"Use this," Wilkie snapped out an envelope from his jacket pocket and dropped it on the table. He stood, glared down at Carter and added, "I expect you on that ship tomorrow, Mr. Carter. Do I make myself clear?"

"Yes sir," Carter coldly replied.

"Good," Wilkie blurted before spinning around and strutting deep into the swelling evening dinner crowd. Instead of trying to chase Wilkie down, Carter sat back and squeezed his forehead as he tried to sort out what he wanted and what he needed to do.

"Mind if I join you, Mr. Carter?" a faceless voice asked from behind Carter. He turned his head enough to see a well-dressed woman standing next to him. Her thin lips stretched into a narrow smile.

"Not at all," Carter replied absently, still reeling from Wilkie's demands. The auburn-haired woman gracefully moved toward the chair vacated by Wilkie and hovered, as if waiting for Carter to respond. When Carter noticed her eyeing the chair, he blushed, realizing the betrayal to his upbringing. "Please, pardon my manners," Carter stood quickly and tugged at the chair, which squeaked loudly against the wooden floor.

"Thank you," she replied, smoothing her long dress before Carter slid the chair underneath her. Carter caught a waft of perfume that reminded him of springtime in Charleston.

'Gardenia,' he thought returning to his seat, still blushing slightly at his own awkwardness. As he settled into his seat, the young woman leaned forward and twitched her eyebrows.

"That rat-faced man you were with before seemed quite rude," the lady commented as Carter took his seat.

"Reporter," Carter lied. "They are always looking for information."

"He didn't sound like a reporter."

"He's — he's my boss," Carter stepped carefully through what he wanted to say.

"I do not believe you are a reporter, but I do believe I think I know what you are avoiding to tell me."

"How do you —" Carter's gaze froze on the woman's eyes.

"But that's fine. I understand," she finished. Carter sensed a familiarity in her soft face, but he could not immediately place it. Her alluring green eyes grabbed his attention.

"My father told me about you," the woman replied after a moment. "As did Consul-General Lee." An inviting smile returned to her face. Carter grew uncomfortable and could feel perspiration seep into his shirt collar. He tried not to stare, but could not restrain himself as he racked his mind to recall where they had met. Her face was too light complexioned to have spent any time in Cuba, he thought and he did not remember any other place where he may have met someone with her apparent affluent background. "The *Olivette*," the woman arched her eyebrows.

Carter startled, suddenly realizing his gaze was fixed

intently on the woman's face. "I apologize. I did not mean to stare," he atoned.

"No offense, Mr. Carter. I assumed you are trying to remember where you saw me?" she then added with a soft giggle.

"Your father was the . . ." Carter clutched, realizing he was about to insult her father. "The sugar baron. McGeehan?" Mentioning the ship was enough to spark Carter's memory. When the nosy sugar baron badgered him about how much the crisis in Cuba was going to adversely affect his business, she was hovering noticeably nearby. Their eyes met several times, but the old man's incessant whining precluded any contact at that time. "Yes, yes, now I remember," Carter admitted.

"He can be such a bore at times. He is always so focused on business and imports, as if he doesn't already have enough," the woman noted.

"I believe you have me at a disadvantage, since you seem to know who I am and the reverse is not true," Carter said.

"Oh, pardon my manners," the woman blushed. "Annette. Annette McGeehan."

"Annette," The name rolled off Carter's lips. "That is a rather lovely name." Carter could not help himself as he regarded Annette more carefully and realized he had seen her several times before. He felt himself stumble over what to say, and then blurted, "Perhaps you would care to join me for dinner? I have not had dinner yet."

"I would, Mr. Carter."

"Sam."

"Yes, Sam, I would like that. Otherwise, I would have to suffer through another business meeting with my father. And that is something I would prefer not to do so," Annette rolled her eyes, and then smiled.

Carter hailed for the waiter, now scurrying about the rapidly filling dining area. When he caught the man's eye, he motioned for two menus. The waiter confirmed with a nod.

"I do appreciate your invitation, Mr. Carter — Sam, but I should at least let my father know I've found more interesting company," Annette said as she pushed back from the table. Carter vaulted up to help, but was too late as Annette was already sauntering toward a table across the room where her father, the nosy sugar baron, had already commenced what appeared to be an ad hoc business meeting. After a few words, he turned and stared at Carter with owl-like eyes, but they quickly softened as he waved.

Carter checked his pocket watch quickly and realized their dinner would need to be cut short. The schedule Wilkie provided left him a short two hours before he would need to be at the docks. If he missed the ferry, he was sure there would be another opportunity in the morning. As he mulled over his options, a faint scent of gardenias wafted into his nose, redirecting his thoughts.

"Perhaps I should learn to be a bit more polite to strangers when I am traveling," Carter commented as he met Annette as she returned, standing at her chair. With a touch more class this time, Carter courteously helped her back into her seat at the table.

"Perhaps you do, Mr. Carter. And maybe even a bit more observant?" Annette said as Carter took his seat. He sensed leaving for Key West tonight had just been made a more difficult task.

"Who knows about this?" President McKinley demanded, his hands demonstratively shaking as he read the Spanish minister's letter. He chewed on his lower lip, clearly perturbed with the written innuendo.

"I am not sure, sir," Wilkie lied as he watched McKinley closely. He sat back in his chair, trying to hide his smirk. He had provided a copy of the letter to Roosevelt as well as a copy to a young reporter at the New York Journal, insisting that it be published as soon as it could. As a former newspaperman, he knew the value of a scoop like this one. He calculated that it would agitate the public into fever since it not only insulted McKinley, but also the fabric of America. McKinley would have to succumb to the public demands for an immediate declaration of war on Spain. And Roosevelt would be ecstatic with him. "Carter indicated he obtained it from belligerents in Cuba. If they have contacts with the press, here or there, it could very well go anywhere."

"I am man enough to take a few insults written in a personal letter, but to state that the United States is weak — that is intolerable," McKinley growled loudly.

"I got here as soon as I could, sir," Secretary Day blurted as he briskly walked into the conference room.

"Look at this. I believe our problem has just erupted into a major issue." McKinley extended his arm emphatically, throwing the letter at Day as he stood and stomped toward the window. He folded his hands behind his back and stared out into the cold January day.

Day's eyes ballooned, bulging from their sockets as he read each line. When he was done, he dropped the letter in front of Wilkie. "When did you get this?"

"As I had informed the President, sir, I just received it from my operative in Havana." Wilkie felt energized with his debauchery.

"Havana? Can't be— de Lôme is here — in Washington." Day's eyes hooded. Wilkie simply nodded.

"You need to discuss this with the Spanish Consulate, William. Perhaps even de Lôme himself. If this is authentic and not some sort of forgery, the least I would expect would be an apology," McKinley directed. Day leaned forward and began taking notes. Wilkie sat back and reveled in the angst filling the room.

"And I personally demand his resignation. The entire Spanish Government, Queen Regent included, needs to know that I am greatly disappointed that even as we have been deliberate in our negotiations, they have not been forthright." McKinley's breathing was labored.

"You do realize sir, that . . ."

"Of course I do. What kind of fool do you think I am? I can already see Roosevelt's teeth gleaming like a damned Cheshire cat." McKinley interjected as he stomped back to his desk. Placing his hands flat on the solid oak desk, he practically bowed as he shook his head. "But we need to ensure he clearly understands this is not, and I stress, *not* a carte blanche invitation to start preaching from his bully pulpit again."

"What about the *Maine*, sir?" Day prodded. "Has this crossed the line?"

"I certainly hope that fool realizes what he has done." McKinley mumbled.

"Sigsbee?" Day asked, confused.

"No. de Lôme. I have tried to be patient with him. I have tried to let him work out his differences with the Cubans." McKinley grabbed the letter and furiously shook it in Day's direction. "But how the hell do I hold off from doing anything now? You do realize what the Yellow Press will do with this one?"

"We do not need to go public with this yet, do we?"

"Mr. Day. This letter was obtained —"

"From a newspaper office in Havana," Wilkie finished for the President when he glanced over to him.

"For all I know, some damned reporter already delivered it to the New York Journal. Hearst has an army of cockroaches crawling around down there. You saw what they did with the Cisneros issue. As embarrassing as that was, it pales in comparison to the outrage this will incite," McKinley icily stared at Day.

"Back to the *Maine* sir. I still do not have a response from Spain concerning sending a 'friendly' military ship to Havana."

"Right now, I don't care. This man and this government have tried our patience once too many times. I dare say the Queen Regent cannot be party to these demonic acts and still expect our friendship."

"Perhaps we can re-direct the *Texas* instead. I believe we can send word for her to break off and go directly into the Harbor rather than head to Key West."

"Who's got that boat?"

"Captain Philip, sir," Day replied.

"No, I know Sigsbee. He's more level headed and I feel he would handle this better. And I am sure the *Maine* will provide enough of a visual reminder that we mean business."

"Send the *Maine* without a response on our request?"

"Just amend our original request to a statement of what we are going to do. Right now, I do not care if they agree or disagree. A clear message must be sent. We will not be used in this manner." McKinley wagged his finger, as if scolding Day. He then added under his breath, "I'll show this bastard who is spineless."

"I understand sir. Send the *Maine*. Do you want me to provide that request to Long?"

"Is that the proper protocol?"

"Yes, sir."

"Consider it your first business when you leave," McKinley said as he grabbed the de Lôme letter and read it again. After a moment, he looked up to Wilkie. "I need you to keep tabs of where this letter is and where it has been. And before some newspaper prints this, which I am sure it will, I need to know. I will prepare my response now so I can properly address the pandemonium when Hearst and his band of cronies publish this."

"And Cuba, sir?"

"I need to know what is really going on down there. I don't care if I get it from Lee, Carter, or anyone else. I need to know what is going on down there — before Roosevelt knows. Is that clear gentlemen?"

"Yes, sir," Day and Wilkie responded in unison.

"Mr. Wilkie, you may leave. Mr. Day and I have some damage control to address." McKinley finished.

Chapter 17

Captain Sigsbee was anxious. He could not wait any longer for a follow-up message. Two days had passed since Consul-General Lee sent his first message. Personally frustrated, he ordered his crew to stand down from full alert status, since maintaining that posture in port had already created a myriad of problems that he preferred not to have to manage. Arguments between his officers and the enlisted men had increased in number and intensity. One sailor was already cooling off in the brig, and another needed medical treatment after a round of fisticuffs had spiraled out of control. Coal reserves had dwindled to such a critically low level that he needed to call up a collier to refuel.

He had heard through Wainwright that a large German battle cruiser had already departed Port-au-Prince for Havana, and several others were on their way. That was one distinct advantage of having a former Navy spy as his XO —good intelligence. His old friend Cyrus McManus, the Captain of the *Olivette*, docked one evening that provided him additional intelligence amidst McManus's complaints of now having to dodge Navy ships on his runs through the Caribbean.

Morning passed arduously with no additional word from Lee. Since it was all quiet at this juncture, Sigsbee needed to work around the rules and get more intelligence about what was really going on. He left Lieutenant John Wood, his brash, primary understudy in command for the afternoon, and with Wainwright, headed off the ship to obtain a more secure communication link to Washington. After departing the *Maine*, he and Commander Wainwright started marching along the pier toward the communications bunker, but when they were halfway there, Sigsbee's attention reversed, recognizing a distinct horn approaching through the west channel.

"*Texas*," he muttered, stopped, and turned toward the sounds. Trailing behind the *Texas* were plumes from at least ten other warships swirling into the sky, commencing a queue for harbor entry. With all the grace of a ship of sail, the *Maine's* sister proudly entered the harbor just before reducing her forward speed. Sheets of water at the vessel's cutwater lost their froth and dissipated to nothing more than a rippled wake. Tugs sitting low in the water motored out and in short order reached the white-hulled cruiser to start their task of bringing her to mooring.

"I didn't reckon they'd be here so soon," Sigsbee said as he watched tugs kiss up to the *Texas*. Over his shoulder, he told Wainwright, "Why don't you head on in and ring up Washington. I've got an old friend to welcome."

Wainwright acknowledged, continuing on toward the communications station while Sigsbee waited for the *Texas* and his old friend Captain John Woodward Philip to dock. He did not have to wait long. The workhorse tugs made short work of mooring the cruiser. Sigsbee beamed when he saw his longtime friend, Captain Philip, standing anxiously at the head of the gangplank. The *Texas's* engines rumbled down to idle as her large propeller shafts were disengaged. Forward movement slowed then ceased. No sooner than the first notes from the boatswain's pipe were sounded, the safety chains dropped and Captain Philip wasted little time heading down the boarding plank.

"Great to see you, Woody," Sigsbee snapped to attention and crisply saluted when Philip's feet touched the pier.

"Heard some scuttlebutt about you, Sigs. Wainwright's your XO now?" Philip whispered as he offered a handshake, frowning as he reconnoitered for listening ears.

"That would be correct," Sigsbee replied.

"Commander Richard Wainwright? ONI?" Philip's eyes

were darting anxiously examining Sigsbee from head to toe. "I thought you wanted Marix —"

"He's a fine XO, Woody. I'm not under investigation, if that is what you're thinking."

"Then is Marix in the doghouse?"

"You know Marix would be an excellent commander. I'm thinking Rosey is running out of good men to run all those ships he's hammering together."

"But Wainwright? There had to be some other officers, don't you think?" Philip still appeared wary.

"I'm guessing Rosey just figured he needed some more Naval Intelligence down here. I'm not about to complain if I can keep the *Maine*."

"Just looks a bit irregular, Sigs, if you know what I mean. It's got a lot of people talking, you know."

"We all have our crosses to bear I guess. Listen, you got time for coffee and a chat?" Sigsbee offered. "They've kept me in the dark lately, and I figure you've got some updated poop, eh? If it's worth anything, I think the swill here is pretty good for a Navy base."

"Maybe I'll grab a quick one, Sigs. You know how Admiral Sampson gets when he's in charge," Philip said as he looked out toward the channel inlet. The balance of the North Atlantic Squadron began queuing into the harbor as five colliers and two ferries yielded patiently for the large ships to berth. One by one, and at reduced speed so as not to create an unmanageable wake for harbor traffic, the battleships lumbered into the port. The last to enter was the *New York*, the flagship of the fleet. "I'll need to get used to it if we're tied up here for a bit."

"It's not that bad, Woody, but it does look like you've got some time now," Sigsbee noted. He figured it would be close to half an hour before the tugs would put the huge *New York* into its mooring, and urged his old friend toward the cafeteria.

Once inside, Sigsbee and Philip hovered for a moment at the table closest to the kitchen, where four coffee mugs had already been set out, as if waiting for them. Philip sat down as a sailor with a bleached white apron appeared with a steaming metal carafe and filled three of the mugs and headed back to the kitchen. Behind him approached a tall lanky officer.

"This is Commander Wainwright, my XO." Sigsbee offered, pointing to his second in command as he approached.

"Captain," Wainwright said as he followed official protocol; stopping, saluting and maintaining an officially correct straight face. Philip stood and returned the salute, then offered a tentative handshake.

"Pleasure to meet you, sir," Philip offered as he sat back down, his eyes still wide and wary.

"*Formerly* ONI," Wainwright added as he sat down. "Secretary Roosevelt asked me to take this position — special assignment."

"Catch anything on the telephone, Commander?" Sigsbee asked Wainwright.

"Couldn't get through," Wainwright admitted as he poured himself a coffee.

"Never thought I'd be considered a courier, Sigs, but I've got this — supposedly from McKinley himself." Philip pulled an envelope out from the inside pocket of his tunic and offered it to Sigsbee as he took a sip of his coffee.

"What do you think it says, Woody?" Sigsbee asked as he slurped a mouthful from his steaming mug.

"There's a lot of saber rattling going on up there in Washington." Philip offered. "Something's definitely brewing. You've been down here longer than we have. You know anything?"

"Squat. We've been ordered mute since we left Norfolk," Sigsbee muttered as he looked over envelope carefully. He flipped it over and noticed the Presidential seal on it. He fondled the envelope a moment longer then slipped a butter knife under the flap and split the seal. He pulled out the message, read it quickly, and then handed it to Wainwright.

"Old Fitzie ought to be happy with this one," Sigsbee commented as he took a mouthful of the coffee. He forced it down his throat with a wince, not expecting the bite it offered this morning.

"So is it true? You headed to Havana?" Philip asked,

placing his cup back onto the table.

"You are to provide American presence there as a 'friendly' visit?" Wainwright chuckled as he read from the orders. He handed them to Philip, who at first did not take the orders. "We are all in the same navy, Captain Philip. I believe you are allowed to read confidential orders once they have been delivered properly."

"I heard the Kaiser has already sent a couple of warships there, Sigs. Sounds like the harbor is going to be a bit on the crowded side," Philip added as he perused the message quickly before passing it back to Sigsbee.

"Well then, Commander, looks like we have some good news for our crew," Sigsbee said to Wainwright, then turned back to Philip, "And I would bet that Roosevelt will soon be getting the nice little war he's been hankering for."

"I wouldn't get too cocky, Sigs," Philip said as he stood. "I think Spain is a bit scared right now, and you know what they say about a cornered rat."

"I've got a good crew, Woody. They'll keep us safe. But if anything breaks out, you will be the first I'll call – as long as you don't let that boat of your's sink again." Sigsbee smirked. The entire Navy joked about the *Texas* having one problem after another, but at least he sensed that Philip would take a comment from him in good humor.

"They've worked out the problems, Sigs. I told them that I wouldn't take it out to sea if I didn't get the guarantee she'd float."

"You take care of yourself, Woody. I got the feeling this will get ugly before God sorts it all out."

"You too, Sigs." Phillip extended his right hand to clasp his old friend's. He covered Sigsbee's hand with his free, left hand as the men exchanged knowing glances of what they may be facing all too soon. The circumstances did not portend their departing as routine anymore.

"Mr. Wainwright, I believe destiny awaits us in Havana," Sigsbee stood, and with Wainwright by his side, headed back toward his boat.

As Sigsbee and Wainwright marched down the pier to the

Maine, they watched the coaling vessels, their hulls low in the grey, green water; kiss up against ships that eagerly awaiting to be refueled. Lines flew out from the colliers to their appointed rounds, and as they were stretched tight and knotted, laborers on top side decks sent bins into the bowels to cradle their life giving black gold to the big white vessels.

The *Maine*, Wilhelm Ziegler chuckled as he overheard the other black-faced coalers on the collier whisper the name of the ship they were cinching up next to. '*People all over the world will remember the Maine.*'

Ziegler had easily worked his way onto this work group, since most of the men at the docks shied away for fear of water. They were all mostly muscle-ripped black men with ragged, dirty shirts, torn pants, and mismatched boots. On the dock, he melded into a pack of laborers, and then slipped in as one of the colliers' crew that waited to head out and load the ships docked at Key West. The ride was not unpleasant, considering it was winter — it was warm enough below decks near the additional piles of coal they would unload.

As the collier approached their intended off-load point, Ziegler sat on the deck of a coal boat, a stone's throw away from what he had discovered was one of the most important cruisers in the US Navy. This was one of the vessels Wilhelm needed to worry about for the "Tirpitz Plan,' as Ziegler called it. It would be a formidable defender — but if his personal plan worked, the balance would shift to the Fatherland.

"Dig!" the order was shouted down from the Captain's bridge, a small coal dust covered shack that seemed to be cobbled onto the collier. Ziegler stood, followed the coalers back down metal stairs and into the dust filled hold, where he was handed a wide mouthed shovel by a grizzly old sailor. The digging was hard work, Ziegler thought as he started shoveling the coal into an empty rigged bin. Choking dust rose quickly around him as he shoveled harder and faster to get the job done, but when he noticed the men around him using handkerchiefs to cover their noses and mouths, he followed suit.

Bin after bin were filled, hoisted over to the Maine, and then returned, hungry and empty for more coal. As the hold emptied and the last bin was started to be filled, Ziegler bent over and rested. He slipped his hand into his front trouser pocket and extracted a small airtight container. Wrapped separately in the small bottle he had carefully placed iron filings, salt, and water with the exact recipe he had calculated would work like a delayed fuse. He cracked the glass, buried it in coal dust he had poured into a thin sock stolen from DeLauro, and then tossed the mix into the coal bin.

The laborers completed their task. The hold echoed in its emptiness as the last bin was hoisted out of the collier. Ziegler dragged himself up the ladder with the other temporary passers, and they all dropped, exhausted, to the deck of the collier, where the hoisters had already laid themselves out to cool off. Ziegler looked up to the *Maine* as the gristly old collier captain took the cue and started turning his boat away, headed back to Mobile. He would have preferred to steal onto the ship to ensure his incendiary device would work, but he reckoned he would need to find another way to follow the progress of his diversion.

"Captain on deck," shouted out a nameless voice as pipes sounded Sigsbee and Wainwright stepping onto the deck of the *Maine*.

"Immediate assembly," Sigsbee ordered to his boatswain.

"Yes, sir," Charles White smiled. He pulled out his pipe and whistled assembly. The tweets echoed out over the ship, stirring everyone into action — hard-soled shoes clomped on steel ladder rungs then hammered the metal decking as they converged on the main deck. It seemed that less than a minute had passed for the entire three hundred and seventy four member crew to gather for the Captain's words.

"We have our orders. Havana." That was all that Sigsbee had to say. A single, short approving roar rose from the gathered men. When enough silence returned, Sigsbee added, "We steam in thirty minutes, gentlemen. Dismissed!"

Sailors scurried out of formation as fast as they had

converged. A line of passers and firemen converged at a stairwell then disappeared into the bowels of the vessel, clomping their boots on each metal step as they headed for the boilers and coal bins. Gunners fanned out to their weapons, unplugged the barrels, piled artillery in holds nearby then started oiling the gears on the guns.

Sigsbee paraded about the upper deck, proud of the way he witnessed his crew responding. His concern for dulled complacency was belied. His men would be ready for anything. From out of the corner of his eye, Sigsbee spotted a collier pulling away from his ship's starboard side. He did not remember signing an order for a fresh supply of coal, even though there was probably a need to top off the bins. *'Perhaps Wainwright placed the order,'* he thought, making a mental note that he would verify that later.

His attention was diverted to the port side of his vessel. Once at the railing, he noticed a youngish man approaching, calling out to the Marines at the head of the dock. The red haired fellow seemed too well dressed to be one of the locals hoping for one last look, or for that matter, one of the tourists that lately seemed to be frequenting the military bases. Sigsbee focused on the Marines as they detained the fellow and inspected a set of presented papers. There was urgency in the way he pointed toward the *Maine*, and after few brief questions, the Marines stiffened to attention and let him pass.

"Would you look at that," Sigsbee grumbled as the fellow hurried down the pier toward his vessel. "Leave it!" he then ordered his men at the gangplank as the fellow neared. The men shot baffled looks toward Sigsbee, but complied, allowing the stranger to board.

"Captain Sigsbee?" Carter gasped for air as he spoke.

"I am." Sigsbee signaled for his men to hold off removing plank. He stoically regarded the comparatively young man before him, inspecting every inch of the civilian who was now trespassing on a Navy vessel. Even worse, his vessel.

"Sam Carter." Carter extended his hand to shake the Captain's.

"What the hell do you think you are doing? Do you realize

you almost got dunked?" Sigsbee growled as he raised one of his bushy white eyebrows and glared disapprovingly at Carter.

"Appreciate the transport to Cuba," Carter bent back over, still trying to catch his breath.

"Let me see what you buffaloed those boys with." Sigsbee demanded.

"Excuse me, sir?"

"Your papers!"

Carter fished the orders out from his jacket and offered them to Sigsbee. The Captain pruned his lips tighter the longer he stared at the papers, then snapped them closed and threw them back at Carter.

"Am I to understand that I am a transport vessel now? I thought that was what the *Olivette* was for?"

"I missed the *Olivette* by a day, and there is urgency that I get back to Havana. I wish no insult to your command, sir but I am essentially working with the government, so that should not denigrate your authority in the least. After all, in the end, we are working for the same boss." Carter cracked a smile. It vaporized when Sigsbee's stone-cold glare iced him.

"I see." Sigsbee seethed.

"And as much as I do not like the military, I prefer this mode of transport to what I have experienced of late."

"I hope you keep that in mind, Mr. Carter. This is not a yacht built for comfort and we are not out for a leisurely sail in the Caribbean. We are hardened sailors, our quarters are designed only for sleeping, and then only in short shifts. Additionally, I certainly hope you at least have some sea legs, since we don't always travel forgiving waters." Sigsbee remained visibly irritated.

"I do not believe he will be a problem, Captain," Commander Wainwright approached. Carter stiffened, showing surprise at seeing Wainwright. Sigsbee tilted his head and looked at Wainwright then back to Carter.

"You two know each other?" Sigsbee quizzed.

"We've met before, sir." Wainwright looked Carter over, and then slipped a knowing grin. "You have lost a few pounds, Carter."

"Pull up the plank!" Sigsbee ordered, continuing his icy stare at Carter. Behind him, his men hoisted up the boarding plank and stowed it for running. The Captain's look clearly told Carter that Sigsbee remained unconvinced he would not be an issue.

"Mr. White, please escort this man to the officer's mess," Wainwright ordered a gruff, middle-aged sailor who appeared. He turned back to Carter and added under his breath, "We will talk later when things are a little less hectic."

"I believe you are in capable hands, Mr. Carter," Sigsbee's words were frosted. "Now if you would excuse us, we all have a vessel to ready for departure."

"Come with me, sir," Chief White grunted.

"Understood, sir," Carter replied to the Captain as he caught White's signal to follow. Carter nodded his acknowledgement of Sigsbee's charge and followed the grizzled Chief toward the rear of the vessel as the Captain began barking orders to his crew.

In the harbor, a pair of pilot tugboats, churning water at their stern, headed in the direction of the *Maine*, a third sped toward the inlet to stop the *Indiana*, a full-sized battleship, before she made her way into the channel for the harbor. An additional pair of tugs then turned and steamed toward the *Maine*. The workhorse tugs cozied up along side the *Maine*, far enough from her outrigger like turrets to keep Sigsbee's blood pressure manageable, then worked in tandem to steer the battleship through the main channel out to sea. Smoke from the *Maine*'s two huge smoke stacks thickened as the boiler fires intensified, bringing the vessel to full steam pressure. The pilot tugs began the chore of turning the vessel toward the open sea, urging the mass of metal in a less than delicate pirouette. The front tug slipped away from the *Maine's* hull, and moved into a position to lead the *Maine* through the channel. The rear tug slipped forward to slow the turn of the *Maine*, churning against the momentum the cruiser had built in its turn.

"Engines ahead slow," Sigsbee ordered from the bridge. Wainwright looked aft, assuring the screw propellers had indeed engaged and started frothing in the water.

"Aye, sir. Ahead slow," Wainwright responded as her lead tug peeled off, then circled to bring itself into position to guide the *Indiana* into port. The other vessel slowed and let the *Maine* continue on her own power past the waiting battleship, where the two Captains talked through their horns before the *Maine* slipped out into the open waters of the Gulf of Mexico.

"Who is he?" Sigsbee asked as he reached over to sound a final adieu to the *Indiana*'s Captain. The return call came quickly.

"I believe he officially works for Treasury." Wainwright replied.

"He said he worked for the State Department?"

"Actually, sir, who reports to who in Washington has been confusing since Roosevelt dirtied his hands in just about everything. Right now, it's safer to assume just about everybody reports to Roosevelt."

"Sometimes I wonder if McKinley does as well," Sigsbee mumbled under his breath.

"But as far as Carter is concerned, I can assure you, sir, you will not have a problem with him."

"How is it you know that, Commander. You said you've met. Is he a spy too?" Sigsbee glared at his executive officer, who arched his eyebrows and grinned slightly. Sigsbee rolled his eyes. "Jesus, first you, then him. You know I haven't had this many people watching over me since my midshipman days at Annapolis."

"It's not you, sir. It's Cuba."

"Certainly looks that way, Commander." Sigsbee's eyes panned up and down his executive officer, choosing not to respond.

A young communications intern with the State Department fidgeted as he waited for the cabled message to start twitching onto the paper roll. Even before the salutation from Fitzhugh Lee had finished, he ripped the incoming message off the teletype. Not wanting to waste a precious second, he immediately broke into a sprint toward the stairs, taking three steps at a time to the bottom where his feet picked up exactly where they left off. As if he was legging out a slow grounder in a baseball game, he churned down the corridor, almost completely passing by Secretary William Day's office. Skidding to a halt, he spun around and then shouldered his way through the large door. After two steps, he froze, realizing he had just interrupted his boss in what appeared to be a very high-level meeting.

"Excuse me, sir," the intern's voice was squeaking as he gasped for air. He raised the paper in his hand and added, "Message from Consul Lee in Havana."

'Now we will see some action,' Roosevelt thought as he smiled with his toothy grin as he looked about the room. Secretary Day appeared docile and understanding. War Secretary Russell Alger was agitated, he was sure. *'This should be amusing,'* Roosevelt thought.

"Come!" Day finally encouraged the young lad to bring him the message. The intern complied; regaining his composure as he steadily approached Day and placed the telegram directly in his open right hand. Day unfolded the crumpled message and started reading it, paled, then looked up to the other men.

"Counsel Lee," Day started, but had to clear his throat. "Counsel Lee indicates that a naval vessel would not be required in Havana. He says the protests have quelled and more time should be allowed for the excitement to settle down."

'Chicken! Let's just get on with it,' Roosevelt thought.

"Well, then, I was correct all along wasn't I?" Alger puffed out his chest and sat back in his seat. He swiveled his head and glared at Roosevelt.

"You should leave Charles," Day said as he turned to his intern. "There may be more messages coming soon."

"Yes, sir," The boy complied and slunk out the door. Day glared at Alger with an expression clearly revealing his disgust.

"Has the *Maine* already left port?" Day inquired.

"Steamed out this morning, if I know Sigsbee," Roosevelt replied, confidently checking his notes.

"Can we recall her?" Day asked quickly before Roosevelt could add another pompous remark.

"She's still under orders to remain silent. We will hear from Sigsbee when they arrive — that is unless the Spanish decide to take some foolish action out in the Caribbean." Roosevelt said.

"We sent a battleship?" Alger's face stretched taught as his jaw slackened. He rose from his chair and immediately started pacing around the office. "We sent a damned battleship?"

"It's done. McKinley agreed to it," Roosevelt quipped smugly, reveling in Alger's agitation.

"What was he thinking? This act alone could be considered an act of war!" Alger protested as he stopped and stared at Roosevelt.

"They are not going in guns blazing, if that's what you are afraid of, Alger," Roosevelt prodded. "Give Sigsbee some credit for prudence."

"A military vessel in an adversary's port is not what I would consider an act of friendship." Alger resumed pacing the room.

"Then explain to me what the hell one of the Kaiser's warships is doing in Havana? And I believe if you read the brief that I had supplied a couple days ago, two more are on their way." Roosevelt stood and stepped in front of the pacing Alger, clicking his teeth in a wide grin.

"Gentlemen," Day tried interceding.

"This is your doing, isn't it Mr. Roosevelt?" Alger wagged his finger in Roosevelt's face.

"There was no disagreement that this had to be done, correct Mr. Day?" Roosevelt twitched his mustache defiantly, baring his teeth in his odd, wide mouthed smile as he crossed his arms in front of him. He twitched his eyebrow as he glanced at Day.

"Mr. Roosevelt is correct. We used diplomatic channels to announce our intensions to the Spanish." Day conceded.

Alger's head spun around like an owl spotting prey. "And where was I in this discussion."

"Beats the hell out of me!" Roosevelt growled at Alger. "Since you are never around when we need to discuss these things, we reckoned there was no need to include you in this discussion. When you are here, you're always half-asleep anyway. The Spanish must understand we mean business." Roosevelt emphatically pounded his fist into his open hand.

Alger's nervous twitches and lip licking grew even more prevalent. He wrung his hands in front of him as his eyes darted around the room, resting on Day and Roosevelt for only a second at a time. "I will lodge my protest with McKinley myself," he then growled, pushing his way past Roosevelt as he stormed out of the room.

"Is McKinley going to have Hobart talk to him soon?" Roosevelt grumbled as he returned to his seat. "John and I are growing weary of pussy-footing around that simpleton. We need someone in that position with some guts."

"Let's get back to the business at hand," Day said with a more refined demeanor. "The question of the *Maine*. Should we —"

"What's done is done!" Roosevelt said, bluntly. "Besides, Sigsbee is an experienced military officer. I am sure he has already plotted out his options if things go awry. And the *Maine* is a rather formidable element, especially in close quarters." Roosevelt said, bluntly.

"Fitz should recover from the shock of seeing her glide into the harbor soon enough," Day reconciled as he started chewing on his fingernails. "Then, that being said, let's get back to the question about what we need to do about the Germans."

"There's not a whole lot we are going to be able to do about them. You read the report, Day. They're in Havana!"

"I think this just became a bit more complicated," Day dropped his head.

"I don't believe that is the case. Once the Kaiser sees that we mean business, I think he'll just high-tail it out of there rather than look down the barrel of one of our cruisers."

"You can't be serious?" Day's head popped up, his face contorted with disbelief in Roosevelt's pompousness.

"You can take that to the bank!" Roosevelt clicked his teeth as he smiled widely.

Once the Keys were cleared, Captain Sigsbee directed the *Maine* on a due east course toward Havana harbor. As he watched the sea stretch out in front of him, he triaged his thoughts, now cascading through his mind. That was the advantage of a quiet sail toward the target — there was plenty of time to logically think through the cascade of events that may or may not occur.

"Anything you need, sir," Commander Wainwright edged up near Sigsbee.

"I don't believe so," Sigsbee mumbled as he stared out onto the open ocean. He continued calculating his vessel's progress against the wave height, thinking about his method of approach. "No, wait! There is something," he then blurted.

"Sir?"

"The coal bunkers. Did you order up some coal while we were in the Keys?"

"Yes, sir, we did. The inventory indicated we were a bit low, and I was concerned we might have some trouble ahead."

"I see. Perhaps you could take a quick tour below decks to be sure everything is how it should be."

"Everything? Do you want a double-up on my rounds?"

"Yes, Mr. Wainwright, everything," Sigsbee nodded. "My gut is telling me something, but I can't put my finger on exactly what."

Wainwright understood the order. It might as well have been an order, he thought as he headed off the bridge. On his way, he detoured to Carter's makeshift cabin, which was actually been a closet that was converted in Norfolk, to invite him along. Carter agreed and the two men rounded the main bulkhead, and then clomped down the steel steps that led to the aft boiler rooms. Wainwright noticed that heads turned at the sight of Carter; the sailors not used to seeing a civilian on board. Especially since they were at battle ready. Carter seemed to take the consternation in stride, politely tipping his head at all the sooty-faced passers and oilers. He even tried to disarm them by flashing a smile, but the return glances were terse since the huge fire pits demanded a grueling pace at their stations.

Wainwright led Carter past the closed fire-room and then to the port side where the coal bunkers lined along the hull, situated between the fore and aft magazines. The Commander opened each door slowly, meticulously checking the thermometers and the recorded data.

"Ever been on a ship with a coal fire?" Wainwright asked of Carter.

"No sir. Is there something I should know?" Carter asked in reply.

"We've got a mix here of bitumen and anthracite — can't get much else in the Keys. It does make it a bit touchy, though," Wainwright noted as the coal passer Lohman stepped through the watertight door.

"Sir?" Lohman asked, his eyes fixed on Carter.

"Put a priority on A-16, Lohman," Wainwright directed.

"Yes, sir. Problem with it?" Lohman shoved a cart at the opening to A-16, marking the bin.

"Just a gut feel from the Captain," was all Wainwright would admit.

"A-16 first, boys!" Lohman called out to the motley looking shift of passers and oilers. Diligently, the men shuttled the coal from the bin to the fire pit, as if they were a colony of bees moving from flowerbed to hive, then back again.

Carter and Wainwright moved on, and once they found an isolated corner, Carter asked, "Is any chance the coal was sabotaged back in Key West?"

"I'd be a fool to believe there is no chance, Mr. Carter. It only takes one or two ne'er-do-wells on a collier to put a load of coal at risk."

"I see," Carter said.

"You appear to be quite suspicious of things, Mr. Carter. Is it because you know something that perhaps I should know?" Wainwright's mustache twitched a bit as he perched his eyebrows.

Carter looked back at Wainwright and thought for a moment that he saw a much different man than he did back in Baltimore. This commander seemed less brash, much less confident, and even less directive. His demeanor appeared more collaborative with him as well. Perhaps, Carter thought, like a fish out of the familiar backdrop of Washington.

"I've learned out here, Commander, that suspicion is a survival strategy," Carter noted as he started back toward the stairs to take him to the upper decks. He stopped and turned as Wainwright paced back to the half-empty bin and stared at what remained of the coal pile. The Commander rubbed his chin in thought, and then turned away just as a passer slipped in behind him to refill his bailer.

"We'll need to work together when we get to Cuba," the Commander noted as he caught up with Carter. "Perhaps when you get to the island proper, you will keep us informed? After all, I do not believe our sailors, or even I for that matter, wandering around in Havana would be a particularly welcomed sight."

"Wilkie may not be warm to that idea."

"I don't really care what Wilkie thinks. We are in the windmill of war right now, and we need all eyes open, git it?"

Carter nodded and started up the stairs toward the main deck without answering. He was starting to like Wainwright, or at least their opinions of Wilkie were in concert.

"At least keep us posted on any threats to that may be coming our way?" Wainwright asked as they reached the main deck.

Collaboration with the military was something Carter was unaccustomed to. He thought about it for a moment, but realized his duty was to his country, and not specifically to an agency or the military.

"I will do what I can without compromising my cover. I am sure you understand that aspect of my business," Carter said. It was the right thing to say, he thought.

Chapter 18

"One-third, Mr. Wainwright," Captain Sigsbee ordered.

"Aye sir, down to one-third," Commander Wainwright responded, then echoed the order down to the engine room through his communications tube.

Sigsbee felt the gears slow and watched the excess steam blow out the stacks as he considered which directives to mete out to his crew. The *Maine* had been at full alert since they had left the comfort of the naval base in the Keys and a fresh shift had assumed their posts. He had already slammed down two cups of coffee before dawn's light revealed the threatening silhouette of Morro Castle cloaked in a cool, hazy morning mist under a gray sky not more than five hundred yards off his starboard bow. '*What orders have the soldiers behind those guns been given,*' Sigsbee mulled as he warily eyed the stark, rock-faced edifice emerging from the sea all the way up to the castle ramparts.

"Channel entrance, three hundred yards," Wainwright noted stiffly as he looked back at the Captain. Sigsbee sensed his XO wanted an immediate response, but instead, he remained stolid, eyeing the fortress that peered down on his vessel.

'*I don't even know if they are expecting us,*' Sigsbee thought. He knew his decisions from here until he orders all stop in the harbor were grueling. '*We can head in and remain on the defensive, turn tail and run, or blast our way in and start the war that everybody said they wanted to avoid — excepting*

Roosevelt. Absent any specific orders, the choice remains ours. No, mine.'

"Two hundred yards, sir," Wainwright nagged, his voice carried more punch.

"New bearing — one-eight-eight. Take her in, Mr. Wainwright," Sigsbee directed as he looked up one last time to Morro Castle. McManus cautioned him about the castle fortifications and suggested not to give the Spanish sentries anything to rattle their cages, but he saw little movement on the walls of the imposing, dark castle. Just a couple of sentries milling about. "Keep us directly in the center of the channel. And don't let those bastards out of our sight."

"Aye, sir. One-eight-eight," Wainwright repeated. The *Maine* responded promptly, listing sharply as she turned into the channel. Sigsbee's eyes remained glued on the fortress as it shifted from starboard, past the bow and then to port. The sun crept a bit higher, to a point just above the walls of the castle, just enough that Sigsbee discerned silhouettes of soldiers behind guns that looked down on him and his crew.

"All guns at sixty degrees to port, sir," Chief White reported as he stepped onto the bridge.

"Understand, angle up sixty to port." Sigsbee confirmed. "No salutes! I repeat, absolutely no salutes," he then ordered. The *Maine* crept by Castle Morro at a lumbering pace. '*Broadside,*' Sigsbee thought as he chewed on his lip. The *Maine* seemed to only inch forward. Sigsbee questioned himself as to whether he should ask for more speed but the progress continued enough that his vessel finally and smoothly steamed out of Castle Morro range, the imposing ramparts now off the *Maine's* stern.

Sigsbee closed his eyes and sighed. With *La Punta*, another disturbing, gun bristled castle remaining just ahead and to his starboard side, he did not want to take the chance that his guns be mistaken to be firing. He regarded *La Punta's* ramparts, a bit less impressive than Castle Morro, but nonetheless, just as threatening. As the *Maine* slid by *La Punta* and into the harbor proper, Havana spread out along the shoreline as grand as any port city he had ever seen.

Sigsbee felt a collective relief rise from the vessel under his feet once his vessel was out of the direct line of fire. "Tell the crew to stand down, Chief. And get Carter up here. I want to keep a close eye on him."

"Aye, sir," the Chief said and scurried away.

"Request permission to enter the harbor, Sparky," Sigsbee ordered toward the telegrapher. Fingers flew as the sailor started tapping away on his machine. Once the young man stopped, everyone in the bridge collectively held their breath.

"What if they refuse?" Wainwright turned and asked.

"We'll cross that bridge when we get to it," Sigsbee commented, then ordered, "Disengage propellers and drift. Keep the boilers hot and ready for action." Wainwright relayed the command down to the engine room and in seconds, the frothing at the rear of the cruiser ceased.

A minute passed. Silence on the telegraph continued. Sigsbee nervously chewed on his lower lip as he fixed his gaze at the station. He sensed that things were about to get frenetic as Carter, dressed smartly in business attire stepped onto the bridge and smiled.

"Morning, Captain," Carter said.

"Vessel headed our way, Captain! Two o'clock!" shouted a lookout. "Possible patrol boat."

"Armed?" Sigsbee asked. He eyed Wainwright and nodded to have the crew prepare for battle. "Carter. Get over by Wainwright and stay there. We don't have time for a tea party right now," he then barked, pointing toward his XO.

Carter stiffened, but immediately complied.

"Possible enemy at two o'clock," Wainwright chattered through the tube.

"No alarm!" Sigsbee barked. "I don't want any damned alarms."

"No audibles!" Wainwright called down through the tubes. The teletype began furiously clacking.

"As soon as you know," Sigsbee called over to the operator. He started chewing his lip again.

"Looks like a pilot, sir," the forward watch called out from behind his spyglass.

"Anything else?" Sigsbee quizzed, condescendingly.

"Buoy four, sir," the operator finally blurted. "We're being directed to buoy four."

Lieutenant Bowers immediately scurried through the map drawer on the bridge and shuffled through the papers until he found the one he was looking for. He snapped the map out from the drawer, pinned it down on a flat table and scanned it.

"Government pilot," the forward watch added.

"Right in the damned middle of the harbor, sir," Bowers grumbled. "We'll be sitting ducks there."

"Depth at low tide?" Sigsbee then asked.

"Shall I have the men stand down, sir?" Wainwright asked of Sigsbee.

"Six fathoms, as far as I can tell," Bowers noted.

"Would you look at that?" the forward watch called.

"Wait!" the Captain replied to his executive officer as he stomped toward the forward watch. "No anchor yet," he then replied to Bowers.

"Sir, German warship. Nine o'clock!" the forward watch pointed toward the eastern shoreline. Sigsbee took the spyglass for himself, adjusted the focus for his eyes then peered at the German vessel. It was the *Gniesenau*, a square-rigged training steamer. He knew she may have been full of cadets, but she could still be a formidable warship if necessary. From her state of readiness, Sigsbee quickly determined she had been here at least a day, if not longer, and that if push came to shove, his vessel and his crew were more than an equal match for her. The fact that she was there made him even more nervous than he already was.

"Confirm for me that she won't be a problem," Sigsbee handed the telescope to Wainwright. He then focused back on the government pilot that had been joined by a heavily rusted tug. "I would presume they will use flags to guide us to buoy four. Ensure you and Bowers are clear on what they want us to do," Sigsbee added, asking the watchman.

"Aye, sir," the watch confirmed.

"At rest, sir. No threat." Wainwright noted, and handed the scope back to the watch.

"Bowers, you have the bridge. Wainwright, have the crew stand down to full alert. Carter, I want you and Wainwright to meet me in my quarters," the Captain growled as he stomped past both officers and off the bridge.

Wainwright completed his duty and with Carter in tow, exited the bridge and marched the short walk to the Captain's cabin.

"What do you two know about the Germans being here," Sigsbee barked before Carter and Wainwright could take a seat at the small, carved teak table. Carter did not mistake the anger in his glare.

"I know that the Kaiser has issued some veiled threats before I left Washington," Wainwright noted, defensively. Sigsbee shifted his glare toward Carter.

"The information I have is not confirmed, sir," Carter started as he sat at the table. In the short two days since Carter had spirited his way onto the *Maine*, Sigsbee had mellowed toward him. With the Captain's sudden rage, Carter grew cautious.

"At this point, I'll take anything. There's a German warship off our port bow that I had no prior warning would be here," Sigsbee waved his right arm in the direction of the *Gniesenau*.

"There is a man in Charleston who claims to have been a spy for Germany for several years. As far as I was able to ascertain, Germany has no desires for Cuba." Carter offered. He sensed it did nothing to quell Sigsbee's concern.

"Do you think they are here to support Spain?" Wainwright interjected.

"That I don't know," Carter grew uncomfortable with the interrogation. "My contact did indicate that the Kaiser was unpredictable when it came to colonies. However, I would offer that Consul Lee would most likely know more about what the Germans stated purpose is here."

Sigsbee paced about his cabin as if he was a caged animal. He then spun around to face Carter and Wainwright. "Then I would suggest that we have Sparky prod Consul Lee and see if he has any idea what the hell we're supposed to do here?"

"Right away, sir," Wainwright bobbed his head in agreement, spun toward the door, started out, but stopped when he ran into the youthful looking telegrapher.

"Message from Consul Lee, sir," Sparky said as he presented the message. Wainwright accepted the offering, but following protocol, as he always did, passed it directly to Sigsbee without reading.

Sigsbee's demeanor softened as he starting reading. "Well, I believe this is our answer, gentlemen. Consul Lee has invited us ashore for a bit of diplomacy this evening with him and our Spanish hosts. A bullfight, no less." The comment earned a scowl from Wainwright.

"As brutal as it is, Mr. Wainwright, it provides us an opportunity to discuss some things with those who have us precariously in their sights right now. Consider it dinner and entertainment," Sigsbee said as he folded up the message and buried it into his jacket pocket."

Wainwright's dour relented. He arched his eyebrows in tentative agreement. Carter remained silent.

"You are welcome to join us tonight if you would like," Sigsbee prodded Carter. "We are supposed to meet the Spanish commander General Parrado."

"I do not think that would be wise for me, sir," Carter respectfully declined. "He may not be as welcoming for someone of my position, if you know what I mean."

"Poppycock! I suspect the Spaniards are pretty much used to spies crawling about their streets by now. Hell, I've heard they've got 'em as thick as black flies back in Washington." Sigsbee penned out a note accepting the invitation as Carter regarded the Captain's words.

"I thank you, but I believe it would be best for me not to attend, sir." Carter noted as he stood.

"You know, Lee did ask about you, Carter," Sigsbee perched his eyebrows. "Been here before, huh?"

"There are some things I really should not talk about sir," Carter grinned and exchanged a knowing glance with Wainwright.

A sultry afternoon arrived in Havana. Captain Sigsbee, in full white dress uniform, turned the *Maine* over to Lieutenant Bowers then moved toward the platform set in place between his ship and the small Spanish colonial government pilot moored next to his cruiser. He stood by as three of the ship's junior officers and Commander Wainwright in procession, all as smartly clad as Sigsbee, maneuvered on the boarding platform and onto the pilot ship. Carter followed the officers, decked out in a smart-looking, contrastingly brown business suit, drawing curious glances from the crew of the *Maine* as well as the Spanish vessel. Sigsbee nimbly concluded the procession, saluting the Captain of the pilot ship as he stepped on board. Without a word said directly to the Americans, the Spanish Captain ordered his crew to kiss off from the *Maine* and head south, allowing their guests the view of the harbor side architecture. Carter listened carefully to their rapid-fire banter, as requested by Sigsbee to ensure they remained guests rather than become hostages.

The only words spoken were those for the business of navigating the crowded harbor as the ferry sputtered south, then bent west toward the docks of their destination, Regla, a small city that sat at the southernmost end of the harbor. Sigsbee, Carter and Wainwright stood at the bow and maintained surveillance of the shoreline. The Captain eyed the fortifications that could easily pose a danger to his vessel while Carter and Wainwright watched for more insidious outlets and hidden coves where adversaries could employ their furtive forays. The half-hour ride ended eventless as the ferry docked and tied up to the pier, where a small group of locals controlled by Spanish officers had gathered. As the Americans departed the ferry, Carter reviewed the faces, looking for one or two familiar ones, but could not see any in the docile, suspicious crowd. His cover remained intact, he concluded.

A commotion then started in center of the mass — the distinctive oddity of Spanish spoken with a southern drawl. "Welcome to Havana, Captain," Fitzhugh Lee's voice boomed out over the local dark faces. As he emerged from amidst the parting bodies, Carter spotted his bowler first, then his paunch.

He raised his hand and waved until he was sure Lee noticed then pointed out the round, well-dressed ambassador to Sigsbee. Despite his welcoming words,

"It is a pleasure to be here," Sigsbee grinned, winking at Lee as he escaped the mass. "I believe you know Mr. Carter?" he added with a whisper.

"I must admit, I was a bit surprised when I heard you had arrived, Captain. I had little forewarning," Lee responded. The rather large man remained stone-faced, slowly moving his head to scan the faces in the surrounding crowd. With only a head gesture, he suggested that they move toward the train station before Sigsbee could start introducing the balance of his party.

"I have been told this is a friendly visit, Fitz," Sigsbee said as the group moved out of earshot of the locals. "A cordial exchange of courtesies. If I understand correctly, the cruiser *Vizcaya* is also on its way to New York."

"I see," Lee said, as the group passed a café full of locals. Wainwright and Carter continued their surveillance, swiveling their heads to study anyone who looked at them. Sigsbee's junior officers were clearly in awe with Regla, never being in Cuba before.

"What do you know about the Germans, Fitz," Wainwright finally and quietly spoke when they reached a stretch of road where they were alone.

"Two others expected. Officially, this is nothing more than a cordial visit. Unofficially, I am still working on that," Lee responded.

"It is making for a crowded harbor out there," Sigsbee chuckled, then added, "Perhaps we can invite the Russians and Britain to drop anchor and we can have an international conference."

Lee ignored Sigsbee's attempt at humor. "Mr. Carter, I believe you have a message back at the Consulate from a mutual friend," he said.

"Then, if you will excuse me Captain, I should see what this message is about." Carter recognized from Lee's tone and facial expression that the message must have been from Washington, most likely Wilkie. "Besides, General Parrado may not take a cotton to my presence, if you know what I mean," he added.

Sigsbee tilted his head, looking at Lee quizzically.

"Southern term, Captain. General Parrado is a very cautious man. He may be a bit more open if he doesn't suspect a spy is sitting with you," Lee explained. Wainwright drew a knowing look from Carter.

"I understand. Good day, Mr. Carter," Sigsbee offered a handshake just as a vacant eyed woman approached and thrust a pamphlet into Sigsbee's hand. Wainwright started toward the woman, but Carter grabbed his sleeve and held him back.

"She's harmless," Carter whispered to Wainwright. "I've seen her before."

Sigsbee looked down at the flyer quickly, keeping a wary eye on the woman's hands while resisting engagement.

"You are not welcome here." The woman wagged her finger at Sigsbee. There was a slight British tone to her words. "We do not welcome your intervention."

Sigsbee thought about responding diplomatically, but Lee shushed him before he could start.

"We know what your warship is doing here. You need to let the revolution run its course." The woman spouted again, and then froze when her eyes met Carter's. She then grimaced, and as she had done before when badgering Carter, skirted off and disappeared back into the crowd. Sigsbee, meanwhile looked back down to the leaflet and tried to read the Spanish, but gave up and handed it over to Carter.

"It is as simple as she said, Captain. Many would prefer no outside intervention," Carter noted, then urged Sigsbee and his entourage to continue toward the train station. Carter shied away from the group as a welcoming pair of Spanish soldiers approached. He watched from a safe distance as the pair offered a cordial greeting on behalf of General Parrado then guided them onto the train. Carter adjusted his wide brimmed fedora to cover his face, waited the few minutes until the train departed the station then headed west along the boulevard, starting his long walk back to the Consulate.

The cusp of evening greeted the entourage as the train arrived a block south of the stadium. After a brief discussion at the entrance, translation provided by the now more jovial Consul Lee, the Spanish soldiers escorted Consul Lee and the American officers into and through the heart of the crowd that had gathered for the evening's main event, the graceful Spanish Toreador Mazzantini plying his trade. Inside the stadium, they scaled the zigzagged stairway and emerged onto a landing.

Sigsbee stopped and drank in the expansiveness of the stadium, to him, as open as the Polo Grounds in Manhattan, where his favorite baseball team, the Giants, played. He looked across the way and saw that the stands were filling rather quickly, as if the first pitch would be nigh. The escorts turned his attention toward the dignitaries section, where General Parrado, a short, stout man in a heavily decorated uniform, stood, flashed a welcoming smile, then waved his cap. Heads nearby noticed the General, and then swiveled to watch the Americans closely as they maneuvered the walkways toward the General.

"General Parrado, this is Captain Charles Sigsbee, *USS Maine*," Lee introduced in Spanish. Sigsbee sensed the introduction and extended his hand. Parrado vigorously shook his hand just as a band, thin of brass but not in volume, announced the entry of the matadors.

"*Sientese y disfrute el espectaculo*." Parrado chirped, extending his hand across the reserved seats.

"Have a seat and enjoy the show," Lee quickly translated for Sigsbee. Parrado began chattering incessantly into Lee's ear, as if he realized that would be the mode of conversation for the evening. Sigsbee realized Lee would have difficulty keeping up with the energetic General, and whispered to Lee paraphrasing would be more than adequate.

Lee sighed, obviously thankful as Sigsbee and the other American officers settled in to watch the matadors enter. A group of picadors followed, mounted on white horses. Each of the bullfighters circled the hard-packed, sand filled ring, stopped and formed a single file in front of Parrado and his guests. When Mazzantini completed his flamboyant jog around the ring, he took his accustomed place in front, and as a team, the group of bullfighters stepped forward and bowed, paying their respects to them all, as Parrado verbosely explained. The opening ritual complete, the group disappeared under the stands at the same location they had entered.

The first matador, looking more like a boy than a man, re-entered the ring alone after a few minutes, his entrance announced by the call from a single trumpet. No sooner than Sigsbee settled back into his seat, Parrado began chattering again toward Lee of how the sequence for the evening would be. The young man, as Parrado explained, was still learning the nuances of the match, marched to the center of the ring and started waving his huge red cape.

A single picador and a rather young bull entered the ring and as Parrado described, the dance began. The General spewed in excruciating detail a continuous explanation as the match moved through its three stages in rather mundane fashion. Sigsbee hoped that he would be more attentive when the final matador set out to please the crowd; since the General's incessant chattering was sharply drilling though his head as viciously as the banderilleros' lances seem to cut into each successive bull's back.

When the carcass of the bull from the last of the preliminary matches had been removed from the ring, and the blood soaked sand raked, removed and replaced with clean, fresh material, the crowd quelled. Even Parrado settled in and focused on the match about to unfold in front of them. Sigsbee grew relieved that this blood sport would finally wind down for the evening.

A series of trumpets announced the final match and through the designated entrance below Parrado and his guests, Mazzantini entered the ring for the final time. The man was a tall, wispy fellow; his stature emphasized by his traditional gold braided, light blue tunic, appearing a size too small for his height and rather broad, square shoulders. He wore a black tri-cornered hat, and his white pants were tied up tight to his knees like knickers. His pink stockings stretched tightly between his trousers and slipper-like shoes.

Parrado, as Sigsbee had hoped, settled down and focused on his boyhood hero as the matador worked through his moves like a graceful dancer, carefully and methodically swerving the large, maroon cape around his body to invite the bull in closer with each pass. Mazzantini clearly pleased the crowd as he parried with the bull, controlling the charging beast as if he could read the animal's mind, directing the beast toward the picadors who lanced their arrow-like spears into the bull's back.

Parrado inched forward to the edge of his seat, eyes trained into the ring. With his final picador stationed, empty-handed along the edge of the ring, Mazzantini unsheathed his sword, and held it behind him with one hand as he waved a rather small cape to attract the immense bull. The animal's charge was slow but steady. Mazzantini flicked the cape as the bull moved closer. He stepped barely aside as the bull passed, then raised up on his toes and struck in a flash, accurately burying the sword directly between the bull's shoulders. A fountain of blood spurted skyward, missing the matador, and then the fluid trickled from the wound. As if it had hit a wall, the bull froze in its tracks, then dropped and rolled onto its flank in a bloody lump. The final stage was quick and merciful, Sigsbee thought.

Parrado leapt to his feet and joined the tumultuous eruption of the crowd. Sigsbee struggled to his feet and joined in the standing ovation, but instead of applauding, squeezed the bridge of his nose tightly, hoping it would relieve his stabbing headache, which now felt as if Mazzantini himself had inserted his sword between his eyes. The crowd settled but remained standing. Parrado signaled for Mazzantini to be awarded both of the bull's ears for his performance. The crowd approved. The picadors complied.

Revelry resumed as Mazzantini paraded around the ring with the bull's ears at the end of his sword, and continued for close to ten minutes. The applause receded only when the matador, with his prize skewered and held high, left the arena. The crowd began to file out. Parrado sat back down and leaned back, waving to anyone that passed and honored him, almost as if he were also one of the bullfighters.

"*¿Le gustó el espectaculo?*" Parrado leaned over and asked.

"Did you enjoy the show?" Lee translated for Sigsbee.

"It was intriguing." Sigsbee replied.

"You should know, my friend, this is an example of our culture," Parrado mused for a bit as he panned out over the arena where Mazzantini's bull was being dragged out by a team of mules. He paused for a moment and then added, "We may be small in comparison, but like what you have witnessed, we are born and live to fight proudly against the odds."

Lee hesitated for a moment before he translated the threat to Sigsbee.

"Tell it like it is, Consul," Sigsbee noted, sensing Lee was considering mollifying the General's harsh words. Lee complied. Sigsbee understood the mentality of the Spaniards. Wainwright recoiled but remained collected.

"Would you and your people be interested in some dinner this evening?" Parrado offered with a grin.

"It has been a long day General. I believe we can talk more tomorrow," Sigsbee replied after Lee's translation. He was not in any mood to continue posturing any longer than he needed to.

"*Buenas tardes*, General," Lee concluded. With that, Sigsbee rose and suggested that Lee guide them back to port and the *Maine*, where he and his officers could get a restful night.

It took all afternoon for Carter to navigate back to the Consulate. As the sun started to set over the western slopes outside of Havana, Carter scurried upstairs to the office and sat down to take a closer look at the flyer. Right from the beginning, the first words he translated were disturbing.

"The moment of action has arrived," he mumbled. Lee and Sigsbee would need to know this information as soon as possible. A noise from Lee's office then startled him. He quickly opened his desk drawer and covered the handle of his revolver, left there for safekeeping. He glared at the door until it cracked open. He started to pull out the weapon, but froze when a familiar face appeared in the doorway, looking as surprised as he was.

"Señor Carter, you're back!" Surprise melted off Domingo Villaverde's faces as he stepped out into the open and smiled. He looked as Spanish as any of the soldiers Carter had dealt with in Havana. He was short as compared to Carter, but average sized for a Peninsular Spaniard. He was lighter skinned, but his hair was still as black and straight as the night. He had come to Cuba as part of the Weyler government, but had grown weary of the regime and its subversion of the Cuban people. Just prior to the escapade to free Evangelina Cisneros, Carter convinced him to turn his back on the Spaniards and become part of the resistance.

"I missed the *Olivette*, but I had papers allowing me access to any other vessel, military or otherwise. That ship in the harbor, the *Maine*, was the first one I could catch a ride with," Carter admitted. He looked back at the flyer and studied it a bit more. Absently he added, "Is there a message from Wilkie?"

"No. I believe it was me that Lee was referring to."

"I see," Carter set the flyer down.

"It's about that." Villaverde pointed to the flyer as he pulled up a chair and sat down next to Carter. "Consul Brice got the same information from a contact he has in Matanzas."

"Is it directed at the *Maine*?" Carter asked as he looked deeply into Villaverde's brown eyes. He could tell that the information was from a credible source based solely on how frightened he appeared. After all he survived with the Spanish regime, not much frightened him.

"He's not sure, but the word about the *Maine's* arrival has reached him. He wanted me to get the information back to the States that they needed to put any ship arriving here on high alert."

"I agree. I will tell Sigsbee as soon as he gets back."

After a quiet night, Captain Sigsbee monitored the mid-morning haze burning off in Havana harbor. His crew had delivered well in their stamina and deliberateness over the past few days; not a single case of insubordination had been registered by any of his officers. The animosity between officers and enlisted men, an infection that had plagued so many other ships over the past year did not appear to have spread to his crew. He understood that good leadership; listening, caring, providing clear and understandable expectations, and holding his men accountable fairly, without bending to those that polished the canon ball; was the best preventive medicine for that unrest. But so was activity. And his ship and crew had been quite active since they departed dry-dock.

Now moored beside the *Gniesenau* was the *Charlotte*, another German school ship, and another puzzle piece for Sigsbee to ponder. She had sailed in just after dawn, at which time he had cycled his crew into full alert again. He had received the report of this vessel's escapade at Port-au-Prince and was concerned that this ships arrival might have brought one too many candles near an open cask of gunpowder. Routine courtesies, as stilted as the language barrier made their messages though, dispelled any immediate concern that being outnumbered presented a threat in the chess board which Havana was quickly blossoming into.

General Counsel Lee as well seemed to be less agitated with the message Sigsbee had sent when the second German ship arrived. His early morning message to the General Counsel received nothing more than an 'all's quiet' from the ambassador. He started to wonder if he was growing paranoid or if the rest of the American influence in Havana had grown complacent.

"Only time will tell who was correct," Sigsbee thought as he sipped his coffee while keeping the *Charlotte* and her sister ship under a watchful and somewhat skeptical eye.

Part Five
February 1898
Washington, DC

Chapter 19

"Good day, gentlemen." William Day greeted as he opened his Washington office door and invited in the two unexpected visitors. He did not usually entertain visitors this early in the morning, but who they were legitimized the information was of critical importance to both him and McKinley. "So, you have some information?"

"Yes sir," John McCook, a New York attorney associated with the Cuban Junta, said as he glanced over to his counterpart. Horatio Rubens, the Cuban Junta's legal counsel took a handwritten paper from his portfolio and handed it to Day. The attorneys stared dour-faced at Day.

"Please, sit down," Day muttered as he glanced at the letter. His face grew ashen, recognizing the salutation and signature on the bottom. It was the same de Lôme letter that Wilkie had presented to McKinley two weeks ago. He had been so consumed with preparing for John Sherman's resignation that it had slipped his mind, and now his inaction had become a grave error.

"The New York Journal contacted us yesterday and indicated they were printing this with English translation in today's newspaper," McCook said. "They wanted to ensure that we would not be jeopardized by them printing it."

"I see," Day noted. "Are you sure this is authentic?" Day asked. He already knew the answer.

"We believe that it is," Rubens noted.

"The crux of this matter, Secretary Day," McCook

injected, condescendingly, "is not whether de Lôme is speaking for the Sagasta government or not, but that there is clearly no interest in withdrawing from Cuba."

Day pruned his lips and nodded his agreement. He started to formulize a ruse of surprise in the letter, but then realized that McCook probably knew the back-story of the letter and his prior knowledge — he never made a statement if he did not already know the details that surrounded it. "I agree. I will call on Dupay de Lôme today and demand a formal apology," Day affirmed.

"Keep in mind, Mr. Secretary, we also know what these conquistadors have done in the past. It is possible your ship — the *Maine* — may be in danger."

"You mean they might attack the vessel?" Secretary Day asked, confused at precisely what Rubens was implying.

"That would not be out of the question," McCook injected. "Our concern, Mr. Secretary, is that your administration has still not recognized our movement's legitimacy and the Spaniards have taken full advantage of that fact."

"Has there been a threat to our vessel?" Day prodded.

"We have heard that there might have been." McCook said with measured words. "Please do not misunderstand us, Mr. Secretary. We do not wish to suggest your course of action, but I personally believe demanding a formal apology would be the least of the actions which need to be taken — a mere shroud to something even more definitive, if you know what we mean. Good day, Mr. Secretary,"

"You may also wish to reconsider who is your real adversary here, Mr. Secretary," Rubens added as the pair rose from their seats.

As the door closed behind the attorneys, Day dropped his head and lamented his inaction. He shuffled through the papers on his desk until he found the draft talking points he had started, quickly brushed them up, then slipped the suddenly infamous letter into his portfolio and headed to the Spanish Consulate two blocks away.

"Ambassador, please excuse the hour of my calling, but this is a matter of extreme delicacy and severe urgency," Secretary Day spoke quietly in his monotone as Dupay de Lôme opened his office door.

"Please, come in," de Lôme opened the door completely to allow Day into his plush office. The Spanish ambassador seemed docile and somewhat pleasant, Day thought, settling into the overstuffed chair closest to the desk. His smile was reserved and colder than his usual greeting. "What may I assist you with," de Lôme added as he hovered behind his large walnut desk.

Day opened his portfolio and took out the letter that had been provided to him earlier that day. He handed the letter to the minister and allowed a minute for de Lôme to scan through it before asking, "Ambassador, do you know anything about this letter?"

"That I do." de Lôme quickly replied, frowning. He carefully set the letter down in front of him, pursed his lips tightly and soured.

"Is it a letter that you had personally written?"

"What would characterize as personally written?" Dupay de Lôme asked as he squirmed in his soft leather high backed chair.

Day glared back at the minister. "Did you write or perhaps dictate this letter?"

"Yes." de Lôme cleared his throat.

Day dropped his head, lamenting as he stared at his own quivering legs. The minister was a man he trusted to be open and honest. There were few others from the European monarchies that he felt had not grown subversive in recent months.

"Señor Day," de Lôme broke the silence. "I would offer that to make things a bit easier for you, I have already cabled my resignation to Madrid. I should be leaving in about a week."

Taken completely by surprise, Day's head popped up and his jaw slackened.

"No formal retraction? No apology?"

"I do not believe so. What I wrote is what I believe." de Lôme's response was terse. He tilted his head as he twitched his lips into a devilish grin. "Now, Señor Day, is there anything else we need to discuss?"

"Yes, there is. I have been provided information that there has been a threat made on the *Maine*, now moored in Havana? Do you know anything about this?"

"Your warship in our harbor," de Lôme broke eye contact. His expression grew cold, as if calculating the exact words he wanted to relay. He drew in a deep breath, fixed his gaze back at the Secretary, and added, "You must be listening to the belligerents, Señor Day. We have welcomed your vessel in our harbor with open arms, have we not?"

"I believe that has been the case," Day stuttered as he asked.

"Then I believe we have nothing more to discuss," de Lôme said and returned to the papers on his desk.

Captain Sigsbee stood on the deck of the *Maine* and stared up at his vessel's immense smoke stacks, where thin wisps from the boilers' smoldering fires escaped into the sky. At their mouths, he noticed a faint blackened ring that had grown since leaving Key West. That would need to be cleaned soon, Sigsbee noted. He did not care much for the filth left in the wake of his vessel's black sustenance.

He had completed his evening rounds early. Below decks, two boilers gurgled at hot standby, the two others were shutdown. The night shift crew was at their stations, less tense than they had been on their entry to the harbor, but still enough on edge to please Sigsbee. He stepped up onto the poop deck and sat down in the chair he had insisted be set out in his open-air office as he called it. He melted into the seat, crossed his legs and relaxed for a moment, admiring the stillness of the early evening. Four hundred yards away, *The City of Washington*, a tourist-filled steamer from the States, had just arrived in the harbor. The passengers waved their handkerchiefs at Sigsbee and his men, bringing smiles to his crew from across the glass like glistening water. As darkness crept in, the crowd dissipated, retreating to the lower decks for their dinner.

Accordion music slipped across the water. Sigsbee noted that the music was from the German vessels. The strands that emanated seemed a bit out of place in the placid Caribbean evening, but nonetheless, they were not filled with anger or agitation, only gaiety. Sigsbee thought about the orders from headquarters that directed them to depart Cuba in two days to be part of the Mardi Gras celebration in New Orleans. The assignment did not bother him much, since his crew well deserved the shore leave in an American port after being stationed in Cuba for three weeks. They were all tired of being on alert twenty-four hours a day, hot bunking, and patrolling on board. With the one exception of the first day in port, when he left the ship for a diplomatic rendezvous with General Parrado, no one, not even him or Wainwright, had taken or been given stand-down time to relax.

The word that they were headed back to the States spread around the vessel like wildfire and that bothered him; more so in that they were headed to a city where alcohol and decadence thrived. Several times over the course of this day past, he spotted crew members on duty daydreaming about the liberty time they would have back home. He knew he had to mete out discipline for their lack of focus, but he too found himself drifting away from the thick and humid air they all were growing accustomed to.

It was time. Sigsbee uncrossed his legs and stood, stretching a bit before he started his walk along the starboard side rail. *Another evening had passed with little commotion*, he thought. The Cubans seemed restful enough, and the Spaniards were not being their usual provocative selves, leaving the merchant ships in the harbor with only their vices for another night.

'February 15, 1898' he started his letter home to his family as soon as he sat down. Evening's two bells had sounded. The night watch had already started and Wainwright had already taken the helm. A quiet contentment settled over him as he started to mindlessly write about his concerns with

his men and that nothing was happening. It was too quiet, he wrote, hoping not to incite any angst for his wife, already as widowed as any navy officer's wife had been,

His letter home to his family continued onto a second page, which surprised him since there was actually very little to write about. He read over the drivel that he had let him mind wander through, and reckoned it was about time he closed it up and got some sleep.

Taps sounded. His bugler started the melancholy nightly ritual. It was too engaging to ignore. The history of 'Taps' was well known to every commander. Sigsbee set his pen down and listened until the last echoes from the instrument faded away. It was time to close up the letter and get some sleep.

A sudden metallic explosion split the night with a deafening roar. Sigsbee felt the deck tremble, shudder, then lurch upwards in waves under his feet, before he lost his balance and tumbled to the deck. He reached for his table, but his hand slipped on the tablecloth and dragged his papers, pens and inkwells on top of him as he fell. Behind him, glassware once neatly arranged on his modest bureau, smashed onto the floor around him in addition to the metallic debris that rained on his cabin from above.

Then it was silent. Eerily silent. For a moment. Sigsbee heard other Captains who had survived disasters talk about the suddenly quiet death knoll — as if the Grim Reaper ceased time in order to sort out the taken and the to be taken. The cabin lights flickered, then dimmed and flickered again before dying out. The *Maine* listed sickeningly under him. His ship and crew were in trouble. Deep trouble. Regaining his footing just as the *Maine* shifted again, this time forward; Sigsbee stumbled toward the starboard cabin ports, executing the practiced escape drill he hoped never to do for real. He opened the door and upon looking out, realized that the passageway leading to the superstructure was clear, but water was already flowing over the passageway. He had to move. Quickly. Feeling his way along and steadying himself along the bulkheads, he felt thick smoke invade his lungs as he neared the outer entrance.

"Pardon me, sir!" a young voice announced as a body ran directly into Sigsbee.

"Seaman, what happened?" Sigsbee asked.

"Ensign Anthony, sir. The ship's been blown up. It's sinking!"

"Attack?"

"Don't know, sir. It's just went!"

"Upper deck, sailor. We need to get to the upper deck." Sigsbee ordered. He grabbed the young man by the hand, and then continued groping his way along the bulkhead. Nothing was hot. The main structure was not afire. *Yet. It was only a matter of time*, he feared. Continuing toward the rear of the vessel, slogging through water that seemed to be rising by the second, Sigsbee dragged his orderly until they emerged from the passageway.

The battery-powered claxon hammered away in the chaos, shorting out to a click sporadically. The main deck was awash in water. Screams, shouts for help and agonized moans filled the air. Splashing water was everywhere — beneath his feet and under others that sloshed by. Below, he assumed in the harbor's waters, he heard more struggling. Once filled, below decks would serve only as a large, cold coffin.

Sigsbee peered around in the smoky darkness; his eyes had acclimated as well as they could. Several figures stood nearby.

"Anybody. Report!" he ordered.

"Wainwright, sir. To your right."

"Hood, sir. Six o'clock."

"Blandin, sir. Nine o'clock"

"Damage?" Sigsbee demanded.

"The forward section's been hit, sir," Wainwright stated.

"From where?" Sigsbee asked.

"Port side."

"Did we fire back?"

"No time sir. Didn't see it coming."

Sigsbee turned toward his left. There were no ships between his listing hulk and the shoreline.

"Are you sure?"

"Positive sir."

"Battle stations." Sigsbee ordered.

"No guns sir. We were hit just below the forward turret. They took out the powder."

Sigsbee triaged the situation from what he had asked as best he could. If they had been attacked, it would not be just one salvo. More should be in the offing. But if there was nothing in the direction from where a shell was supposed to have come, it couldn't have been an actual attack.

"Everyone to the poop. We've got to know what we've got," Sigsbee ordered. Without pause to question, all within earshot moved as quickly as they could, slogging through the rising water on the main deck toward the rear of the ship, hobnails now slipping on the slick wooden planks in an uphill climb. The *Maine*, his *Maine* was sinking quickly, it seemed bow first, into the harbor.

As Sigsbee reached the poop deck, he climbed up onto the guardrail and held on to the main rigging. The poop awning had collapsed into a sagging tarp, succumbed to the fallen debris. Sigsbee looked forward, trying to discern anything to the front of the ship that would reveal a hint if what he could do outside of just order his ship to be abandoned.

"Wainwright," Sigsbee called out. "Post sentries."

"No sentries, sir. The Marines were lost in the explosion." Wainwright replied.

Casualties, Sigsbee thought. He shuddered. There was no war. They were on a friendly mission. Even the Germans acted cordiality. It was non-sequitur that his ship would be in such hell. Through a clearing in the smoke, Sigsbee saw that even if he had sentries to post, the entire forward section of the ship was underwater, listing badly to port. There was clearly a breach in the center of the vessel.

"Flood the forward magazine," Sigsbee ordered without thinking.

"It's already underwater, sir," Lieutenant Hood replied.

"Aft?"

"Blandin, sir. It's underwater." Lieutenant Blandin replied to his captain's query.

Flames suddenly burst out over the central superstructure, illuminating the entire vessel for Sigsbee.

"Cover!" he yelled. "Where is that coming from?"

"It's us sir. The *Maine* is lost," Wainwright insisted.

Through his boots on the rail, Sigsbee felt his ship groaning as it filled with water. The main mast, tilted, still stood like a sentry in the center of the flames, but was subsiding slowly into the murky waters below. He struggled with the reality, reeling through what he and the crew needed to do to save the ship. He could not accept what he saw in front of him — what Wainwright was insisting — his ship was lost.

"Wainwright — the spare ammunition in the Captain's pantry — any hope for recovery?" Sigsbee barked through a sore throat.

"Can't get there sir. You must order abandon ship." Wainwright growled.

Sigsbee's eyes darted around the poop deck, slowly dying beneath him, becoming engulfed with water. Little of his vessel, once the proud battleship *Maine*, remained above the harbor surface. Faint cries continued rising from the water where he saw bodies, some thrashing, some just floating. An explosion reported from the front of the sinking hulk. *Another magazine consumed by the flames*, he reckoned.

"Damn it to hell! Lower all boats! Abandon ship!" Sigsbee swallowed hard. He never wanted to say those words while he was in command. No captain ever did.

"Only two boats available, sir." Wainwright replied. The brightly burning fire amidships gave Sigsbee a view of a number of rescue boats headed in their direction. Searchlights from the other ships in the harbor, awakened by the demise of his vessel swept across the surface. Rescuers slowed, dragging in writhing bodies as they passed, helping recover what little remained alive with the crew.

"Drop them. Collect up the wounded. Get as many as you can over to those rescue boats yonder." Sigsbee ordered.

"But sir." Wainwright pointed to the gig, the smallish boat that was the designated Captain's escape route.

"Come back for me when you are done."

"Aye sir," Wainwright slogged into the gig and headed out to gather up the survivors.

Underneath Sigsbee, the *Maine* writhed from water pouring into her belly. He had commanded her for six months, and been with her since birth. He knew every inch of her now twisted metal. She was dying before his eyes and there was nothing he could do. Not even salvage just a small memento of her. Exhausted, Sigsbee grieved for her from his perch as his men collected up the wounded, transferring them to the flotilla of rescue boats bobbing on the harbor waters as they rushed to her aid. Exhaustion consumed him. He dropped his head and prayed.

"Sir, it's time," Wainwright's voice startled Sigsbee. The Captain shook his head, as if clearing cobwebs. He must have dozed off while the whirlwind that was this night continued on around him. He opened his eyes and could clearly see by the light of the fiercely burning mass that the rail on which he stood was even with the gunwale of the gig. Between the two of them water had risen enough that the poop deck was now under water. Sigsbee hesitated.

"The ten incher, sir. It's engulfed. You need to leave now before it explodes." Wainwright whispered.

'This is not what I came here for,' Sigsbee thought as he stepped from his rail into the gig. '*I will not rest until I find who is responsible. It must be a mine.'* The spare ammunition from the pilothouse was now engulfed and was reporting in detail. Black clouds mushroomed through the crimson blaze. As Wainwright and Sigsbee headed into the darkness, they warned the remaining boats to leave the vicinity of the wreck for their own safety. With ammunition exploding in the distance, Commander Wainwright and Captain Sigsbee reached and boarded the civilian liner *The City of Washington* while emergency crews from every other vessel in the harbor worked to recover survivors and the dead. The gleaming faces that only hours ago smiled in respect, now only gazed in disbelief.

Fitzhugh Lee could not believe his eyes. Under the moonless, sultry evening, from his perch on the third floor of the Consulate, he witnessed an explosion that ripped through the center of the *Maine*, sending sooty flames into the night sky. Stunned, he watched her steel bow lift off the oily black water, high enough to expose the keel under her forward cutwater, then drop with a sickening splash. Smoke and flames poured out from amidships as debris rained from the sky.

"What the hell was that?" Ambassador Fortin, the visiting Consul from the Eastern Cuban provinces, asked as he stumbled, sleepy-eyed into the room.

"The *Maine*."

"Who in hell opened fire? Was it the Germans?"

"I don't know. It just blew up," Lee said, still unable to believe the debacle unfolding in the harbor.

"It just blew up?" Fortin groped along the desk and toward the window. He flinched from the brightness of the erupting forward magazines on the *Maine*. Shells screamed into the sky; whistling feebly as they wobbled upward, died in mid-air, then fell directionless to the water. "I can't see anything incoming."

"Son of a bitch. We've got to report this to Washington, right away," Lee turned and headed to the telegraph room while Fortin remained at the window, engrossed by the successive, forceful explosions rocking the *Maine*. Through the open window, he heard screams echoing and claxons throbbing into the night. Searchlights from the other vessels combed the oily black surface. Water near the capsizing hull broiled as it listed further to port. Lifeboats from all the vessels in the harbor crawled about the water like maggots on carrion. Within minutes, there was little remaining of the *Maine* that anyone could see in the dark, moonless night.

"It is done. I am sure this is war," Lee mumbled as he left the telegraph room and rejoined Fortin at the window overlooking the harbor. "How could we have missed this?" he mumbled, feeling a sense of failure that he had not properly connected the dots.

Footsteps stammered up the stairs.

"Counsel Lee!" Lee recognized the voice. When the office door burst open, Domingo Villaverde stepped through, his eyes wide enough to expose white rings around his brown pools. His dank, burnt smell continued into the room even as he stopped to suck in air.

"It is bad," Villaverde muttered, bending over, still breathless. "They are as shocked as we are."

"Who?" Lee arched his eyebrows.

"The Spaniards. They are surprised. They did not expect this."

"But Carter said he heard Ramón say he heard some officers describe the *Maine* as an insult to Spain and her sinking would be a just reward. You remember that, right?" Lee asked, baffled.

"No, no. I was listening to the officers. The explosions surprised them as well." Lee's and Villaverde's eyes met. Without facts, they both knew what conclusion Washington would come to and what the consequences may be. "Will they listen to you?" Villaverde asked.

"All I can do is try." Lee shook his head. He headed back to the telegraph room and started tapping away as Villaverde joined Fortin at the window.

Sam Carter could not believe what he had just witnessed. From the deck of the *City of Washington*, where he had been monitoring a group of potential counterfeiters, he heard a low rumble, followed by the explosion of the *Maine*. Her steel bow rose from the oily black water, exposing her cutwater and keel, and then dropped with a sickening splash back onto the harbor surface.

"Send out rescue boats," the *Washington's* Captain ordered as he stepped out onto the main deck. Carter, stunned, thinking of how he could help, watched the crew dutifully comply with their orders. Shackles squealed as line spun through pulleys. Wooden rescue boats skittered toward the water, and then splashed as they hit the surface. "Lights! This side," the Captain barked as smoke continued pouring out from the *Maine*, the ship now twisting itself into grotesque wreckage. Flaming debris escaped with each ensuing explosion then rained aimlessly from the sky.

Carter watched the *Washington's* calcium searchlights as

they sparked to life then joined the search lights of other moored vessels, the myriad of light beams seemingly sword fighting out over the harbor. Methodical sweeps combed the surface, fixing sporadically on movement near the vessel. Some of the men flailed while others floated with a sickening stillness. Screams punctuated the night, echoing over the chaos until drowned out by additional explosions. He followed the searchlights carefully as they explored the oily black surface. Movement caught his eye in one of the light streams. Ripples. He thought he had spotted a rippled, spreading wake headed away from the wreck. He took out a small pair of binoculars he had stuffed into his jacket and scanned more closely, but by the time he focused, the disturbed surface was calm again. The searchlight moved on again, back toward the men thrashing in the water, skipping over the bodies that floated in the bay like contorted driftwood.

Chaos reigned throughout the harbor. Rescue boats from every ship moored in the harbor, military and civilian alike, splashed into the water and joined the amoeba-like flotilla whose extremities reached out ever closer to the wreckage to consume the maimed. Explosions from the swamped sections of the dismembered warship died out, leaving a macabre twisted hulk in the center of the harbor. Carter gravitated toward the boarding platform, and joined with the crew to help the first of the survivors onto the deck of the *Washington*. He eyed the burned and tattered men as they limped with help toward commandeered cabins for triage.

Captain Charles Sigsbee and Lieutenant Commander Richard Wainwright were the last two men to board the steamer. Sigsbee bowed his head as he walked by, his trousers soaked to his waist. An ink spot stained the belly of his white shirt. Wainwright glanced up at Carter, stopped and stared blankly for a moment. The assured expression that Carter had always seen on his face was now wiped clean and replaced with one more of astonishment. The officer nodded a nearly imperceptible acknowledgement before being skirted away for needed medical attention.

Carter understood the sign. He looked back toward the

wreckage. There was little more that he could see left of the *Maine* in the dark, moonless night. The only thing that was certain to him was that this changed everything.

"My God, Sam. How could this happen?" a soft, female voice said behind him. Carter looked over his shoulder as Annette nuzzled up close to him.

"I don't know," was all he could say. Without thinking, he placed his arm around her shoulders. "You and your father need to get to the Hotel Inglaterra as soon as you can."

"But . . ." Annette started, but stopped when Carter placed his hand over her lips.

"And then home. Nothing good will come out of this." Carter noted.

As the chaos dissipated, a stunned pall settled over the *Washington*. It was already midnight. Carter did not have any opportunity to talk with Wainwright, but he knew he would need to soon. None of this made sense to him. The Spaniards weren't itching to get the United States involved, but if this was their doing, there had to be some reason.

There was nothing more he could gather tonight and morning was just a few hours away. He knew he would be back here soon enough — he would need to be at his best to try to make sense out of what had just happened.

Carter took full advantage of the stream of ferry boats now headed back to the shore, and personally assured that Annette and her father were safe in a land hotel for the night. He headed back to the Consulate, a short walk from the docks, blinded and confused by the myriad of possibilities and probabilities. Carter reached the Consulate still trying to piece together clues, and then navigated the stairs in the old plantation house. Lee had fallen asleep at his desk, head buried in the cradle of his folded arms. Exhausted himself, Carter melted into the cot in his office, dozed for a moment, then slipped into a fitful sleep that let the months before this now fateful night ramble aimlessly through his mind.

"Secretary Long. I have an urgent message," the

communications orderly hammered on Navy Secretary Long's bedroom door. Long rose from his chair, in which lately he had taken to napping. He was having trouble sleeping, partly due to the cold he had acquired in the recent spate of cold weather, and partly from the tension spreading in Washington as everyone waited for the next flare-up in Cuba to occur. He stumbled through the living room, aided by the light from his study, until he reached the door and cracked it open.

"I have urgent messages from General Consul Lee and from Captain Sigsbee," the orderly announced. Long's adrenaline immediately sped up his already pounding heart.

"Come in, please," Long opened the door further, and then closed it immediately behind the orderly. He fastened the buttons on his night coat as he took the messages from the shaking orderly's hands. He did not have to read the telegrams to know this news was bad — the ashen expression on the young man's face spoke volumes.

"*Maine* blown up and destroyed tonight at 9:40 pm," Long read aloud. That was all he could muster. His jaw gaped open.

"Yes, sir. Shall I inform the President?"

Long felt his legs grow weak. He stumbled back to a chair and sat down awkwardly. He again looked at the messages, but was unable to focus and read further.

"My God, what have they done," Long mumbled.

"Sir?"

"Who is on duty tonight?"

"Commander Dickens, sir."

"Dispatch Commander Dickens to the White House immediately with this information. I am sure McKinley will want to assemble the War Council immediately."

"Yes sir," the orderly replied and headed out, leaving Secretary Long alone with the messages.

'This was a grave time for the country,' Commander D. W. Dickens thought as he waited in front of McKinley's desk for the President to be awakened. There was little doubt in Dickens' mind that this meant war. President McKinley entered the office, shuffling in his slippers and fidgeting with his red

housecoat over his nightgown. He combed back his thinning gray hair from his face with his fingers and stumbled toward his high backed leather chair. Dickens laid the telegrams on his desk immediately in front of him as he sat down.

"Secretary Long received these just now," Dickens muttered as the president rubbed his eyes. McKinley sighed deeply as he fumbled to unfold the letter. As he started to read, his face grew longer than it already was. His eyes darted back and forth over the words until he dropped the first letter on the desk. He sighed deeply again.

"How?" McKinley asked, handing the letter back to Dickens.

"No details, sir," Dickens replied. McKinley twitched his hand, urging Dickens to give him the letter back. Dickens complied.

"Two hundred and sixty men, at least," McKinley mumbled. He looked up at Dickens and again handed the telegram back. "Was it deliberate? Any warning? An accident?"

"We don't know sir."

"We need to know. How could Spain even consider doing this?"

"Spain is already denying involvement."

McKinley motioned for the letters again, still seemingly in disbelief. Dickens complied, and the President again read over the messages. "It says here it was blown up. It says that the *Maine* was blown up."

"There was an explosion which destroyed the *Maine*, sir. Secretary Long is asking for the War Counsel to be convened."

McKinley mulled over the telegram again. He shook his head and closed his eyes. After a deep breath, he raised his head and glared at Dickens.

"I would like to speak to the Spanish consulate immediately. We need to get to the bottom of this regretful act. I certainly hope this is an accident, but if they are responsible in any way, they need to know this provocative behavior will be reprimanded to the fullest extent."

"The Ambassador resigned, sir. A replacement has yet to

arrive."

McKinley stared up to Dickens with bloodshot wide, sleep deprived eyes. It took a moment for him to remember that fact, perhaps since it was the only way to save apologizing for the letter.

"Wake Secretary Day. We need to get a dialogue started with the Spaniards." McKinley slurred most of his words as he started to nod off back to sleep.

"Yes, sir," Dickens replied and stood. He stopped at the doorway, turned to McKinley and added, "Secretary Long should be here shortly. Shall I also inform Secretary Alger?"

"Yes, yes," McKinley grumbled as rose from his seat. "We will need everyone involved in this to ensure we come to the correct conclusion."

Not more than an hour had passed from the time the President had received the news about the *Maine* that the War Council convened while the balance of Washington slept.

"Gentlemen, I realize this situation appears to have a simple, plausible answer, however I have some rather intriguing information from Lee and Captain Sigsbee that we should clearly consider," McKinley, still dressed in night clothes wrapped by his scarlet housecoat, opened the discussion.

"There can be no doubt who the perpetrator is," Roosevelt groused. His fist slapping punctuated each of his words.

McKinley, his complexion still blanched from his early awakening, raised his hand to silence the Assistant Secretary. "Lee and Sigsbee both suggest that an accidental explosion is unlikely but cannot be ruled out. They both urge us to remain calm. He does not believe that General Blanco or other high officials are responsible for this action."

"Then who does he think is responsible. The Cubans?" Roosevelt squirmed in his chair. "Or maybe the Mexicans paddled over in a banana boat to frame the bastards. Or perhaps the Germans decided it was time to test our will?"

"Mr. Roosevelt!" McKinley interrupted loudly.

Roosevelt shuddered, and settled back in his chair. His

furrowed forehead remained as folded as a spring-plowed field.

"We should seriously consider these comments," Secretary Day noted. "If the investigation reveals an accident on board was the cause, we would be inappropriately rushing into a conflict."

"Investigation? What the hell are we going to investigate?" Roosevelt hammered his fist on the table. "The *Maine* has been blown up, gentlemen. Blown up! Our boys have been killed. This is war, gentlemen. It is as plain as the nose on my face!"

"I would suggest Commander Wainwright as the ideal person to conduct this investigation." Commander Richardson Clover added.

"If he survived. Do we have any information about who survived this murderous act?" Roosevelt chattered as he clicked his teeth.

"No. Commander Wainwright will need to collect and provide information. We need someone else." McKinley noted. His castigating glare was fixed on Roosevelt as the secretary fidgeted in his chair, as if waiting for a morsel of information that he could pin on the Spaniards. After a pregnant pause, he demanded, "I would like a list of officers who would serve well on a board of inquiry, Mr. Long, I am sure Commander Wainwright understands the significance of the results, but to protect his integrity, he should only be a witness rather than a judge on that board. Understood?"

"Yes, sir."

"And I am sure the investigation will be thorough and complete."

"I beg your pardon, Mr. President, but this is a catastrophe!" Roosevelt clenched his fists in front of him.

"We agree, Mr. Roosevelt, but I do not propose to be swept off our feet by it. Our duty is plain and simple. We must learn the truth and endeavor, if possible, to fix responsibility," McKinley replied sternly.

"We need to act now! We can't trust them. You've already seen that with de Lôme," Roosevelt wagged his finger at McKinley. "Waiting only lends credence to his spineless accusation."

"This country can afford to withhold its judgment and not strike an avenging blow until the truth is known. This Administration will prepare for war, but still hope to avert it," McKinley replied in a raised voice. He scanned the room to assess agreement. Roosevelt, he felt, was clearly outnumbered.

"I suspect this was planned all along. de Lôme is gone. He accused you of being weak. How much more evidence do you need?" Roosevelt growled. Veins bulged from his temples.

"Mr. Day, I would provide Ambassador de Lôme's replacement a message that we are showing as much prudence as we can in this situation, and will not rest until we ascertain the truth," McKinley ordered.

"Yes, sir," Day responded as he looked about the room. He did not remember whether he had told McKinley that de Lôme's replacement was still a month away, but with the piranha in the room, this was not the time to discuss that.

"In the meantime, gentlemen, as Consul Lee has requested, we should remain patient until the investigation has been concluded. That is all."

Chapter 20

Sam Carter arrived at the harbor just after sunrise, exhausted from a fitful night replete with nightmares of the horrific explosion. The temperature was not more than fifty degrees, cool for Havana — cool enough that the few gathered locals had slipped on jackets to rubberneck at the twisted metal hulk in the harbor. Carter read dismay, anxiety and concern in the faces — faces that saw a great American vessel, a warship at that, crippled in their harbor, at the behest of a Spanish military contingent squatting at the best vantage point for photographing the twisted wreckage.

Carter inspected as best he could what remained of the fireballs and explosions that had torched into the previous evening. In forty feet of water, the forward section of the center structure of the *Maine* had been blown upward and to starboard. Along with the bridge, pilothouse and conning tower, the entire structure was peeled back, partly submerged. He reckoned determining the cause for the explosion would be impossible from the surface.

'*The cause*,' he mused. No question. It was an explosion. But the reason and who was culpable still eluded him. The more he thought, the more questions blossomed. He shifted focus to the Steamer *City of Washington*, now called to duty as the primary rescue ship. At her rail stood a single, perfectly still figure, gazing over to the pillar of smoke still rising from his destroyed ship. It was Captain Sigsbee. From the distance, Carter could not see the expression on his face, but he could sense the melancholy — perhaps anger at the demise of his command.

Carter assumed there would be investigations. There had to be. The Spaniards were already collecting information. The American Navy was obligated by regulation to perform their own. Wilkie would want to get some details as well, he was sure. The newspapers, acting in the public interest they would say, would want to dig into the sordid details to drive their own agendas. His own curiosity was eating at him to find out who was responsible and most importantly, why, since he was not sure whether any of the interested would provide a clean, unbiased story based solely on facts.

'There was only one way to find out for sure,' he thought as he headed down to the ferry launch to survey from that angle.

"¿Puede llevarme en ese barco?" Carter asked a crusty looking old fellow sitting on a stool at the end of a rickety dock. As he extracted a dollar bill from his pocket and pointed toward the *City of Washington*, the old man looked up from his whittling, then looked out to the steamer, then shifted his glance back at Carter.

"¿Ahora?" The old man smiled a toothless grin.

"Sí," Carter handed the bill to the old man. The fellow spryly rose from his stool and climbed into his motorized dingy. He yanked three times on the starter rope and on the third try, blue smoke spewed from the engine. The old man held back a giggle as he waved Carter into the skiff. He dropped the spinning blades into the black, oil-filmed water as soon as Carter sat down and the pair puttered out into the bay.

The monotone drone from the small engine was loud enough that Carter realized talking over the buzzing motor with the old man would be useless. Instead, he thought about the *Maine*. It did not make any sense to him it could be anything but an accident. If the Spaniards were responsible, admission of guilt would be suicidal. The photos being taken by the militia at the shore would clearly construct the story of how the vessel imploded with their own armament, perhaps even internal sabotage. If the evidence for an external detonation could not be refuted, the culpability would clearly be crafted to be the work of malcontents or even the Cuban revolutionaries attempting to frame the Spanish colonial government.

Carter was also certain that the United States Navy would skew any evidence gathered to construct an external explosion theory in order to manufacture a reason to plunge into war. He could not help but recall the vivid debrief with Roosevelt and Wilkie. He wondered even if the evidence was irrefutable that the explosion was initiated from within, whether the investigators would provide an unbiased conclusion. Was it beyond Roosevelt and Wilkie to have this staged? Considering all the emotions now swirling around the *Maine* like a lightning rod, Carter realized if he did not see the point of explosion with his own eyes, he might never know the ultimate truth of the matter. Even if he did see it, he might still be left bereft for clues.

As the small boat pulled up to the side of the *City of Washington*, Carter convinced the old man to wait for his return. The old fellow agreed, cinched up to the steamer, pulled out his carving knife and resumed his whittling as Carter boarded and headed to the railing where he had seen Captain Sigsbee earlier. When he rounded the bulkhead, he noticed that Wainwright, out of uniform and in a dry business suit, had joined the Captain, and together, the officers in examined what little of their vessel they could see from this vantage point.

"Commander?" Carter asked as he approached. Wainwright turned, revealing a weary, haggard face. Sigsbee remained fixated on the remains of his ship. "Could I have a moment with you?" Wainwright obtained agreement from Sigsbee and with Carter, moved toward the stern of the ship.

"Mr. Carter. I did not expect you." Wainwright said under his breath. His unshaven face was drawn and pale, clearly victimized by lack of sleep.

"I assume there will be a dive team." Carter pointed to the twisted metal that poked out from the harbor's grimly gray surface.

"Likely," Wainwright pursed his lips.

"I understand this may not be a usual request, but I would

appreciate if I could be part of the team. I don't know who you may have lost," Carter said as he tried to sense Wainwright's response.

"You do surprise me, Carter." The Commander scrunched his face and cocked his head. "I didn't know you were an experienced diver?"

"Yes, sir," he lied. His stomach knotted as he swallowed hard. He had done some snorkeling, but he had never been in a full dive suit. He reckoned he might be able to fake his way through it, having seen the equipment used before, at least until he got into the water, at which time, it really did not matter. As long as he did not panic and understood most of the mechanics, it was worth the gamble. Wainwright's face remained grim and expressionless, unrevealing to Carter if he believed him or not.

"I do not see why that could not be accommodated. You would of course need to be debriefed when you surface. It will be an official Navy operation."

"Thank you, sir," Carter replied with a touch of trepidation. He wondered if he had become too eager.

"We have cabled out for divers and some equipment," Wainwright's tone was cold and calculated. "All we had is now below the surface."

"I've seen marine salvage shops in town. I know the ones in Charleston have them," Carter noted, remembering that there were a couple of dive shops in the city near Regla.

"We had someone scour the streets for that last night. No luck. The *New York* should be arriving later today, maybe tomorrow. It has the gear and a couple experienced salvage divers," Wainwright added.

"Do you think they would mind if I join him?"

"I will try to clear it through command," Wainwright noted.

"I understand," Carter replied. "Please let me know when the *New York* arrives and I will assist your diver in the investigation. I will be at the Consulate."

Wainwright nodded his head, then left and returned to Sigsbee's side as Carter returned to the old man's skiff. In minutes, he was back on shore and headed directly back to the

Consulate, convinced that a message from Wilkie would be there when he arrived. As Carter headed up the boulevard, a particular image that he had seen the previous night haunted him. The surface of the water between him and the carcass of the *Maine* rippled. He was sure it was the wind today, but it was right where he saw the wake last night. He began to question if Moser's revelation was sub-consciously planting that image or if he really did see something submerged and moving away from the ship. In either case, if the Spanish did have an infernal machine plying these waters, it was something not only he needed to know, but any other American captain that ventured into the harbor.

Carter found Fitzhugh Lee sequestered in his office, working on a letter, when he arrived back at the consulate. The old general looked up with eyes as bloodshot as if he had been on an all-night binge, and then waved Carter in with his hand.

"Wilkie's telegram arrived — as you had suspected," Lee noted as he leaned back into his chair. He sighed deeply as he gazed at the mottled ceiling. Carter settled into a chair in front of the desk.

"What do you think? Do you think General Blanco is lying?" Carter asked.

"Nothing indicates that, son. Villaverde did say last night that the Spaniards were just as surprised as we were. And if it is someone from their ranks, I cannot accept that it was at all sanctioned."

"Huh?" Carter asked, not following Lee's logic.

"You've seen the warnings. Not a one of them came from a group that was associated with Parrado or Governor-General Blanco. They were all splinter groups, anarchists, Weylerites, and the like."

Carter scowled and tried to follow Lee's thought process.

"You remember when the *Maine* arrived? General Parrado invited Captain Sigsbee and I to a bullfight. A gesture of peace, you know, when in Rome?"

"I remember."

"Well, you remember this, don't you?" Lee retrieved a paper from his desk and handed it to Carter.

"Yes," Carter said as handed it back to Lee, who squirreled it away back in his desk.

"I didn't think anything of it at the time," Lee continued, rather disengaged. "I just thought it was a simple anarchistic protest. Young people are like that, you know, always screaming for attention. But I kept receiving threats, each one successively stronger and more direct."

"Are you thinking the Weylerites did this?"

"Just like they were behind most of the riots this past month. Just two days ago, I received another warning that contained a direct threat against the *Maine*. Yes. I should have listened to the signals."

Carter recalled Ramón's message as well. It was pretty clear to him that there was at least one plot to destroy the ship."

"I should have been more attentive," Lee continued to lament.

"So you have ruled out an internal explosion already?"

Consul Lee closed one eye and craned his neck forward, looking dumbfounded. The old man shook his head, then got up from his chair and wandered toward the window overlooking the bay. "What in tarnation are you thinking, son?" he finally mumbled.

"I don't know. Sabotage, maybe. A coal explosion — perhaps. I just think we shouldn't rule that out quite yet," Carter explained. He let his thought drop, rather that reveal he may have been taken by an informational ruse. He turned away and moved toward the bookshelf, then leaned into the musty odor of old, damp paper.

"We can't dispel that completely, but it will be a bit difficult to prove." Lee acknowledged.

"Or disprove," Carter added.

"You may have something there, Sam," Lee said as he stood from his desk and moved toward the window. He folded his hands behind his back then stiffened. "What in God's name are they doing?" Lee uttered as he scrambled back to his desk, grabbed the spyglass he had kept for surveillance, and scurried back. He focused the instrument, and then harrumphed.

'*Sooner than he thought,*' Carter thought as he joined Lee

at the window and saw the *Olivette* pass Castle Morro at flank speed, sheets of the harbor peeling off her cutwater and steam directly into the harbor.

"Do they realize what the hell they are doing?" Lee said, his voice tainted with disbelief. His glance toward Carter turned into a puzzled expression. "You knew about this?"

Carter nodded. "Yes. I was just on the *City of Washington* talking with Wainwright. The *Olivette* is taking most of the survivors back to Key West. There will be other ships arriving shortly, with divers. I am going down to take a look."

Lee glared at Carter, his face etched with concern. His eyes moved up and down as if inspecting every inch of Carter's body. "You know how to dive?"

"I know what I am doing," Carter lied as he headed out the door.

"I hope you do, son," Lee said, chuckling under his breath.

Wilhelm Ziegler wandered into Wilson's, a small eatery a few miles from the Norfolk Navy Yard, and gravitated toward a corner table where he was confident he would not be bothered. He settled into a strait backed wooden chair, and then unfolded the newspaper he found lying on a concrete bench outside. He ordered up a cup of strong coffee with a pastry, a donut the round-faced cook called it, and while he waited for his breakfast, began reading the front page.

'U.S.S. Maine blown up in Havana Harbor,' the banner headline pronounced. Ziegler sat back in his chair, smitten. His plan had worked. He had clearly added enough iron and salt to the load to ignite the coal and create the explosion. He reckoned the drama would have been enhanced if it occurred in open waters, but that did not matter now — what was done was done.

He read on in the article, piecing together the English words he knew to gather the essence of the story. It was interesting to him that the Americans clearly believed that Spain was responsible somehow, and retribution was already being demanded. He snickered, realizing that it was his work that initiated the Kaiser's plot – the diversion had gone off as planned. McKinley and Roosevelt were bound to take revenge and send everything in the arsenal to teach Spain a lesson — half to the Philippines and the other half to Cuba. Just as the Kaiser planned. The coast would be left defenseless. It was now in the hands of Tirpitz to come through when this place emptied of protection.

Ziegler glanced up and noticed the waiter appeared from behind the counter bringing his coffee and pastry. He hovered for a moment near the table, looking over Ziegler's shoulder.

"Now if that don't get some blood boilin'," the waiter said as he pointed to the article. He wiped his hands on the towel hanging from his apron. Ziegler looked up to him quizzically, not familiar with the expression. "I would bet that old Roosevelt will finally get his way," the waiter then added.

"How is that?" Ziegler turned his attention to the man.

"Where you been, man?" the waiter cocked his head. "He's been waiting for somethin' like this to happen so he can rally the cause."

A set of tiny bells on the door drew Ziegler's and the waiter's attention. A group of uniformed men entered and converged at the counter, bantering loud enough that Ziegler could overhear their conversation.

"Let me get these boys set up," the waiter said as he knocked on the table. "Coffee?" he then yelled out. The officers all nodded and raised their hands almost in unison as they settled in near Ziegler.

"Going to three shifts, I hear," the taller of the officers noted. His uniform was bit crumpled, but still in better condition that the other three.

"Yep, and we got a whole fleet of merchant ships coming in for refit after these new ones are done," another one revealed. "Guns have already been ordered and on the way. Old Rosey had this one figured out a long time ago!"

Ziegler thought about the comments as he feigned continuing to read the article. He sipped at his coffee and devoured the crusty pastry, reckoning the information he was hearing was important. The Kaiser's plan to invade through Norfolk and Hampton might not be as unchallenged as Tirpitz had believed. As he suspected, Baltimore might be a more viable target.

"Woe is the Spanish ship that ventures into this harbor. We'll blow them clear back to Madrid." Ziegler took mental notes as he listened to the taller officer spout off. He finished his donut, wiped his hands on the worn napkin lying on his table, and drained his coffee cup. He dropped a coin on the table and waved to the waiter, something he had seen others do customarily here, then stuffed the folded paper under his arm and headed back out to the chilly Norfolk streets.

Ziegler wasted little time reaching the vantage point he used to look into the now bustling Navy yard. His observation confirmed what the officers said. Progress had been made on the ships — enough progress since the last time he was here that Tirpitz's planned incursion could be jeopardized. Flat cars overloaded with stacks of war materiel waited outside the chain-linked fence in a queue to be unloaded and moved deeper into the yard when the cars inside the compound were unloaded. Workers moved about the yard like army ants he had seen in the tropics, from the trains to the buildings, and then out to the waiting hulls, most of them close enough to completion that they floated in a long line along the piers.

He had collected enough information, Ziegler thought as he turned and slipped back into thick pines surrounding the yard. If he stayed, he would need to find a way to cable this information back to the Kaiser, in code, since he was sure there were no secure lines in this town. And soon.

Carter grew more anxious each additional hour he waited at the Café Luz. The vessel promised to bring the needed diving gear was overdue. Long overdue. Two coffees worth overdue so far. Out over the wreckage, vultures appeared, first one, then two more, queuing into a wide macabre circle over the wreckage, as if calculating their approach toward the surfaced bodies that drifted with the tide toward the southern seawalls. Cuban workers with kerchief-covered faces combed the shoreline, collecting detritus as it washed onto the oil-stained rocks and sand.

'How many more would float to the shore today,' Carter thought as he slowly sipped at his third cup of coffee. Nineteen sailors had already been buried here, a capitulation Sigsbee had to make since Havana lacked adequate embalming facilities. He counted three more blanched bodies floating close enough to the shoreline that a pair of Cubans were ordered to fish them out of the water.

Carter set his cup down and looked out to the mouth of the harbor again. Morning had now warmed from its crisp start. Finally a contorted steam plume. A single plume appeared west of Castle Morro. *'A single stack?'* he mused, remembering the *New York,* the cruiser that was supposed to arrive, had two stacks. Or was it three. It really did not matter — it was more than one. A vessel was arriving and it probably had diving gear. He dropped money onto the table, headed to the ferry slip and in fifteen minutes, he was aboard the *City of Washington.*

The *Bache,* registered as a transport and survey ship, drifted into its mooring just to the west of the *City of Washington* as a small ferryboat, already halfway between her and the pier, approached. Commander Wainwright stood at the bow of the ferry with Carter, and as soon as the skiff drew alongside the transport, the pair scrambled aboard. Sailors on the *Bache* unloaded another pair of tethered, flat-bottomed boats into the water on the opposite side of the vessel. Gear flew between hands and into the metal barge-like skiffs that looked more like tin tubs. Motors, hoses, canvas coveralls, copper metal dive helmets almost spewed out of stump-like lockers, filling the barges to the gunwales as Lieutenant Collins presented his dive team to Commander Wainwright.

"Rescue, if there are any air pockets first," Wainwright ordered.

"Aye, Sir," three divers concurred in unison.

"Recovery follows. Anyone still in the holds. Then preservation of evidence. Recover what you can, make note of what you can't." Collins added, emotion absent from his directives.

"Aye, sir," the team replied and climbed aboard the transports. Carter followed under intense scrutiny from the team.

"This is routine for them Commander," Collins scowled at the *Maine's* Commander. "They're a bit crusty, but they are the best in the world at what they do. Treat 'em that way."

Wainwright nodded as he stepped over the breach between the vessels as the outboard motor coughed to life with a spew of blue smoke. The skiff maneuvered widely before buzzing in a beeline toward the carcass of the *Maine*. As they closed the distance, a flotilla of three small motorboats, officers aboard, maneuvered into a blockade and forced the equipment ferries to stop short of their intended target.

"*No va*," a young Spanish officer announced as he stood defiantly at the bow of the lead patrol boat and waved off the approaching American boats.

"Bull shit," Commander Wainwright cursed under his breath. He stepped to the gunwale of the equipment skiff and pointed to what little of the *Maine* remained above the surface. "I am Commander Wainwright and that is our ship there."

The officer turned to another sailor and after a brief huddle, turned back to Wainwright and repeated, "*No va. Ahora se trata de español.*"

"Bastards!" Wainwright spit. He chewed his lip for a moment, and then turned to his signalman. "Can you get Sigsbee here? Maybe they'll listen to him."

"Yes, sir," the young sailor replied. He took out his flags and postured with a flurry of positions back toward the *City of Washington*. After several series of maneuvers, he turned back to Wainwright and said, "On his way."

Wainwright puffed up and glared back at the Spanish officer, who remained standing defiantly at the bow of his own patrol boat. For a minute, the stare down continued with neither officer backing down. Several of the officers cinched up their rifles while the Americans covered the handles of their revolvers.

"Incoming vessel!" the signaler called out to Wainwright as he noticed a small skiff headed toward them.

"We'll see what the bastards have to say now," Wainwright whispered toward Carter. After a tense wait,

Sigsbee's craft pulled alongside of the equipment skiffs. The Captain puffed out his chest and stood tall and sturdy, legs parted, arms crossed.

"What's the problem, Commander?"

"We're being held back, sir. They are claiming it is theirs."

"Bullshit!" Sigsbee groused as his vessel kissed the gunwale of Wainwright's skiff. He climbed aboard, then stomped accurately across the hoses and diving gear laid out in the belly of the boat, then stood next to Wainwright and faced the Spaniards.

"I am Captain Sigsbee and that is my vessel down there," Sigsbee growled as he pointed to his epaulets. "I demand that you allow us to dive on that wreckage."

"*No va*," the Spanish officer repeated, more indignant than before.

Carter could see that Sigsbee was fuming. He hoped that the Captain would properly evaluate the unevenness of armament.

"It is probably better to withdraw for now," Sigsbee finally spit out. Carter sighed, relieved as Sigsbee motioned with his hand for the pilot to return to the *Washington*, then turned back to the Spaniards and threatened, "We will be back!"

"Capitulation, sir?" Wainwright asked.

"Discretion, Commander," Sigsbee turned to Wainwright, his face clearly etched with an anger Carter had not seen before. "Telegraph Consul Lee and have him demand a meeting with General Blanco. And while I get this mess straightened out, get these men some rest and something to drink."

"Yes, sir," Wainwright replied then turned to the men on the skiffs and ordered the return.

As Captain Sigsbee's official motorized dingy reached the pier, he stood, arms crossed, directing the skiff toward the dock where Consul-General Lee paced in front of a small assembly. Before the boat had even stopped, Sigsbee stepped up onto the pier, met Consul Lee with a quick, deliberate handshake, and then walked through the center of the gathered onlookers and directly to the palatial office building, arriving in less than ten minutes. Sigsbee marched into the building first, briefly taken aback by the posh accoutrements along the corridor headed toward the General's office. With Lee at his side, he was sure Blanco would avoid slipping into some guttural Spanish he did not understand. At the end of the long hallway, a soldier sitting at a tiny desk looked up and crudely demanded credentials from Sigsbee.

"Captain Charles Sigsbee, United States Navy. I demand to speak with the General," the Captain barked, angered by a low ranking soldier's lack of respect for his rank. He crossed his arms and scowled at the soldier, refusing to submit any papers.

"*Momento*," the soldier said as he slowly stood up. He stepped toward the tall, narrow wooden doors, cracked them open, then leaned in and spoke to someone, most likely the General himself. The young soldier leaned back as General Blanco opened the doors fully and gestured Sigsbee and Lee into his well-appointed office.

"There appears to be a bit of a misunderstanding, sir," Sigsbee growled as he walked through the threshold, not waiting to sit down before he started. Secretary General Congostino, Blanco's close aid quickly and efficiently translated Sigsbee's opening statement while Consul-General Lee monitored the words closely.

"*Tal vez podría explicar*," Blanco replied, stiff-lipped, with a cocked head and wide eyes.

"My vessel, the *Maine*, had come to Havana on a legitimate errand, and had entered the harbor with the consent of the local authorities." Sigsbee waited for the translation before continuing. "By international law, therefore, even the wreckage remains American territory. I should not be denied access to her."

Congostino efficiently translated Sigsbee's words. The General rubbed his chin slowly, and then responded through his translator, "That may be true, but Spanish law requires that any disaster on our soil be investigated by us first."

"My vessel is not your jurisdiction," Sigsbee fumed. "And I am not going to sit back and wait until you —"

"Captain, it is our honor that is involved in this case. Perhaps we could make this venture together, you know, our divers and your divers?" Blanco countered.

Sigsbee thought for a moment, and then turned back to Blanco. "We agree that you have the right to investigate, and in fact, we would endorse that investigation. A joint venture however, would need to be cleared through Washington. I do believe, though, that Washington would encourage separate investigations, and perhaps share the information that each of us discern. After all, we both want to come to an understanding of what truly occurred, yes?"

Blanco leaned toward Congostino as the translator rattled through the interpretation of Sigsbee's words. Sigsbee meanwhile conferred with Lee using a whispered voice, and for the moment, only whispers filled the room. Blanco referred to a paper on his desk several times in his conversation, clearly displeased he had been cornered. Blanco finally cleared his throat and waved to Congostino to recommence translating.

"How will I know that you will not create, shall I say, false evidence of responsibility?"

"I have dead men down there," Sigsbee clenched his teeth and leaned forward. "It is my duty as the Captain to discern the truth of this matter."

Blanco recoiled and stared at Congostino as he waited for the translation. When his translator was done, Blanco arched his eyebrows and skewered Sigsbee with a disapproving glare. After a tense moment, he nodded.

"You are free to explore. General Blanco would see to it that your team is no longer refused access." Congostino said with a harsh tone. He then tilted his head, looked directly at Lee and asked, "Is there anything else you need today?"

"No sir." Sigsbee replied icily, stood and hand pressed his uniform. Choosing not to seal the agreement with a handshake, he turned and left the office with Lee close behind.

"Cold enough?" Sigsbee commented wryly as they headed

directly toward the pier.

"I would say so, Captain," Lee replied. "We can radio the go ahead from the Consulate, if you wish. It would be quicker."

Sigsbee agreed and even before the last scratchy comment came through the radio, Wainwright climbed down into the lead skiff, stood at the bow and directed the pilot to head back to the wreckage. Wainwright stood at the ready for confrontation, but as his craft slowed and slipped past the stone-faced Spaniards, he could not resist smugly grinning. Now inside the circle, Wainwright ordered the pilot of the lead craft to maneuver toward the middle of the crippled *Maine*. The engine starved until it coughed and ceased puttering, leaving momentum to sling the barge close enough to the wreckage.

Carter began having second thoughts, suddenly feeling unprepared for this venture, but there was no turning back. Having already slipped into the canvas coveralls provided him by the diving crew, he and the other three divers waited in the metal barge for their tenders. Dive plans were reviewed verbally. Carter peeked over the edge — the murky gray water would challenge their ability to see, even with powerful electric lamps attached to their helmets. Revealing details would be hazy at best, invisible at worst. But it would have to do. These were the only tools they had.

The barge bobbed as the tenders jumped from the pilot boat to the diver's barge, then worked over to the additional diving gear. Carter took advantage of the delay to study the wreckage above the surface close up. In front of him was the clearly torn away stern, listing slightly to port. The deck lay only a few feet below the surface, the tall rear mast still above the surface and towering ominously over the wreckage. The front half of the ship had clearly suffered the most severe damage. Almost exactly at the middle of the ship, the front half appeared to have been thrust upward and twisted to port. The green under plating of the hull on the starboard side was exposed, resultant of the gaping hole on the port side that had sunk the battle ship. The metal was twisted and scorched from the fires, but no other damage was visible.

The impact, whether it was internal or external, Carter

thought, must have been at that point where the two halves of the ship had been split. Over his shoulder, he noticed that several Spanish war ships sat silent on the water, to the starboard side of the wreckage, where they were the night before, a line of sailors maintaining their watch. Carter resumed his dressing, reaching down and strapping on his twenty-pound lead shoes. They clanked loudly onto the metal bottom of the boat.

"Air on!" shouted out one of the tenders. The air compressor started, spitting and coughing until it smoothed out to a low rumble. Air seeped through the lines into the helmets at first then hissed more strongly and steadily.

"Hats on!" Charles Morgen, the dive team leader ordered. Carter took one last glance to the front of the wreckage, where he and the team would be headed for their inspection. The tenders responded, lifting the fifty pound brass helmets above each of the diver's heads.

"Hold still. This'll break yer nose if yah don't," a tender barked at Carter, who immediately stiffened and let the tender slip the musty smelling casing over his head. The gruff old sailor latched the neck plate into place over Carter's shoulders as stale air hissed inside the helmet and bathed his face. The tender tightened the brass nuts along the neck plate, moved to the still open faceplate, and sneered. "Don't suck up too much here. It'll be hell on yah when yah come up. That's iffin yah come up," he then noted with a grin that revealed three missing teeth.

Carter took heed relaxed, hoping his breathing would follow. He wondered if the tender could tell he was inexperienced. '*It didn't matter now,*' he reconciled to himself.

"Dive time limit, two hours," Morgen reminded. Carter's tender closed his faceplate. "I have inside with Folsom, Carter you have outside with Briggs." Carter barely heard the words, but signaled with a 'thumbs up' sign anyway. Silence reigned. With the exception of the hissing air slipping life into his brass helmet, Carter heard nothing but an occasional squawk of a seagull. He watched as his tender further tightened the outside bolts one by one. He felt a tug at the top of his helmet. '*The lamp'* Carter reckoned as he focused through the thick face plate glass at the dive team lead for hand signals.

Morgen signaled up. Carter felt his tender roughly hog-tie him, then hoist him with arms buried in his armpits. He stood in line and watched as Morgen rolled over the side and secured his lead shoes between the top rungs of the barnacle covered wooden ladder. Morgen's helmet sank methodically then disappeared below the gunwale. After a minute, enough time for Morgen to clear the ladder, the second man in line plunged into the water. Another minute, then the third. The helmet disappeared below the gunwale.

It was Carter's turn. He focused on his breathing, trying to hold his panic at bay as he stepped toward and worked around the ladder. He hooked his lead shoes onto the top ladder rung as he had seen the others do. Descent. A rung at a time. The water line inched up and covered his faceplate. He then exhaled, explosively as he had been told, then continued to work down the ladder as far as it reached. He waved his foot for a moment to be sure he was at the end of the ladder, then stepped off and drifted a couple more feet down until his shoes hit and sank into the soft murky bottom of the harbor.

Carter closed his eyes and focused on breathing slowly and steadily rather than his building fear and twisted stomach. He didn't remember ever being as vulnerable — a grizzly old sailor literally had his life in his hands. He would have rather faced the barrel of a gun. Carter closed his eyes and started thinking, *'What was it that Garcia said? If one is always afraid about saving his carcass, he would never get his rewards?'* Those were good words. Against his tender's orders, he sucked in a deep breath and focused on the work he had to do. He opened his eyes, pushing them as open as far as he could with the air that blew in his face, oriented himself in the direction he sensed the front section had to be, then plodded forward like Frankenstein, hands outstretched in the direction of an eerie glow.

The deeper water started sapping body heat through Carter's suit, chilling him by the time he could discern light beams out in front of him. He remembered the plan. He and

Briggs were to inspect what they could outside the bow of the vessel while Morgen and Folsom walked through the stern. The clamminess of the suit against his skin raised a full crop of goose bumps by the time he reached Morgen standing stiffly at the fissure where the *Maine* had been severed into two pieces. Morgen appeared frozen and stiff; his light beam was still, directed forward and into the twisted hull. Carter moved closer to the wreckage as quickly as the water resistance and his lead shoes allowed. He dragged his feet, defensively so that he would not fall if he plowed through some of the timber that had been shattered and lay on the harbor floor. When he reached Morgan, he looked inside the broken hull, turning his head enough that his light crossed Morgen's and Folsom's in the vastness of the hull and gasped. Amid the turbid, dark water, shattered timbers, twisted metal beams, and collapsed bulkheads, dismembered limbs floated toward them, as if caught up in a feeble current. Deeper in the hull, bloated bodies, their faces burned beyond recognition, drifted into the lighted pathway, then back into darkness. Carter felt a building surge of vomit but he closed his eyes and held back the purge. He slogged a few steps closer to Morgen before placing his hand on his shoulder. Morgan probably knew many of these men.

Morgen's catatonia broke. He turned toward Carter and slowly nodded. Carter hand signaled he was heading out away from the wreck. He needed to move away from the death ship, partly to gather his wits from the floating mass of bodies and partly to see what other evidence may lie on the harbor floor around them. He slipped the rope off his shoulder and wrapped it around a timber that had been pummeled into the harbor floor like it were a post, assuring a method to grope his way back to the murky world surrounding the ship.

Carter took deliberate steps. The memory of his father's fate some thirty-five years ago seeped into his mind. His stepfather never revealed the details of that fateful night, but perhaps it was more because he was not there to witness it. *'Did the Hunley implode under the pressure of their own charge, its force expelled when it detonated inside the*

Housatonic? Did his father and the rest of the crew drown like these men? Did he suffer as these men did, sucking in water into his lungs, struggling for even a bubble of stale air trapped in the hull? Did he float away, bloat, decay and be left as detritus for sharks and scavenger fish?'

Carter stumbled, but caught himself before falling over. He gently placed his right foot forward as if testing the water in a lake before a refreshing swim. Under his shoes was the lip of a crater that had been filled in with a mud softer than the rest of the harbor floor. He worked himself down in a zigzagged manner until his lead overshoe clunked against a metal fragment. It was a large, intact shell.

Ordnance. One of his questions had been resolved. What he saw sculling away from the *Maine* last night was most likely this shell, propelled from the ship by the explosion, and once the momentum dissipated, it dropped to the harbor floor and discharged more like a dud than an explosion. This was what he thought was a submarine, he was sure. He climbed back out of the crater and scanned further toward shore, where the water was marginally clearer. Nothing. Nothing else had travelled this far. Satisfied, he turned back toward the wreckage, and recoiled the rope as he shuffled back toward the death ship, as he now knew it.

Carter reached the wreckage and began working his way back down the hull. He stepped closer and closer until he noticed the plate where the explosion had occurred. It seemed oddly bent. The rivets that were used to hold the plates together were missing. He shuffled closer, enough to see that four rivets were missing in the center of the plate. He moved his head lamp closer still and noticed there was a distinct bulge from the inside on the lower plate. He studied the plates as closely as the murky water allowed, making mental notes that he would need to decipher. Looking at it just wasn't adding up for him.

Carter felt a pull on his air hose. It was the signal for time to head back to the dive entry point and muster. He looked around, but suddenly saw nothing but blackness. His light had burned out. He felt his heart pound faster and harder as the reality that he was out of his element grew stark and evident.

He could feel his breathing labor. His panicked breaths grew shallower as his breathing started to labor. Paralleling the hull, he worked his way back, struggling against tangled rigging from the forward mast as he stepped. Methodically, he slogged back in what he thought was the rendezvous location at the breach between the fore and aft sections. He stumbled again, struggling to keep his heavy dive shoes from becoming entangled in any wreckage.

An eerie glow emerged from the darkness. He reckoned it had to be another diver, so he plodded directly toward it. When he reached the light, he realized it was Briggs. He relaxed — resting and waiting for Morgen and Folsom to emerge from inside of the hull. He did not have to wait long for the dim light to suddenly appear, shadows of bodies floating in and out of the beam as it grew closer. Finally, Morgen's silhouette appeared, struggling through the twisted metal and body parts, but ploddingly making progress, followed closely by Folsom.

They all trudged together back to the drop point, tied their lines around their waists and tugged on their lifeline to signal they were ready. Carter rose first, working as best he could to pull himself up the ladder, all the while letting the surface crew help him navigate closer to the real world.

"Exhale more than ya inhale on yer way up," Carter remembered the tender's words as he stepped up the sixty feet of rungs on the ladder. As he rose, he counted the rungs. The ladder seemed more like a mile than a couple dozen feet. Finally, the surface. He could see again. Exhaustion sapped any elation he felt with the escape. Water slid off his canvas suit as he emerged from the water. He reached up onto the gunwale and then hand-over-hand moved to the lever-like platform placed on the rail of the barge. Three tenders groaned as they tilted the platform that brought Carter parallel to the water's surface. He crabbed his body enough to turn his boots toward the inside of the launch as the platform pivoted and deposited him in the skiff, his boots clomping onto the boat's metal floor as he collapsed.

"Hold still or I'll twist yer head off," Carter heard his tender growl as he spun the large wing nuts to open his helmet.

As he watched Folsom's tender start the process of extracting the diver from the water, his faceplate was popped open and he sucked in the deepest breath of his life. The air, even as it was tainted with salt, never tasted as good as it did at that moment. He leaned back against the side of the barge and sat, trying to muster the energy he needed to remove his waterlogged diving gear.

Morgen was the last diver to emerge and thud into the bottom of the diving skiff. Carter noticed that as soon as his metal helmet was removed, a tall, wispy man swooped down on him and commenced a very pointed debriefing. Wainwright had warned Carter about this particular investigator — Ensign Wilfred Van Nest Powelson; a dowdy sailor of little personality and less compassion. Few in ONI had cared much for him, but he was always able to get the information he needed.

"It was horrible!" Morgen leaned over to catch his breath. His face was pale and ashen. Morgen's tender helped him to the bench so he could sit upright and recover as he responded to Powelson's interrogation.

"Explain," Powelson barked. He craned his neck forward and stepped up on the gunwale with his foot, using his thigh to balance his notebook and record the information.

"As I moved into the wreckage, the dead rose up to meet me. They floated with outstretched arms, as if welcoming a shipmate. Their faces . . . bloated with decay, most burned beyond recognition."

"The vessel, sailor. What about the vessel," Powelson demanded.

"But here and there the light of my lamp flashed upon a stony face I knew," Morgen's voice dropped off into a monotonous crazed soliloquy, which rambled on as if not hearing Powelson's demands. "Which when I last saw it had smiled a merry greeting, but now returned my gaze with staring eyes and fallen jaw."

Carter struggled up from his sitting position and inserted himself between Powelson and Morgen. "Give him some time," he growled. "You have no clue how gruesome it was down there. Floating, bloated bodies completely choking passageways. I watched Morgen as he worked his way through doing his duty. He had to elbow his way through them as if he was on a crowded street. Give the man some time!"

"Body to port!" One of the tenders then called out. Powelson glanced over and saw a half-naked corpse breach the surface, then slowly drift toward the barge. He gagged, stepped down into the barge, and moved to the far gunwale. Carter heard him purge violently over the other side of the boat.

"Recover it," Powelson ordered as he returned, spitting to clear his mouth of vomit. He then glared at Carter and added, "Let me make myself clear, Mr. Carter. We need to get all the information documented as soon as we can. Perhaps that is too much for a non-military rubbernecker to understand."

"I am here on official government business, sir, directly from the President. All I am suggesting is some hint of courtesy rather than cannibalism for your own kind." Carter snapped around on his bench and finished sliding off his musty smelling coveralls. As Morgen glanced up to Carter, a thank you expression spawned on his face.

Powelson quivered, clearly angered by Carter's quip. He bit his lip and turned back to the tenders. "Wrap them up in those sheets," he barked, and then stumbled across the hoses, ropes and other diving gear strewn about the launch to get back to Morgen.

"Tell me again, Mr. Morgen. What else did you see?" Powelson asked with a more conciliatory tone. He pulled the clipboard out from his belt where he had stowed it, then settled down on the plank next to Morgen.

"While I examined twisted iron and broken timbers, they brushed against my helmet — touched my shoulders with rigid hands, as if they sought to tell me what happened," Morgan started again, his tone as macabre as if he were reading a Edgar Allen Poe story. Powelson let him ramble this time. "I often had to push them aside to examine deeper into the hull. I felt like a live man in command of the dead. From every part of the ship came sighs and groans. I knew it was the gurgling of the water through the shattered beams and battered sides of the vessel, but it made me shudder. Turn which way I would, I was confronted by another corpse."

"Could you reach plate seventeen?" Powelson prodded. Carter took note and tried to remember what might have been different about that plate.

"No, sir. Not on this dive. It will take some time to get that deep into the hull." Morgen bowed his head. His voice seemed to have returned to reality. "On the outside, it is pretty treacherous with all the rigging debris there."

"Do we need to extend the dive times?"

"Yes, sir. And perhaps a few more men would help," Morgen noted.

"I will get the men. We need to find the answers," Powelson conceded, placing his hand on Morgen's shoulder. "Rest up, sailor," he added as he turned and headed to the rear of the barge. The ensign sat down on an oak plank and examined the locations on the wreckage he could from the surface, taking notes as he pointed to each of the grotesquely bent metal frame parts.

Carter's lungs ached as if he had run a mile in a driving, cold rain. His body throbbed, feeling as abused. The dive had taken more out of him than he expected, and was not sure if he could even dive again. He still needed to see what the *Maine* looked like from below, but he was not sure if he could personally continue performing dives on a daily basis. He reckoned that if he didn't go in, he would have to work with Powelson and share information. Perhaps he could do that, he thought, at least for the short term.

Chapter 21

Alone in his office, President McKinley poured over what little information had come in from Cuba. None of the details came from official sources, although the facts did provide enough clues for him to make an educated guess on the probable outcome of the investigation. He understood that naval regulations forbade Captain Sampson or any of the inquiry board to release any information, including conjecture, until the investigation was completed, facts corroborated, conclusion solidified and made ready for delivery. He knew he had the means to exempt Sampson from that rule, but he chose not to exercise his Executive Privilege. Contrarily, he expanded the rule to include Captain Sigsbee and Consul Lee, considering how impactful the findings would be in the coming months. It concerned him that even with his own secure means of communication, some people with less than honorable intentions might intercept and twist any preliminary information to further their agendas. For now, he could justifiably hide behind a 'nothing official' statement.

McKinley fondled his cigar as he perused the papers and thought about his dilemma. He was not convinced that anyone in the Spanish government or military would be so brash as to concoct this incendiary action, especially at this critical juncture, but it was difficult to rule it out since the alternative was not without its own set of consequences. If the explosion was internal, whether a coal fire or sabotage, then by protocol, he had to hold Captain Charles Sigsbee, a dear friend, accountable. Having his friend Court-martialed was as unpalatable as heading off to war.

He also knew he had to be the stabilizing factor in his personal Cabinet, now seemingly more emotionally charged than ever. Up to now, he felt he controlled the gadfly in Roosevelt. The spectacle-wearing rogue Secretary's charisma was more consuming than even he could have imagined. His boisterous outbursts in public catapulted his popularity. McKinley was certain it was Roosevelt who slipped information to the media, most of which was devastating to his image, characterizing him as weak for not taking immediate and swift action. Nevertheless, prudence was the President's personal talent, and he firmly believed that facts yet to be uncovered in the *Maine* incident would exonerate him, revealing a more benign truth. He was the leader of the country and before he jumped off halfcocked on an irreversible path, as Roosevelt seemed to have done, he had to be sure that the event was clearly an act of sabotage on Spain's part. The consequence of a wrong decision now would have historically lasting impacts.

Looking up, McKinley noticed Vice-President Garret Hobart standing at the open doorway, leaning into the jamb. He waved him in. Hobart complied, melting into a chair next to McKinley's desk. An aura of calmness surrounded the stout man, and his robustness, reminiscent of a St. Nicholas fable, mislead many to believe the man to be nothing more than jovial and aloof. McKinley had seen exactly the opposite. He had come to recognize in his short tenure that Hobart was wise beyond his years, despite what he and others thought of him prior to the election.

"Not much from Havana?" Hobart asked. McKinley remained silent. He looked up to his second with a stare worn blank by sleepless nights. "We have no choice but to make preparations, Mac," Hobart added.

"What do you think I should do with Alger, Garrett?"

"I think you know, Mac," Hobart fidgeted for a moment, unbuttoning his tight, restricting vest to let his paunch expand. "His memory is weak. He clearly cannot foresee even the most obvious of conclusions. His decision making is circuitous, at best."

"An albatross, then."

"Hmm," Hobart grunted agreement. He slipped his finger between his neck and stiff, upright shirt collar and pulled.

"If I get rid of him now, how would that look? I've already pigeon-holed Sherman, and if I sack another of my cabinet, would I be seen as despotic?"

"If it is the right thing to do —"

"I would rather be seen as a fair and wise man rather than some tyrant who went to war, especially over a mistake in judgment," McKinley lamented. Hobart stroked his thick eyebrows as he glanced toward the ceiling. His eyes swept across the ceiling before they rested on his boss. McKinley then added, "Am I as bull-headed as Johnson with these moves, Gus? Is Congress going to rally for Articles of Impeachment like they did with him?"

"Are you convinced there is no side road we can take to move away from this war?"

"I believe I am now at this point, Gus; the delays from the Queen Regent, the de Lôme letter, the *Maine* . . . it's all adding up to one thing. And Roosevelt already has half the Navy on alert and declared he's packed and ready to go to the front."

"Then I believe you already have your answer on the latter question, Mac. All we can do is to stall long enough for preparations and hopefully a swift conclusion. Waiting for the investigation's conclusion should give us that time."

"And then what? Do we just hand the whole thing over to the resistance? You know if we don't maintain some presence it would be a disaster." McKinley buried his head in his hands and grumbled. "Have you seen anything from Lee? He is our best set of eyes down there."

"He's asking for time and help to get our people out of there. His actions are providing your answer."

"In the end, perhaps I am headed down the correct pathway," McKinley bemoaned. "But you know as well as I that Alger simply cannot be trusted to rally up the troops. He would most likely drag his feet so long that the Spanish could become strong enough to defend the island."

"That is unlikely."

"Or worse, combine forces with the Kaiser. Who's to know what he's been doing over there. Hell, they may be even strong enough combined to take back Florida."

"You want me to talk to him?" Hobart asked as McKinley pensively glanced up to the ceiling. "Once war is declared, you are in charge anyway, so you would only be bridging the gap between now until then." Hobart finished.

"I see," McKinley scanned the ceiling again. When his eyes returned to Hobart, there was a clear conviction in them. "I'll let you know after this meeting. I'd like to give him one more chance to show me something of a backbone. If he is still recalcitrant, you may inform him that his services are no longer needed."

"I can do that for you, Mac." Hobart said as he rose from his chair and started out. He stopped before stepping out into the hallway and turned. He folded his hands behind his back for a moment, but he released his right so he could wag his finger in a friendly, direct manner at McKinley.

"As a business man back in Jersey, I learned a very valuable lesson. You can manage all the sordid details for periods of time, but only brief periods of time. That is a very important position, especially considering the direction we are headed. You will need to choose a replacement quickly — a strong replacement that you can trust to make decisions aligned with yours, articulate it well, execute the details, as well as deal decisively with Roosevelt."

"Maybe bring the tiger into the fold?" McKinley finally cracked a grin.

"I would not advise that, Mac."

"I'll need your help with the selection. I can't recall anyone that could fill those shoes," McKinley noted, then returned to his papers and combed through the disheveled pile. He then looked back up to Hobart and tipped his head. "A different subject Gus, if you don't mind. What do think about John Wilkie?"

"That too is a rather loaded question, Mac," Hobart

sauntered back in toward McKinley and sat down in front of his desk. "What do you need help with?"

"The economy is crippled. Hell, we've got so many people out of work right now. And on top of that, the entire currency issue that Hazen promised would stimulate growth had to be withdrawn because of all this counterfeit crap going on."

"Hmm," Hobart nodded his agreement. He chewed his lower lip.

"I thought Hazen could handle that by himself. I didn't think I needed to get involved but he is just not getting off square one. He's got a whole office full of agents to ferret out where these two-bit criminals are. I would have expected him to catch this before it exploded into the ugly mess we have on our hands now."

"You're asking for help?" Hobart twirled his mustache.

"You know how fragile the banks are right now, and you know what could happen if they fold up. Inflation. Strikes for more money. Business spirals downward. More people out of work. More strikes. Stock market crash. More people out of work. Just one hellatious spiral if we're not careful."

"Then perhaps a nice little war is just what we need. It does create a strong cash flow, you know." Hobart stated matter-of-factly.

"Perhaps, but Hazen could always juggle. He should have been able to at least keep track of what was going on."

"Maybe he's the wrong person for the job, Mac." Hobart said bluntly.

"If I sack another Cabinet member, I'll be running the entire government on my own. You can see how this is quite embarrassing for our whole administration, Garret. The country knows most of us are businessmen and this says that we can't manage money safely?"

"Then you've got to make that change too, Mac." Hobart's lips pursed. McKinley nodded absently. "I don't know much about Wilkie, but he does seem to have Roosevelt's favor. I'd say do it. You need the peace of mind, especially on the home front." Hobart stated bluntly.

"I hear you. Can you take care of that while I work on Alger some more?"

"Consider it done, Mac," Hobart said, turned and disappeared into the corridor.

McKinley returned to the papers he had in front of him again, scanning the notes he had scribbled in the margins. He rubbed his eyes as if hoping that some divine intervention would tie everything up neatly so he could resolve a conclusion before his ad hoc war council convened.

"Morning, Chief!" Roosevelt announced as he strutted into the office. There was a quickstep in his gait and a high pitch to his voice.

"Too late," McKinley mumbled to himself. Roosevelt never called him Chief.

"Incredulous news, eh?" Roosevelt blurted as he marched vigorously around the table, stopped for a brief glance out the window to the snow dusted ground, then finished his round and took his seat at the table. He expelled a huge breath, then grinned. "Even I can't believe they could do something so stupid."

"We still do not have the full report from the investigation," McKinley cautioned. "Both Lee and Sigsbee insisted we proceed with caution, and I fully agree with that."

"I don't think we need a map to figure this one out. Something bad has happened and someone has to be held accountable for it. There is only one explanation," Roosevelt snapped back as Russell Alger stepped through the open door. "I firmly believe we have reached a tipping point in history."

"The potential still exists that this may have been an accident," McKinley provided cautiously.

"This was not an accident!" Roosevelt argued adamantly, pounding his fist into his open palm. "We all know the Spaniards are responsible for this. I am sure this investigation will reveal nothing more than we already know. They planted a damned submarine mine at that mooring point purposely."

"We have no proof of that," McKinley rebutted.

"How the hell are we going to find proof of that? It blew up! Eyewitnesses said there was a water plume. What more do you need?"

"The report from the board of inquiry will provide the details. Until then —"

"Are you serious? You know it flies in the face of reason that we have not gone to war already."

"Do you realize what you are saying, Mr. Roosevelt?" Alger said. His voice trembled with tentativeness.

"I believe I do," Roosevelt replied. "So much that I am willing to put up a reward to identify and detain the perpetrator at the root of this outrage! How does fifty grand sound? This was clearly an attack. An outright, deliberate attack. I know that, you know that, the press knows that, and most importantly, they know that."

"I am as much distraught by these events, especially since we have expended months negotiating with the Spaniards. But we must use caution as we proceed." McKinley insisted.

"We can't wait any longer. If we let this pass without decisive action, we will be a laughing stock," Roosevelt insisted. "If nothing else, we need to prepare ourselves for action."

"If we do, we risk war." Alger protested.

"Then we bring it on. Our men on the *Maine* cannot have died in vain." Roosevelt insisted again. "How about you just give me a regiment, Alger and I'll go take the damned island myself!"

"Ludicrous! Do you realize what you are saying?" Alger protested. His head swiveled between Roosevelt and McKinley.

"Month by month their Navy has been put into a better condition to meet us. Do you realize that they were negotiating the purchase of two Brazilian military cruisers under construction in England?"

McKinley recoiled. He glared at Roosevelt, silently asking if he was grandstanding.

"I didn't think so," Roosevelt's lips were pursed and turned down. He squinted behind the monocle he chose to use rather than his pince-nez. "While we've been waiting for them to respond to our feeble diplomatic calls, they've been building up. And have they told Secretary Day that morsel of information?"

Roosevelt crossed his arms in front of his chest. McKinley felt his eyes drill through him. "Didn't think so," he added.

"Buy them. I'll authorize it right away. Whatever it takes, buy these ships just so that they don't have the chance at them," McKinley directed.

"Now you're talking, Chief!" Roosevelt chirped as McKinley weakly stood, eye lids drooping from lack of sleep.

"I believe we must accept that we are now at crossroads, gentlemen. I fear that we must prepare for war even as we hope that some other answer will come back from Captain Sampson's investigation. I trust him, and I am confident he will come to the correct conclusion."

Kaiser Wilhelm impatiently waited for Admiral Tirpitz to arrive. He marched about his office like a caged animal, stopping to stare only for a moment at his grandfather's oversized, gold-leaf framed portrait on the wall. He stopped briefly at the window to look at the crusted snow in the courtyard, and then marched back to his desk to review Ziegler's cable again. The news of the destruction of the *Maine* pleased him. Whether Ziegler received recognition for it did not matter to him. He had done his duty, nothing more, nothing less. The fact that what was meant as a magnet for the American forces did nothing more than spin off an investigation rather than react as he or Admiral Tirpitz had predicted concerned him.

"Your Excellency, Admiral Tirpitz," the Kaiser's aide announced as he opened the large double oak doors and allowed the hefty, fork-bearded officer to enter.

"Sire." Tirpitz genuflected with his greeting. Wilhelm looked up from his desk and with his wide eyes, directed Tirpitz to sit in the overstuffed chair in front of him.

"Ziegler reports that the Americans continue to bring armament to Norfolk," Wilhelm waved the cable in from of him as Tirpitz settled into the chair. "They are even refitting merchant ships to increase the number of vessels available."

The old Navy Captain scowled. He reached over the desk, took the cable from Wilhelm and holding it arm's length away, grunted and harrumphed as he read the details. He placed it back on the desk when done and looked past Wilhelm to the frosty window with glassy eyes.

"Perhaps we should consider an alternate plan, Admiral?" Wilhelm proposed.

"I have already considered alternatives, Sire. If not Norfolk, then New York. If not New York, then Charleston," Tirpitz growled, shifting his bloodshot eyes back toward Wilhelm. "We could also consider blockading Cuba, or for that matter the Philippines." Tirpitz spouted arrogantly.

"Ziegler has suggested Baltimore as an alternative."

"Ziegler should be more disciplined so as to do what he has been told to do," Tirpitz scoffed.

"And have you thought more of this underwater boat?" Wilhelm prodded.

"No," Tirpitz spit out curtly. "There is little value in this type of machine. Too much risk."

"I sense you are afraid of these machines, Alfred?" Wilhelm's voice was condescending.

Tirpitz stiffened and growled.

"Or is it you are too much an old man to consider a new concept. You do know this boat could provide the stealth we need," Wilhelm continued his agenda. Underwater boats had fascinated him even since his discussion with McClintock years before.

"Or we could simply place our plans on hold until this fracas between Spain and America is resolved. Is that an adequate addition to your list of alternatives?" Tirpitz offered.

"What of the money I have allocated!" Wilhelm exploded, slamming his fist on his large oak desk hard enough to rattle the Pickelhaube helmet that sat on its corner.

"Forgive my rudeness, Sire, but I am but a messenger at this point. We cannot fight anybody with money. We need iron on the water for any of these plans to bring you glory. Simply put, production needs to improve." Tirpitz sat back in his chair, as if expecting Wilhelm to explode at him again. The Kaiser's temples pulsed as his forehead flushed red. He glared directly at Tirpitz, pursed his lips and ground his teeth from side to side.

"Are you telling me that production is behind schedule?" he squeezed the words through his clenched teeth.

Tirpitz closed his eyes and nodded. "Yes, Sire. Only half of what I need to be successful is seaworthy. And some of that had to be reworked, causing further delays."

Wilhelm seethed. He recognized the time to act was slipping away. He did not want to admit to Tirpitz that the alliance with the other European monarchs was falling apart, and with it, his vision to wrest world dominance was fading. Perhaps his top naval officer already knew that. "Is there anything else?" Wilhelm asked, more subdued.

Tirpitz hesitated a moment before answering. "Yes, Sire. We also need to increase recruitment. We have barely enough men for the vessels we have now."

Wilhelm squeezed his waxed mustache against his face as he groaned and bowed his head. He trusted Tirpitz's judgment more than he had anyone else's, but the news that the Admiral had presented irritated him. The opportunity to collect his coveted Cuba was slipping away. He knew Sagasta would not be timid for long. He couldn't be. And when he did finally grow some balls, he would surely exert himself as a strong Spanish leader.

"I will visit the factories myself," Wilhelm said as he thrust his head back and jutted out his chin. He corralled his helmet and slid it toward him, swinging the Pickelhaube precariously close to his neck.

"I will prepare a list of factories we need to challenge. I will have that in your aide's hands by day's end." Tirpitz noted.

"And Admiral Tirpitz, you will be by my side to show these workers how they have disappointed not just me with their sloth, but the entire Reich." Wilhelm vaulted up from his chair and shook his clenched fist above his head.

"Yes, Sire. We can reconvene tomorrow, if that is your desire."

"That will be acceptable, Admiral," Wilhelm dismissed

Tirpitz. As soon as the Admiral exited, Wilhelm marched to his tactical map and leaned over, staring and stewing at the elusive lands in the Western Atlantic.

Roosevelt hoofed directly to the Navy Department's offices after leaving the White House. The brisk winter winds whipping around him did nothing to quell the fire now burning in his chest. Crisis and the lack of sleep that accompanied it energized him. As did the discovery that Secretary Long had taken the afternoon off to recapture some of the sleep lost in the days since the *Maine* explosion. He sensed the opportunity to act should not be lost while waiting for permission. He penned an urgent cable for Wilkie, ripped it from his writing pad and stormed out to the telegrapher.

"Right away!" he directed, slapping the message flat on the desk. Wide, young eyes gazed up at him. His fiery return stare incited scrambling for quick action — the telegrapher's fingers went immediately to work.

Roosevelt returned to his desk and started issuing a stream of directives. He didn't need to think about what needed to be done. Plans had already been hashed out several times during the past few weeks. The first cable was directed to the Washington Navy Yard; an order to transport as many five and six inch guns available to New York, confiscate the merchant fleet, and refit the ships as auxiliary cruisers. He then drafted a cable to Naval Operations at Key West, ordering the North Atlantic Squadron to cancel maneuvers and head back to port where they could coal up and be ready to sail at a moment's notice. His third cable was for Admiral Dewey in Hong Kong; assemble the Asiatic squadron in Hong Kong, coal up and be at the ready. He further explained that at the imminent declaration of war, the Admiral was to take the Asiatic fleet to the Philippines, engage the Spanish squadron, and trap it along the Asiatic coast. The blockade was to be followed by an offensive move to eradicate the Spaniards from the Philippines. Permanently. As he completed his final cable, a feeble knock rapped on his door.

"Come," he barked as he assembled the cables to be sent

in a neat pile in front of him. He then looked up over his pince-nez and noticed a familiar thin figure. "Ah, Mr. Wilkie. I am pleased you could make it."

"Yes, sir," Wilkie sat down near Roosevelt's desk.

"Tell your boss Hazen to pull his strings at the Treasury and buy those Brazilian cruisers right away. I've got McKinley's approval. More metal in our hands is a good thing, I say," Roosevelt scribbled through the word 'cruisers' on his list.

Wilkie squirmed in his chair. "Money is in short supply. Counterfeit scandal. We may not have the cash to complete the transaction."

"Well don't you boys over there make money?" Roosevelt leaned forward, glaring sternly at Wilkie. He pruned his lips and craned his head forward. "This is an issue of national importance, Wilkie. I didn't think I had to repeat anything with you, but let me be crystal clear — I have McKinley's concurrence to make it happen. What more do you need?"

"I understand, sir," Wilkie replied sheepishly.

"Your boys still in Havana, yes?"

"Carter, sir."

"And poking at this inquiry, I presume?"

"Yes, sir." Wilkie squirmed. "My request."

"What have you picked up?"

"The cables have been quiet, sir."

"I'm not sure what that means," Roosevelt leaned forward and clicked his teeth in a wide straight grin. "It has to conclude it was an external explosion, got it?"

Wilkie did not respond.

"Let me be perfectly clear, Wilkie," Roosevelt launched out of his high-backed chair and stomped about the room, circling once before leaning over the expanse of his desk. He glared at Wilkie menacingly. "I can't afford to have any more delays in this tidy little war we need down there, understand?"

Wilkie finally nodded.

"Nor can I afford to lose someone of Sigsbee's caliber. If Carter comes up with something other than a torpedo, it shall remain Havana's secret. Are we clear?"

Wilkie nodded again.

"Then, what are you waiting for, man? Don't you have some ships to buy for me?" Roosevelt's grin grew wider as he reached for his humidor, pulled out a cigar and offered it up. Wilkie declined as he stood.

"I understand, sir," Wilkie said and left.

The Consulate remained morgueishly quiet. Consul Lee had been so consumed with Captain Sigsbee that he had for all practical purposes moved into the Hotel Inglaterra. Sam Carter read his scribbled notes that captured his personal dive observations and compared them to the information he obtained from the other divers. There was clear correlation between the two sets of observations, other than the divers had used technical terms for the ship's components. Numbered from the front of the vessel, each metal sheet riveted together carried a plate designation. There was no visible damage to plates one through fifteen on the starboard side. He did not record anything for sixteen. Plate seventeen had been peeled away, outward, as if pushed out by a huge explosion. As were eighteen and nineteen. Underneath these plates, the hull had an odd, inverted V-shape. And an odd ragged edge, he remembered.

Carter took a sip of the coffee he made earlier that evening. It was bitter and cold, but enough to keep him from falling asleep. Ensign Powelson's notes were next. He rolled his eyes and took another sip of the coffee — if his notes were as droning as he was, more coffee was essential. The young officer had added some cryptic notes near each of Morgen's revelations that followed each of the dives. Several comments appeared to have been blacked out, perhaps censored, Carter reckoned. Powelson had also added rough sketches of the ship and the position of the plates with his notes. No mention of the inverted V-shape. It seemed odd that Morgen or Powelson would miss that distinct detail.

Carter stood up from the paper-strewn table, stretched and yawned. He could not help but groan since his lungs still ached whenever he inhaled deeply. He stumbled toward the window and looked out over the city to the harbor, where bright lights remained on, illuminating the *Maine's* carcass as if it were a monument.

'*He's already made his conclusion,*' Carter considered as he stifled a yawn and let his eyes slip closed for a moment. '*But something's telling me that it's just not right,*' he thought, as he slid the window open and let some of the cool night air infiltrate the office.

"Señor Carter?" a familiar voice called from the rear staircase entering the Consulate office. It was Domingo Villaverde, the Cuban telegrapher. As Carter shuffled in his stocking feet toward the table piled with papers, Villaverde softly but not silently entered the office. "They have sent their report."

"And?" Carter prodded as Domingo relaxed in a straight-backed chair.

"As expected. Internal explosion. Coal. That set off the magazines," Domingo revealed as he looked suspiciously at the dark coffee on the table.

"An accident? Didn't expect any different," Carter said as he dropped into a chair at the table and looked at Villaverde. "And they concluded that without any divers," he added sarcastically.

"General Blanco said their photographs revealed enough." Carter looked over his papers again, and then wrapped his hand around his coffee cup reflexively. "You are drinking that? Cold?" Villaverde asked as he scrunched up his face as if he had taken some of the acrid swill.

"Yeah," Carter admitted, taking another mouthful of the bitterness. "Anything else? Anything with the Germans? They seem too quiet in all this mess."

"I did hear Blanco agree to a direct reprisal to the Kaiser," Villaverde offered.

"Reprisal? For what?" Carter's curiosity was piqued.

"One of their sailors never returned from a shore leave."

"Before or after the explosion?"

"I am not sure, but I believe it was before."

Carter's neck prickled as a thought crossed his mind. "Do

you know what happened to him?" he asked. Villaverde recoiled. Carter noticed. "Ah, you do."

"A body has not been found yet," Villaverde noted sheepishly, squirming in his seat. His eyes widened as Carter sensed him reading his thoughts.

"You suspect he knows something."

"Señor, you do not want to speak to him."

"He suspects Arturo, doesn't he?" Carter badgered. Villaverde sighed. "Domingo, amigo. It is not like you to hold information back," Carter pried. He arched his eyebrows and slowly waved his index finger at the Spaniard.

"Yes, he might know something."

'Arturo. The renegade,' Carter thought. The man was violently radical, had a mercurial temperament and was partial to chaotic anarchy and his own convoluted brand of justice. Carter knew he and a handful of insurgents wanted more control, and after being shunned, chose to split from Garcia's coalition more than a year ago. Since then, it had only been rumored, something he could not confirm but still suspected, that Arturo welcomed them into his seemingly invisible cadre. The brutal evidence of his terror continued though — maimed, decapitated soldiers, brutally tortured loyalists — would appear several days after they had gone missing. Carter was convinced Arturo was more than alive — he was active.

"I need to be headed home, as it is," Villaverde said as he stood.

Carter wasn't listening. Instead, he was thinking. A missing German and Arturo were two more possible suspects for sabotage. Arturo would probably not commit the act, but he could not divorce himself from believing the Germans may been responsible for what turned out to be a suicide mission. It was something he had to know, and there was one person who probably knew.

Villaverde grabbed Carter by the shoulders and looked directly into Carter's eyes "Señor Carter, you know Arturo is the devil and he would just as soon cut you as talk to you."

"We cross many bridges in our lives, Domingo, and if I am worried about my carcass all the time, I would never cross that one bridge that leads me to the truth," Carter pontificated. Domingo simply nodded his understanding before turning away. As he disappeared down the back stairs, Carter organized his papers in a neat pile and squirreled them away for later review as the grandfather clock in Consul Lee's office chimed twice. He shuffled to his small room off the conference area and melted into his cot. He drifted off to sleep, anxious. Going to Arturo was a chance he had to take if he wanted to know who was really responsible for the *Maine*.

Carter woke with the sunrise, shivering since he had left a window open through the night. He was stiff as well — he had not moved a muscle since dropping into his cot four hours earlier. He twisted, popping vertebrae, three he counted, then changed into a fresh set of drab cotton clothes that would let him blend in. His wide-brimmed Panama hat covered enough of his red hair so he could disappear into crowds. As he passed the conference table, strewn with papers, he stopped and quickly scribbled a note for Lee, just in case he returned, then disappeared through the rear entrance.

Carter maneuvered down toward the docks, settled at a table at the Café Luz, and ordered a coffee from the attractive young local girl. He sat back in a cold metal chair as he waited and watched the activity near the *Maine* carcass, where steam rose in wisps from the water's surface. Carter spotted Morgen and the other divers commencing their daily preparation for another excursion to the sunken vessel under Powelson's watchful eye.

"Señor Carter, it is a fine day, is it not," a familiar voice broke his concentration. He looked up and noticed Manuel behind a blackened eye and a nose that must have been forcefully moved out of place.

"*Buenos dias*, Manuel. It is good to see you," Carter replied, and offered his former guide a seat. Manuel moved easily between the eastern part of the island and Havana under the guise of a fisherman whose trade was plied along the southern coast of Cuba. Manuel eked out a peg-toothed smile under his own wide brimmed hat. "Your 'tattoos' appear to be healing well. How is your father faring?" Carter asked.

"He is beginning to understand in his old age that he may not be able to do what he would like without help," Manuel noted furtively.

Carter understood the codified words. General Garcia had finally capitulated to the reality that an American intervention in Cuba was not only inevitable, but also necessary. He would have preferred to talk personally with the insurgent General, but an excursion to the other side of the island, which would take days away from his own reconnoitering, could not be accommodated. Messages and information would need to go through couriers like Manuel.

"And our estranged cousin?"

"The answer to your question, Señor, I believe will be no," Manuel offered as he sat. He glanced around to be sure he was not being watched.

"But it is possible, isn't it?" Carter asked as he turned and caught the attention of the young girl. He signaled for a second coffee as Manuel nodded quickly.

"*Gracias*," Carter said as the waitress set two steaming coffee cups on the table in front of each man, then gracefully set down a half-filled sugar bowl in the center. Manuel and Carter silently and politely smiled until the lady turned away to another arriving customer.

"This is important, Manuel. I need verification. I know no one else will know." Carter sipped at the coffee and let the warmth trickle down his throat.

"I do not believe you need to, Señor."

"Then who do I have to talk to?" Carter prompted.

"I don't think this is wise, Señor." Manuel warned.

"Where would I find him?" Carter prompted. Manuel stiffened. He had his answer.

"Señor Carter, you do not want to sit with Arturo. He is not stable."

"Perhaps, Manuel, but I need to know the truth of this incident."

"He is evil. His trustworthiness is questionable."

"One way or another, I am going to sit with Arturo. I'm

going out there, Manuel, whether you give me a hint of where he is or not." Carter sipped at his coffee as Manuel hesitated.

"He has a camp up near Castle Morro, last we all knew." Manuel capitulated.

Castle Morro, Carter thought as he placed his cup back down on the table. '*Right under their noses and close enough to raise hell. Yes, Arturo had the opportunity.*'

"*Bueno*." Carter responded as he fished through his trousers for coins.

"But, Señor —"

Carter held up his hand and stifled Manuel as he finished his coffee with a satiated "Aah,." He chinked a pair of coins onto the table.

"Raul has a stable near the arena at Regla. He will help you. You will need a machete to get through the jungle," Manual reluctantly offered.

"Much obliged," Carter noted and headed off.

Havana proper was easy to maneuver through for Carter, and within an hour, he had negotiated his way to Regla. As he passed the bullfight arena, he heard the whoops and hollers of some young boys who snuck onto the field to scrimmage with a football. Carter reckoned the Spanish authorities would discover their trespass before long and then chase them out. After walking another half-mile, just east outside the reaches of the city, an open field of small green plants, jalapeño and habanera peppers spread out in front of him. Toiling in the field a wispy old man crouched, tending the tiny plants.

"*Buenos dias,*" Carter called out as he spotted the old man. Raul looked up and slid his wide-brimmed hat off his forehead. He lifted his hat briefly, long enough for the old man to spot his red hair and bring a crease to his face. Carter continued into a fallow pathway, reseated his hat and approached.

"Señor Carter? *A donde vas?*" Raul hobbled toward Carter with his bowed legs.

"*Castillo Morro. Voy a ver Arturo,*" Carter said. Raul's face instantly blanched as white as his deep bronzed complexion allowed. He bowed his head and shook it slowly as

Carter added, "I need a machete."

Raul looked back up to Carter with an expression that asked if he had lost his mind. "It is something I must do," Carter replied. Raul frowned disapprovingly, shrugged his shoulders and then waved at Carter to follow him. The pair meandered toward a small shack near Raul's dilapidated stable where plowing mules were foraging on a bale of cut grass. When Carter rounded the corner of the stable, he spotted Raul's grown son, Gabriel, sitting on a three-legged stool, filing the edge on a sling blade.

"*Machete, por favor, Gabriel.*" Raul said in a soft conciliatory tone. His son stood, swung open the wide, weatherworn-planked door and revealed a series of cutting tools. Gabriel inspected the tools for a moment before taking down a two-foot blade and handed it to his father.

"*Él va a ver Arturo,*" Raul whispered to his son as he inspected the blade briefly, brushing it across his scruffy cheek before checking it again. His impish smile confirmed for Carter that it did not need sharpening. Gabriel's eyes widened before he slipped a sly grin toward Carter and winked.

"*¿Comida?*" Raul then asked, but before Carter could respond, the old man hobbled on his bowed legs to a chest outside the door where he ferreted for a moment before extracting a small sack. Still stooped over, he held it blindly over his back. Carter took a handful of the boiled beef chips and slipped them into his mouth. Raul's peppery seasoning scorched his cheeks and singed his tongue. Carter offered a gracious nod.

"*Buena suerte,*" Raul added as he stood up and patted Carter on his back. With high noon approaching quickly, Carter realized his time was growing short. Negotiating the forest before dark would be his only assurance of catching Arturo. Bidding his farewell, Carter left and continued east.

The machete became useful as soon as Carter left the city limits. The hills along the shoreline leading to Castle Morro were thick with palms and tuberous undergrowth that only stubbornly succumbed to his two-foot blade. After an hour of bushwhacking through the thick emerald canopy, greenery which seemed to have trapped the heat from the past hurricane seasons, he finally broke through into a clearing, as Miguel had suggested he would find. He surveyed the horizon for the any indication of encampments until he finally spotted the telltale wisps of smoke. He set his bead and started back into the thickness.

A sudden clutching at his boot pulled his feet out from under him. Stumbling forward, he broke his fall with his forearms, covering his face with his hands. Prone, he lay still, listening for any sounds nearby. There were none. He turned his head enough so his ear set square on the dirt. Still nothing.

'*Maybe just a trailing vine*,' he thought. He started to push up to his hands and knees, but when a boot pressed into the small of his back he immediately understood it was not a vine. A cold sharp machete blade then pricked at the nape of his neck. He cautiously lowered his face back to the musty forest floor.

"American!" Carter said purposefully in English. His heart raced. It was a chance. He hoped he had found who he was looking for, but if he did not, and these thugs were Spaniards, he was dead. Another boot then pinned his left hand and his machete to the forest floor. Behind him, a squabble in Spanish ensued, but only briefly.

Steps crackled across dried leaves, then stopped. His hat was then skewered away from his head. He wondered if Manual was correct. The silence seemed to last for hours, although Carter knew it was only a minute or two. Additional boots crunched through dried leaves.

"Let him go," a faceless voice directed in English. Carter sighed in relief as he recognized the voice. "Sit up on your ass and face me," Arturo added.

"Get your thugs off me and I can," Carter replied.

"*Liberas*," Arturo ordered. Boots withdrew off Carter's arms. He rolled over, sat up, and then planted his butt on the ground. In front of him stood Arturo, his eyebrows singed clean, his face as horribly pockmarked as Carter remembered. His lips wore a thin smile, barely enough to let his teeth seep through. He wore the same khaki shirt and trousers that his henchman wore. Arturo pompously folded his arms, tipped his wide-brimmed hat back, and tilted his head to the right. His eyes drilled into Carter. "I hear you are looking for me?" he asked in broken English.

"Yes, I am."

"And what is it that you want from me?"

"Information." Carter noted. Arturo's men wrapped Carter's hands together at his wrists with a scratchy, heavy rope.

"You've come a very long way just for information."

"How else was I supposed to get some answers? Send you a letter?"

Arturo smiled. "I always admired your bravado, Señor Carter. What kind of information?"

"What kind do you think?"

"How long do you wish to play this game, Carter? I do believe you are aware of my limited patience, yes?" Arturo bent over until he was nose to nose with Carter. "*Apretadas*," he growled. The ropes were tugged tighter.

"You know there was, let's just call it and accident, with a ship."

Arturo's smile widened. He pulled out a cigar from his pocket and chewed the end. He slipped it into his mouth, let it emerge slowly, lit the end, and sent a thick stream of blue smoke toward the sky. "Ah, yes I do. I heard you had a little problem over there. And I suppose you want to know if I did it?"

"The Weylerites say you did," Carter lied. Arturo tilted his head, squinted then glared. Carter struggled to read through his subtle gestures.

"And you believe those spineless drones?" Arturo erupted with a loud bellicose laugh, infectious enough that his comrades joined in.

"Didn't say I did. I wanted to hear it from you."

Arturo backed off, paraded around to Carter's back, and then stopped. Carter felt Arturo's boot step on the ropes chaffing into his wrists, pulling him backwards. Arturo leaned forward, close enough that his sparse stubble scratched at

Carter's neck.

"The thought did cross my mind, Carter."

"So you did not sabotage the ship?"

Arturo laughed loudly, then backed off and finished his march. He stomped the ground in front of Carter.

"Do I have the means and material? Yes. Do I want to waste my supplies to make some statement? Well, that is for you to decide. You can believe me or you can believe them. And since you believe both of us lie, it still remains your choice what is the truth."

"Do you know who did it?" Carter then asked.

Arturo laughed loudly again. He knelt down and faced Carter, blowing a cloud of grayish-blue smoke into his face. As it cleared, Arturo's face grew evilly serious.

"So you believe me, Carter?"

"We may not have always agreed on what was the right thing to do, Arturo, but I do know you have always had good information," Carter prodded.

"I told them it would not be wise," Arturo growled, then turned to his men and ordered, "*Tráelo aquí.*" From amidst the thick undergrowth, a bound and gagged German sailor stumbled into the opening, then fell, face-first onto the forest detritus.

"He did it?" Carter said breathlessly as he watched the young sailor, now a prisoner of Arturo, roll over and reveal his bruised and beaten face.

"Not him, but it was one of them. That is what he confessed — after some coercion," Arturo said. Carter had at least a partial answer.

"*Patrulla!*" one of Arturo's men interrupted. Arturo startled and sprung up from his haunches. His men scattered, disappearing into the jungle. Carter whipped his leg out, catching Arturo's shin. The rebel stumbled but quickly scrambled to his knees and glared at Carter.

"At least give me a chance," Carter demanded. "You know they will make me tell them where you are."

Arturo grabbed the machete and started toward Carter, who closed his eyes, bowed his head and waited for his fate. It was death or freedom. He heard leaves crunching under boots behind him then a machete blade whoosh. Warmth trickled down his back. His hands were freed.

"Remember this, Carter," Arturo said as he stomped toward the German, now scrambling to free himself. With one thrust, Arturo skewered the sailor's chest, sawed the sharp blade up to his suddenly limp neck before extracting the blood-covered blade. "Bastard!" he added, threw the machete toward Carter and followed his men into the forest.

Carter needed more information, but there would be no more to be had. Instead of chasing down Arturo, he scrambled to cover until the patrol passed by, then headed back the way he came, hoping to reach Regla by nightfall.

Chapter 22

Fitzhugh Lee boarded the *Mangrove*, a non-descript lighthouse tender that had settled in with the international myriad of vessels now choking Havana harbor. He sensed that finally after a month of conjecture and official silence about what happened to the *Maine*, the book would be closed and the fallout would begin a new chapter in the Cuban saga. He felt it was his duty to attend at least the opening session of the official Court of Inquiry on the destruction of the *Maine*, although being the only civilian in the room made him rather uncomfortable. The hard wooden chair along the cold metal bulkhead of the *Mangrove* as well did nothing for his comfort.

Through General Blanco, Spain had officially requested to be part of the inquiry, which he was directed by McKinley to deny. Lee surmised they would be put out by the denial, since their board had already met and essentially concluded the incident was accidental. He reckoned their request was more a ploy to detract the direction of Admiral Sampson's board rather than provide salient information.

"I'll be relieved when this is finally over," Captain Sigsbee said as he settled into the seat next to Lee.

"Yes, sir. It will be a welcomed relief," Lee responded. Sigsbee looked the model Navy officer — perfect posture in his straight-backed chair, white-gloved hands folded precisely three inches above his knees, a well-groomed and trained mustache, and an expression that exuded an utmost personal confidence.

'Does he already know the verdict?' Lee wondered to himself as he squirmed in his chair. The clock on the conference table, set up in the center of the *Mangrove's* converted dining area, indicated ten before ten.

"All rise!" a smartly dressed sailor acting as a bailiff announced as the rear portal-like door opened. Everyone in the room complied as Admiral William T. Sampson, commander of the *Iowa* and now serving as the president of the board, entered first and stepped smartly toward the table. He sat stalwartly at the far end, allowing him full view of everyone in the cramped room. Lee was aware of Sampson's lengthy history — a lifetime officer, well versed in ordnance and the physical effects of underwater explosions. He had served as the Chief of Ordnance and as Commandant of the torpedo station at the Newport War College. As the stately looking Admiral settled into his seat, he glanced down at some handwritten notes then looked up at the clock before arranging his papers in discrete piles in front of him.

The next officer to enter was Lieutenant Commander Adolph Marix, selected as the court's judge advocate. Lee sent a sideward glance to Commander Wainwright, understanding that Marix knew the *Maine* well, having served as her executive officer before being replaced by him. He mused that there might be some animosity between the former and present executive officers, and wondered if Marix might use the court to forward his own agenda. The youngish man as compared to the rest of the grayed men in the room, settled in at his station, the drop desk table near Sampson, then fixed a gaze on Wainwright.

Captain French Chadwick, commander of the *New York*, and Lieutenant Commander William Potter, seasoned officers who were well experienced with sabotage and spontaneous combustion, followed Marix into the room. Lee knew little of these men other than they, as Wainwright, had spent time serving in the Office of Naval Intelligence. Lee had heard that Potter had recently chaired the investigation of the coal fire explosion on the *Cincinnati* — a board which included Wainwright.

The bailiff clanked the door closed behind Potter then called out for those assembled to be seated as the spry looking Commander assumed his position at the table.

"This Board of Inquiry is now in session," Sampson announced as the clock moved to ten. He tapped at the bell in front of him and turned toward Marix. "Commander Marix, please read our charge from Admiral Sicard."

"Yes, sir," Marix cleared his throat and stood. "The duty of this court is to diligently and thoroughly inquire into all the circumstances attending the loss of the *USS Maine* on fifteen February of this year, eighteen-ninety-eight. This court is to report whether or not the loss was in any respect due to fault of negligence of part of the officers or members of her crew. This court is to also report its opinion as to the cause of the explosion, including other incidents that bore directly or indirectly on the loss of the *Maine*." Marix concluded. He set the paper from which he was reading to his left, and then assumed a recording position with paper and a pen at the roll top desk.

"I am sure the Board understands that we have only one fact from which to begin," Sampson droned through his opening statements. "And that is that an explosion occurred in one or more of the forward magazines. What caused the explosion is another matter, and that is what we have been tasked to determine."

Ensign Powelson fidgeted in his seat along the bulkhead. Under his arm, he squeezed the overfilled portfolio where his collection of diver's depositions and his personal conclusions were stowed. He started to stand, but a glare from Sampson appeared to change his mind.

"We will hear Captain Charles Sigsbee's deposition to start this session," Sampson's voice changed, booming through and filled the room.

"Thank you sir," Sigsbee said as he stood and smartly approached the round oak table. He calmly took a seat at the table and folded his hands in front of him.

"Commander Marix, will you conduct the first examination." Sampson ordered.

Sigsbee remained in his chair as Marix scooped up his papers and marched to a position facing Sigsbee. He adjusted his glasses, cleared his throat again, and began.

"For the record, state your name, rank and present station."

Sigsbee replied properly. Marix continued, and with each additional question, Sigsbee responded with short concise responses. When Marix finally asked for the Captain's statement, Sigsbee detailed the arrival of the vessel, and how the *Maine* came to be moored at buoy number four, a location that had seldom been used, no less one used by a battle-cruiser. He explained how diligent his crew had been in the monitoring of the coalbunker temperatures as well as the stowage of any paint that could have been volatile enough to start an internal fire or explosion. Sigsbee spouted the exact times the rounds in the bunkers had been completed, tracking each event on his paper with his finger, until he concluded his statement with "and at 9:40 pm on the fifteenth, the explosion occurred."

"Thank you Captain Sigsbee," Sampson said as he swiveled his head to view the board members. His head swiveled around as if silently asking the members if they had any questions for the Captain. Seeing no movement, he added, "With no further questions from the Board, I understand that there is no probable or salient evidence for an internal explosion to be the root cause of the loss of the *USS Maine*."

Sampson scanned the Board one additional time before dismissing Sigsbee. The Captain stood and saluted, but instead of leaving, took a seat against the wall. Lee did not know whether this was proper protocol or not, but since it was Sigsbee, and it was his vessel, he thought that it must have been allowed.

Lee sat baffled. He realized he had little say in the inquiry however, it did seem to him that the potential for an internal explosion had been brushed aside as quickly as it had been raised. Having not been in contact with Carter recently, Lee wondered if Carter had also dispelled the internal explosion hypothesis as quickly. Unless, he thought, addressing the theory in this manner was what had been agreed to at some higher level so that the expected conclusion would be arrived at more quickly.

Sampson then called Ensign Powelson to the stand to provide the details he collected from the divers. Powelson approached the table, settled into a seat next to Sampson, then opened his portfolio and assembled two piles of papers neatly in front of him.

"Gentlemen, at the behest of Secretaries Long and Roosevelt, I have compiled a complete description of the wreckage from the diver's reports," he started with a droning monotone, and then detailed each of the divers' observations in excruciating detail. He explained that the examination of the ship was fraught with formidable difficulties starting with the poor diving conditions. Visibility was hampered by filthy and nearly opaque water. Soft ooze, some feet thick, hampered walking on the harbor bottom. Pieces of twisted and torn wreckage presented a great danger to lifelines and air hoses.

Morning moved slowly into the afternoon, and without a break for lunch, Powelson's continued drone created a catatonic assembly. The ensign's lethargic pace continued through the afternoon and into the evening hours, lulling Lee and several others to nod off into brief naps. Lee realized that even though he had fallen asleep several times during the deposition, he missed only a sparse few details of Powelson's lengthy deposition.

As evening began darkening the room, Sampson mercifully ordered an adjournment for the day. Lee's head hurt from the constant barraged of droned details from the first day's testimony, quickly exited onto the deck of the *Mangrove* and queued into the lines for the ferries headed back to the city.

Evening crept in from Havana harbor as a chilled Sam Carter dragged himself up the rear stairway at the Consulate. With each step, pain shot through his back where boots had ground into his lower spine. His bruised arms and head throbbed. Once Carter reached the second floor, he stumbled to the table where his notes remained in piles from the night before and collapsed in the chair in front of them. He laid his head down in his arms and tried to make sense of the facts as they began swirling around in his aching head. Closing his eyes, he tried to remember precisely what he had seen on his dive. He relived dressing in the musty, canvas suit. That seemed routine. His helmet went on next, and while it was secured into place on his shoulders, he inspected the harbor surface.

He then recalled that he noticed something odd about the surface, but could not remember exactly what that was. He combed through his memory of that particular sight; the water surface was covered with oil soaked debris, human and wooden, deathly still in the morning calm. The hulk of the *Maine* barely breached the surface, her plating at the forward section extending out like craggy old oak tree limbs at a fishing hole. Muffled groans emanated from the deep, sometimes gurgling, sometimes moaning as the hulk sank and settled deeper into the muck on the harbor floor, like a giant rolling over in fitful sleep. Bubbles swam to the surface, emanating muffled pops as they released their contents. Bodies drifted aimlessly toward the surface, some bloated, some burned, some dismembered.

How the Germans could be involved, as Arturo said he extracted from his hostage nagged at him. They weren't fired upon, that was clear. It was true that they would have the explosives powerful enough to burst through the double plating with which the *Maine* had been constructed, but it was irresolvable how a torpedo —a weapon needing to be the size of two men — could be planted unseen by any of the sailors on board.

And there were clearly two explosions. The majority of the damage was obviously the result of the second, more powerful explosion of the forward magazines. It was the first explosion that was the catalyst, and it had to have occurred at the exact location that would detonate the magazines. And if what Arturo said was true, there was only one conclusion — a saboteur.

"Fish!" Carter yelled as he popped his head up. He sat erect in his chair, slammed his fist on the papers then started shuffling through the notes. *That's why the surface looked odd,* he thought. *There were no fish.* As a boy, he used small fireworks in bottles, dropping them in the shallow ponds to stun fish so he could collect them when they floated to the surface. Any fish feeding off the barnacles and slime that had grown on the *Maine's* hull would have certainly been stunned by the concussion — unless the explosions came from inside the vessel.

"That's it!" Carter muttered as he continued digging through the diver's reports. Just one would dispel his theory, but diver after diver said nothing of working through dead fish. '*Navy men would have noticed that,*' he thought. They would not have missed that detail.

"Ah, Sam, you're back," Consul Lee said as he entered the foyer. His face long and pale, his shoulders slumped, clearly exhausted from sitting through the deliberations, Lee dragged himself toward his office but stopped and inspected Carter. "Hell, son. You look like you've been in one beauty of a scrap."

"I think I know what happened," Carter said as the teletype began clacking away.

"If you can tell me in less than a minute, I'm all ears. Do you realize how much that boy Powelson can talk?" Lee chucked as he headed into his personal office and melted into his large cushioned chair. He slipped off his shoes, leaned back and propped his stocking feet up onto the corner of his desk.

"It had to be sabotage," Carter blurted.

"Hope you got some solid proof of that, son," Lee said as he lit up a fat black cigar. He puffed a few clouds out, and then yawned widely. "Don't think the Board will take too kindly to that."

"Arturo got that German that disappeared to confess," Carter said as he looked up at Lee.

"And you believe Arturo?" Lee grunted as he dropped his feet from the desk. He shuffled over to the teletype and pulled off the cable. Before he started reading, he added, "At this point I think we are just wasting our time."

"Wasting our time?"

"I believe everybody has already drawn their conclusion — Powelson, Sigsbee, Sampson — even though from what I heard, the evidence is thin. The harbor is not letting your secret out, son."

"They're wrong." Carter protested.

"It really doesn't matter at this point." Lee expelled a heavy sigh as he plopped back into his cushioned chair and read the cable. He then leaned his head back, covered his face and mumbled, "Unless you can come up with some real evidence, it's a done deal."

"I think we are too focused on the wrong side." Carter offered as Lee rubbed his eyes.

"You do mean an explosion from the inside?" Lee let his hands slide down his face. A scowl scrunched his face. Carter nodded. "Like an accident?" Lee shook his head. "Not likely. You know Sigsbee and Wainwright. They are sticklers for routines and procedures, especially disposing of ashes and wastes. Paints and other materials were clearly well managed. They already dispelled that at the inquiry."

"No, not an accident," Carter said as he slogged through his files.

"And Commander Wainwright was also an expert on the use of coal," Lee continued, clearly not hearing Carter. "He inspected the records personally to ensure they were meticulous. As was the housekeeping. I heard it all for hours on end."

"General, it was not an accident! It was sabotage and the Germans did it," Carter vaulted up from his chair and glared at Lee. "I just have to figure out how they got on board.

"I don't think it really matters anymore. Read this." Lee dropped the typed cable in front of him and waved Carter over to read it. Carter stomped over to Lee's desk and took the letter. He first glanced at the bottom. *Wilkie, Director, Secret Service*.

"Director?" Carter asked. Lee shrugged his shoulders. Carter returned to the top and read the message. When he finished it, he dropped his hands to his side and looked at Lee with a blank stare.

"This is ludicrous." Carter sighed then looked at the message again. He leaned back, stretching and disturbing the long, thin scab down his back, courtesy of Arturo. It cracked open, but for once, it remained dry.

"I really don't think it all matters much anymore, Sam. If they are hell bent on war, we have to leave, either voluntarily or by force. And before we leave, we have some cleaning up to do."

Carter pursed his lips and let his anger seethe. If the confession Arturo extracted was true, there was something more insidious that Kaiser Wilhelm was plotting to implement once war broke out.

"If you're fixing to clean up papers tonight, you can start with this one," Carter growled as he balled up the message, threw it at Lee's feet and left the Consulate.

Senator Redfield Proctor, a close ally of McKinley and a former Secretary of War, watched closely from the port side rail as Captain Cyrus McManus shut down the *Olivette's* engines and moored her east of the Maine's wreckage. He had decided that since the debate of whether or not to go to war had risen to be the most prominent daily question discussed on the floor of the Senate, some member of Congress, and he decided it was him, had a duty to uncover the real story about conditions in Havana. As he headed to the harbor ferry, he stopped by the bridge and waved to catch the Captain's attention.

"I wish to thank you, Captain," Proctor said with his gravelly voice. "I've been on many a vessel up North, but never have I been treated to such a smooth sail."

"My pleasure, Senator," MacManus saluted the Senator, then leaned over and asked in a hushed tone, "How long do we have?"

Proctor stiffened, jutting out his chin at the Captain. He squinted with a sideward glance and scowled. "That is a bit presumptuous of you, isn't it Captain?"

"I've seen what's going on there, sir. If you ask me, we would be doing the people here a great service if we drive the

Spanish out once and for all."

"Please be sure that Consul Lee is at the dock when I arrive," Proctor snapped and stalked into the line for the ferry that would take him to the shore. McManus obliged. He quickly scribbled a note to be sent by telegraph to the Consulate and handed it to his signaler. The signaler quickly read the message, then cocked his head and stared at MacManus.

"Lee needs to know this old man is as craggy as they come," MacManus whispered as he looked over his shoulder to be sure Proctor's ferry had already left. "Now send it."

"Yes, sir," the signaler promptly cranked the magneto and began punching the message on the single key.

"Welcome to Havana, Senator," General Consul Lee greeted cordially as the tall, thin, bearded politician stepped onto the pier. Lee had received the message and took a break from the elimination of many of the sensitive papers he and Carter had collected in the Consulate to meet the Senator at dockside.

"I am not here to inquire about the proceedings with the *Maine* disaster, and to be perfectly honest with you, General, I don't want to hear anything about that. It simply does not matter now. Do I make myself clear?" Proctor growled.

"I do not recall you indicating your purpose, sir," Lee recoiled. He did not think he had done anything to imply he was going to coerce the senator with any innuendo.

"And don't call me sir. I knew my parents," Proctor glared at Lee.

"Yes, sir," Lee swallowed the words before they left his mouth. He didn't think MacManus explained how touchy the old Vermonter was to the cultural differences between New England and the South, just that he was a crotchety old coot.

"*Buenas dias,*" a thin Cuban greeted, joining the Consul-General and the Senator.

"This is Hernandon Gomez, Senator," Lee introduced. Proctor examined Gomez with a scowl. "I have arranged for him to show you around. Mr. Gomez knows this area better than I do, and he may provide for you a better perspective."

Proctor looked back up to Lee with a tilted head before slipping a slight grin.

"Thank you," he noted. He then pointed to the open-air tables at Café Luz. "Perhaps a cup of coffee to start this day," Proctor added, and the pair headed toward the bistro as Lee headed back to the Consulate.

Theodore Roosevelt stomped around his office, seething at the conclusions of the article he had finished reading in the Washington Evening Star, an article that had been published a week earlier. He stood at the window for a moment, harrumphed, then rambled to his door and swung it open. Outside, a young ensign sitting at the long narrow desk filing papers for the secretary, turned and stared at the grimacing Roosevelt.

"Get your ass in here," Roosevelt demanded, then turned and marched back to his desk. The ensign immediately vaulted from his chair as if he had been electrically shocked and followed the Assistant Secretary back into the office. He sat down on the chair in front of Roosevelt's desk, peered up to the huge moose head that hung mounted on the wall between bookshelves, then down to the desk where paper and pen had been set out for him.

"Address this to Admiral O'Neil," Roosevelt started.

"Confidential, sir?" the ensign asked sheepishly.

"No, this is far from confidential. Hell, Spain probably already knows about this spineless attempt at derailing justice. Treason. I say." Roosevelt seethed as he lit a cigar and started puffing away furiously. "He should be strung up on a yard-arm."

"Understand, sir," the ensign replied.

"I understand that one of your professors at the Naval Academy, one Lieutenant Phillip Alger, has raised questions about the explosion which caused the sinking of the *Maine*. A published interview with him states that he knew of no submerged mine that could have caused the explosion. He also stated that in seeking the cause of the disaster, it was not necessary to look beyond the same hazard that had nearly caused similar explosions in the past, that being coal bunker fires. This is insidious innuendo, which I find as close to treason as a free press is allowed to print.

"I submit that Mr. Alger cannot possibly know anything about the accident. We have a sitting Court of Inquiry assigned to not only to evaluate the facts as they are, but also resolve culpability. It is unadvisable for any person, no less a person connected with the Navy Department to express such a treasonous opinion publicly. I urge you to reprimand this ill-informed stoat, if not altogether drumming him out of the Academy at once. Sign the message, Assistant Secretary Theodore Roosevelt."

"Yes, sir. Shall I have this letter delivered today or through regular mail," the ensign asked innocently.

"Immediately! If I have to carry the damned thing up to Annapolis myself, I will. I want it in the Admiral's hands today," Roosevelt insisted, punctuated by pounding his fist onto his solid walnut desk.

"Yes, sir," the ensign replied with an octave jump in his voice. He scurried out of the office and immediately began typing the message for Roosevelt's signature.

Carter passed the Café Luz and watched the sun sink further into the western sky behind him. It was as beautiful a sunset as he had ever seen, with the streams of red and orange streaking across a deepening sky. Normally, he would take the time to enjoy these occasions at the café, but seeking out Commander Wainwright before he left for Washington himself was an imperative.

The Hotel Inglaterra was a posh establishment, perhaps one of the more luxurious in all of Havana. The exterior reminded him of the huge plantations that remained intact in Charleston, with large white pillars in front of the structure exalting three stories high. The gaslights on the balconies had already been started, allowing silhouettes of those visitors who sat out enjoying the sunset to waver on the walls. Carter stepped inside the foyer, maneuvered directly to the front desk.

"Commander Wainwright, please," he asked. The clerk

nodded and started through his file. As he did, Carter slogged to the waiting area where he found a cushioned chair. He melted into it and began dozing, exhaustion from the emotional rollercoaster he had been on catching up with him.

"Mr. Carter," a familiar voice startled Carter awake. He cracked open his eyes and saw the tall thin figure and long face of Commander Wainwright standing in front of him, clean-shaven, but as drawn as he had ever seen the officer.

"Commander," Carter shook off his sleepiness as Wainwright took a seat next to him. "I am concerned that the inquiry may not be coming to a truthful conclusion."

"I have little information on that matter, Mr. Carter, and even less that I am able to share at present." Wainwright stiffly responded.

"I am not looking for information, sir. I have information. Information that may be of vital importance," Carter noted. Wainwright cinched forward in his seat and turned his head.

"Where did you get this information?" Wainwright asked, suddenly curious rather than defensive.

"It's more a conclusion based on what I had seen and have found out since. Remember you had let me be part of the first dive team on your vessel?"

"Yes, I do. It was a rather gruesome sight," Wainwright replied with clearly measured and carefully chosen words.

"When I entered the water, there was nothing but bodies and debris. There was something odd — something missing that for some reason did not register with me until a short while ago."

Wainwright squirmed slightly in his chair, obviously not sure where Carter was leading him.

"Fish," Carter stated.

"Fish?"

"There were no fish, Commander. I would have expected at least a few fish floating with the debris, but there were none. Do you remember seeing any dead fish floating near the wreckage?" Carter asked as Wainwright slid back in his seat, rubbing his chin with his hand. "You are an explosives expert. An explosion outside of the ship would not go in just one direction, is that correct?"

"That is a matter of physics," Wainwright said as he nodded.

"The concussion from that explosion would head out in all directions, correct?"

"I am not sure where you are headed, Carter."

"That concussion would stun if not, kill any fish swimming near the vessel."

"Perhaps they were washed out with the tide?" Wainwright countered, his words still measured.

"The same tide that pushed the bodies toward the sea walls? I find that irresolvable," Carter said. Wainwright's face remained expressionless. "I can not believe the initiating explosion was exterior to the ship."

Wainwright was silent. Carter felt the Commander's eyes fix on his face. In a very hushed tone, he noted, "Mr. Carter, I do not believe you understand the gravity of your implication."

"I believe I do, Commander. If it was an internal explosion that initiated the magazine detonation, the truth is that the Spaniards were not responsible."

"Let me be clear, Mr. Carter. The insinuation of your accusation is that Captain Sigsbee is responsible. That is something we cannot afford, especially if we are headed into a conflict."

"Let *me* be clear, Commander," Carter's voice grew quiet and deliberate as he stood. "I am accusing no one."

"At the risk of violating my oath to the inquiry board, I shall offer that the overwhelming evidence suggests a submerged mine was the initiator, not a coal explosion." Wainwright's tone grew grim and demeaning.

"Not a coal explosion, Commander. You yourself scrubbed the records meticulously. And I can validate that, being there. It was sabotage."

Wainwright's face grew ashen. He arched his eyebrows and mouthed, "Who?"

Carter leaned forward and whispered, "Germans."

Wainwright recoiled. His expression registered disbelief. "I inspected the holds and every inch of the lower decks. You were with me. There were no stowaways."

"That I concur with, but there was a coaling at Key West, yes? Anything odd that you can remember?" Carter prompted.

"How did you know about the coaling?"

"Your records, sir. You keep and demand meticulous records," Carter noted. Wainwright's eyes looked up as if he was trying to recall.

"Just before we left. All the ships were coaled up. I didn't care much for that since the coal was in large part bitumen, but that's not uncommon for that part of the country." Wainwright divulged. "But I checked that coal," he added.

"Did you dig into it? You and I both know there had to be something more than just coal burning to do the damage that it did."

"Then the rest of the Squadron needs to know to check their coal bins."

"Yes, sir, I agree." Carter said. He waited for a minute to ensure his concerns sunk in with Wainwright and then headed back out into the warm but comfortable evening.

Part Six
March 1898
Berlin, Germany

Chapter 23

Kaiser Wilhelm had grown impatient with the progress on his idea for the formation of a European coalition to assist Maria Cristina, the Queen Regent of Spain against the growing power of the United States. Exacerbating his sense of failure to forge that concerted front, the miserable winter lingered in Berlin — cold, snow, and a bitter wind that frosted windows as far south as Bavaria. Even if he had been able to convince the other monarchs of Europe to join with him, his Navy, the cornerstone of the coalition's defense, was still not ready despite his and Tirpitz's enthusiastic visits to the foundries and shipyards.

"We cannot force anyone into this coalition," Bernhard von Bülow calmly stated. It was not what Wilhelm wanted to hear.

"You want me to believe that France is the only other nation willing to support our neighbor? France?" Wilhelm hung his head in disbelief, grumbling as he stood and began pacing around the office. He stopped at the window and watched the snow fall for a moment before turning back to von Bülow, who was comfortably sitting in the overstuffed chair in front of the Kaiser's desk fondling his notes.

"Only France has committed," von Bülow responded when he had eye contact.

"Russia!" Wilhelm thrust his pointed finger at von Bülow. "What about Russia?" Wilhelm emphatically marched back to his desk and dropped into his chair.

"Nicholas has expressed willingness, lukewarm at best, as has Austria," von Bülow said, his face growing long and dour. "But, Sire, it seems everyone has some insidious internal issue brewing that demands their attention. No one wishes to take the lead in this matter. Of them all, I would only count on Austria, since the Queen Regent is after all a Hapsburg as well."

"Has Maria Cristina approached England at all, or is she cowering in her little castle, waiting for someone to ride to her rescue?" Wilhelm dropped his head and stared at the desktop, where a European map had been spread across.

"That I cannot say, Sire, but the information I have is that she has not."

"What is she waiting for? How the hell does she expect me to leave my school vessels there without any additional support? Doesn't she recognize when a gift is handed to her?" Wilhelm slammed his fist on his oak desk, rattling his Pickelhaube helmet that rested on the corner. Von Bülow let the Kaiser rant, chewing on his lower lip as he considered an appropriate response.

"I cannot postpone my needs to assist her any longer. I have already talked with Tirpitz and he agrees that tactically, we need to withdraw our vessels from Havana and have them re-coaled." Wilhelm began scribbling a message to withdraw the *Gniesenau* from Cuba. "They need to be at the ready if McKinley suddenly becomes frisky and decides to take action in retribution for their vessel being destroyed," he added absently.

"Take action? The Spanish inquiry has already determined that this was a coal explosion." von Bülow recoiled.

Wilhelm suddenly realized his gaff. Von Bülow had not been briefed on Ziegler's activity in America. "And the Americans have accepted that is how it happened?" he asked before exploding with a belly laugh that reverberated each of the frames on the portraits on the walls. "Bernhard, you are attempting to humor me with feigned aloofness, yes?"

"Perhaps," von Bülow cowered in his chair, clearly embarrassed.

"You do understand if they admit to an accidental

explosion, it is tantamount to suicide?" Wilhelm patronized, his tone oozing condescension. "Bernhard, you may know diplomacy, but you are a bit naïve when it comes to the blood of war."

"You are correct, Sire," von Bülow atoned. It did little to dull Wilhelm's sharp criticism.

"Let me make this clear for you — the Americans will determine some submarine mine, or some other explosive set by the Spaniards, exploded under the vessel. Then they will demand reparation of some sort. When Maria Cristina and that weak willed, flaccid minded Sagasta realize they are cornered, they will have to go to war."

"Then where does that leave us," von Bülow asked, as if he was fishing for direction.

"I want you to talk to Maria Cristina about England," Wilhelm noted rather calmly. "She needs to understand the importance of her taking that step so that we at least know where England stands. She does not need to know that we still, even after all the money I have poured into the Krupp Works, do not have enough ships to help her and defend our own coast if England decides to side with the Americans." Wilhelm finished with the words seeping from between his teeth, barred in anger.

"And the school ships in Havana?" von Bülow asked absently.

"I am drafting an order to recall them to Port-au-Prince — for fuel and rest. I am sure my schoolboys must be getting a bit nervous with all the activity around them. We can send a stronger vessel with an experienced crew in their place."

Von Bülow nodded his head in agreement, left the room, immediately heading back to his office at the other end of the Reichstag. The files he had been reviewing when Wilhelm had called him down to his office remained on his desk. Returning to them, he worked his way down the list of his foreign agents that he could contact to get more information about what exactly was transpiring in Havana.

His forefinger crossed the name Rudolf Moser. There had been little information received from Moser since he landed in

Jamaica. He knew Wilhelm had assigned him to Haiti, but the lack of intelligence made him wonder if Moser had been compromised. Perhaps he had simply died, considering he was on in years, he thought.

"One more mission, Rudolf," von Bülow mumbled as he started a telegram with a mission for Moser to the German Consulate in Jamaica.

Sam Carter finished filling a second large green trunk, swung the lid closed, then secured the latches. He had been packing since Secretary Day sent an urgent message to all Consulates that a general evacuation of American interests was warranted. He then dropped into the leather-backed chair next to Consul Lee's now naked desk — the desk which usually had some pile of paper or several open books that had constituted Lee's research — and then wiped the sweat trails from his face with a handkerchief. The previous day's heat, unusually hot for early spring in Havana had not dissipated overnight, making the scurry to pack away sensitive material that much more laborious. He eyed the pile of papers near the fireplace waiting to be burned, and decided they would need to wait until it cooled off at least a degree or two. Then Consul Lee entered the office with another armful of papers, and added them to the pile to be burned.

"Surely going to miss this place," Lee lamented as he ambled to the window. Carter watched the old man stare out over the harbor, noticing a touch of melancholy creep in until his eyes suddenly grew wide. "Son of a bitch!" Lee then shouted, reaching forward for the sash and throwing it open.

Intrigued by Lee's sudden astonishment, even as tired as he was, Carter rolled out of the chair and joined Lee at the window. He scanned the harbor and noticed the tender *Mangrove* heading out to sea.

"The Court's going to Key West to question the balance of the survivors. Thought you knew that," Carter mumbled, and then thought, '*Seems like a moot point at this juncture. They've already drawn their conclusion.*'

"No, son. Look over there!" Lee pointed to the German

school ships, which had also drawn anchor and were being escorted by Spanish tugs out toward Castle Morro. "So what do you think of that?"

Carter stood slack-jawed and baffled. If the German ships were leaving, where were they headed, he wondered. He was certain that the German ships would remain as a deterrent for an American attack on the Spaniards. "Washington needs to know this," he them muttered.

"Go ahead," Lee said, maintaining his gaze at the German ships that were now firing their boilers hard enough to spew a heavy bluish white smoke from their center stacks.

Carter took the cue and headed down the hallway to the telegraph room. Without sitting down, he wrote out what he wanted to send. '*Stiles. German ships leaving Havana. Destination unknown. Purpose unknown. Find Moser. Should be in Charleston. Carter.*'

"Cain't tell if they fixin' to head east or west," Lee moved away from the window. He walked down the hallway and joined Carter in the telegraph room. "What's got you all spun up, son?"

Carter, now sitting, remained silent, looking over the words he had written. He debated whether the message should be sent or taken by courier. He knew the telegraph was not secure enough and if the Germans intercepted the message, it could expose Moser. Hell, Moser might not even know what the Kaiser was positioning himself to do.

"Do you need me for anything more?" Carter asked as he folded up the message and started tearing it up.

"I don't think so. I reckon our special project is about done. And last I heard, Secretary Day was sending some help down on the *Carthage* to process our people out." Lee noted, matter-of-factly.

"What about the *Olivette*?" Carter asked.

"She's been commandeered by the Navy. I think Sampson finally figured out a way to bring McManus and his vessel into his fold."

"Then the *Carthage* it is. I need to go to Tampa now. Send my stuff home if all hell breaks out before I get back," Carter replied. He squeezed his fingers together, cracking two of his knuckles, then cranked up the magneto and typed in Morse code, '*Send Stiles to Tampa for a package.*'

Queen Regent, Maria Cristina, a daughter of the Austrian royal house, lamented each day of her regency for her son, Alfonso. She hoped she could turn over a Spanish empire that was thriving, virulent and expansive, rather than one which was faltering, disrespected and shriveling into nothing more than a weak monarchy on the Iberian Peninsula. As she looked out from her palace window into the rainy March morning, a day that her subjects slogged through to reach their daily toil, she felt her trust in each of her Cabinet of Ministers being washed and eroded away. The men she once trusted for their candid truth were now pompously beating their chests to pronounce that Spain had not spiraled down into ineptitude and unimportance in world affairs. She knew better. Even the information she had obtained from her Minister of Marine contradicted what she knew about the readiness of her navy and their fighting will.

Her one lasting pleasure in her life was her husband's namesake. Her encouragement for athletics had turned a delicate boy into a strong, energetic young man. Her desire for a deep and broad education was fulfilled — her conversations with her son warmed her heart. He would be well prepared once he came of age to assume the throne, a crown that now felt to her more a burden than honor.

"*Buenas dias, Reina,*" Maria Cristina's private secretary arrived at the open, massive double doors for their morning discussion. Jorge was an older man of Basque decent; short, muscular and dark-skinned. Maria had found his counsel useful. Besides her son, he may have been the only man she felt she could trust anymore. He respectfully bowed to Maria before settling into a small cushioned ladder-backed chair directly underneath a larger than life sized portrait of her belated husband, Alfonso XII.

"Any reply from England?" she asked, turning back into the wide expanse of the room. Jorge's bowed head and solemn expression was all she needed to see. She read in it that her appeal to Queen Victoria for support in the Cuban situation had been ignored once again. Worse yet, her request may have been seen as begging, revealing her weakness in dealing with the other monarchs in the fragile European alliance.

"Perhaps, Ambassador Dubsky will convince Franz-Joseph that Austria will take part in this coalition?" Jorge proposed.

"This has ridden me with guilt, Jorge — asking support from family when I have my own recourses that should be adequate." Maria walked gracefully to the center of the room and settled behind a large ornate table crafted from Cuban mahogany that Governor Blanco presented to her as a gift.

"Nonetheless, you needed to ask, no?" Jorge's lips twitched as he arched his eyebrows.

"Perhaps not, dear Jorge. I have discovered through some conversations that my once very unpopular idea has gained a very influential ally," Maria said slyly.

"The Church?" Jorge asked.

Maria nodded and cracked a tiny, thin-lipped smile. She leaned forward and lowered her voice. "I want you to understand, Jorge, that this matter requires the utmost secrecy and sensitivity. Only Ambassador Woodford is to know about this. He is to assure you that any discussions about this will take place privately and exclusively with President McKinley." Maria leaned back to let Jorge put the innuendo together.

"So that I understand correctly, your Majesty," Jorge frowned and sat forward in his chair as his eyes focused directly at Maria. "You are considering —"

"Reconsidering," Maria corrected.

"Reconsidering selling Cuba to the United States?"

As her words were spoken by Jorge, Maria suddenly felt as desperate as her words sounded. Remaining silent for moment, she then agreed with a brief nod. "My fear is that it has become likely that one way or another, we shall lose Cuba. I believe this unfortunate explosion of the American ship at Havana has unraveled our future."

"Have you conceded then that we would lose any battle

with the Americans?" Jorge asked as Maria stood and slowly walked back to the large expansive window that overlooked the spring flowers arranged neatly in her palatial garden. Birds flitted through the bobbing heads, gently tossed by the warm breeze that had floated in off the sea. Maria then turned back to Jorge, her eyes wide.

"No, Jorge, I have not," she started with a whisper. "But if there is a way to relieve the assured agony that presses on the heart of this mother, the agony of the blood that will be shed in any war over this tiny spit of land, I must pursue it."

"And reparations for the battle ship?"

"Yes, Jorge, we should consider that as part of this offer as well. If McKinley's administration can immediately sanction fifty million dollars for a war effort to free this island and her indignant inhabitants, then I believe money holds little value for them."

"Then I shall deliver the message to Ambassador Woodford immediately," Jorge stated as he stood and bowed again to his Queen Regent.

"I have already prepared the message," Maria nudged an envelope toward Jorge. "I am sure that Mr. Woodford and President McKinley will see sincerity with it being written in my own hand."

"I understand, your majesty," Jorge said as he took the letter, slipped it into his jacket pocket, and exited the room, leaving Maria alone at her desk. She knew it was her last hope to avoid war, but was confident that what she had learned of President McKinley's pacifism would help continue the dialogue. She looked up to the gilded portrait of Alfonso on the wall and began to sob.

"You are in fine health, Mac," Assistant Attending Surgeon Leonard Wood concluded, putting his stethoscope away after his routine physical examination of the President. "You could use a bit more sleep, which may be why you feel these bouts of lethargy during the day, but to this point, you have staved off any infection."

"Thank you," McKinley noted, stepping down from the

examining table and recovering his shirt. "And how about your counterpart? How is his health?"

"TR is doing fine at this point," Wood replied, starting to place the stethoscope into his medical bag.

"And Edith?" McKinley asked.

"She finally had the necessary surgery," Wood organized the instruments in his black medical bag and weakly grinned. "It took some coercing getting through his thick head, but TR finally relented. Dr. Osler found an abscess near her hip and successfully removed it. She's doing much better at this juncture."

"He did attend the surgery, yes?"

"He was right there with her, but only after I refused to continue our wrestling matches unless he did," Wood said with a chuckle.

"I am pleased to hear that. Perhaps there is a heart in that man, after all." McKinley buttoned up his shift and tucked the tails back into his trousers. Wood tidied up his medical bag and snapped it closed. He then hung up his white lab coat meticulously, stowed the black leather satchel into the closet, and checked the time.

"So have you and Theodore declared war yet?" McKinley joked as he looked into the small desk mirror and adjusted his tie around his raised shirt collar. He knew Wood and Roosevelt had both indicated they would like to be returned to active duty in the Army to lead forces into Cuba. McKinley had always shook off Wood's requests as flippant, as had Long of the demands of Roosevelt, but their persistence had not dissipated in the least.

"No sir," Wood replied then added as he headed out the door, "But we think you should."

Within minutes of leaving McKinley in the White House to continue his day full of meetings with Congress, followed by the press briefings, Wood met up with Roosevelt, who appeared more agitated than usual. Their daily brisk walk was ritualized; their pace, steady and strong. Roosevelt upped the speed enough that by the time they plunged into the park, their pace was more running than walking.

"I have not heard from Admiral Davis," Roosevelt started. "I admit that I inflict so much advice to my boss that I fear I have now become more a detriment than an advantage."

"I am sure he recognizes your judgment and perceptions are sharp, useful and on target." Wood punctuated his statement with a punch to Roosevelt's shoulder. His pace then quickened, preventing immediate retaliation.

"So I wrote to General Tillinghast this morning," Roosevelt noted as he caught up with Wood.

"New York?"

"National Guard." Roosevelt confirmed. "I thought I would try that route since the Guard would indeed be called up once hostilities broke out. Alger, or whoever McKinley puts in that chair, will surely look that way when he sees what few regulars we truly have."

"And?"

"You doubt me?"

"Well, did you ask about me?"

"Of course! I noted that you would be a fine addition to the regiment when called up. I so want to be at the front, Leonard. I believe you understand, unlike most others." Roosevelt finished as he took a swipe at Wood, but the agile young doctor was able to dodge the impact. Wood rammed his shoulder into Roosevelt's in response, and then curled up his arms in self-defense of the secretary's retaliation.

"We'll have to work on your reaction time, Teddie," Wood taunted. "Otherwise I would not want you next to me trying to take some hill from those bloody Spaniards."

"That's TR," Roosevelt growled and launched himself into Wood. The men began grappling at each other like a pair of schoolboys in the yard until Wood squirmed out of Roosevelt's hold, and then began dancing around the heavier man.

"That desk job of yours is dulling your senses, Teddie."

"My point exactly," Roosevelt sprung forward, gripping Wood by the shoulders and wrestling him to the ground. With quick hands, he latched onto Wood's arms and pinned him, face down, with the doctor's arms bent and stretched behind his back. Wood groaned.

"Perhaps yours as well," Roosevelt crowed, accepting his friend's capitulation. He then rolled off, laughing gutturally as he clacked his teeth behind his wide grin. Wood quickly scrambled to his feet, and the two men moved onto a grassy knoll where they could continue their rugged play, testing their personal moves at hand-to-hand combat, preparing for the day they would become war heroes for their nation.

A hot afternoon melded into steamy evening in restless Havana. Sam Carter had navigated around the gathered American newspaper correspondents in the Café Luz and headed to the dock for his voyage back to the States. Before he could reach the ferry that was to take him out to the *Carthage*, he noticed Consul Fitzhugh Lee stepping out of a carriage full of fleeing, wide-eyed Americans. Carter stepped out of line and allowed them in front of him.

"I know you are not much into politics, Sam, but hear me out," Lee started as he waved Carter closer so they could talk in private. "Everyone has been itching to start something. Roosevelt, Blanco, hell, even the Kaiser has been saber rattling. You'd think we just need to throw down the gauntlet and get it over with."

Carter glared at Lee, taken by surprise by his comment.

"Think about it, Sam. Almost forty years ago, our own country was hankering for something to happen because we had made a canyon between regional definitions of states' rights. You know we, the South, formed our own nation over this interpretation and the powder keg still didn't blow. It wasn't until we poked the skunk at Sumter that all hell broke loose."

"And so it will be with the *Maine* since the Board will most likely conclude it was a mine," Carter replied as he looked over his shoulder and watched the line boarding the ferry dwindle to less than ten. "But if the truth is something else — something more insidious, especially sabotage, we need to know who and why."

"It won't matter. Either conclusion will provide the same
404

result. If the verdict is an internal explosion, Spain accuses us of a set-up, takes us to task because of it, and we have war. If the verdict is that a mine blew up, Spain is accused and we go to war as well."

"Listen to me," Carter pushed the words through his teeth. His eyes had widened large enough that he could feel the strain on his face. "If this was sabotage, and not at the hands of the Spaniards, we have another problem — a different problem — a bigger problem. I've come to realize we're running hell bent into a war that was inevitable anyway. I really don't give a damn about that any more. What is imperative, and dangerous, *right now*, is that we don't know who planted that bomb on the *Maine*."

Consul Lee titled his head and stared silently at Carter. "You are convinced of that, then?"

" Yes, I am. Something was planted on the *Maine* by someone. Other ships could be targets as well. We don't know who, I have my suspicions, and we don't understand why. I am not convinced, General, it was just one isolated occurrence. Something more is afoot and we need to figure it out.."

"I see your point," Lee rubbed his beard and cocked his head.

"I gotta go, sir," Carter said as he looked back at the line for the ferry. Everyone in line had been processed. "I think I know who did this, but I need to talk to someone back in the States to confirm what I am thinking."

"What are you going to tell Wilkie," Lee asked as Carter headed toward the end of the dock and waved to catch the boson's eye.

"I don't know. He probably won't listen to me anyway," Carter finished and ran the last fifty feet to the ferry. He waved to Lee one last time, smiled and boarded. No sooner than Carter sat down, the boatswain started the ferry's motor, plunged it into the dark harbor water and turned out toward the *Carthage*.

Chapter 24

Ambassador Woodford looked out his small office window and watched a cold, drizzling rain welcome a late March morning in Madrid. The usually cool morning, followed by a quick warm-up once the sun worked its way over the eastern mountains would not be the case today. It seemed that there was indecision in the clouds, fickle in choosing whether to pour down or just blanket the area with a gloomy thick mist.

'These days are seldom encountered though,' Ambassador Woodford thought. With the exception of the tension with the politics, he had enjoyed the weather and his time in Spain. Having a chance to learn more about Spanish culture was an added bonus that he would remember for a long time after his civil service days were done.

If he could help it, that day, the day that he had to leave would now be far in the future. McKinley approved him to negotiate of the sale of Cuba to the United States as a way to save face for the Queen Regent and Spain. It would also help prevent what would clearly be a brutal, bloody war over the Caribbean island.

Yes, this was going to be a glorious day for him, he thought as he took the five long legged steps back to his small walnut desk and wormed his backside into the thin but soft cushioned chair. With a copy of the specific elements which the President insisted be included, he dug in, working feverishly to cobble together the final proposal which he would personally deliver to the Queen Regent herself before the morning was done.

Woodford tried to contain his excitement with each clause so that the final copy would be clear and legible. This would be his breakthrough moment, he thought as he leaned back and imagined how well he would be received back at the State Department for such a clever feat of negotiation — wresting a peaceful settlement when everyone, even him for a brief period, felt the teeth of the jaws of war had already begun snapping wildly.

A commotion at the front door caught his attention, but he ignored it since he had already arranged for the Consul General to handle any visitors this morning. He needed to be left undisturbed to complete what he was sure to be touted as an international triumph.

'The Woodford Treaty of 1898.' That's how it would be lauded, he thought as he reviewed the paper one last time. The sections included cost and terms of the sale, recognition of Cuba as a free state, withdrawal timetables, and finally reparations for the *Maine*.

He heard the Consul greet the guest, and invite him in. They talked briefly. Then silence. As Woodford glanced back down to his work, there was a knock on his door.

"Ambassador Woodford. Mr. Jorge Xerada is here to see you." The Consul announced as he opened the office door.

'No, I was supposed to go there and meet with Maria Cristina,' Woodford thought then stepped out from his desk and met Xerada half way with an open hand.

"Ambassador Woodford?" Xerada stepped through the open door.

"Jorge, it is a pleasure to see you again. Please, let me take your coat." he offered.

"No, thank you. I will only be a moment. I have a brief message from her Majesty."

"And you came all the way over here in the rain? I was scheduled to see her Majesty later this morning," Woodford felt an ominous chill run up his back and tingle his neck.

"Her Majesty does not wish to pursue this matter of Cuba after all," Xerada said quietly and precisely as he lowered his head. Woodford sensed that the man was as disappointed as he was. "Your meeting with her this morning will not be necessary."

"I understand," Woodford lied. His dream of notoriety suddenly spiraled away. "I presume that is all."

"Yes, sir," Xerada replied in English, which his had improved in the short time Woodford had known him. Slowly, the Spaniard turned around and sulked his way out the door.

Woodford dropped his pen. There was no need to continue his work. He waited at his desk until Xerada left the building, then stood up and looked out the window, watching the Queen Regent's aide head back into the city. All of his dreams of grandeur, of being the one man who was able to avert a seemingly inevitable conflict — a conflict he knew would probably decimate the Spanish fleet — had been washed away, like the rain did to the dust on Jorge's jacket.

Woodford wandered dejectedly into the teletype room and sat down to compose a message to McKinley. As he searched for a pen to collect his thoughts, he noticed there was another cable on the desk. He picked it up and noticed it was from an active agent in Cadiz, the port city in the south.

"It is truly over," he mumbled as he sat down to compose a message to McKinley. "There will be no negotiation for Cuba. The Queen evidently lost courage between yesterday afternoon and today," his message started. "I also have received a report that a flotilla of torpedo boats and torpedo boat destroyers have departed Cadiz and are destined for the Caribbean.

As Senator Redfield Proctor passed through Lafayette Park, he brushed close enough to the lemon yellow forsythia blossoms that pollen dust streaked onto his drab gray suit jacket sleeve. He would have normally smiled since he enjoyed spring blossoms that colored and scented the Washington air, but this morning he felt consumed by the inhumanity to the Cuban population he had witnessed first-hand on his fact-finding voyage. Instead, he maintained a stone-like frown on his long, weathered face as he walked up the Capitol building steps and into the legislative chambers.

The Speaker of the House called order to the combined session of the House and Senate, and then invited Senator Proctor to the center of the amphitheater. Proctor rose from his seat in the gallery and calmly approached the podium. The tall, thin, bearded man marched stiltedly to the front of the chamber, laid his papers down, and like a preacher in the pulpit on a Sunday morning, surveyed the settling congregation before clearing his throat.

"I have been alleged to have said that there was no doubt the *Maine* was blown up from the outside. This could not be farther from the truth. The fact of this grave matter is that I hold no opinion about it for myself, and have carefully avoided settling on any conclusion," Proctor started in a humble voice. Those present had become mesmerized by the Lincoln-esque demeanor of their seasoned colleague.

"In Havana, everything seems to go on much as usual. There are the typical skirmishes between the locals and the Spanish overlords, not much different than we have seen here in recent years. However, outside Havana, there is not peace. There is not war. There is solely desolation, misery and starvation." The Senator spoke in variable tone for emphasis, as skilled as any speech he had delivered before his colleagues. His voice grew in volume, with descriptions more aghast than the previous as he described the debacle that Spanish rule had become in Cuba.

"I conclude that the strongest argument is not the barbarism so evident in the countryside, nor is it the destruction of the *Maine*, but the spectacle of thousands of people, the entire native population of this once wondrous island, struggling for freedom and deliverance from the worst misgovernment of which I have ever known. I now see it as not only righteous to intervene on behalf of these down-trodden people, but it is our obligation and our duty to do so," Proctor concluded. The floor erupted in agreement with the Senator, showering him with a standing ovation that lasted through him neatly folding up his notes, slipping them into his tweed jacket pocket, and exiting the chamber.

Roosevelt, who had heard every word the Senator preached, grinned widely and clacked his teeth together with as much fury as he slapped his palms in applause. He waited patiently for Proctor at the chamber's tall, narrow doors. The Senator caught Roosevelt's glance as he strode up the red-carpeted chamber step-like levels, and nodded to meet him out in the foyer, where the noise level was sure to be reduced.

"Great speech, Senator," Roosevelt grabbed the Senator by the shoulders and winked. "I would certainly hope that the President recognizes your qualifications when he eradicates Alger from his Cabinet."

"Perhaps you should consider the difficulty of that position before you damn the man, Mr. Roosevelt," Proctor stated, matter-of-factly. He regarded Roosevelt and his crass statement for a moment before adding with his usual grim-faced self-deprecation, "I believe I have already served in that capacity, Mr. Roosevelt. Some would say I was as well ineffective. If I were President, I would select someone with a bit more vigor than what this old man has to offer," Proctor responded with his usual wry grin.

"Yes, yes," Roosevelt tempered his enthusiasm as Proctor, released from the Secretary's grip, headed toward the building exit. Roosevelt scrambled to catch up with the Senator as he stepped outside into the bright sunshine, and then asked, "I need to present some proposals to begin the defense of Cuba to McKinley. You would not mind if I use some of your images?"

Proctor continued walking in silence toward Lafayette Park, in the direction of his flat, with Roosevelt double-timing behind him, trying to keep up with the old Vermonter's strides. Proctor finally stopped, turned to Roosevelt, and handed him the notes he had squirreled away in his jacket pocket.

"Use what you would like," Proctor grumbled, and without a grin or additional words, turned and continued on his way.

The *Carthage* entered Tampa Bay only minutes after sunrise, and even considering the time of day, the Captain announced his arrival with three long blows of his ship's horn.

He maneuvered his vessel around the breakwater and into the bay crowded with moored military transports teeming with soldiers. Nearby a squadron of sleek torpedo boats bobbed gently on the glassy, slight roll of the surface. Gunboats cobbled together from commercial and private vessels lay in-between the *Carthage* and a berth at the docks.

The Captain called for a full stop. The engine room complied and the thunk of the propellers being disengaged loudly enough that those who dared sleep through their approach were shaken awake by the vessel's shudder. A series of tugs steamed out from their berths and wormed their way around the tonnage in the harbor as the *Carthage* drifted into shallower, calmer waters. With four water mules plying their trade, the *Carthage* was pushed and prodded until she was wedged amidst transport vessels and the wide, wooden pier.

Sam Carter departed the *Carthage* with Annette McGeehan, who had surprised him by being on-board. He remained silent and comfortable as he escorted her from the *Carthage* to the train station, a short walking distance from the port. He felt almost discrete with her, courteously holding her arm with one arm while his other carried her heavy, book-laden luggage. When they reached the train station, Annette queued into the ticket line while Carter silently waited and watched from a short distance. He caught her wandering glance at times, to which she feigned shyness when her eyes met his.

"I must thank you Annette. This was one of my most pleasant voyages that I can remember," Carter admitted as she returned with her ticket.

"The pleasure was mine, Sam," Annette replied, bowing her head coyly. "It is not often I can talk about my bird study without being ostracized for being a woman doing man's work."

Carter felt different about Annette now than he did when he first met her. Her directness and openness no longer made him nervous. She drew out feelings he had repressed for years. Being able to talk freely about his own inner feelings was something he had not been able to do, no less do with any woman before. He was what he was and Annette accepted him

411

as he was. '*What more could I ask from a friend*,' he thought.

Behind them, the train announced its imminent departure. Annette took her overstuffed cloth satchel from Carter and fished through one of the side pockets. She took out a small, notebook-sized paper and handed it to Carter.

"This is where I live in Charleston. We have a nice porch where I can look out over the marshes."

"We?" Carter recoiled.

"It's actually my Aunt's house. We do rent rooms if you decide you would like to be closer to the water."

Carter glanced at the address briefly. It was very familiar. "Has your Aunt rented out a room . . ." he started, but deferred and let Annette finish.

"To an older man?" Annette finished. "Why, yes she did. And you know, he is a very intelligent man. He even told me about you."

Carter felt suddenly naked.

"Please come and see me sometime. Perhaps when you visit your Mr. Moser?" Annette grinned, leaned over and kissed Carter on his cheek. She then hoisted her bag, turned and hailed the conductor to wait, then quickly boarded the train, leaving Carter at the podium still astonished at Annette's departing revelation.

As the train peeped its departure whistle, Carter headed back to the posh Hotel Tampa where he had arranged to meet Stiles. Nearing the block, he slowed, taken aback by the grounds having been overrun with officers and soldiers, nervously awaiting the inevitable order that the war had begun. Through the milling crowd, he squeezed into the foyer and looked into the dining area where he spotted two men at a corner table — Jack Stiles and to Carter's surprise, Rudolf Moser.

"Welcome home, Sam," Stiles rose from his seat as Carter emerged from amidst the stiff blue uniforms milling about.

"Good to be back, I think," Carter firmly shook Stiles' hand. He dropped his satchel next to the table and melted into the seat across from Moser as Stiles waved to the waiter for service. "Glad you understood my message."

"You were a little more beat up the last time I said that to you," Stiles noted.

"*Guten Tag, Mr. Carter*," Moser lifted his eyes, twitched a smile, and nodded his head politely.

"How 'bout something to eat, Sam?" Stiles asked as the waiter finally arrived at the table. "I bet it's been a while since you've had some good old American food."

Carter noticed the waiter was Cuban. There was calmness in his face that seemed so much in contrast to what he had seen in Havana. He wondered for a moment if the young boy would be called up, possibly even impressed and sent to trudge through the jungles with his lost brethren, side-by-side with American boys that had no clue what their fates would be on that hot humid island. "Now that you mention it, Jack, shrimp and grits," Carter looked at the waiter, grinned, and added, "With three pats of butter."

"I'll have the same," Stiles noted then looked at Moser.

"*Krapfen und kafe*," Moser said with an elfish grin. The waiter cocked his head as a vacant stare covered his face.

"Oily cakes — doughnuts," Stiles interpreted.

"*Ja, ja*, doughnuts *und kafe*," Moser repeated. The young waiter tipped his head then headed back to the kitchen.

Stiles leaned forward. "What's this urgent information you discovered about the *Maine*."

"There were no fish in the water, Jack. That tells me the explosions, both of them, not just the second one came from the inside." Carter insisted.

"You've got to be kidding me."

"It was an internal explosion Jack. Sabotage." Carter completed his thought from earlier as the waiter returned with their breakfasts. The young Cuban placed the food in front of each of the men, then took out a small bottle filled with green sauce from his apron pocket and placed it in front of Carter.

"Jalapeño," Carter grinned as the waiter winked and turning away.

"Mr. Carter is probably correct, Mr. Stiles," Moser mumbled. As he took a small bite from his doughnut, a crumb fell into his coffee. "It is what the Kaiser would do. A

413

diversion. *Ja*, Tirpitz would want that. *Ja*, I believe Samuel is correct. Wilhelm had one of his agents place an explosive on your ship," he added absently as he rescued his broken pastry with a spoon.

Stiles stared at Moser, visibly stunned. "You can't be serious?"

"His Excellency and Admiral Tirpitz have plotted to invade America for some years now. I know this. I have seen plans," Moser wagged his finger at Stiles, before taking another bite of his breakfast.

"That all makes sense, now," Carter noted, splashing his grits with the green sauce. "The *Maine* was a diversion — a way to get McKinley's focus on Cuba and Spain. Once we send all of our ships there, we are left naked in our home ports."

"Ziegler," Stiles whispered.

"*Ja, ja.* Ziegler is here," Moser added. His eyes widened as he swallowed hard. "*Und* he knows explosives."

"I was tracking him with an anarchist named DeLauro, but they both disappeared just before all the saber rattling starting spinning out of control. Wilkie lost interest in that and he's got me chasing Cuban spies now," Stiles noted.

"I've told Wainwright before I left Havana to get the Navy to check the other ships' coal storage for sabotage. I believe he'll follow through." Carter noted.

Stiles checked his pocket watch, then pushed his breakfast away and leaned over to Carter. "Wilkie's got to know this whole thing. Roosevelt as well."

"That's why I needed to come home personally. I couldn't just put over the telegraph that we know what the Kaiser is up to," Carter said.

"*Ja, ja.* He can hear." Moser injected before taking another bite of his doughnut.

"Alright, then," Stiles wiped the corners of his mouth and dropped the cloth napkin on the table. His tipped his head back and looked to the ceiling, as if planning. "I've already left a decent suit for you in your room. I'll take the noon train with Moser and you can follow on the four o'clock. That gives you some time to clean up. I'll set up a meeting for you with Wilkie tomorrow."

Carter nodded as Moser pleasurably finished his doughnut, followed by a mouthful of the black coffee.

"If I'm going to catch that train, I'd better be going. I'll make sure there is a ticket waiting for you when you get there," Stiles said as he stood and slipped his seat under the table.

"*Danka*," Carter said as he glanced at Moser. Stiles dropped a ten-dollar bill on the table and with Moser, quickly exited the hotel, leaving Carter alone amidst the troops that had gathered for the Cuban incursion. He reveled in his plate of grits, and after looking around to be sure no one was watching, slid over the plate that Stiles had started and worked through that one as well. For now, it was good to be home, he thought.

President McKinley nodded off in his high backed cushioned chair as he waited for his daily meeting with his cabinet. He bemoaned his daily cabinet meetings now, knowing that Roosevelt would be badgering him to start the war right away. Waiting for the official report of the *Maine* explosion had visibly taken a toll on him. Bags of blued and bruised skin sagged under dulled eyes; his expression had grown sullen, his skin pasty. He still took his slow methodical walks during the sunny weather, but this did little to stave off his degradation. The added worry of this turmoil's effect on Ida, her fits and episodes growing more frequent and violent, did not help his melancholy.

'Resolution,' he prayed. The drive for a resolution by conflict resonated from not only Roosevelt, but also the press. Public consensus had burgeoned in favor of faulting Spain and taking her to task. Alger reported that enlistments were up, and to pacify Roosevelt and Long, McKinley personally ordered his War Secretary to commence troop build-up in preparation for what now seemed inevitable.

McKinley returned to his office at the stroke of ten, having finished a wandering morning walk around the White House, hoping it would improve his circulation and his thinking. As he walked into the Yellow Room, his Cabinet had already arrived, taken their seats, and commenced their daily round of bickering and finger pointing. He ambled toward his cushioned seat at the head of the table, folded his hands in fig-leaf posture and peered out with a deep-set expression in his eyes at the convened Cabinet.

"Good Morning. I regret that I still have no report," McKinley stated.

"I have provided to Secretary Day that Spain has already started their insolence with a flotilla steaming across the ocean," Roosevelt immediately squawked, banging his fist into the table. "Is this not an act of war, Mr. President? I submit that we should act accordingly."

"What do we have available?" McKinley asked.

"Ten vessels out of the Revenue Cutter Service. We can arm them up with a few guns, and perhaps a torpedo or two. They may be a bit slower than the flotilla, but it is the best we can do until the refits are complete in the Navy Yards." Roosevelt noted.

"I will consider that, Mr. Roosevelt," McKinley's voice echoed his exasperation.

"William, I have decided that we need to submit to the Queen Regent a final offer," McKinley said, turning to his old friend from Ohio. Day had replaced the increasingly ineffective Sherman in the post and as McKinley expected, was already providing a steadier stream of information. "Senator Proctor's speech the other night provided a clear enough vision that the undeclared war against the Cubans must immediately cease."

Secretary Day took notes fervently while McKinley spoke. As he finished his scribbling, he looked up to McKinley, at the ready, expecting more.

"She needs to know this is our last chance. Get Woodford involved. We need an immediate answer to accountability for the loss of the *Maine*, what reparations will be afforded, and this needs to be emphasized — a timetable for withdrawal and Cuban independence."

"Yes, sir," Day responded. He looked up and added, "Consequences if these demands are not met?"

"Gentlemen, there is only one consequence," McKinley

416

looked back up to the group, where the only smiling face was Roosevelt's. "I believe we are grasping at our last hope for peace. Our efforts, as valiant and restrained as they have been to avoid an armed conflict, have borne no fruit. Once the report from the Board of Inquiry is submitted to the Congress, which will be soon, I truly believe I will be requesting their authorization for armed intervention."

The room remained gravely silent. McKinley scanned the room, stopping only for seconds to lock eyes with each of his Cabinet members. "I believe we all have things to do. Good Day," McKinley announced as he stood. Slowly, he exited the room and meandered down the hallway, leaving his Cabinet to muse on when the report was to arrive.

Chapter 25

Wilhelm Ziegler was astounded at his fortune. When he had received the urgent cable from the Kaiser that stated he suspected Rudolf Moser's defection, Ziegler knew what had to be done. He never thought that he would be able to complete his new assignment so quickly; concerned he would need to find transport to Haiti. Finding an old man in a country full of old men would be nothing more than a wild goose chase, he reckoned, but there he was, sitting on a park bench on a quiet Washington afternoon, alone, dressed in a gray suit with a gray fedora. The dim gaslights in the park provided adequate illumination that he was assured it was Moser. He tapped his jacket, then covered his right hand over the thirty-two caliber Iver-Johnson revolver hidden in the inside pocket.

The old man had to be silenced. Moser knew about Tirpitz's plan. Ziegler knew that. Wilhelm wanted him sent to Haiti to get him out of the way. Even if they targeted somewhere other than Norfolk, missing the element of surprise, the plan would rapidly become a debacle, and the Kaiser would be embarrassed on the international stage again. Even worse, Moser could very easily expose him to the American authorities, rendering him ineffective. Ziegler enjoyed his freedom of movement too much.

He scanned the area from one corner of the park to the other as he slowly approached. No one was nearby. It was time. Ziegler passed twenty feet to the left of the bench and without raising Moser's suspicion, verified his target. He circled back in the grass, and then started his furtive approach from behind. "*Guten abends*, Rudolph," he said in a hushed tone, then quietly sat down next to Moser.

Moser looked up. His face registered recognition. "Wilhelm," he stated calmly.

"I want you to know that I once respected you," Ziegler said. His left arm twitched. The grips of the revolver felt cold in his hand. He looked around one more time. They were still alone. As quickly and fluidly as he could, Ziegler grabbed Moser's jacket flap, yanked it open, pulled out the revolver with his right hand and placed the barrel into Moser's rib cage. The gun popped as he pulled the trigger.

Moser turned his head toward him and looked at him with ghostly eyes. His expression showed surprise. Only briefly. He tried to utter something, but nothing emerged from his open mouth except a thin trail of pink froth. His body slumped forward.

"That was before you crossed me and His Excellency. You should have never come back here," Ziegler growled. He picked up the satchel and thought about removing any papers he had carried. It didn't matter, he resolved, then used it to prop up Moser's limp torso. He opened the old man's right hand, wormed the pistol into his fingers, and laid it back on the bench.

Ziegler looked around again. All remained quiet. He would be gone before anyone discovered the slumped old man on a park bench was actually dead. Ziegler rose from the bench and calmly strolled away from the park toward the train station.

Pausing briefly at the steps of the palatial looking pillars that marked the impressive entrance to the Treasury building, Carter looked up briefly to regroup his thoughts. He dug into his pleated trousers, still feeling they were uncomfortably fancy for him, and took out his now salt-tarnished pocket watch. He risked being late if he dawdled any longer, and he had come to understand that in the eyes of Director Wilkie, being late was as close to a sin as anything. He snapped his watch closed and hurried up the steps two at a time and plunged into the massive structure, worked his way down the tall, imposing corridors, and then into the expansive waiting area outside Wilkie's office. Without a clerk to greet him, he rapped on the door.

"Come," a faceless voice responded. Carter complied and stepped inside. Alone in the room behind a desk that appeared much too small for the spacious office, Wilkie sat in a high-backed leather covered chair, stiff backed, with his hands folded in front of him.

"Mr. Carter, you are late," Wilkie noted curtly as he glanced over his spectacles at the far corner of the office where a tall grandfather clock ticked away. Carter noted it was five minutes faster than his watch. "Have a seat," he then added, nodding to a plain wooden chair in front of his small desk.

"Thank you, sir." Carter complied and anxiously sat down. He didn't know what to expect from Wilkie in his own office, especially now that he attained the top position in the organization.

"You say you have some revealing information concerning the *Maine*?" Wilkie craned his neck forward and glowed at Carter.

"Sir, I believe the *Maine* was not destroyed by a Spanish mine."

"*That* matter has been settled, Mr. Carter." Wilkie responded, more curtly than before.

"Perhaps for everyone else, sir, but not for me," Carter noted. Wilkie scowled as he tilted his head, appearing to be listening, or at least, entertaining Carter's thoughts. "There were no dead fish when I accompanied the first dive. And the plates were bent at an odd angle —"

"What does that have to do with anything?" Wilkie cut Carter off. His face registered skepticism.

"You know as well as I, the concussion resultant from an external explosion would have killed any fish in the area."

"Perhaps there were no fish in the area to begin with?" Wilkie spit out.

"There were many —"

"Carter, think about what you are saying right now."

"I already have," Carter responded, defiantly.

"Let me make myself clear, then," Wilkie rose slowly from his seat. He glared over his spectacles and leaned forward on his hands. "If the explosion was internal, Captain Sigsbee is accountable for that accident. Since we are headed into a war, one that will certainly be rife, if not almost exclusively focused on naval encounters, we will need Captains. We cannot afford to have Sigsbee or any other Captain on some administrative leave for losing a ship when we are headed into war. Does that make it a little clearer for you, Mr. Carter?"

"Sir, it is more insidious that that." Carter stood his ground.

"Mr. Carter, the conclusion of what has happened has already been made," Wilkie's tone was condescending. "And if you want to continue your employment with the Secret Service — then you will leave your little secret about the fish in Havana. No one will know any better. And since there is enough evidence that points to a mine, then a mine it is. End of story."

"I see," Carter bit his lip, stewing inside. He bowed his head and closed his eyes, realizing that Stiles must not have talked with Wilkie.

"Mr. Carter, you have been out of the country for some time now and you have probably lost touch with what is going on here in Washington," Wilkie said as he broke his eye contact and returned his focus on the papers on his desk.

"Sigsbee is not at fault for this. It was sabotage," Carter said, ensuring Wilkie heard his concern. The Director did. He dropped the paper in his hands he was reading and looked at Carter with an incredulous expression.

"Do you realize what you are saying, Carter?"

"That I do, sir."

"Then explain yourself."

"I am not exactly sure how they were able to do it, but somehow, a German agent or agents planted a bomb inside the *Maine*."

"And you want me to believe you solely on your word?" Wilkie appeared to be listening, Carter reckoned.

"Not just me sir. I met with Arturo — the Cuban

revolutionary? While I was questioning him who could have done this, he dragged out a German sailor their group had captured. The sailor admitted he know of a plan to blow up an American ship."

"You want me to believe something Arturo said? Half the people in Cuba don't believe him."

Carter sighed. "No sir, the *sailor* admitted it." Wilkie's eyes widened a bit as he cocked his head. "The sailor knew about the sabotage."

"That's one man. Arturo probably kidnapped him and put him up to it."

"Arturo didn't know I was coming. And when I met with Stiles a few days ago, trying to figure out the loose ends, Moser said that Wilhelm had placed an operative here in the States that was familiar with explosives."

"Ziegler?" Wilkie whispered.

"Yes, sir. Ziegler. Moser said that's who it was," Carter grew excited, sensing that Wilkie might actually be starting to believe him.

Wilkie fell silent. His attention reverted to the papers on his desk as he squeezed at his temples. Carter sensed that for all practical purposes, he was not there. Wilkie worked through the papers in front of him slowly, as if in deep concentration.

"And physics tells me that the explosions had to be from the inside. The plate where the explosion occurred was bent twice. That's why it had the odd V-shape."

"Does Roosevelt know this? Secretary Day?" Wilkie mumbled, glancing up for a moment.

"Wainwright does," Carter started.

"Why?"

"He had to know," Carter replied. "The *Maine* might not have been the only ship set up. I could get the information out faster that way."

"You don't know whether he has told Roosevelt or not?"

"What would that matter?"

Wilkie removed his glasses and dropped them onto the pile of papers in front of him. Carter felt his eyes stab him directly in his chest. "You really don't understand how things work around here in Washington, do you Carter?"

Carter was ready to blurt out what he thought, but chose to hold back. It really didn't matter much to him how things worked. The fact of the matter to him was that Spain was not their only concern. "No sir, I reckon I don't," he then replied.

"Don't tell anyone else. We need to keep this our secret so that the whole country doesn't dissolve into a general panic," Wilkie said. Carter squirmed in his chair.

Carter reckoned that Wilkie now believed him. "If we don't do anything, sir —"

Wilkie tucked his chin, his glower stopping Carter in mid-comment. "Carter, let me tell you something about what all goes on in this town. I have to deal with a myriad of problems all at once. So does Roosevelt. And the President. Right now, we've got this Spain-Cuba crisis on the horizon. We still have counterfeiters running around hell bent on spinning the economy out of control. Thousands of people are still out of work because President Cleveland did nothing to prevent it. And you think that some renegade anarchist who probably got lucky with blowing up a Navy ship is our major concern?"

"It's not some anarchist. It's a damned spy."

"Did you hear me?" Wilkie scowled. Carter dropped his head, conciliatory. "I didn't think so." Wilkie slipped the wires of his spectacles behind his ears.

"So what is my next assignment, sir." Carter noted.

"I want you and Stiles to find this Ziegler. I need to know what he is up to. At least until this Cuba thing finishes up, we've got to keep him quiet."

"Yes, sir," Carter mumbled as he fidgeted in his seat. He stared at Wilkie for a moment before uttering, "I understand sir," he added and rose from his chair. Slowly exiting the building, he stopped for a moment and looked back at the posh Treasury building. Wilkie was correct — Washington was not his kind of town. He preferred openness. He preferred wide-open fields, acres of forests, and expanses of marshland. The marble, granite and concrete buildings that seemed to be growing like weeds along the streets of this city appeared cold and imposing.

Carter headed north toward the train station, cutting through Franklin Square Park. He ambled along the brick walkway, gazing at the emerald leaves on the oak boughs that reached over his path, until he noticed a commotion directly in his pathway. The small crowd of people gathered near a secluded bench appeared aghast at what they were witnessing.

Closer still, he slowed. "Did anyone see what happened?" he heard one of the three police officers ask. There was no reply.

"Looks like he killed himself, Charlie," another of the officers stated, matter-of-factly as Carter walked near enough to see a stain that had seeped through the entire right side of his gray jacket. The morning breeze, slight and with a touch of spring sweetness on it had blown his fedora off and onto the bricks in front of him. "There's only one bullet in the gun and it looks like he used it."

Carter stepped closer, and then froze. He recognized the pasty white, drawn face. He cocked his head and tapped one of the police officers.

"I need you to stand back, sir," the officer grumbled, then turned and ordered. "See if you can find a wagon, Charlie."

"I know him," Carter said breathlessly. It didn't make sense that Moser would kill himself, but it certainly appeared that way.

"Who was he, son," the attending officer asked.

"Rudolph Moser," Carter said. "He was — a friend of my father." The words spilled over Carter's quivering lips as he held back tears. He suddenly felt empty. Moser was the only person he had met that knew his father well. He had hoped that when he got back from Cuba that he would be able to find out more about the Gunter Rohlenheim or Sam Miller that was an enigma to everyone. Anyone but Moser.

"We've got to take him to the morgue before he starts stinkin' up the place. Can you get to whoever needs to know to claim the body?" the officer everyone called Charlie asked.

"Yeah, I can do that," Carter sighed as he reached over and touched Moser's shoulder. "*Auf Wiedersehen, alt freund,*" he whispered, then continued on to the train station.

Epilogue
April 1898
Charleston, South Carolina

Epilogue

Sam Carter sauntered along the Battery and gazed at the darkening sky over Charleston Bay. There was only a lazy roll to the water — nothing more to the surface than a lazy round crease that shimmered in the fading sunlight. A slight breeze swept over his shoulders, wafting the aroma of Charleston out to sea. Magnolias were in blossom, as were cherries and peaches. He stopped at a concrete bench and sat.

Out beyond the breakwaters, faint steam plumes swirled toward the clear sky. '*Cruisers headed to Cuba*,' he thought. The Court of Inquiry returned the expected verdict. Spain was at fault. McKinley declared war, stated eloquently for the betterment of the people of Cuba and their freedom from oppression. The intent though was lost by the Congress and the presses — for them it was retribution for the *Maine*. Why else would McKinley have waited so long to declare war, they wrote.

And someplace out there was his father. Somewhere below the rolling surface, there were secrets.

"Is it not just a beautiful evening, Sam," a woman's voice broke through his thoughts. He looked up and saw Annette standing beside him.

"Something just doesn't make sense, Annette," Carter perched his head on his open hands.

"Something?"

"I came to Charleston and thought that I might, just might be able to find out about my father. Then, by chance, by chance alone, I meet the one man who could fill that void. Now he's gone."

"Maybe you are looking in the wrong place, Sam," Annette said as she sat down next to him. She gently worked her fingers through his thick hair.

Carter turned and looked at Annette, puzzled.

"An older gentleman once told me that you are your father," Annette slid her hand down Sam's arm. She clasped her hand over his, then stood and started to pull him up. "If you walk with me, I'll tell you some of the secrets he told me."

As Carter stood, he looked into Annette's eyes and for a moment thought he could see his mother's. "I would like that," he then said, and with proper Southern manners, placed her hand in the crook of his elbow and the couple headed south along the Battery.

ABOUT THE AUTHOR

Guntis Goncarovs is an analytical chemist by education, historian by interest, amd storyteller by passion. His discoveries and analysis of the details surrounding the mysterious demise of the H.L. Hunley led to his novel, Convergence of Valor. Havana's Secret, the culmination of Goncarovs' research into the sinking of the USS Maine in Havana Harbor in 1898, is his third historical novel.

Goncarovs and his wife, Joan enjoy the wonders of New Hampshire with their dog, Sasha. Aquatic and terrestrial gardening, spotted with trying to keep up with three grown daughters keeps them hopping.

Books by Guntis Goncarovs

Telmenu Saimnieks
Convergence of Valor
Havana's Secret

36325967R00239

Made in the USA
Columbia, SC
03 December 2018